10-18

INTRODUCTION

Young Tom Hall: His Heartaches and Horses came very near to serialization in *Punch* in 1851: Mark Lemon, the editor, an old friend and admirer of Surtees, had the first chapter or chapters set up in proof before deciding that it would take up too much space for too long. Surtees was not put out—indeed, he was soon helping Lemon to set up *The Field*, which Lemon also edited, with Surtees as its hunting correspondent, "general adviser and helper-editor-in-reserve," but offered the novel to another friend, Harrison Ainsworth, for his *New Monthly Magazine*, in which *Mr. Sponge's Sporting Tour* had just come to a triumphant end. In doing so Surtees stipulated, as he always did, that it should be published anonymously: "I find I can write much better and with far more pleasure to myself when I am free to deny an article if I like." (Not that he ever did...)

Ainsworth was delighted, and *Young Tom Hall* got off to a good start: every monthly cheque for twelve months was accompanied by editorial compliments, but only a month after a flattering letter from Ainsworth, agreeing to another six months' run, a notice appeared in the December 1852 issue, announcing the next instalment and explicitly giving Surtees's name. Then followed this exchange of letters:

> William Street, Sunderland,
> 28th December 1852.
>
> Dear Sir,—I cannot permit the use you are making of my name, and must request you will immediately withdraw it from the New Monthly advertisement.—Yours truly,
>
> R. S. Surtees.

> The Club, Brighton,
> 1st January, 1853.

Sir,—I beg to enclose cheque on Coutts & Co. for £6 in payment of the present chapters of 'Tom Hall.'

I shall be glad if you will wind up the tale as soon as you conveniently can.—Your faithful Servt.,

> W. Harrison Ainswirth.

> 5th January 1853.

Sir,—I beg to acknowledge the receipt of your note and cheque for the January portion of 'Hall,' which it is not my intention to continue.—Yours obedtly.,

> R. S. Surtees.

> The Club, Brighton,
> 6th January 1853.

Sir,—I have to acknowledge the receipt of your letter announcing your intention of discontinuing 'Tom Hall' in the Magazine. I do not think this fair to the Magazine or to me. But I have no wish that the tale should be continued.

In closing our correspondence, I must remark that the courtesy and consideration with which you have always been treated by me during your somewhat lengthened connection with the New Monthly ought in my opinion to have rendered your present communication and that which preceded it less abrupt. I was very sorry that the advertisement occasioned you annoyance, but I had not the slightest idea that it could do so. On your request it was immediately withdrawn; and if this request had been made in terms consistent with our previous intercourse, I should have felt no occasion for further remark—except to express regret at any unintentional interference on my part with your other arrangements, if such was the case.—Your obedient servant,

> W. Harrison Ainsworth.

Whether Surtees's anonymity was breached by accident, or by accident-done-on-purpose; whether Surtees was too arrogant or Ainsworth too touchy, or whether both were at fault—these questions have been much debated. All that concerns us here is that *Tom Hall* was never completed, as serial or as book, even in its uncompleted form, until E. D. Cuming, Surtees's biographer, rescued the fifty chapters from the files of Ainsworth's magazine, to be published in 1926 by Blackwood and Sons of Edinburgh.

Tom Hall was something like two-thirds done; characters and plot had taken shape: Surtees could have finished it quickly and easily. Why did he not?

War in the Crimea was still a year away, but rumours of war were in the air, and the public had a mind to it. Less than a couple of months after Surtees's last letter to Ainsworth *The Times* published a warning that Franco-British policy towards Russia might well "embroil Europe", and an allied fleet was preparing for the Black Sea.

It must surely be that Surtees decided that this was no time to put before a glory-greedy public a more complete portrayal than he had already afforded of the shifty louts of the Heavysteed Dragoons and their Colonel Blunt, "a great, coarse, blackleg sort of man," and the popinjays of the Royal Lavender Dragoons and Hyacinth Hussars, "heavies in the morning and hussars at night. Red coats and horse-haired helmets, with leather tights and jack-boots were the marching order, while richly silver-braided, ermine-trimmed, lavender-coloured jackets and pelisses, and the aforesaid marmalade-coloured tights, with silver-tassel'd Hessian boots, annihilated the ladies of an evening..."

Surtees laid it on pretty thick, as usual—which is why he is such a joy to read—but he was not so far off the mark. In spite of the Peninsula and Waterloo the British public was not so fond of its soldiers as it has become after two world wars, and the cavalry in particular, whether regular or yeomanry, was far from being idolized.

At Waterloo, well within Surtees's lifetime, Ney's cavalry flung itself time and again in vain at the squares of British infantry, whereas Lord Anglesey, in his *History of the British Cavalry* (1973), writes of the cavalry his ancestor commanded there that "one of the inherent flaws of the British cavalry of this date was their tendency to break up in pursuit ... the colonels of the Greys and Royals, as soon as they saw that their men had got out of control, sacrificed their lives in vain efforts to rally them." Throughout the Peninsular campaign, Wellington "tended to distrust the 'cavalry spirit' ... the sheer incompetence of some of the senior cavalry officers was quite alarming."

Captain Gronow, who served in the Peninsula and at Waterloo as a young ensign in the Guards, quotes Wellington time and again in the two volumes of his memoirs, 1810–60 (published by the R.S. Surtees Society) on "the harum-scarum customs of our cavalry officers" and reinforces Wellington's opinion with that of the French marshal, "one of the most experienced cavalry officers of the day", who pointed out not only that British cavalry officers were convinced that they "can dash and ride over everything; as if the art of war were precisely the same as that of fox-hunting" but that they were so "tightly habited that it was impossible for them to use their sabres with facility."

Not much more than a year after *Tom Hall*'s untimely end the Poet Laureate, Tennyson, and the war correspondent of *The Times*, William Howard Russell, immortalized the Light Brigade, but Cardigan, who (at 57, never having been in action) led the charge, was not all that unlike Lord Lavender, "who had the soul of an army tailor in the body of a nobleman." Cardigan, whose arrogant quarrelsomeness lost him the command of one cavalry regiment—he fought two duels, almost the last in England, one about the colour of a bottle, one about the size of a teacup—made the 11th Hussars the smartest in the service by spending on it for years a quarter of his income of £40,000. Lucan, his brother-in-law and superior officer, camped with his men and shared their privations: Cardigan lived in his luxurious yacht in Balaclava harbour, ministered to by a French cook.

He did go into battle, though, and bravely—times had changed at any rate that much in the forty years since Gronow had come across the "officer of the 18th Hussars ... young, rich, and a fine-looking fellow, who joined the army not far from St. Sebastian. His stud of horses were remarkable for their blood; his grooms were English and three in number. He brought with him a light cart to carry forage, and a fourgon for his own baggage. All went well until he came to go on outpost duty: but not finding there any of the comforts to which he had been accustomed, he quietly mounted his charger, told his astonished sergeant that campaigning was not intended for a gentleman, and instantly galloped off to his quarters, ordering his servants to pack up everything immediately, as he had hired a transport to take him off to England." (He got home in time to sell out of his regiment before the despatches arrived ordering a court-martial.)

That was the sort of cavalry officer that Lord Lavender's yeomanry aped and Surtees detested—kin to his Cut 'em Down captains of the shires. And then there were such yeomanry regiments, officered by counter-jumpers in the towns, hobbledehoys in the country, as that which rode down the reformers at Peterloo, and Lord Marney's, which "fired on and sabred" a peaceable demonstration in *Sybil* (1845), the novel by Surtees's precise contemporary, Disraeli—they were born within a year of each other—and fellow-Tory.

Surtees was too humane to stomach the one's brutality, too reserved himself not to despise the pretentiousness of the other. But his quality as a story-teller is that his feelings are never translated into indignation or sentimentality: all is fun.

Whatever his reason for not carrying on with *Tom Hall*—I can think of none other than the one already given—he used it as a character-cupboard from which to people his next two books. Tom, the booby whose papa wants to make him "a gent", becomes in *Ask Mamma* "Fine Billy", the Richest Commoner in England, and his father is born again in *Plain or Ringlets?* as Old Goldspink, the Banker, with the same muttered monologue of "Sivin and four's ilivin, and eighteen is twenty-nine."

Lord Heartycheer becomes Lord Ladythorne in *Ask Mamma*, and his pimping huntsman, Dicky, is Thorndyke in the earlier novel, Boggledyke in the later. Angelena Blunt, the grimly determined husband-hunter, becomes Miss de Glancey who, like Angelena, loses her looks and her hold on her elderly admirer when, as they hack home, they are caught in a rainstorm, and "the smart hat and feather are annihilated; the dubious frizette falls out, down comes the hair; the bella-donna-inspired radiance of her eyes is quenched; the crinoline and wadding dissolve like ice before the fire ... she has no more shape or figure than an icicle."

Look, though, at Leech's brilliantly drawn, all too drenchingly evocative, wood-engraving of the unhappy return in *Ask Mamma* and at G. D. Armour's wishy-washy depiction of Miss Blunt's similar discomfiture in the only (1926) edition of *Young Tom Hall*. Here is one explanation, I suggest, of the wide differences of opinion about the merits of the unfinished novel. To Leonard Cooper, for instance (*R. S. Surtees*, 1952) "it is, as far as it goes, a masterpiece", but to John Welcome (*The Sporting World of R. S. Surtees*, 1982) "no great loss."

Had *Young Tom Hall* been published, even in its unfinished form, with Leech's illustrations, and had the author's admirers been able to read it *before* meeting many of the livelier characters in two books which, to my mind, are its inferiors, then they might well have ranked it with the three top-notchers—*Handley Cross, Sponge* and *Mr. Romford's Hounds*.

The set pieces are as brilliant as any that Surtees did elsewhere—Colonel Blunt's uproariously offensive social call on the banker; the *thé dansante* in his married quarters, and dinner in the mess—and so are such character sketches as that of Ruddle, the pastrycook turned railway-director turned house-painter turned portraitist; of the colonel himself, his shady hangers-on and his designing daughter. So, too, the sartorial descriptions, not only of the misses and their mammas but of the soldiery and the civilian sawbucks. This unfinished book alone would justify one critic's claim that Surtees "in the richness of his detail ... is the best guide of all to the clothes, transport, food, furniture and fun enjoyed in England between the first and the second Reform Bills."

Albany, London,   CYRIL RAY
March, 1986

YOUNG TOM HALL

HIS HEART-ACHES AND HORSES

LORD HEARTYCHEER'S QUIET BYE-DAY.

YOUNG TOM HALL

HIS HEART-ACHES AND HORSES

BY

ROBERT SMITH SURTEES

AUTHOR OF
'HANDLEY CROSS,' 'MR SPONGE'S SPORTING TOUR,'
'ASK MAMMA,' ETC., ETC.

WITH ILLUSTRATIONS BY G. DENHOLM ARMOUR

THE R. S. SURTEES SOCIETY

CONTENTS

ILLUSTRATIONS

YOUNG TOM HALL:

His Heart-aches and Horses.

CHAPTER I.

MR HALL AND OUR TOM.

" OUR Tom shall be a gent ! Our Tom shall be a gent ! "
exclaimed old father Hall to himself, with a hearty slap
of his fat leg, as, after a careful casting-up of the sum
" tottles " of many columns of many books, he at length
faced the nervous total, and found he was worth—we
don't know how much. The observation escaped the
worthy man in the partitioned-off nook of a dingy counting-
house, through a four-square window of which he could
contemplate the clerks, ranged on either side of the
banking and wool-stapling departments. For five-and-
forty years old Hall had laboured assiduously in the two
callings, having commenced as an office-sweeping-out
errand boy, with twopence in his pocket ; thence, passing
up the sliding scale of clerkships into the heaven of junior
partnership, he at length loomed out into Hall & Co.—
the Hall being our friend, and the " Co." himself also.
Young Tom—the youth that was to be a gent—was to
old Tom pretty much what a new keepsake or annual is
to a faded one. The bald turnipy-shaped head of the
father was reproduced in the round, light, hyperion-
locked one of the son ; the still keen but now watery
grey eye again shone forth in cerulean blue ; the very

A

dimples in his grizzly cheeks reappeared in the downy ones of his son, whose gaudy-coloured, exaggerated Joinvilles gave ample scope and latitude to a fine double chin, which the old gent kept a good deal within the folds of a puddingy white cravat. Their figures, too, were the same — round, fat, humming-top-shaped men, upon whose plump limbs the flesh wobbled and trembled as they walked.

Figures, figures, figures! Old Hall's head ran upon nothing but figures. His mind seemed to be formed of three red-ink columns, up and down which his thoughts circulated in the shape of pounds, shillings, and pence. He was wary, cautious, and watchful. He always seemed to be thinking that the party he was speaking to was setting a trap to do him out of money, perhaps to get him to discount a bad bill, or buy some damaged wool. He could not answer a common observation about the weather without doing a little mental arithmetic while he thought the thing over.

" Fine day, Mr Hall," farmer Barleymow would say as he stumped along to the market.

" Sivin and four's elivin, and eighteen is twenty-nine. Yes, sir, it *is* a fine day," the banker would reply.

Sivin and four must have stood Hall in good stead at some season or other of his life, for, to whatever length his calculations ran, he invariably commenced with " Sivin and four's elivin," and built up his column on that superstructure.

But to the " gent " department, as they say at the Crystal Palace.

The emphatic slap with which we opened the chapter startled the clerks and astonished " our Tom," who happened to be engaged on the wool-stapling side of the counting-house, arranging an ingenious piece of mechanism, by means of which he fished off old Mr Trueboy the cashier's scratch-wig, suspending it in the air, like the top of a Dioropha carriage.[1] Tom, who was only half educated, was just of an age and calibre to be ready for anything—anything except business. His father had had

---

[1] *Vide* Messrs Rock & Corben's specimens of carriages—not wig-tackle—in the Crystal Palace.

" Our Tom shall be a Gent ! "

to take him from a private tutor's, to prevent his marrying Miss Jane Daiseyfield, ninth daughter of Mr Mark Daisey-field, of Butterlaw Farm—a most amiable and elegant young lady, but who, like her sisters, was a " treasure in herself." Miss Jane, however, was not Tom's first heart-ache ; he had been desperately in love with Miss Sowerby, daughter of his respected tutor, who had completely wheedled and talked herself into his good graces, notwithstanding she was quite as fair and almost as fat as himself. He was *desperate* for her, and the lady, though a trifle older, was equally enamoured of him. How this, his *premier* heart-ache—of which, we are concerned to say, he has since had many—might have ended, is immaterial, for Jane Daiseyfield's slim angelic figure, raven locks, and bright Italian complexion, once seen, completely turned the cream of his affection for Miss Sowerby, and made him wonder how he could ever take up with her. Then Mrs Sowerby, with the honest outraged feelings of maternal pride, unable to see a " mere *boy* " so put upon (though it was as good as forty pounds a year out of their pockets, notwithstanding our Tom had a good appetite), wrote to old Hall, cautioning him against the designing Daiseyfields ; and Hall forthwith removed his son, and shortly afterwards complimented the Sowerby candour with a " T. Cox Savory " teapot with a silver handle. And Miss Sowerby returned our Tom the hearts-ease and forget-me-not entwined white cornelian brooch with a dignified but not altogether despairing note ; and our Tom passed the brooch on to " dearest Jane," with a schoolboy scrawl of very infirm English, vowing that nothing but death should prevent his making her Mrs Thomas Hall. And all these things being accomplished, he presently took a second-class fare home, falling desperately in love with his fellow-passenger, Lady Bedington's pretty maid, who he was only prevented offering to by the station-master at Fleecyborough refusing to book him on by the train she was travelling in. So Tom was left, cursing his luck and kissing his hand to her from the platform.

CHAPTER II.

INTRODUCES MAJOR FIBS.

FLEECYBOROUGH, the new scene of our hero's exploits, though more of an agricultural than a manufacturing town, was large enough to have many of the attributes of a manufacturing one : fairs, assizes, races, and so on ; also a theatre and assembly rooms, where town and county met in scornful defiance. In this not unfertile field old Hall had amassed money in a quiet, unobserved, unobtrusive sort of way, until Young Hopeful looming on the scene caused people to be suddenly struck with the fact that Old Hall must be very rich. Nor did " Tummus," as his father called him, keep his candle under a bushel ; on the contrary, he was continually polishing the flags of Lark-street along with Mr Padder, Mr Capias's swell clerk, or Mr Yawney, Mr Drugmore, the doctor's young man, or standing with them at the corner of Spooneypope Street, sucking his cane-handle, gazing at the passing vehicles, or criticising as much of the ladies' ankles as could be seen for their draggling dresses. He was always arrayed in the brightest, most glaring colours, the gaudiest shirts, with the most inexhaustible wrist-bands, the most varied and glittering studs, the most bepocketed Baden-towel waistcoats, the queerest, scrimpiest, little jackets, and the widest, boldest-patterned trousers, with the tiniest lacquer-toed boots peeping out below that ever were seen. So our Tom stood " a gent "—a character that in old Hall's estimation simply meant a man with plenty of money and nothing to do.

The worst feature of Fleecyborough for a gent was that there were no gents to keep him company—at least,

not till the afternoon. All the other gents were only
gents from three or four o'clock or so ; consequently
our Tom's time hung rather heavily on his hands. He
had fished off old Trueboy's wig until the operation had
ceased to create a laugh, and his practical jokes upon the
other clerks had exhausted themselves by repetition.
' Bell's Life,' though a pleasing paper and full of varied
information, would not last him a whole week ; and
even Miss Isinglass the pretty confectioner's vapid
simper oftener set him yawning than she inflamed him
by the regularity and beauty of her features. Fortune,
however, soon after his arrival came to our friend's
assistance. So marked a young man could not but
attract attention, and one afternoon, as he was disporting
himself on three chairs in the bay-windowed coffee-room
of the Salutation Inn, after the manner of St James's-
street club swells, as his friend Padder assured him, the
well-known Major Fibs of the Heavysteed Dragoons, then
quartered at Fleecyborough, entered the room. The
major was a tall gaunt man, with full, wide-extending,
sandy moustachios, that curled out into points like
antelope's horns. The major was about fifty years of
age, nearly five-and-thirty of which he had spent in the
army, and he had long taken an M.A. degree in all that
relates to the ways of the world. What a mentor for a
man of our Tom's inexperience ! Let us get him introduced as quickly as possible.

The military being to a country town pretty much
what the nobility are to London town, Tom's first impulse
was to get up and offer the major the chair ; but recollecting that he was a gent, and well qualified, as his mother
often assured him, to " hold up his head," hinting, woman-
like, that he might even aspire to one of the lord-lieutenant's daughters, he just rolled a fat leg off a chair,
and gave it a sort of outward twist towards the man
of war. The major's strapping figure relaxed into a
pokerified sort of bow, while a sardonic smile played over
his hirsute features as he scanned the young greenhorn
with his greenish-grey eyes. ' Bell's Life ' being a far
better ice-breaker than the weather, or even the Crystal
Palace itself, the major at once proceeded to ask Tom

if he would have the " Goodneth," for he lithped a good deal, " to tell him if Charley Brick's little dog had won the great rat match at Edgebathton."

Now Tom had just been reading the column " Canine," and knew all about it ; so he detailed to the major, with remarkable accuracy, how the little animal had won, and expatiated on the beauties and delicacies of the affair. The old major listened with marked attention, and, having discussed that point, he asked Tom if he thought he could pick him out the winner of the Rascal Stakes at Chippenham. Tom could not, but referred the major to the very promising column of prophets in ' Bell's Life,' to one of whom—viz., the genius who advertises " that his tongue is not for falsehood framed," though we should think it was framed for nothing else—he thought of applying for racing information. The major then assumed the office of mentor, cautioning Tom against these impostors, who, he assured him, were the veriest scum of the earth, who knew nothing at all about " horthes," and would infallibly bolt if they got any money into their hands. The major was warm and energetic on the point, feeling morally certain that he was equal to easing Tom of any superfluous cash he might happen to have, as he had eased many a youngster both in his regiment and out of it. And after a little more such agreeable and instructive conversation, the major tendered his hand, saying that he was glad to have had the pleasure of making Mr Hall's acquaintance, and so departed.

CHAPTER III.

TOM IN GOOD HANDS.

" Sivin and four's elivin, and eight's nineteen—I don't know that that'll do you any good," observed old Hall, when Tom boasted at dinner that he had made Major Fibs's acquaintance.

" I don't know *that*, my dear," observed Mrs Hall, coming to the rescue. " I think it's just the sort of company our Tummus should be in."

" Sivin and four's elivin, and forty-five is fifty-six—don't like the mil*in*tary," replied Hall, busy with a chicken leg.

" That's only because Captain Sloper bit you," replied his wife. " You shouldn't judge of all by the faults of one. The army's a most honorable profession."

" Middlin'," replied Hall, who had had the offer of many other " bites " besides Sloper's—for escaping which he was more indebted to his own acuteness than to the candour of the would-be biters.

Tom, too, with the generous sympathies of youth, defended the major, whose action in cautioning him against the advertising turf swindlers he eulogised ; and what between his wife and his son, old Hall soon found that he might as well hold his tongue.

Next day, as he was peering over the dingy green blinds of his bank, and saw Tom strutting by on the arm of the red-jacketed major, in the full enjoyment of the curious pleasure some little men feel in walking with very tall ones, the old man felt more pleased than pained at the sight. The major and Tom walked the streets for two hours, in the course of which time they met Mrs Flareup's gold-lace hatted coachman, nine times watched the Miss Skippingtons into seven milliners' and other shops, and got innumerable salutes from the soldiers. Their conversation was chiefly about " horthes," which the major criticised, or rather denounced freely as they passed, pronouncing one to be a rip, another a brute, a third a devil, a fourth a screw, and so on—opinions to which Tom freely assented, though he knew nothing whatever about them.   Seeing the swaggering way in which Tom brandished his cane whip-stick, the major asked him what hounds he hunted with, and being told that he had never been out but once, and then on foot, with old Mr Bloatingford's beagles, he particularly recommended hunting to his attention, assuring him that the very best introduction for a young man of figure and fortune like him was to be found at the cover-side. He then entered into a dissertation on the relative merits of Lord Heartycheer's and Sir Harry Bulfinches' hounds, commenting on the skill of their respective huntsmen, and the powers and performances of their packs.

He also glanced at the composition of their respective fields, denouncing this man as a " jealous dog," that as a " fine 'orthman," and concluded by asking our Tom to dine at the barracks on the morrow, being band-day, to which our friend readily assented.

To this enlivening scene let us now adjourn.   Although Fibs was not considered quite the thing in the regiment —at least not by some of the saucy subalterns, who, after all, might be no great judges of propriety, or might, perhaps, mistake for cheating what in reality were most useful lessons in the ways of the world—although Fibs, we say, was not considered quite the thing in the regiment, yet, being an intense toady of the colonel's— Colonel Blunt—who was no great shakes himself, they pocketed their dislikes and wined with our Tom in the hearty liberal sort of way of men who have got to pay their share of the shot.   The colonel, who sat opposite Tom, led the charge with a great stentorian voice, an example that was quickly followed by the major, taken up by Captain Pippin opposite, responded to by Mr Mattyfat down below, followed by Captain Dazzler higher up, repeated by Captain Spill from behind the epergne, re-echoed by Captain Whopper in the vice-chair, chorused by Mr Stalker on his left, and squeaked by little Mister Jug, the junior cornet, who was very industrious in the drinking way, and generally got too much wine every night. They all took wine with our Tom—the adjutant twice.

The consequence was that our Tom got a very considerable quantity of hot heady wine during dinner, and soon felt at home among these jolly cocks instead of rising from table as unacquainted with them as when he sat down, according to the frigid rules of high society, where people are neither introduced nor make acquaintance by asking each other to wine. We really think it would be an improvement on the modern practice if a host were to calculate how much a dinner would cost, and send a share of the money to each guest, with, " Company not required," as undertakers do with mourning at a funeral—a solemnity that a modern dinner-party very much resembles. Not so our mess, however, where everybody wined with our Tom ; and what with the novelty of the scene, the dash of the uniforms, the tall liveried footmen, the massive plate, the general glare and glitter of everything except the plate, which was dull and pewtery-like, when the profane Cardigans mingled with the cut-glass decanters, and the band struck up, and the orderlies went round with their books, our Tom felt as though he had imbibed the spirit of the Duke of Wellington, and could lead whole armies on to glory and renown.

The conversation, however, did not take a military turn, for Colonel Blunt, being a great, coarse, blackleg sort of man, soon turned it into his favourite channel, and after a very critical review of the previous week's sporting transactions, as detailed in the Sunday papers, he evoked an expression of opinion as to the propriety of matching his bull-terrier, Griper, against Bullhide the butcher's Holdfast, and the band striking up " Rory O'More " in the course of the discussion, he sent the adjutant to dismiss them as a noisy set of scamps. Having got rid of them, he resumed the subject, frequently directing his questions and observations to our Tom, who felt

flattered by the attentions of the great commander, and
his offer of allowing any one to go halves in the match
rather hanging fire, Tom boldly closed with it, leaving
it to the colonel to make it for any sum he liked. Having
attentively scrutinised Tom's fat vacant face, and considered whether he had better pigeon him or let his
daughter have a run at him, he came to the conclusion
that he might do both, and being in the secret of the then
great coming cross between Sledgehammer, the blacksmith, and Granitenob, the miner, the colonel accom-
modated Tom with the favourite at evens.

He then introduced the subject of some leather-plating
they were getting up among themselves—quite select—
" *small* stakes—just for amusement, and to please the
country folks—five-pound forfeits—*only* five pounds,"
and Tom dashed at them too. In fact, he was ripe for
anything ; but the prudent colonel thinking he had done
enough, and many of the officers having retired on the
appearance of a bottle with a white paper cravat, the
colonel looked significantly at the major, who forthwith
proposed retiring to his room and having " thum thardines
or anthovies, or bitter ale and grilled bones, or thumthin'
of that thort." The fat boy and the fat colonel then
rose together, and the fat colonel seeing that the fat
boy rather lurched in his gait, thrust his huge arm through
his, and led him away before the now tittering remnant
of his regiment.

" What a youth ! " whispered one.—" Green as grass,"
observed another.—" In good hands," said a third.—
" The old 'uns will draw him," tittered another.—" Never
mind, he's plenty of wool on his back ! " exclaimed a
fifth.—" Right shop for getting it shorn in," rejoined the
first speaker, who had had practical experience both of
the colonel and his major. But we must accompany the
departing worthies.

Colonel Blunt being quite a martinet in money matters,
never compromising a good bet, or letting a youngster off
a bad one, or out of a bad horse deal on the plea of inebriety, which he used to say was only an additional
reason for enforcing the bet or the deal, were it only to
cure him of the foul propensity—the colonel, we say,

being quite a martinet in money matters, was anxious to "compare" with Tom Hall in private, so that there might be no mistake or misunderstanding in the morning. Seeing, too, how freely Tom rose at all manner of bait, he thought he might feel how the land lay with regard to entering him for his daughter—a most lovely and angelic girl, as her mother told the gents, or a fiery little fiend, as she occasionally told the young lady herself. Accordingly he stuck to our friend Tom, even after he had got him safe down the stone steps of the mess-room and into the spacious star-canopied barrack-yard, looking so different in the dull sombre garments of night to what it did when he entered in the bright glare of day. Whether it was the night air, or the stars, or the young moon, or the young port, or the old cheese, or the green salad, we know not, but Tom's head ceased to serve him even as indifferently well as it had been doing, and his legs seemed inclined to rebel too. However, the colonel got him over the ground, and up to the end of a spacious wind-whistling passage, through which darkness was made visible by a few glowworm-looking lamps, aided by occasional gleams of light from partially-opened doors on either side, disclosing adjourned scenes of revelry, or emitting the fumes of tobacco. The major's soldier-servant, anticipating his master's coming, had got a couple of composite candles lighted, which cast a cheerful radiance over the crimson furniture and fancy fittings of the little room, and had even been so considerate as to lay a pack of cards on the table.

"Thit down, my dear feller—thit down," lisped the major, wheeling a semi-circular chair behind our friend Tom, which, taking him just behind the knees, sent him souse into it. The colonel then took possession of one opposite. Tom's head now began to swim. He thought the carpet was undulating, like the sham sea at a theatre, and clutched his chair manfully with both hands.

"I wish this chair mayn't come down with me," observed the colonel, as his chair began to creak under his enormous weight, for he walked seventeen stone.

"That would be ve—ve—very *awk*ward," stammered Tom, staring wildly.

"Oh, no; it things (sings) with me," observed the major from the adjoining cupboard of a room, whither he had gone under pretence of arranging his supper tray, but in reality to give the colonel an opportunity of taking Tom through hands.

"Well, I hope Bullhide won't whop us," observed the colonel, reverting to the dog-match, slapping his great brawny hands on to his enormous knees, and contemplating Tom just as a cat contemplates a mouse before pouncing. "I hope Bullhide won't whop us," repeated he in a louder tone, Tom not noticing the observation.

"That would be ve—ve—very *awk*ward," replied Tom after a pause.

"If the Nob beats the Hammer I shall want two ponies of you," observed the colonel, slowly and sententiously.

"That would be ve—ve—very *awk*ward," replied Tom.

"Humph!" grunted the colonel, fixing his eyes on the now open-mouthed, drooping-lidded, chubby-faced boy, and thinking whether it was worth while continuing the effort.

Just then Tom thought he felt the room begin to rock, and started forward with a violent stamp on the floor. Finding his mistake, he gave an idiotic sort of laugh, as if nothing particular had happened, and then essayed to sit bolt upright.

The colonel thought he would make one more attempt.

"You understand the terms of the Warrior Stakes," observed he, speaking very loudly, and leaning towards Tom. "It's a fifteen-guinea stake, ten guineas forfeit, and only five if declared by the 15th. If you don't mean to run, you'll have to pay five guineas."

"That would be ve—ve—very *awk*ward," replied Tom with much labour.

"Ay, but if you don't declare in time, you'll have to pay *ten*," rejoined the colonel, with a knowing jerk of his great bull head.

"That would be ve—ve—very *awk*ward," replied Tom as before.

"Hang your awkwards!" growled the colonel, rising

from his chair ; and, going to where the major was still busy among his condiments, he whispered him " that the boy was drunk, and he (the major) must see that matters were right in the morning."

This the obsequious major promised to do, and bidding Tom " Good-night " the colonel rolled off home, to take the usual revenge upon his wife and daughter that he did when things didn't go right.

And the major got a fly and took our Tom home to his father's.

CHAPTER IV.

MARTIAL ARDOUR.

MAJOR FIBS was in town betimes the next afternoon, having double duty to perform—namely, to call the colonel's bets over with our Tom, and to caution him against the men in the regiment who he thought likely to enlighten Tom as to their joint propensities. The mess dinner having made Tom common property, the major felt the urgency of the occasion ; for though few of the men had been long in the regiment—which, indeed, seemed to act the part of conduit-pipe to others—yet they could all tell something against the colonel or the major, or both.

Not falling in with Tom in High-street, or Cross-street, or at the corner of Spooneypope-street, and seeing nothing of him over Paddington the tailor " from London's " blinds, between the brush and soap bottles of Bergamot the hairdresser's window, or in the coffee-room of the Salutation Inn, the major drew on to Miss Isinglass the confectioner's, where he found our jolly friend sitting backwards in his chair, contemplating the young lady over a conical tumbler of capillaire and soda-water. The major clanked in with his long brass spurs and coarse iron-heeled boots.

" Ah, my *dear* fellow, how d'ye do ? " lisped he, as if the meeting was the veriest accident in the world. " Good mornin', Miss I.," continued he, addressing the lady, with a military touch of his gold-laced forage cap. " Hope I don't intrude ? as Paul Pry used to say," looking significantly at Tom ; at which the lady smiled and hung her head, showing her auburn ringlets to great advantage.

The trio then entered upon the interesting subject of the weather : the major wanting rain, to soften the ground, to train a ticklish-legged horse ; Miss Isinglass wanting it fair, as she was going by the last cheap excursion train to the Great Exhibition ; and Tom Hall not knowing exactly what he wanted. So they talked a very edifying pastrycook-shop sort of conversation. At length, having finished his beverage, and told Miss Isinglass to "tick it," Tom rose from his seat, and, with a parting leer, linked arms with the major, and sallied forth for a stroll, Tom observing confidentially to his friend that his "coppers were hot."

"I thought you were rather thleepy last night," replied the major, suspecting that Tom might be wanting to cry off his bets on the plea of intoxication. "I thought you were rather thleepy," repeated he ; adding, "That beethly band's enough to thet anybody to thleep."

The "sleepiness" was not the only reminiscence of the previous night's carouse, for, in addition to the ghost of a tune with his headache, Tom had awoke with a desperate military mania. Nothing would serve him but he would be a soldier. As he lay cooling his throbbing head against the pillow, he thought over the glories of a military career, the magnificent uniforms, the splendid dinners, the enlivening bands, the brazen trumpet's sound, the honour of belonging to the "Rag"; and he fancied himself capering about the streets on a splendidly caparisoned charger, with a red-and-white feather floating gracefully from his cocked hat.

"I tell you what," said he, squeezing the major's arm confidentially—"I tell you what, I've been thinking— that is to say, I've been considering—I mean, I've half an idea—I should like to go into the army."

"Hem!" mused the major, thinking how that would fit.

"And I should like to go into your regiment," continued Tom eagerly ; adding, "D'ye think I've any chance ? "

"Not im*poth*ible," replied the major, making a good mouthful of the *poth*—"not im*poth*ible. The colonel's parthal to sthtout men—likes them fat."

"Indeed," replied Tom, who didn't consider himself at

all out of the way in that respect. " D'ye think he'd give me a commission ? " asked Tom.

" Why, as to that," mused the major—" why, as to that, I dare say he'd give you his interest, and he's thick with the old Dook ; has a bed at Apthley Houth whenever he goes to town. Indeed, I've no doubt the Dook would be only too happy to therve him. But thee him yourthelf, my dear feller," continued the major—" thee him yourthelf, and ask him the question."

Tom walked on in silence, not exactly knowing how to set about it.

" You might call under pretenth of talking over your last night's beths, you know," suggested the major, " and that would give you an opportunity of theeing his daughter Anthelena, the most lovely creature you ever thet eyes on —things like a theraphum ! "

The lady temptation was for the moment lost upon Tom by the sudden irruption of Granitenob and Griper, and Bullhide and the Warrior Stakes, upon his recollection. He now felt that, if he hadn't made the colonel's acquaintance thereby, he would rather not have made the bets ; for, like the great John Gilpin, although on pleasure bent, Tom had a frugal mind—a deal of his father's caution about him.

" If you have any therious thoughts about the army," continued the major after a pause, " it wouldn't be a bad plan to humour the old gentleman by making a few more beths with him. It isn't the money he cares about," continued the major, " he likes the ecthitement of the thing. Money !—bleth ye, he has more than he knows what to do with. I'll be bound to thay, Anthelena will have fifty thouthand punds—not fifty thouthand stock, but stock that will prodooth fifty thouthand tholid thubstanthal thovereigns."

And Tom felt cheered by the assurance, and thought he saw his way through the Granitenob and other difficulties. If excitement was all the old boy wanted, he could accommodate him with that to any extent ; and though aspiring to so great an heiress might appear presumptuous, Tom was not prepared to say but he was ready for the attempt.

" Is she pretty ? " asked Tom, flourishing a cane whip-stick in an off-hand sort of way.

" *Beeau*-tiful ! " drawled the major. " The most *beeau*-tiful figure and complexthon you ever thaw."

" Indeed," replied Tom. " I'll have a look at her."

" Do," replied the major. " I athure you, as a friend, she's well worth it."

" Hum ! " mused Tom, wishing he hadn't given Jinny Daiseyfield the brooch, and wondering how he could get it back.

" The colonel's an ecthellent cretur," observed the major as they sauntered along.

" He seems so," replied Tom.

" *Ecthellent* cretur," replied the major, with an emphasis and a twist of the points of his ferocious moustachios ; " quite a father to all the young men in the regiment— far too good for some of them, indeed."

" What sort of chaps are they ? " asked Tom.

" Why, between ourselves," replied the major in an undertone, and hugging Tom's arm as he spoke—" between ourselves—in strict confidence in course, for one doesn't like to speak ill of one's brother-offithers—there are some queerish blades among 'em ; that Dathler, for instance, and Whopper " (both of whom the colonel and major had recently cheated in horses), " and Pippin, is no great things ; but you've no occasion to trouble yourself about any of them ; the colonel's the boy for you—stick to him. It's a far finer thing to be thick with field-offithers and colonels of regiments than with little whelps of boys like that little Mithter Jug, and Shuffler, and so on."

And Tom thought so, and fancied that he, too, might come to have a bed at Apsley House. The major inter-rupted the reverie by entering upon the more imme-diate object of his mission—namely, that of ascertaining how far the youth's memory retained the recollection of the overnight's transaction ; and finding that he was pretty well " up " in them, he next sounded him as to his means of carrying them out, particularly as regarded the race for the Warrior Stakes. Hearing that his hunting-cane then constituted his whole equestrian stock-in-trade, the major hinted at the desirableness of getting horthes

B

directly, so as to get them into condithon before the season, observing that condithon was half the battle with a hunter—a fact that Tom was wholly unconscious of, being of opinion that a horse, like a carriage or a steam-engine, was always ready to go when wanted. In short, Tom knew nothing at all about horses, and in more ways than one seemed to have been sent for the especial benefit of the gallant Colonel Blunt and his able and indefatigable coadjutor, Major Fibs. The major then proceeded to show how, if Tom got a nice orth or two, thummer'd *à la* Nimrod, which the major pronounced to be the most orthodox thystem, Tom might do a little cocktail rathin, and perhaps win a goodith sthake, all of which was extremely comfortable to our young friend's comprehension. The major even hinted that he knew a very likely nag to do the trick; but he just mentioned this in a casual incidental sort of way, addressing himself as much to the wall as to Tom Hall; and after a protracted saunter, the major at length parted with his amiable young friend, assuring him of his distinguished consideration, and returned to the barracks to report to the colonel; while Tom turned in for a four o'clock dinner at his father's, his head still harping on the army, and aching with the fine military port of the previous day.

CHAPTER V.

MRS HALL'S AMBITION.

" SIVIN and four's elivin, and ninety-four's a 'under'd and five," exclaimed old Hall in astonishment, planting his knife and fork erect with a thump of each on the table when our Tom broached the subject of soldiering. " Sivin and four's elivin, and ninety-nine's a 'under'd and ten—*wot the doose should you go into the army for ?* " gasped he.

" Serve one's queen and country," stammered Tom, blushing, not expecting such a note of exclamation.

" Serve one's queen and fiddlestick ! " replied old Hall, who, like Mr Cobden, was all for peace and politeness.

Mrs Hall was equally opposed, though on a different principle. She couldn't bear the idea of her dear boy being cut up by the Caffres, or burnt by the Indians, or peppered by the Irish, or prodded by the French. " No, no, Tummus mustn't be a soldier. He must stay at home and comfort his father and mother."

But Tom was obdurate ; and having always got what he wanted by standing out, he worked the subject morning, noon, and night. The old people took counsel together. Many were the expedients and diversions they suggested.

" It's a pity, but we could get him into Lord Lavender's army," at length observed Mrs Hall to her husband one night after Tom had been unusually persecuting. " He would look uncommonly nice in marmalade-coloured tights, and it's just the sort of company Tummus ought to be in."

Now Lord Lavender was the preterpluperfect tense of dandies ; his hussars were the pink of the yeomanry cavalry of England, and officered by noblemen and swells of the first water. The facilities of railways enabled many listless, lounging, London bucks to bebeard and bespur themselves, and take up their quarters at his noble mansion for fourteen days, eating and drinking and playing at soldiers in the park. His lordship, who had the soul of an army tailor in the body of a nobleman, spent endless time and countless cash in the advancement of this his favourite hobby; and though in reality commanding but one regiment, it was as good as having two, for they were heavies in the morning and hussars at night. Red coats and horse-haired helmets, with leather tights and jack-boots were the marching order, while richly silver-braided, ermine-trimmed, lavender-coloured jackets and pelisses, and the aforesaid marmalade-coloured tights, with silver-tassel'd Hessian boots, annihilated the ladies of an evening.

None but the wealthy, or men with good credit, could go into the corps, for all the appointments were studiedly expensive, no German silver allowed, and the lace was laid on as if it was impossible to get it thick enough. Into this "Heaven of Heavens" Mrs Hall was desirous of intruding our Tom, or rather her Tom. We diverged at the point where she introduced the idea.

"Sivin and four's elivin, and sivin's eighteen—there wouldn't be much difficulty about that," replied old Hall.

"D'ye think not?" exclaimed Mrs Hall in delight.

"Sivin and four's elivin, and eighteen's twenty-nine— I think not," replied her husband cautiously; "at least I take it not—I apprehend not."

Old Hall had been recently reading that great work of information his bank-ledger, wherein he had a concise view, not only of his lordship's affairs but of the affairs of many other great men of the county, and finding that his lordship had what he called "overdrood most desprate," he had very little doubt that he could have whatever he chose to ask for.

His wife, of course, urged him to ask for a commission for our Tom; and our Tom, though he had been desperate about the Heavysteed Dragoons, yet feeling, on reflection,

that all the splendour in the world would be little worth
if he hadn't dear Fleecyborough to exhibit it in, with
becoming reluctance at length came into the arrangement.
Old Hall, after duly considering whether he should
address his lordship on the subject of the overdrawn
account, and allude to the commission in a postscript—
or address him on the subject of the commission, and
allude to the overdrawn account in the postscript, at
length chose the latter, and finally despatched a very
business-like letter, beginning as high up the page as if
he meant to fill the whole sheet, though, in reality, he
only got through a third of a page, stating that his son,
a very promising young man, who had just finished his
education, was desirous of joining his lordship's regiment,
and that he (the father) would esteem it a favour if his
lordship would appoint him, for which he would be ready
to pay whatever was required, adding that he was his lordship's obedient humble servant to command ; and, as
if by way of showing how little he was his servant in
reality, he added this :—

" P.S.—My cashier has just drawn my attention to
your book, which he would like to have a little more
evenly balanced before Christmas."

CHAPTER VI.

LORD LAVENDER AT HOME.

WORDS cannot express the rage Lord Lavender was in when he received the foregoing missive, which he did as he sat at breakfast with his family, who, as they will occupy a somewhat prominent position in our story, it may be well for the reader to become at once acquainted with.

His Lordship, though past the heyday of youth, had not been able to persuade himself of that fact. Indeed, he laboured the other way, and, by dint of belts, bands, washes, cosmetics, and dyes, managed to set half a century at defiance as successfully as any made-up gentleman we ever saw; and but for three full-grown buxom-looking girls, to say nothing of a son or two out of sight, might have passed for a gentleman a little turned of thirty. The girls, unfortunately, looked older than they were, and, instead of the father's high-bred air and Italian-like complexion, took after their mother, who was fair, and now somewhat dumpy. Lady Lavender, though painfully aristocratic, now that she had scrambled into the peerage, might have been a little higher bred without disadvantage. Indeed, it was not exactly known whence she came, the stud-books of humanity merely entering her as daughter of John Smith, Esq., thus offering a wide field for the speculations of the curious. Be that, however, as it may, she was very highty-tighty, fully appreciating the advantages of position, and entering into the outraged feelings of her husband at such overtures as Hall's.

"Such impudence! Such presumption! What next,

I wonder ? Passes all comprehension. Will be offering to one of the girls next," observed her ladyship, throwing the wide-unenveloped letter from her with disdain.

" Who is it ? " inquired Miss Maria Henrietta Jane.

" Oh, nobody—only your pa's banker writing about a cub of a boy of his," replied her ladyship.

" What, old fat-throat ! " exclaimed Maria, whose other two names we will now take the liberty of merging.

" What do *you* know about fat-throats ? " demanded his lordship with a frown, which might be caused either by the familiarity of the expression or the inconvenient postscript to the banker's letter.

" Oh, nothing," replied Maria, with a blush ; " only we see a great porpoise of a boy in all the colours of the rainbow hanging about the streets and shop doors at Fleecyborough, and—and—and—somebody christened him old fat-throat."

" I dare say the somebody was yourself," snapped her ladyship ; " you are always demeaning yourself with undue familiarity."

" Always ! " exclaimed his lordship, who wanted some one to be angry with.

" Indeed I know nothing about him," replied Maria quite innocently.

" *I* should hope not ! " replied the lady-mother. " *I* should hope not ! " repeated she, with great dignity. " I should hope no daughter of mine would demean herself by a plebeian connection." So saying, she rose from the table and sailed out of the room, with as much stateliness as a dumpy lady all stomach up to the chin can assume, followed by her daughters, giggling at the idea of our Tom forming one of their select family circle.

Although his lordship had made use of at least a bushel of bad words in declaring his fixed determination not to sully his corps by admitting such a snob as our Tom, and had mentally consigned him to all manner of out-of-the-way and uncomfortable places, yet when he found himself in the solitude of his own room, with the ill-omened document before him, and a strong file of last year's unpaid bills at his elbow—some, indeed, beginning with the ominous words, " To bill delivered " so much—

he thought better of writing in the indignant strain to old Hall that he at first contemplated ; indeed, he believed it was best to be civil ; most likely it was ignorance ; the man mightn't mean to be rude—didn't know the regulations of his corps, and so on ; so he would write him a polite put-off note, beginning, " Lord Lavender presents his compliments to Mr Hall, and regrets exceedingly," &c.

Before he had got an answer combed out to his mind, a servant announced that Mr Drearyman, the land-agent, was waiting for an audience, and that dread functionary being admitted, and at length induced to take a seat, proceeded to pour out such a catalogue of grievances, such wants, such distress and poverty among the tenants, aggravated by the tedious prolixity with which Drearyman dwelt upon each item, that, before he was done, his lordship felt he would be fortunate if the estates did not bring him debtor instead of his having anything to receive.

Mr Drearyman, indeed, drew a lamentable picture of the state of the country—a striking contrast to the pen-and-ink prosperity of some of the newspaper press. But there are no people so confident of the capabilities of land as those who have none.

When Drearyman at length took his departure, his lordship saw things in a different light. So far from gratifying Mr Trueboy with an adjustment of his account, he felt satisfied that he would have to increase his obligations ; and after a strong struggle between pride and pocket, pocket at length gained the mastery, and the haughty lord humbled himself before the griping banker, and, sinking all notice of Hall's postscript, wrote that he would have great pleasure in appointing Mr Thomas Hall to a cornetcy in the Royal Lavender Dragoons and Hyacinth Hussars. By the same post he increased the weight of his obligations to the bank, by sending Madame Dentelle a cheque for her ladyship and daughter's long-standing account, for which he had had innumerable applications and assurances that the money was wanted to enable madame to meet a heavy bill coming due the then next week.

CHAPTER VII.

COLONEL BLUNT CALLS.

OLD Hall's house was in the heart of the town of Fleecy-borough, in Newbold-street, and, though substantial and well-built, could not vie with the more modern plate-glass-windowed mansions that had sprung up in the outskirts and newer streets. It was a dingy brick mansion, with heavy woodwork windows, a massive green door, and an old iron railing enclosing nothing. Newbold-street at this part was rather narrow, and only flagged on Hall's side, but some fifty yards to the west was an airy market-place, and the bank, forming part of the house, was what was called extremely " used " for business, the farmers popping in and out like rabbits in a warren. Though the bank was as dark and as dirty as a place could be, and the little partitioned-off nook, wherein we introduced the banker to our readers, was all the " sweating room " he possessed, it was wonderful the amount of business he did, and the agonies parties underwent in that nook. " Sivin and four's elivin, and nineteen's thirty—I'm afeard this bill won't do," Hall would say to a ponderous farmer who wanted a little accommodation, or perhaps a good deal, to enable him to meet his rent. " Couldn't you get some 'un to join in a note ? " or, to another, " Sivin and four's elivin, and fifteen's twenty-six—it's not convenient just now," returning the gaping goose his hopeless paper. " Ay—w-h-o-y—ar'll call again in haafe an hour," perhaps replies the innocent, not understanding the delicacy of the refusal.

But we are entering into the mysteries of Hall's calling, whereas our object is only to introduce his residence to our readers, preparatory to receiving company. We will now suppose our worthy friends in receipt of Lord Lavender's letter, and, the first transports of joy over, Mrs Hall castle-building—imagining a match between our Tom and one of the Miss Myrtles, his lordship's daughters.

"Our Tom shall have an honourable for a wife!" exclaimed she.

"Sivin and four's elivin, and forty-one is fifty-two— I don't know that that would do him any good," replied Hall.

"Not do him any good!" retorted his wife; "why, it's the very thing that Tom ought to have—a high-bred lady for a wife, who'll take him to court, and into distinguished society, and make a first-rate man of him."

"Sivin and four's elivin, and eighty-three is ninety-four—I don't know that he'd be any better of that," replied the imperturbable banker.

"Not any better of *that!*" retorted his wife, who was all for advancement, and saw no reason why our Tummus should not marry a lord's daughter as well as Miss Nobody-knew-who Smith marry Lord Lavender; and so Hall and she got into a discussion on the point.

Their dialogue was interrupted by the most violent pounding of their hitherto peaceable, brass, lion-headed knocker, and before the astonished couple had recovered from the surprise, or speculated whether the bank was broke, or the house on fire, a second assault, if possible more furious than the first, thundered through the mansion, and caused a simultaneous rush to the drawing-room windows to see what was "oop," as old Hall said. A tall, gold-laced hatted, moustachioed footman, in a dirty drab greatcoat, was in the act of returning to a high mail phaeton, yellow picked out with red, drawn by a pair of silver duns, in which was seated an enormous Daniel Lambert-looking man in undress uniform, and a little shrimp of a woman in a mixed costume of faded finery, in the shape of summer and winter clothes. A green terry - velvet bonnet with a yellow feather, a large ermine tippet over a light-blue muslin gown, with a machinery-lace-covered pink parasol, bright yellow-ochre-coloured gloves, and black velvet bands, with long ends and bright buckles round her wrists, as if she had sprained them. Altogether—man, woman, vehicle, horses —a very remarkable turn-out. The servant is now waiting for orders.

"ASK IF MISTRESS WHAT-HER-NAME'S AT HOME," bellowed the monster, in a tone that sounded right into the house, and was heard by the curious on either side of the street, who had been attracted to their windows by the unwonted pounding of the door—" ASK IF MISTRESS WHAT'S-HER-NAME—HALL'S AT HOME," repeated he, catching the name, and flourishing his whip triumphantly over his stout Hanoverians.

"*O lauk!*" exclaimed Mrs Hall, in dismay. "I'm not fit to be seen! I've got my old gown and a dirty cap on," glancing at herself in the eagle-topped mirror, as she hurried out of the room. "Not at home, Sarey!— not at home!" exclaimed she, leaning over the banisters to the maid, who, startled over the remains of a currant dumpling, was rushing pale and frightened to the door. "Not at home, Sarey!—not at home," repeated Mrs Hall, almost loud enough to be heard outside.

"Not at home!" blurted out Sarah, before the question was put at the half-opened door; and forthwith the lady in colours produced an elegant mother-o'-pearl card-case, and handed the footman an assortment of various sized cards for the not-at-homeites to help themselves to when they returned.

"Master's at home," observed Sarah, in a tremulous voice, with a laudable regard for the honour and credit of the bank.

"I THOUGHT YOU SAID NOT AT HOME," roared the officer, in a voice of thunder.

"Master *is*, missis is not," replied the maid, timidly.

"AH—WELL, I'LL JUST GO IN AND SEE WHAT SORT OF A TIGER HE IS," observed the officer in the same tone after a pause; and, depositing the whip in its case, he handed the pipeclayed reins to the lady, and descended with a swag that shot her up in her seat like a pea.

He was indeed a fat man, and his crimson-and-gold belt was lost in the folds of fat at his sides. Having alighted on *terra firma*, he shook himself to see that he was all there, and then proceeded to labour in on his heels, paddling as it were with his short fat fins of arms.

The tiger had got himself into his lair ready for a pounce before the heavy man got creaked upstairs to the door which Sarey had left wide open, after a hurried half-frightened exclamation of "The gentleman, sir," hoping she was right in letting him in—fearing she was wrong.

"Sivin and four's elivin, and forty-five is fifty-six— what the deuce can the feller want with me?" muttered old Hall to himself. "Sivin and four's elivin, and ninety-five's a 'under'd and six—he'll stand a dooced bad chance of gettin' a bill done after that impittence," thinking of his calling him a tiger. "Sivin and four's elivin, and a 'under'd and fifteen is a 'under'd and twenty-six—what a time he is in gettin' up," thought he, as the ponderous heavy-breathing man still laboured at the ascent. At length he appeared at the door.

"Mr Hall (puff), I believe (wheeze)," gasped the officer, snatching his gold-laced foraging-cap off his great round head, and giving an uncouth bow with a kick out behind.

The banker acknowledged the impeachment without rising from his seat.

"I've called (puff)," roared he,—"that's to say, Mrs Colonel (wheeze) Blunt and (puff) I have done Mrs (wheeze) Hall the (gasp) honour to call. I mean to say," continued he, waddling across the room to an easy-chair as he spoke,— "I mean to say, Mrs Colonel Blunt and (wheeze) I have done our (gasp) *selves* the honour to call on Mrs (puff) What's-her-name," sousing himself into the chair as he spoke, "to ask you to come to a little (puff) entertainment —music—mornin' hop, *thé dansante*, as she calls it, or ear-ache and stomach-ache, as I call it; and your (puff) son—how's your (puff) son? James, that's to say—fine young man (wheeze), great favourite of mine (puff); great (wheeze) pleasure in making his (gasp) 'quaintance. And your daughter; oh! I beg (puff) pardon, you haven't a daughter. It's Mr Buss who has the daughter (puff); you townspeople are all so (puff) alike, you

puzzle one. It's Mr Buss who has the daughter—(puff)—
dev'lish ugly girl she is too (wheeze) ; ugliest girl I ever
saw—nasty-looking girl, I should say. He—he—he !
Haw—haw—haw ! Ho—ho—ho ! "

Hall accompanied this speech, or rather parts of a speech,
with the following mental commentary—

" Sivin and four's elivin, and forty-nine's sixty (what
a fat man he is), and sixty's a 'under'd and twenty, and
ninety's two 'under'd and ten (I wonder whether he'll
be asking me to do a bill), and twenty-nine's two 'under'd
and thirty-nine " (that's a piece of impittence callin'
Tummus, James—knows his name's Tummus as well as
I do), and forty-five's two 'under'd and ninety-four (Miss
Buss *is* an ugly girl) ; " and as Hall hated old Buss,
the censure of the daughter rather expiated the offence
of calling Tummus, James.

" Thank you, sir,—that's to say, colonel—that's to
say, sir—that's to say, Colonel Blunt," replied Hall,
after the monster had exhausted himself. " Mrs H.
and I are much obl*e*ged by the compliment of this call.
Tummus, not James," continued Hall, eyeing the monster
intently,—" *Tummus, not James*," repeated he, " will
have much pleasure in accepting your note,—that's to
say, your *invitation*," continued he, with an emphasis,
lest the inadvertency should lead to the production of a
bill-stamp.

" Oh, but *you* must come too," roared the now recruited colonel ; " you must come too—*you* and *Mrs
What's-her-Name*, and all—hear my daughter play—finest
performer in the world !—quite divine ! "

" Sivin and four's elivin, and forty-eight's fifty-nine—
there's a darter in the case, is there ? " mused Hall.
" Thank you, sir—that's to say, colonel," replied he,
aloud. " You're very good ; but music's not much in
my way."

" Why, as to that," replied the colonel, with a shrug
of his great shoulders—" why, as to that, I've no great
eye for music myself ; but the women like these sort of
fandangoes, and we must knock under to them sometimes, you know—he, he, he !—haw, haw, haw !—ho,
ho, ho ! " his fat sides shaking like a shape of blancmange.

" Sivin and four's elivin, and eighty-three's ninety-four—my black shorts wouldn't show well by daylight," mused Hall, " and Mrs H. would be sure to want a new gown to go in. No, I thank you, Mister Colonel," resumed Hall, aloud ; " you're very good, but it's really quite out of my line, and Mrs H., though very well at home, won't do to take abrooad."

Just as Mr Hall made this unfortunate declaration, the lady who " didn't do to take abrooad " made her appearance, a splendidly revised edition of the one that had fled. A fine fly-away cap, with full forty yards of pink ribbon, graced the back of her silvery-streaked head, while an elaborately-worked collar drooped over a shot-silk dress that assumed a variety of colours according to the light.

" Oh, here's Mrs Buss ! " exclaimed the colonel, as she entered ; " here's Mrs Buss herself ! "

" I say, Mrs Buss, what d'ye think your husband says ? " roared the military monster, treating her just as he would a barmaid—" what d'ye think your husband says ? He says, by Jove ! that you're very well at home, but you don't do to take abroad—he, he, he ! Now *I* should say," continued he, eyeing her intently—" *I* should say that you're a devilish deal better-looking woman than he is a man—haw, haw, haw !—ho, ho, ho ! But, however, never mind," continued he, checking his guffaw ; " I'll tell you what I've come about—I'll tell you for what I've come about. Mistress Colonel Blunt and I have called to ask you to come to a *thé dansante*, or dancing tea, as she calls it ; or ear-ache and stomach-ache, as I call it—you and your husband, and my friend Charles—so now you must come."

He rose and rolled out of the room, leaving old Hall and his wife to settle the question of looks between them at their leisure as soon as they recovered from the petri-faction of astonishment into which his condescending visit had thrown them. The Colonel then stumped downstairs, and climbing up into the phaeton, resumed the whip and reins, roaring out as he squashed himself into his seat, " RUMMEST COUPLE I EVER SAW ! " He then flourished the whip over the Hanoverians, the tall footman clambered up behind, and the rickety vehicle went jingling, like a tambourine, over the uneven pavement, to the delight of the children and the admiration of the country folks, who thought it a most splendid turn-out.

CHAPTER VIII.

THE *THÉ DANSANTE.*

NOT having the Fleecyborough census-paper at hand, we are unable to say what age the lovely Angelena— Miss Blunt—returned herself at, but her mamma admitted she was out of her teens, while a rival mamma would very likely set her down at thirty or more. Be that, however, as it may, she had all the worldly experience of a woman of thirty. She had flirted with and jilted half the young men during their passage through the regiment : Cornets Cubley, Disher, Dazzler, Dibs, and Shaver ; Lieutenants Dancewell, Wildblood, Bouquet, and Gape, courting as a soldier's daughter ought to court—by the word of command—making up to this man when told he was a "catch"—chopping over to that when advised he was "better." Her present *liaison* was with our little pig-eyed friend, Cornet Jug, a beardless boy, equally enamoured of his bottle and her. He would be an honourable when his grandpapa, old Lord Pitcher, went to the "well." Invincible Tom was now coming to cut him out.

Singularly enough, the band struck up "See the conquering hero comes" as Tom dashed up to the door of the colonel's barrack-house in a Fleecyborough fly on the day of the *thé dansante.*

"Mr Hall !" "Mr Hoar !" "Mr Horn !" announced three consecutive Heavysteed Dragoon footmen, as our fat friend elbowed his way upstairs into the colonel's little rooms, now looking less by the profusion of hairy heavies simpering their vapid inanities over the perspiring, and therefore thoroughly happy, rank, beauty, and fashion of Fleecyborough. Dancing teas not being much in vogue in that neighbourhood, some were attired in evening, some in morning, dresses. Miss Blunt being of the slim, not to say scraggy order, capable of improvement by millinery, was in an elegant Turkish trouser-sleeved tarlatan double-skirted muslin dress, that seemed undecided whether it would be a morning or an evening one. It was made as a tunic, both skirts trimmed all round with plaited pink ribbon and very broad machinery lace. She also wore a black lace jacket with most voluminous sleeves, showing her arms well up to the elbows. These were heavily laden with jewellery, for though her well-disciplined mind would not allow of her thinking for "one moment" of a man without her "beloved parents' approval," she nevertheless exercised a sound discretion of her own with regard to keeping their presents, and her hands and arms were perfect trophy-bearers of her eyes. There, in the shape of rings and lockets and chains and bracelets and armlets, glittered the spoils of war—the honours of many sieges. She could have furnished a conquest department in the Crystal Palace. One might almost read the characters of her lovers in their presents. In the mild, fairy-like web of that turquoise-studded Venetian chain breathes the soft languishing notes of Lieutenant Wildblood; in that plain gold armlet with the sparkling diamond heart we read the cruel case of Cornet Dibs; that showy, never-going armlet watch tells the deception that was practised upon honest Gape; the bacchanalian-grouped cameo proclaims the taste of little Jug. But to our dashing Tom.

There was a general lull and stare, and nudging and putting up of eye-glasses, as, red-faced and hot, our friend forced his way into the room, the officers eyeing him with pity as the next victim, the ladies feeling somewhat hurt at Mrs Blunt trenching, as it were, on their preserve. "Not that they, &c.,—*but*, &c."

"How ARE YE, HALL?" roared the colonel, who was standing in full uniform, looking like a red-hot globe in the centre of the little room, the perspiration standing on his bald but still darkly-fringed head. "How ARE YE, HALL?" repeated he, extending an enormous fin

c

of an arm. And drawing Tom towards him, he shot
him forward with a force that cannon'd him against his
wife and daughter.

" Let me introduce my darter," observed the former,
on recovering her equilibrium.

The happy couple made their obeisances like combatants
entering the arena, and again the surging roar of conversation rose and overwhelmed what followed. The
small room was crammed to suffocation ; and the gallant
men were so intent on guarding the fair, that they seemed
to have put on all their accoutrements, and brought
everything, except their horses, into the room.

" Oh, my toe ! " squeaked little Miss Smiley, as Captain
Dash came down upon it with his spur.—" That's my
foot, sir ! " exclaimed Mr Benson, as Captain Pippin
began to drum upon it with his sword.—" Would you have
the kindness to move a little that way ? " asked Mrs
Makepiece mildly ; " the peak of your helmet is piercing
my back." But we must leave these minor casualties in
favour of the greater actors in this our drama.

Most regular flirts have a set form of attack, and
Angelena's was of the most direct and positive order.
She always advised young men to have their pictures
taken. " Oh, dear ! she thought it such a pity for men
not to be ' pinted,' " as she called it, for she had an elegant
way of making her a's into i's, and committing other
extravagances with the English language. " She thought
it such a pity for men not to be ' pinted ' when they
were young and handsome. Wouldn't he now—wouldn't
he have his portrait ' pinted ? ' " and she would look in
the goose's grinning face in the most winning, beseeching
way possible. She had sent a dozen fools to the "pinter's,"
and was just advising little Jug to have his unmeaning
mug taken when the new conquering hero arrived. She
went at Tom most vigorously—eyes, nose, mouth, ears,
hands, and all. After an icebreaker about the weather,
she diverged at once into the army. " So he was going
into Lord Lavender's Hussars ! Well," continued she,
clasping her hands, and turning her eyes up to
the ceiling. " Ah ! she had heard—she had hoped—
but no matter—Lord Lavender's was a lovely corps—

the finest out of the line. Such uniforms! Heavies
in the morning, and Hussars at night! Wouldn't he
now—wouldn't he have his portrait pinted? In the
hussar uniform, with his busby on? Nothing so becoming
as a busby. It was such a pity for men not to be pinted
when they were young and handsome," dropping her
voice as she uttered the word handsome, and looking at
Tom as if she was utterly annihilated by his beauty.

" I say, Hall! I've made the match with Old Hide,"
roared the colonel, at this interesting period. " You
know what i mean, Griper and Holdfast! It's for
Friday—ten sovs.—P.P.; so you come and see it,
and dine with us after; and now, Angelena, my
dear," continued he, at a signal from his wife, " sing us
' Marble Halls,' ' The Soldier Tired,' or something
to keep us warm. He—he—he! haw—haw—haw!
ho—ho—ho!" the colonel mopping the perspiration
from his head with a great snuff-coloured bandana.

And Fibs and Stalker and Pippin, and all the jolly subs,
" he—he—he'd " and " haw—haw—haw'd," as if he
said the wittiest thing in the world. Wondrous are the
pleasantries of the powerful!

" How tiresome!" muttered Angelena, aside, to our
Tom ; adding, in an undertone, as the intelligent youth
stood with his mouth open, " well, come, you must
hand me to the piano, and turn over my music for me ; "
so saying, she ran her arm through Tom's, and went
pushing and pardoning and excusing her way through
the crowd, the lady making way for Tom, instead of Tom
making way for her. Arrived at the piano, she ungloved
her little white hands, and holding up her arms to shuffle
her manacles into their places, she again cast an imploring
glance at our hero, and whispered, " Now, *don't* forget
about the pinting."

All this was done in full sight of little Jug, who stood
biting his lips, his right hand clutching his sword
while he kept thinking what a subject Tom would be to
exercise it upon.

Then Miss ran her taper fingers gaily along the accustomed notes of the old tingling instrument. Her mamma
cried " *H-u-s-s-sh!*" the colonel rapped with his sword

against the floor ; Major Fibs clapped his red hands ;
Mrs Makepiece whispered Mrs Jenkinson, " What a bore ! "
Mrs Jenkinson observed, it was " just a show off for
themselves ; " while Mrs Loveington looked at her three
charming daughters, and thought how much better any
one of them would look at the piano : above all which
envy, hatred, malice, and other uncharitableness, the
rich clear notes of the syren arose, gradually prevailing
o'er the noise. As for Tom, he stood pilloried, looking
as sensible as young gentlemen in similar circumstances
generally do. He was now on show like a " lively turtle "
before dressing.

When the song—an Italian one—was over, loud and
vehement was the applause, the stamping, the clapping,
and thumping. Captain Spillman, who wanted a month's
leave of absence to go and have a turn with Sir Richard
in Leicestershire, cried, " *Bravo, bravo, bravo, bravissimo !* "
and clapped his hands till he burst the seams of his
eighteenpenny kids. Jug, too, squeaked his best, though
he couldn't but feel that Angelena was playing him
false. Still he thought she would never take such a lout
as Tom Hall in preference to him. It must just be because
Hall was a stranger ; and he doubted not all her former
affection would return as soon as they were together
again. So Jug squeaked a good squeak, and belaboured
his hands as well. The ladies, too—dear, truthful creatures
—applauded, and some drew nigh, complimenting the
corpulent colonel on his daughter's extraordinary execution, others flattering his wife ; while Mrs Makepiece,
who had just passed it as her private opinion to Mr
Mackintosh that " the girl had no more voice than a
peacock," rushed up to Angelena, and, seizing both her
hands, swung them like pump-handles, declaring she
reminded her of Catalani in her best days. The artless
girl gave a deprecatory shake of her prettily-shaped head,
now dressed in the madonna style, and replied, " If she
sang well enough to please her perhaps too partial friends,
it was all she desired ; " and our Tom, who was still
hard by, thought he never heard a more angelic speech.

The band outside then struck up another tune, giving
freedom of speech to the lately suppressed voices ; and

little Jug, having been primed by Captain Dazzler that
he oughtn't to let that d——d civilian cut him out,
advanced, with a noisy, free-and-easy, arm-squaring
air, and thrusting his little person before our fat Tom,
exclaimed—

"Now, Angelena, give us ' Drops of Brandy ! ' "

Angelena, who had now resumed her seat at the piano,
took no notice of him, but turning her die-away eyes up
to our Tom, said—

"What's your fivorite tune, Mr Hall ? "

And, most fortunately for Tom's musical reputation,
the lovely Jane Daisyfield had been much addicted to
"Jim Crow," which enabled Tom to cap "Drops of
Brandy" by asking for that lively air. Thereupon
Angelena struck it up most vigorously, setting all the
heads a-bobbing, and even the ponderous colonel's feet
a-shuffling. Great applause followed the execution, and
Tom felt that he had performed quite a feat in calling
for it.

After this there was an evident signalling and sign-
making going on in the room, and presently the band
struck up " The Roast Beef of Old England ; " whereupon two tawdrily-dressed dragoon footmen—much such
looking gentlemen as we see rush upon a stage to clear
it of chairs or other properties—commenced an assault
upon the wooden partition at the back of the piano,
and presently succeeded in exposing the colonel's bedroom, now fitted up with blue-and-white calico as a tent,
with a table of refreshments in the centre. At one end
of the table were tea and coffee—the *thé dansante* that
the colonel spoke of when he called to ask the Halls—
while the other was occupied with red and white wine
negus-jugs, cut decanters, and glasses. On the centre
of the table stood a thing like a glass dumb-waiter, surmounted by three tiers of calves'-foot jelly glasses, and
flanked on either side by the mess epergnes, tastefully
piled with fruits and flowers, the handiwork of the lovely
Angelena. Between the epergnes and the silver trays
at the ends of the table were wine-coolers, with nothing
in them. Both Mrs and Miss had tried hard for a few
bottles of cheap champagne, but the colonel had most

resolutely resisted any such extravagance, observing, that if they once began to give champagne, there was no saying how much a mob of that sort would mop up, and that they would abuse them far more, if they didn't get enough, than praise them for giving any. Indeed, the colonel had been bent upon giving as cheap an entertainment as possible, having first of all calculated that twenty or five-and-twenty shillings, judiciously expended in fruit and confectionery, aided by the great attractions of " our band—finest in the service," of course—would give such an ear-ache and stomach-ache as would amply requite any attentions they had received at the hands of their Fleecyborough friends.

As usual, however, with such undertakings, the programme extended as the arrangements proceeded, and long before the appointed day the five-and-twenty shillings had grown into a five-pound note. This was, perhaps, caused a good deal by the lithping major going about the town talking of the " great preparathons they were making for the ball at the barrackth—the e-*nor*-moth ecthpenth the old colonel wath going to ; " darkly hinting that " it wathn't impothible the old Dook might be down." This had the desired effect, and many people who gave good dinners, but not to the military, began to think they would make an exception in favour of the Heavysteed Dragoons. They didn't say, point-blank, let's go and card the colonel, and see if we can get an invite, but Mrs Freebody said casually to her husband, as he was smacking his lips after his fourth glass of port wine, " F., my dear, don't you think you might as well (hem) call (hem) at the (hem) barracks ? "

" *Call at the barracks !* " retorted Freebody (a substantial brewer), firing up. " What the deuce should I call at the barracks for ? Barracks indeed ! Why these people get their beer at the Jerry-shop ; what should I call at the barracks for ? " he repeated, fixing his bloodshot eyes on his astonished wife.

" Oh, just to be civil to the military," replied his wife.

" *Civil to the military !* " exclaimed Freebody. " *Will they be civil to me ?*—eat my dinners—drink my wine—

and call me a base mechanic behind my back. Just as
they do old Jack Gooseman. No—no—no barracks for
me, I thank'ee ; " and thereupon he filled himself an
overflowing bumper.

" Oh, that was those saucy hussars," replied his wife.
" It was just like their impittance—thought there was
nobody in the town good enough for them to 'sociate
with ; but these gents seem quite different sort of gents ;
amiable agreeable young people ; dance with all the girls
at the balls—at least, all those whose houses they dine
at ; and the colonel's daughter seems a most genteel
young person—quite a desirable 'quaintance for our girls.
Besides, they're going to give a ball. The Busses are
asked, and the Chinneys are asked, and the Plummeys
are asked, and the Halls are asked, and it *would* be such
a thing if our girls were not there."

And Freebody, who hated the Halls more than there
is any occasion to describe, principally because old Hall
had " sivin-and-four'd " one of his bills at a time when
Freebody was not thought so " highly respectable " as
he had since become ; Freebody, we say, hating the
Halls, and other considerations him thereunto moving,
was at length induced to card the colonel. And many
others being similarly instigated, the five-and-twenty
shillings soon stood a very poor chance of satisfying
the requirements of the occasion. However, the colonel
consoled himself under the increased expenditure by
thinking that he had good six months to eat his returns
out in before the regiment was moved, and that it might
not be impolitic to endeavour to enlist the townspeople
in aid of his designs upon Hall. Accordingly, he saw
the calves'-feet jelly, and porcupine sponge cakes, and
finger cakes and fruit—above all, the job calico for the
tent—arrive without kicking up any of those tremendous
shindies that he was in the habit of doing when things
went contrary to his wishes. And this reminds us that,
having got so far in the entertainment as the opening
of the banqueting bedroom for the stomach-ache part
of the *thé dansante*, it may be as well for the reader and
guests to enter together.

Looking at the *coup d'œil*, it did not seem as if the

colonel had misnamed the entertainment ; for hard-featured apples, harder - featured pears, sour - looking plums, and bunches of questionable-looking black things, that Angelena not inaptly called " gripes," formed the principal feature of the feast. However, they were well set on, tastefully decorated with flowers and ever-greens, and a pleasantly-disposed public accorded the usual indulgence granted to bachelor and barrack efforts. Old Miss Fozington, to be sure, with her accustomed curiosity, went prying about with her eye-glass, guessing that this was borrowed, that hired, the fruit a cheap bargain, pinching the table-cloth to test its quality, and even fishing for the mark to see that it was their own. But even she, with all her talent for detraction, could not but admit that the entertainment was " not so bad," and much better than anything that Mrs Loving-ton, or even the Empress of Morocco—as they called Mrs Halfhide, the tanner's wife, who essayed to lead the Fleecyborough fashion—ever gave. Indeed the whole thing—the name, *thé dansante*—the unwonted hour—the mixed and uncertain dress, the tent-like room, the boisterous band—above all, the dear delightful barracks, with sentries and real soldiers, and simpering officers in all the pomp and circumstance of war—led the im-aginations of the excitable ones into the airy regions of romantic flight. From these pleasant excursions, just as the thing was in full swing—the band uproarious, and all hands settled to their game, Miss Spencer at Mr Fielding, Miss Weathertit at Mr White Brown, Miss Tinney at Mr Thompson, and Angelena languishing at our Tom, as she offered him some more " gripes "—a loud tapping was heard at the top of the table, and presently Sir Thomas Thimbleton rose, and gave indica-tions of eloquence. Sir Thomas, whose father had been a great army tailor, was a Dublin Castle knight, but, like all truly great men, condescending withal—and no feast or *fête*, or wedding, or christening, in Fleecyborough, or within a radius of three miles, was considered perfect without Sir Thomas Thimbleton of Thimbleton Park (so he called his villa with twenty acres of land). He always took the palavering department as of right, and, though

a man of few words, he contrived to stretch them over an
extraordinary space of time, always, if possible, making
a mess of the thing. He was a terrible man for treading
on peoples' corns. Anxious mammas trembled when
they saw his vacant visage rise on its substantial star-
bedecorated pedestal, lest he should nip a rising *liaison*
in the bud, or connect a couple in a toast who hated the
sight of each other. The most unimaginative listener
knew what he was going to say long before his dwelling
tongue came up to the words. On this occasion he began,
as usual, with "Ladies and gentlemen," and having
got so far, placed his right hand in his richly-buttoned
velvet-collared blue coat, and pondered a little, as if
he *was* going to say something original this time. Then,
having raised the expectations of his audience, he gave
a loud cough, and again said "Ladies and gentlemen,"
which produced renewed tapping and a dead pause.

"Ladies and gentlemen," said he, for the third time,
"I consider it one of the proudest privileges of rank and
station"—("Old story over again," whispered Miss
Tinney to Mr Thompson. "Old fool! his father was a
tailor," muttered Mr White Brown to Mrs White Brown
that was to be)—"I consider it one of the proudest
privileges of rank and station to be permitted on this
occasion"—a pause, while he considered whether it was
a birth, death, marriage, or meeting of the Conservative
Club, where he had a lease of the toast, "The health of
the Duchess of Fleecyborough," the Lord-Lieutenant's
lady; finding it was none of these, he backed the train
of his thoughts a little, repeating the words, "to be
permitted, on this occasion—this festive occasion"—
applause from those who thought he had got himself
into a fix—"this *most* festive occasion," repeated he,
cheered by the encouragement, "to propose the health
of the distinguished—*illustrious*, I should say—givers—
donors of this sumptuous—this most sumptuous—this
most elegant and sumptuous——" (dead pause)—

"EAR-ACHE AND STOMACH-ACHE!" roared the old
colonel, coming to the rescue.

The old knight, nothing disconcerted at the outburst
of laughter that followed, stood, taking impressions

of his inverted wine-glass on the table-cloth, till the noise had somewhat subsided, an interval that enabled him to consider how he should wind up his oration. Child's health there was none to propose; "married couple" were equally out of the question; but a quick-minded world often setting parties out for each other before they are aware of it themselves, it now occurred to Sir Thomas that he had heard something about Tom Hall and Miss Blunt, and seeing the interesting couple looking sweet at each other, with his usual propensity for blundering, he jumped to the conclusion that they were betrothed, and proceeded to announce it as follows, being his usual form of speech for wedding breakfasts—

"This sumptuous *entertainment*," continued he, with an emphasis on the word that had brought him up short, "an entertainment ushering an event that he hoped would be as conducive to the happiness of the interesting young couple," looking at Tom and Angelena, "as he was sure it would be pleasing to their respective parents and friends." Applause from the mischievous, with "Poohs!" "Pshaws!" "No, noes!" "Stuff and nonsense!" "What's the man about?" from the colonel and Mrs Blunt.

Nothing daunted, the doughty knight turned up his glass, and filling it with hot elder wine, called on the company for an overflowing bumper to the healths of Colonel and Mrs Blunt, Mr and Mrs Hall, and Mr and Mrs THOMAS HALL, the last names being received with the most uproarious laughter and applause. The knight was quite cock-a-hoop; he thought he had done it wonderfully well—everybody else thought he was mad. The fair Angelena blushed a real blush, and hung her head; Tom Hall gaped with astonishment; Jug looked as if he would eat Tom; and there was such a battering and clattering on the table that three-and-sixpenceworth of glass was demolished in no time; the dumb-waiter-looking jelly-stand quaked, the Ripstone pippins, pears, and grapes came rolling from their places, and great was the relief when the colonel, clapping his great mutton fists, announced that the late concert-room was ready for dancing.

" What a man it is ! " (meaning Sir Thomas) exclaimed
Angelena, running her arm through Tom's, clasping her
hands like a bracelet on the top of it, as she led him
away to the head of the quadrille, already forming by the
obsequious heavies, all anxious to do honour in the
colonel's *fête*.

Now Tom's education had been neglected in the dancing
as in other lines, but having no option given him, he
just took his place, and went rolling and bumping about,
getting in everybody's way, and getting smart tastes
of the spurs of the soldiery. Angelena did her best to
keep him right, but before the quadrille was over, the
happy couple had monopolised the attention of the
whole room. However, Angelena was not easily put out
of her way—at least, when it was her interest not to be—
though she could read the " riot act " as loudly as anybody when she had no interest in being amiable.

Having at length worked the fat and now profusely
perspiring youth through the intricacies of the dance,
she gladly led him back to the refreshment-room, where
she began to make the most of her time in a series of
pertinent questions, beginning with, " Was he going to
stay altogether at Fleecyborough ? Was he going to
dine at the Emperor of Morocco's on Monday ? Would
he be at Mrs Moneytin's party on Tuesday ? Was he
acquainted with the Fergusons of Thorneyfield ?—Well
now he ought to know them—indeed he ought—most
agreeable people—Sophy Fergey was a particular friend
of hers—*such* a nice girl ! *so* unaffected ! " And as she
was explaining how Sophy and she met every other
Friday when Sophy's father was justice-ising at Fleecyborough, at the cottage by the windmill on Heatherblow
Heath (Mr Mattyfat of the Heavysteeds, we are concerned
to say, making a third, to meet the fair Sophy), little
Jug, nothing daunted by his former rebuff, again swaggered
up and claimed Angelena's hand for a waltz. The fair
lady pretended not to hear him, and flaunting her handkerchief, went on expatiating on the merits of Sophy, who
she was sure our Tom would like to know, suggesting
that the heath was such a charming place to ride upon,
asking if our Tom was fond of riding ?—declaring, without

waiting for an answer, that she *delighted* in it herself,
asserting that she had the sweetest lady's horse in the
world, that the queen had sent to buy it, and her father
wouldn't let her have it.   When little Jug tired of admiring her back, he got round to the front, and said, in an
angry tone, " Well, Angelena, are you going to dance
with me or not ? "

" To be sure I am ! " replied the fair lady, starting
as if she had never heard the previous question, and
looking most lovingly at our Tom, she suffered herself
to be led away by the now triumphant Jug, who whisked
her and twirled her, and twisted her and jumped her,
till Tom, in his turn, was troubled with jealousy.   As
they every now and then swept past his nose, he determined, if he laboured all night, that he would learn to
waltz.   In the midst of this resolution, and certain
imaginary arrangements for licking Jug, the band suddenly
struck up " God save the Queen "—the *thé dansante*
was over.   Adieux, hunting for hats, shawls, and cloaks
quickly followed, mingled with protestations that of all
agreeable parties that was the most so ; and when at
length it came to our hero's turn to take leave, Angelena,
looking archly in his face, as she held his fat hand,
whispered—

" *Now, don't forget to be pinted.* "

And Tom went home with a desperate heart-ache.

CHAPTER IX.

"CONSIDERING" A HORSE.

MAJOR FIBS pretended to be thorry that Tom Hall had
got a commithon in Lord Lavender's Hussars, observing
that the colonel had written to old Wellington to give
him one in the Heavysteed Dragoons, and he was sure
old Wellington would only be too happy to have it in his
power to oblige their old boy.

The fat colonel, on his part, patronised our friend
extensively, and when he read that Thomas Hall, gent.,
was appointed to a cornetcy in the Royal Lavender
Dragoons and Hyacinth Hussars, *vice* Lord Shockingdog
retired, he bethought him of mounting Tom becomingly.
Now Captain Smallbeere of the Heavysteeds (then absent
on leave) had a second charger, a horse that, without
speaking too disparagingly of it, "might have been
better," and the colonel's sagacity suggested some good
might be done with it. Accordingly he bought him—
a time bargain—forty pounds, with liberty to return
him at the end of a week if he didn't like him—that is
to say, if he couldn't make anything of him. He was a
nice-looking horse ; indeed, his looks were the best part
about him. He had two good ends, as the horse-dealers
say : a nice light, well set-on head, an arched neck
with a flowing mane, and a full, well set-on, life guards
tail. He was not deficient in middle-piece either, being
round in the barrel, well ribbed up, and altogether a
taking-looking animal. Indeed, he had taken many
people in. He had taken young Mr Simpkins in, he had
taken middle-aged Mr Gooseman in, and he had taken
old Mr Gammon in. He had been twice unsaddled for

dead in the hunting-field, and only escaped repetition
of the scene by knocking up before he got to the meet.
He was a washy, weak, good-looking, good-for-nothing
animal, that with coddling and pampering and linseed-
teaing and hand-rubbing could come out of the stable
a very fine showy creature. Colour, a dark brown, with
tan muzzle, four black legs, and a star.

" I know a horse that would suit you to a T," observed
the colonel, the first time he met our friend after the
above-mentioned arrangement with Smallbeere. " Just
the thing for the yeomanry—used to troops—such a
one to salute the general upon at a review ; " the colonel
performing the evolution with a great, baggy, brown
alpaca umbrella as he spoke.

" Sivin and four's elivin, and twenty-four's thirty-
five—I don't know that soldiers are good folks to buy
horses of," observed old Hall, filing away at his chin,
when his son told him what the colonel said. " Should
say, if they had a good 'un, they'd keep him among 'em—
at least, I think—I take it so—I apprehend so."

" I think so too," replied our Tom, who had no more
fancy for being " done " than his father, " only," added
he, considering the instability of his seat—indeed, his
utter inexperience in the saddle—" it might be as well,
perhaps, to have a horse that knows his business, and
that wouldn't unship me."

" True," replied old Hall, after a pause, and a little
more mental arithmetic. " True, and therefore I'd
look at him ; but I'd be cautious about buyin'—buy
in haste, repent at leisure—buy a good 'un when you
do buy. A good horse costs no more keeping than a bad
'un ; a bad 'un 'ill eat as much as a good 'un, perhaps
more, because he's got more time."

Tom pondered all this in his mind, and having heard
a good deal from dear Jane Daiseyfield's brother Tom,
who was rather an adept at cheating in horses, how
they tricked them up for the market, and how they
gammoned the greenhorns (if ever there was such a
thing as a self-admitted greenhorn in horse-dealing, which
we very much doubt), Tom went to look at the horse by
appointment, without much expectation of doing business.

Though he went, as we say, by appointment, the diplomatic old colonel, whom he found playing at quoits with the Vet at the back of the riding-school, pretended to have forgotten all about it, and assuming that Tom had come to see the ladies, he offered to show him his daughter's pad on his way—"a perfect lady's horse— one that he had been offered no end of money for— but, poor thing, he couldn't bear the idea of selling her. Angelena was so fond of her," continued he, as he shuffled himself into his frock-coat, and adjusted his forage cap, for the day was warm, and he had been taking it coolly. He then waddled away to the stable, where, between two elephantine chargers, stood the model of perfection, an Arab-like cream colour, with a flowing silvery mane, and a tail reaching down to the heels.

"There!" roared the colonel, as the soldier-groom swept the clothes over its hind-quarters—"there's (puff) shape for you!—there's an Arab-like head—there are clean well-shaped legs and an elegantly set-on tail," continued he, as the mare began to flourish and switch it in return for the tickling of the groom. "That's the sort of thing now," continued he, in a lower tone, drawing across the line of scent, "that Lavender would give any money for to mount one of his band upon; indeed, the Dook's always at me for it for the Life Guards; but what's the use of parting with one's comforts,—one's child's comforts,—one's daughter's comforts. Couldn't do it!—couldn't bear the thought of it!—couldn't, by Jove!" added he, boiling up, and kicking out with his right fin. Then, after a pause, and passing sundry compliments on his other quadrupeds, and anathematising the soldier-groom for not having the scanty straw laid out to air, he suddenly pretended to remember that Tom had turned a soldier, and would be wanting something in their line. "Shouldn't wonder now," continued he thoughtfully, as he held his chubby chin in his hand— "shouldn't wonder now, if Smallbeere's horse would suit you. Does anybody know anything about Captain Smallbeere's horse?" continued he, staring around, an inquiry that failed to elicit an answer from the well-drilled stablemen. "Send the adjutant here!" roared

he. " The adjutant will know all about it," continued
he, addressing Tom ; adding, " these noodles never
know anything."

Adjutant Collop was a trusty man, and, having been
in a good many robberies with the colonel, was extremely
useful as well in forwarding the transactions as in keeping
Major Fibs in order, who might have been more exorbi-
tant in his " regulars " if he had had no one to compete
with. So now to the deal.

The sentries had had orders to acquaint the adjutant
the next time our friend Tom entered the barrack-
ground ; and, having got the information, he had been
busy during the time the colonel was expatiating on the
beauties of his stud in removing a sweating bandage
from the brown horse's near fore-leg, and offering him
sundry little attentions that the uninitiated are, perhaps,
as well ignorant of. The colonel's summons found Collop
in the act of biting a piece of ginger, which he handed
hastily to the groom, and hurried away to obey the
great commander.

" Ah ! there he is ! " observed the colonel, as the
adjutant whipped round the canteen corner ; " always
at his desk—always at his desk ; greatest consumer of
ink in the service—sometimes tell him I think he must
write the ' Edinburgh Review,' or ' Bell's Life in London,'
or the ' Lives of the Chancellors,' or some of those sort
of fandangoes—he's always so full of employment."

The adjutant now approached with a pen in one hand,
making a full deferential swing of salute with the other.

" Well, old inky fingers, how are ye ? " roared the
colonel. " Hope you find your cash all square, and
don't cheat yourself out of any halfpence. ' Take care
of the pence, and the pounds 'ill take care of themselves,'
my grandmother used to teach me. Haw ! haw ! haw !—
he ! he ! he !—ho ! ho ! ho ! "

And Adjutant Collop he, he, he'd ! haw, haw, haw'd !
and ho, ho, ho'd ! just as if he had never heard the saying
before.

" Well, Col," resumed the colonel, as their risible
faculties subsided, " well, Col, you're the man ! Wish
I had a dozen such. This is my friend Hall ; believe you

know Mr Hall; dined with us at the mess, you know. Now, can you tell us," continued he, still speaking at the top of his voice, though they were all close together, "can you tell us anything about Smallbeere's horse?— the brown, you know; the one he rode with Jugginson's harriers."

"The brown," repeated the adjutant, thoughtfully— "the brown. He's sold," added he, after a pause, "to Bartley."

"Sold!" exclaimed the colonel, throwing up his fins in well-feigned disgust—"sold! That is a pity!—that is a pity!—very horse to have suited our friend Hall here; gone into the Yeomanry; wants a charger or two."

"Oh, you mean the *charger!*" exclaimed the adjutant, with an air of sudden enlightenment—"you mean the charger!"

"To be sure," replied the colonel, "to be sure. You don't s'pose I meant that rotten devil Samson? Wouldn't take him in a gift—dashed if I would!" added he, with a crack of his thigh with his right fin.

"Oh, the brown charger is in," observed the adjutant deferentially.

"Ah, come, I thought so," replied the colonel, eyeing Tom encouragingly; adding, what he considered *sotto voce* though quite loud enough for Collop to hear, "My adjutant isn't quite so bright as he might be this morning. Got muddled with his accounts, p'r'aps." Then, turning to Collop, he roared out, "Well, now, does anybody know anything about the horse?—I mean, has anybody any instructions about him—about selling him, I mean?"

"Yes, I have," replied the adjutant promptly.

"You have?" responded the colonel; adding, "that's business-like, now. Let's see him out."

"Certainly," replied the adjutant, leading the way to the stable.

The colonel then got himself on to his heels, and, accompanied by Tom, went wad, wad, waddling across the barrack-yard; the farther he went the farther he was left behind by the swift-footed adjutant, who hastened to see that all was right in the stable.

"You'll not be wanting to ride far, p'r'aps?" observed

the colonel, recollecting that a young gentleman at Norwich
had once ridden one of his officer's horses to Ipswich
and back on trial; "you'll not be wanting to ride him
far, p'r'aps?" repeated he, as he puffed and laboured
away on his heels.

"Oh, no," replied Tom, glad of an excuse for not
mounting at all. "Oh no," repeated he. "Indeed—
in fact—to tell you the truth—I—I—I—only want to
look at him."

"Oh, you can *ride* him," said the colonel—"you
can ride him; only don't bucket him cross country,
you know, or ram him at any impossible places. The
horse can hunt, no doubt; but what I recommend him
to you for is as a charger. There I think he'll excel.
Colonel Peters himself couldn't have made him more
perfect. Indeed, if I wasn't certain about it, I wouldn't
recommend him to you, for who shall counsel a man
in the choice of a wife or a horse, as Solomon, or some
other gentleman of fortune, asked. Haw, haw, haw!—
he, he, he!—ho, ho, ho!" the colonel inwardly hoping
he might have to suit Tom with both.

Prudent people may think that the colonel would
have done well to confine himself to one endeavour, but
his rule was never to lose a chance; and he had seen
the failure of so many of Angelena's bright prospects,
that he thought the horse might be the best chance of
the two.

The reader will now have the kindness to suppose
our fat friends arriving at the stable door just as the
horse's tan muzzle pioneered his glossy body, radiant
with grooming, and fresh from the operation of mane
and tail combing and brushing, to say nothing of other
figments. Whatever might have been Tom's misgivings
and suspicions—whatever his previous determinations
about buying or not buying, they entirely vanished
under the influence of the colonel's honest interest and the
pleasing appearance of the horse. He stepped out of
the stable so lightly and quietly, and as Tom marked
his blooming coat, clean unblemished legs, and placid
eye—above all, the flowing flourish of his well set-on
tail—an appendage that has led more young ladies and

gentlemen into mischief than the uncandid will care to acknowledge—Tom's only fear was that they would be asking an impossible price for him—two or three hundred perhaps.

"There!" exclaimed the colonel, striking out his right fin towards the horse, "there! that's a neat horse! He's not a great horse, nor a grand horse, nor an over-powering horse; but he's a neat horse—a gentleman's horse—a horse that a man may ride down St James's-street before all the bow-window beggars that ever were foaled, and snap his fingers at the 'ole lot on 'em "—the colonel accompanying the declaration with a hearty snap of his own. And Tom stood mute, simply because he didn't know what to say, and didn't like to let out that this was his first deal. "Good shoulders—deep girth—fine, expressive, blood-like head," continued the colonel. "How old is he?" demanded he of the man.

"Seven off, sir," replied the groom, with a respectful touch of his forelock.

"Seven off," repeated the colonel, "seven off. Thought he'd been older. Devilish good age," whispered he to Tom. "Wasn't handled till he was four; did nothin' till he was five. Easin' 'em at one end puts a deal on at t'other. That horse'll be fresh at twenty." And Tom still stood mute, for the colonel's logic was all Greek to him. He was as ignorant as Pickwick in all that related to horses—didn't know whether they lived to twenty, fifty, or a hundred. He would have given anything for an idea.

"Get on him, Hall," at length roared the colonel, tired of Tom's staring. "Get on him," repeated he, "and give him a round in the riding-school."

"Thank'ee—no," replied Tom, in an easy, indifferent sort of way, as if he didn't think the horse likely to suit, but in reality to avoid the chance of a spill.

"Well, as you please," responded the colonel, in a huff, with a kick out of his right fin; "as you please, as you please—only don't keep the horse starvin' there, or we shall be havin' his death at our door."

"Let me lay my leg over him," interposed the adjutant, anxious, if possible, to save the deal, though he feared

things were going against him, he too suspecting Tom
had been reading some of the mischievous books that
recommend youngsters not to try horses they don't think
likely to suit, less they should afterwards be talked into
buying them.

Adjutant Collop then approached the passive animal,
and, mounting with a military stirrup, proceeded to
point his toe and show off, turning right left about on
the horse's centre, fore and hind-quarters, and so on,
to the evident satisfaction of Tom, who fancied himself
the equestrian, with his lady-love looking at him.

At the close of each well-performed evolution, Tom's
fear increased that the price would be an impossible one.

The adjutant, having twisted and turned and tickled
the horse about, at length drew up beside our friends,
with the horse's head towards the rising ground, and,
making him extend himself, he proceeded to dismount.

" How is he under you ? " roared the colonel, as if
the adjutant was a mile off.

" Sweet 'orse," replied the adjutant, who was a bit
of a Cockney. " Sweet 'orse," repeated he.

" Now will you mount him ? " demanded the colonel
of Tom.

" Thank'ee—no," replied Tom, in an easy, indifferent
sort of tone, "thank'ee—no," repeated he, turning away,
as if he wasn't going to be tempted. The fact was, he
saw little Jug and Mattyfat watching him from behind
the red curtain of the messroom window, and he didn't
know how many more might be in the bush.

" Take him in, then," roared the colonel, disgusted
at Tom's stupidity ; and, wheeling round, he proceeded
to retrace his steps to the quoit-ground, thinking what
an ass he had been to give himself so much trouble.
Tom followed passively, fearing he had offended the
opulent man.

" What's the price ? " at length asked Tom timidly,
after walking for some time in silence by the side of
the rolling man-mountain.

" Price ! " exclaimed the colonel, brightening up.
" Price ! " repeated he; "faith I can hardly tell you
about price—don't belong to me—belongs to one of my

young people—Captain Smallbeere—you know him—
ugly conceited feller—great head, button nose—away
on leave—old Collywobbles there (meaning Collop) has
the selling of him. Should say—though mind, I don't
know for certain," continued he, dropping his voice
as he scrutinised Tom's vacant face—"should think
that he might be had reasonable—say sixty, or p'r'aps
se—ven—ty guineas—*sixty* p'r'aps," continued he, as he
saw Tom's countenance fall.

And when Tom said, with a long-drawn *h-e-m*, that he
would " consider," the colonel saw he had made a mistake,
but his sagacity did not tell him where.

" Well," said he, " do as you like ; buy in haste, repent
at leisure's an old sayin', and not a bad 'un. But mind
ye ! " continued he, raising his voice, " the horse may
be sold while you are considerin'." So saying, the gallant
colonel lashed out with his right fin and struck across the
barracks to seek consolation at the hand of his friend,
Major Fibs, leaving Tom to dispose of himself as he
thought proper.

CHAPTER X.

COLONEL BLUNT CONFIDES IN MAJOR FIBS.

" Ah! I thee how it ith, thir! I thee how it ith!"
lisped Major Fibs, when the colonel told him what had
taken place, " I thee how it ith—the fact ith, thir, you're
too conthiderate—you don't do yourthelf juthtice—you
should have asked him a hundred, or a hundred and
fifty, and you'd have got it."

" D'ye think so ? " exclaimed the colonel in disgust.

" *Thure* of it," replied the major, " thure of it ;
never was a boy yet that wanted an orth under a
hundred."

" But d'ye think that old griffin of a governor of
his would have forked out the tin ? " asked the
colonel.

" No doubt about it, thir," replied the major, " no
doubt about it. Bleth ye, that old buffer's rolling in money
—has a hundred thouthand pounds in the funds—not a
hundred thouthand stock, but stock that'll prodooth
a hundred thouthand tholid thubstanthal thovereigns."

" And lives like a mouse in a cheese ! " exclaimed
the old colonel, throwing up his hands in disgust. " Well,
it's a pity," added he, " it's a *great pity*."

" It *is* a pity," replied the major thoughtfully ; " but,
excuse me for thaying it, you really throw away the
advantages of your high pothithon. What's the uth of
being colonel of a crack cavalry corps if you don't improve
your opportunities ? You don't s'pothe Andrews throws
chances away like you ? Not he, by Jove ! Two 'under'd
and fifty, or three 'under'd, and not all the Mr Watsons,
Q.C., could indooth an honest British joory to believe

that it wasn't an upright transaction. It would be a Q.C., or queer concern, if, because a man's a colonel, he's not to sell an orth for as much as he can get."

" It *would* be a pretty go indeed," assented the colonel. " I like these common councilmen thinking to teach us what's right and proper, as if the army isn't the real school for honour and morality."

" To be thure ! " rejoined the major, " to be thure ! Her Majesty's commithon wouldn't be worth holdin' if one mightn't turn an occathonal copper by orthes."

The two then sat mute for some time, the huge colonel contemplating his enormous feet, occasionally lifting one up, as if to see they were fellows, and the gaunt major stretching his legs to their utmost longitude, wetting his finger and thumb, and twiddling his truculent moustachios into points. No noise disturbed the scene, except the occasional tap, tap, tapping of the terrier dog's tail against the uncarpeted corner of the room where he lay.

" I think we might manage it yet, thir," at length observed the major.

" D'ye think so, Fibby ! " exclaimed the colonel, starting up.

" *Think* tho, thir ! " replied the major, cautiously but deferentially.

" I wish you'd try, by Jove ! " roared the colonel, " for I'm reg'larly in Short's-gardens—never was so hard up in my life. May call me *Blunt*, but I know I never have any. Don't know where to lay hands on a halfpenny ; and there's that beastly Mrs Bussleton's dunnin' me almost every post for her ' little bill,' as she calls it—eighteen pund odd."

" 'Deed ! " replied the major ; " doesn't deserve the honour of the ladies' cuthtom. However, I'll tell you what, thir, if, as I thuspect, this young gentleman was put off buyin' the orth on account of the prithe, we can accommodate him either with this orth or another."

" You'll do the State great service ! " exclaimed the colonel—" you'll do the State great service ! " repeated he. " I always say her Majesty hasn't a more meritorious officer than yourself. The Duke's services are nothin' compared to yours. Well, now, tell me how you think it can be done ? " continued he, dropping his voice, and leaning forward in his chair towards the major.

" Why," replied the major, " it must be done gingerly. I must endeavour to find out what his objecthon was to this orth ; and if it was merely prithe, I'd try him on again with it ; but if he has any tholid thubstanthal dithlike to him, then we must look out for another. There are plenty of orthes in the world, and it wouldn't do to let such a promithin' young gentleman go on foot for want of one."

" Certainly not ! " exclaimed the colonel, " certainly not ! In my humble opinion, however," added he, in a lower tone, " this horse is the very one for him—quiet tractable animal, used to troops, and all that sort of thing ; no great constitution p'r'aps, but that's matter of opinion—de gustibus non est somethin'—I forget the word," added he, with a shake of his head, " but you know what I mean ? "

" Perfectly, thir," replied the major, who had all the colonel's sayings stereotyped in his mind.

Another dead pause then ensued, broken only by the renewed tapping of the tail as before.

" He's no great horseman, I imagine," observed the colonel, at length breaking silence.

" Not a bit of one," replied the major, " doesn't set up for one indeed ; but his money's just as good as if he was—indeed, better, for as it is he can't compare notes— thay this orth is not so good as my old bay, or so fast as my young grey ; or this orth would have been better if he'd had four legs, or a thuffithenty of wind ; or make any unpleathant reflecthions of that sort."

" Very true," replied the colonel, " very true ; and therefore, Fibby, I'll confide the whole of this delicate affair to your management. Do what you think best, only don't kill the goose, you know, that lays us the golden what d'ye call the thing-um-bobs—you twig, eh ? " said the colonel, putting as much expression into his great red apple face as he could—meaning, " Don't forget Angelena's in the case."

" I understand, thir," replied the major.

" And be quick about it," rejoined the colonel.

" Of courthe, thir," replied the major ; " but, in the meantime, p'r'aps you'd have the goodneth not to do anything more in the matter yourthelf, or mention it to any one," added he, drawing his long legs up to further the colonel's departure—meaning, " Don't let Collop have a further finger in the pie."

" Certainly not ! " exclaimed the colonel, " certainly not ! Too many cooks spoil the broth. Should never be more than two at a deal—that's to say, if you expect to deal. Besides," added he, as he waddled away on his heels, " it's no use keepin' a dog and barkin' oneself."

CHAPTER XI.

THE MAJOR KNOWS OF ANOTHER HORSE.

"You did well not to buy that Thmallbeere orth, I think," observed the major confidentially to Tom, after having exhausted the usual topic of the weather, the dirtiness of the streets, the fewness of the foot people, and the number of horsemen, as he found our friend a few days after the misdeal sucking his cane-handle at Miss Isinglass's door, waiting for Padder and Proggy, and the young Emperor of Morocco, to join arms and polish the flags, and take up their usual stations at street corners. "You did well not to buy that Thmallbeere orth, I think," observed the major, after criticising two or three that passed along. "The fact ith, he'th a nice orth and a neat orth, but Beer—Thwipes, as we call him—wouldn't have parted with him if he'd been quite the thing."

"Well now, that's what I thought!" exclaimed Tom, "that's what I thought! I was sure there was something wrong when I heard the price."

"You thowed your judgment," replied the major, brightening up, "you thowed your judgment; but please have the goodneth not to tell the colonel I thaid tho, for the betht of us are liable to be dethieved, and I'm thure the colonel's great regard for you would prevent his theeing you impothed upon knowingly."

"I'm sure of that too," replied Tom, "I'm sure of that too," and he thought of Angelena, and her singing, and her fifty thousand pounds, and how he would like to be pinning the heartsease and forget-me-not white cornelian brooch upon her beautiful chemisette. Then

he thought he'd better get the brooch back before he
appropriated it to another, and wondered whether he
could safely entrust old Trueboy, the cashier, to negotiate
the return of it, and the promise of marriage letter, the
next time old Daiseyfield came to their bank to get a
bill done.

These pleasant reflections were interrupted by the
major resuming the subject of the horse.

"What you should have should be a nith, steady,
well-trained orth, that's been used to troopth, and the
firing of vollithes, and so on; much such an orth as
Thwipes's, in fact—only a little gamer, higher couraged
animal—*more* of an orth, in short. You are stout—I
don't mean to say *fat*," continued the major, looking
down on Tom's great puffy figure, "but full-limbed,
just what a man ought to be, and should have an orth
to correthpond. It's a bore being under-orthed, feeling
that you should be carrying the orth instead of the orth
carrying you."

"So I think," replied Hall, "so I think,"
adding, "I liked the cut of Swipes's horse uncommonly."

"Did you?" replied the major, "did you?" adding,
after a pause, "Well, then, do you know, I think I can
tell you of one very like him, as like as Voltigeur to the
Flying Dutchman; liker, indeed, for he's got never any
white about him. He belonged to poor Charley Chucklehead of the Bluths, who drank himself detheased. Thweet-
est snaffle-bridle orth I almost ever thaw; can canter
round a hat, and throw the dirt in the faces of all those
bragging Heartycheerites who think nobody can ride
but themselves. It's no uth keepin' an orth that can
only do one thing," continued the major, "ethpethially
now that you've made up your mind to go into the
yeomanry instead of our corps. Bleth ye! why a mere
charger would be no more uth to you than a thimney-
piece ornament the greater part of the year. He'd be a
deal worse than a thimney-piece ornament, for he'd be
constantly having his pecker in the manger, and peckers
in mangers cost money, as you and I know," the major
thinking it might be convenient to invest Tom with

a little more equestrian knowledge than he really possessed.

"Well, but I could ride him on the road, and on the heath, and so on," observed Tom, who had been repeatedly reminded by Angelena of the projected excursions to Heatherblow Heath.

"Oh, in courth," replied the major, "in courth; only a twenty-pound 'ack would do all that; but when we talk about orthes, we mean valuable animals— 'undred or 'undred and fifty guineas' worth, and so on— orthes that do a gentleman credit, and not cat-legged cripples, that look as if they'd ethcaped from a cothermonger's cart."

"Well," mused Tom, "I should like to get a good 'un."

"Take my word for it, my dear feller," replied the major, "there's nothin' like a good one—there's nothin' makes a man feel so bumpthously conthequenthal as being cocked a-top of a good 'un. So now, if you really feel inclined for a creditable animal, a good-looking animal, and don't mind prithe, why I would really advise you to send for this blue orth, and to be quick about it, for he'll soon be caught up. Good orthes don't hang fire in London."

"Well," mused Tom. "Well," repeated he, remembering what his father had said about not buying an officer's horse, "I should like to look at him—there'd be no harm in that, you know."

"True," replied the major, fearing that Tom was one of that numerous tribe, the looking sort—one of those weary fellows who are always wanting horses and never buy them; the major, we say, fearing Tom was one of the wrong sort, and that it was going to be all labour lost, at once pinned him by asking if he should write and have the horse down by the rail to look at; and after much humming and hawing and hesitation, Tom at length gave his consent, induced, perhaps, not a little by the observation that it would *only* be the expense of the rail if Tom didn't buy him, that little word " only " being extremely useful in leading people astray.

And the major having enjoined our friend to secrecy,

lest any of the "dealers" should be beforehand with them, took a most affectionate leave of him, and went to report progress to the colonel, whom he found half-frantic with rage at the ear-ache and stomach-ache accounts that were pouring in upon him.

CHAPTER XII.

CLENCHING A BARGAIN.

Two days after, Tom and the major were at the Fleecy-borough station, waiting the arrival of the 2.30 train from town, which, coming with its usual punctuality, about three-quarters of an hour after time, the last joint of the tail, in the shape of a horse-box, was chopped off, and the snorting monster presently pursued its course, without appearing either better or worse for the operation.

The train having whisked out of sight, all eyes were turned to the amputated member, which, arriving so easily, now took half a dozen porters to coax to a siding. Having at length accomplished the undertaking, a side wing was let down, disclosing a horse, in a complete set of new clothing, attended by a melancholy-looking groom, with a band of crape puckered mournfully round his cockaded hat. He saluted the major with a sorrowful look, as if the meeting was productive of painful recollections ; and the pent-up horse being released from confinement, came clattering over the boards, making as much noise as Timour the Tartar's at Astley's. Having reached *terra firma*, he stood shaking and stretching himself, and staring about at his leisure.

"What, you've clipped him, have you?" observed the major, eyeing his bright mouse-coloured coat.

"He was getting rather woolly," replied the man.

"And plaited his mane, too," added the major, as the groom stripped off the hood, and exhibited a racing mane.

"Didn't lie very well, sir," said Joe, a complaint that could not be laid to his door.

Major Fibs sells Tom a Horse.

" Captain 'All wants a charger, not a racer," observed the major.

" He'll get both if he gets this 'oss," replied Joe, with a sigh, sweeping the clothing over his tail.

" What ! he's been raced, has he ? " asked Tom, thinking of his nomination for the Warrior Stakes.

" Raced, yes ! " replied the groom, as if surprised at the question. " Raced, and won, too. Won the Gammon Stakes at Stewpony—not in the ' Calendar,' and so much the better, for he won't have to carry hextry weight as a winner."

He was very like what the major had described— very like Swipes's horse, only clipped, with a bang tail instead of a life-guard's one, and a leaded mane instead of a flowing one. His action, too, was much the same ; " Easy as a chair," as the major said, on alighting, after a canter round on Mr Ploughharrow's pasture.

" Try, him yourself, Hall," said the major, handing Tom the rein.

The coast being clear, and the elastic-seated saddle roomy, with raised padding for the knees, Tom screwed up his courage and mounted. After a very quiet walk down Soberton-lane, he ventured back into the field, and, with due caution, worked the horse from a trot into a canter, without eliciting any of those inconvenient ebullitions of spirit that sometimes attend the too sudden transition from highway to turf. And Tom tit-uped about very pleasantly. The major saw, by the self-satisfied grin on Tom's face, as he at length returned with the slack rein of confidence, that it was a " case," and was fully prepared for his " tender question."

" I'll tell you in two words," replied the major, in reply to Tom's tender question as to how much, " I'll tell you in two words. Chucklehead gave a 'under'd and sixty for this orth. The ecthecutors, to effect an immediate sale, will take a 'under'd and twenty ; but you must be quick about it," added he, " for the groom tells me that Mr Meyers has been to look at him for the Printh."

And Tom gaped and gasped as usual, for the money, he thought, was a vast, and he would have liked to have

consulted his father, and Mr Trueboy and Padder and
Proggy and the street swells of Fleecyborough, to say
nothing of any chance opinion he might be able to pick
up; it being a remarkable fact that, however deficient
men may be in intelligence or general information, there
are very few who are not equal to giving an opinion
about a horse. The major, who had been in at as many
deals, good, bad, and indifferent as most people, knew
there was nothing like clenching a bargain at the satisfied
moment, and observing to the man "that he oughtn't
to have let Mr Meyers see the orth before they were done
with him," whispered in Tom's ear, "that if Meyers
thought him good enough for the Printh, Tom might,
perhaps, path him as good enough for him "—a suggestion
that had considerable weight with our friend, who stood
staring and wishing to pick a hole if he could, but fearing
to commit himself in the attempt.

"'I don't advithe,' as the City merchants write to
their country correthpondents, nor do I wish to influence
your dethithon," continued the cunning major, "but I
really think he's very much the sort of orth you should
have. He has all the temper and dothility of Swipes's
orth, combined with higher courage and more strength—
a gayer and better animal altogether—a fitter animal
for a gentleman of your figure and thubstance; and,
besides being a perfectly broke charger, is a very thuperior
'unter—isn't he, Joe?" continued he, appealing to the
man.

"I believe ye," replied Joe, with a snatch of his hat.
" If you'd seen him the day the Queen's Jelly-calf Staggers
met at Maidenhead Thicket, how he thro'd the dirt in
Davis's face and Bartlett's face and Cox's face, and in
all the London hell-keepers' and horse-dealers' faces,
you'd have said he was an oss to go indeed. That's
wot set Meyers arter him for the Prince," added he.

"No doubt," assented the major, "no doubt. An
orth that distinguithes himself is soon thnapped up,
at any prithe. Now," continued he, turning to Tom,
" you'd better make up your mind, and remember, if
a well-broke charger is desirable, a well-made hunter is
equally so. It would never do for a gentleman of your

fortin and accomplithments to be tumbled about in the dirt like an orth-breaker's man. Half the pleasure of hunting consists in being carried comfortably."

And Tom thought there was a good deal in that ; for though he had never been out, on horseback at least, he had studied ' Punch ' attentively, and thought some of Mr Briggs's predicaments anything but pleasant ; and there were a series of " Alkens," in Grammar the book-seller's window, representing red-coated gentlemen in every species of discomfiture, some on their nobs, some on their horses' nobs, some on their backs, some dashed into melon-frames, some hurried into rivers, some into ditches, that made Tom think it was desirable to have a tractable horse.

" It's a vast of money," at length said he, after a good suck of his whip-handle.

" I'm afraid you won't get it for leth," replied the major ; " at least, if what the man tells me is correct. But you had better talk to him yourthelf, and see."

Tom stood mute.

" The captain thinks the orth dear at the money," at length observed the major, turning spokesman.

" Does he ? " replied the man, with the utmost in-difference. " Won't get him for a copper less," added he, preparing to replace the clothing, muttering something about " fool for coming."

Tom still stood agape, not knowing what to do.

" You'd throw the clothin' and thaddle in, at all events ? " observed the major.

" I've no instructions to do nothin' of the sort," replied the man, tartly but firmly.

" Ah ! that's all Mr Meyers's doing," whispered the major to Tom. " Made them independent."

" Humph ! " mused Tom, staring vacantly.

" Well, you'd better thettle it one way or other," at length observed the major ; " the man will be wanting to go back by the next train."

It then occurred to Tom that he would have to pay the railway expenses if he did not buy ; and, like many people involved in one expense, he went on in hopes of retrieving it.

E

"Well, but I can't pay for him now—at least—I mean—I haven't got the money in my pocket," stammered Tom.

"Oh! never mind that," replied the major; "give the man five shillings, and we'll arrange that together. Here, my man," continued the major, pulling out two half-crowns, and giving them to the groom, "Captain 'All will take the orth, and I'll write to your people by to-night's posth, and if they require the thaddle and things back, they shall be thent, but I don't expect they'll be thuch screws."

"Very good, sir," replied the man, pocketing his *douceur*, adding, "You'll be wanting him taken into town, won't you?"

"No," replied the major, not thinking it prudent to let this man have the run of any of the town taps; "I'll get a man here," jerking his head towards the railway station.

Having got the horse and a railway porter, they nodded their adieux in return to the groom's parting salute, and set off on the well-cindered white-posted footpath, with the horse led alongside them on the road.

"You've done a wise thing, I think," observed the major, squeezing Tom's fat arm, as they tramped along. "I'm sure the colonel will approve of it, and there's no man has your interest more warmly at heart than he has. You've got a very nith orth—a very neat orth—a very gentlemanlike orth."

"Yes, I think he is a nice horse," replied Tom, eyeing him as he stared and sauntered leisurely along. "Where shall I get him a bed, think ye?"

"Oh, haven't you a stable?" asked the major.

"Yes, we have a stable," replied Tom, "but it's full of coals and casks and empty bottles and things."

"Well, but they could be emptied out. Is it damp?"

"Yes, I think it's damp," replied Tom; "at least, there's green upon the walls."

"Ah, that won't do. Orthes should be kept dry and warm."

"Do for one night, I suppose," said Tom, with an offhand sort of air.

" Do for your orth, if that's what you mean," rejoined the major. " Orthes don't take so much killing as some people suppose. No, no ; you'd better take him to the Thalutation, or one of the inns, till you get him a proper stable of his own."

So saying, he gave the word of command " to the Thalutation," and horse and groom and friends turned up Spooneypope-street accordingly ; and as Tom chanced to look back, he saw heads popped out of windows and shop doors, and a general commotion on his track, so acceptable is a little excitement in the country. The news soon spread that Tom Hall had bought a horse. Young people said he was going it, old ones shook their heads and said they wished he mightn't make the old man's money fly.

CHAPTER XIII.

SATISFACTION OF THE COLONEL.

WHILE the incidents of the last chapter were going on, the old colonel, eager and anxious at all times, was now doubly so, in consequence of having received a dunning letter from his accoutrement maker, threatening an appeal to the Horse Guards if his bill for 1849-50 was not immediately discharged, the writer, of course, having "to meet a large one himself the next week;" nay, so excitable had the colonel become that he could not contain himself in barracks, but putting himself in mufti— to wit, in a tight brown Newmarket cut-away, with a voluminous bright-buttoned buff waistcoat, scanty tweed trousers, and high-lows, with a drab felt wide-awake, proceeded to carry his corporation in the direction of the railway station to make an observation, relying on the disguise for Tom not knowing him; as if there was any disguise that would effect the concealment of such a figure as his. However, off he set, and there is no saying but his impetuosity would have carried him to the field of action, had not a lofty pile of Birnam native oysters, in Grundsell the greengrocer's window, attracted his attention, and caused a diversion. There, as he stood, with his great stomach resting on the counter, devouring bivalve after bivalve as fast as Mrs Grundsell could open them, the light tramp of a horse's hoofs fell upon his ear, and, looking round, he saw the well-known steed stepping gaily along, followed by the gaunt major, with his long arm thrust through our Tom's.

The colonel saw by the radiance of the major's usually heavy brow, and the airy swagger of his walk, that it was a deal ; and, nearly choking himself with the huge oyster he was in the act of swallowing, he clapped down half-a-crown on the counter, and was only prevented giving chase, and most likely spoiling sport, by the time Mrs Grundsell took fumbling for the change.

When he got rolled to the door the group had turned up Spooneypope-street, and feeling satisfied that it was a case of delivery (the road to the barracks being right up the town), he gave vent to his gratitude by ordering a gallon of rum, a Dutch cheese, and a dozen red herrings, to be sent to the major's rooms directly. When, however, he fingered the *flimseys*, as he called them, though *greaseys* would have been a more accurate description of " Hall & Co.'s " dirty five-pound notes, his gratitude expanded ; and besides chucking the major a fiver for his trouble, he ordered him two dozen of strong military port, exclaiming, as he gave the order, " Mind, let it have a good grip of the gob ! "

He then went rolling about the town with a plethoric-looking tarnished-blue purse, paying his ear-ache and stomach-ache bills, and talking as if he was going to buy all the things in the shops. Mrs Bustleton got her money, and wrote a most obsequious letter, " hoping to be honoured with their future orders." So the money was not altogether wasted, and the deal furnished abundant conversation for the town, the horse being made the representative of all sorts of imaginary sums.

There were such solemn consultations—such feelings— such handlings—such trottings out and sittings in judgment on the unfortunate animal. What with the post-boys and flymen continually going in and out with their horses, and young gentlemen dropping in to pass their opinions, the door of the stable was continually on the swing. What a diversity of opinion the horse elicited ! No two people thought the same of him. Buttons, the postboy, thought he'd done a deal of work with his legs, while Bricks, the boots, thought he'd done a deal more with his teeth. Mr Weathertit thought his body too large for his legs, while young Mr Spoilwater, as they called Freebody, the brewer's son, thought his legs too large for his body. The young Emperor of Morocco

thought the fetlocks too fine ; Mr Smiley took exception
to the elbows ; Mr Fielding pronounced the hocks to be
curbey ; Mr Clapgate suspected he had been at his
prayers ; while Mr Bright thought he detected incipient
cataract in the right eye. No one, however, hinted that
he had seen the horse before, or suspected that it was only
Captain Smallbeere's horse clipped, and his tail squared.
To crown the whole, the old colonel waddled down from
the barracks in a shell-jacket and high-lows to pass his
opinion upon it. After making a most critical examination,
beginning with the horse's head and ending with his heels,
grasping his windpipe and punching his sides, he exclaimed,
with admirable *naïveté*, after straddling with his great
fin ends in the bottom of his dog-earey overall pockets,
as if making his calculations between Swipes's horse and
it, " Well ! dash my sabretache, if there's tuppence to
choose atween 'em ! "

CHAPTER XIV.

THE HEAVYSTEEDS AT DINNER.

THE county papers, after coming out blank, or as good as blank, all the summer, at length gave symptoms of returning animation, and Eureka Shirts, Parr's Pills, and Dental Surgery advertisements found themselves " slap by cheek," as Colonel Blunt called it, with " Hunting Appointments." Three varmint-looking short-tailed pinks that had long been ornamenting Scissors & Tape's window disappeared ; Felt, the hatter, had imported some best-made London caps ; Corns, the bootmaker, exhibited rows of variously-tinted tops ; while Gag, the saddler, placed a whole sheaf of highly finished whips, and long lines of glittering spurs, in his bay-windowed shop. A few frosty nights had brought the leaves showering from the trees, while four-and-twenty hours' rain had saturated the ground, making it fit for that best of all sports, fox-hunting. Big-breeched, knock-kneed, brandy-nosed caitiffs began to steal into towns from their summer starvings, offering themselves as grooms, or helpers, or clippers, or singers, or shavers, or anything— anything except honest work. All things bespoke the approaching campaign. Our military friends partook of the mania.

"Let's give old Cheer a benefit," exclaimed Colonel Blunt, from the right of the president of the mess, on the evening the fixtures appeared—" let's give old Cheer a benefit at his Park meet. Let's cut a dash with the drag, and I'll drive," added he, the above being roared out in his usual stentorian strain, slightly impeded by the quantity of roast pig he had eaten, or rather devoured.

" I vote we do," lisped Major Fibs, from the opposite side of the table; adding, "Who'll stand an orth?"

"Goody Two-shoes is much at your service, sir," observed Captain Dazzler, who wanted a little leave of absence.

"That's right!" exclaimed the colonel, with a thump of his fist on the table.

"Cockatoo also," bowed Adjutant Collop, who was in strong competition with Fibs for the colonel's favour.

"I'll stand Billy Roughun," observed Pippin, from the bottom of the table.

"That's right!" repeated the colonel. "Goody Two-shoes, Cockatoo, and Billy Roughun, that's three—only want another to make up a team."

"You are welcome to old Major Pendennis," squeaked little Jug, "if you don't mind his knuckling-over knees."

"Oh, hang his knees!" responded the colonel; "four horses are four horses, and if he does tumble down he'll get up at his leisure; but when the weight's off their backs there's no great temptation to tumble. Well," continued he, "that'll do—Goody and Cock for wheelers, and the Major and Roughun for leaders; or s'pose we put Roughun at the wheel, and Cock and Pen leaders."

"Nothing can be better," observed Fibs.

"Nothing," ejaculated Collop.

"We must have the drag overhauled," continued the colonel; "and I vote we have the ballet-girl—Taglioni, or whatever you call her—painted out, and a rattling Fox with a 'tallyho' painted in. It'll please old Cheer, and p'r'aps get us invited to the castle—they tell me the old man has an undeniable cook."

"I'll tell you what we'll do!—I'll tell you what we'll do!" he went on. "We'll go and breakfast with the old boy. He gives a spread—cold pies, pork-chops, pigeons, porter—all the delicacies of the season in short,—at least he did the last time we were quartered here, and I make no doubt he does still."

"We'd better not go on speculation, I think," observed Captain Mattyfat, who was very fond of his food. "How would it do to have a jolly good breakfast here and lunch with his lordship?"

" And have that fat Hall up and make him muzzy,"
suggested Jug, helping himself to an overflowing bumper
of port.

" Oh, Hall's a good fellow," growled the colonel;
" I won't have him run down."

" We don't want to run him down," squeaked Jug,
" we only want to make him comfortable."

" I'll make *you* comfortable," roared the colonel, his
bloodshot eyes flashing with indignation—" I'll make
you comfortable," repeated he, " with an extra drill on
that day " — a threat that produced a hearty guffaw
from the company.

Jug bit his lips, for he saw that Hall was the
favourite, as well with the colonel as with Angelena and
mamma.

" Well, but about the wrag," resumed the colonel,
" how shall it be ? Breakfast or no breakfast—that's
the question."

" Oh, breakfast by all means before you start," exclaimed several voices.

" Have your breakfast before you go, whatever you do,
and what you get extra will be all so much gained,"
assented Mattyfat.

" True," replied the colonel—" true. Pass the bottle,
and I'll tell you what we'll do—I'll tell you what we'll
do. We'll make a day of it—we'll make a day of it ;
we'll have a light breakfast here—slops (catlap, you
know) and so on—then drive there and have a regular
tuck-out ; broiled bones, sherry coblers, sausages, and
so on," the colonel munching and smacking his lips
as if he was engaged with a plateful.

" And send the horses on, I suppose ? " observed Mr
Gape.

" Oh, of course," replied the colonel—" of course ;
you wouldn't disgrace the regiment by riding your own
horse on—that would never do. No, send them to Heartycheer's, get them fed, and so on : cost nothin'—old man
has plenty of money. One groom will take two horses.
Servants will come back in the drag, you know."

" That'll do capitally, thir," observed Major Fibs.

" *Capitally !* " exclaimed the opposition toady, Collop.

" You've a wonderful talent for arrangement," observed Major Fibs.

" *Wonderful !* " echoed the other.

" Yes ; I don't think I'm deficient in that way," replied the self-satisfied colonel, taking double toll of the port as it passed.

Conversation then became general and brisk, turning altogether upon hunting—or rather upon riding—each man having some wonderful recollection of some wonderful feat he had performed in some other country. The colonel's heretofore pig-impeded voice presently rose to the ascendant in details of the doings of his day ; when he used to ride—when he used to beat everybody—when nobody could hold a candle to him—heavens, how he used to go ! And he turned up the whites of his eyes as if lost in amazement at the recollection of his temerity.

Fibby and Collop egged him on, as if they had never heard his lies before ; while Mattyfat and Pippin, and Dazzler and Gape, and all the jolly subs winked and nudged each other under the table.

" Yeth, thir, yeth," observed Major Fibs ; " I've alwayth heard that you were firht-rate acroth country."

" *Heard* it ! " exclaimed Collop ; " I *know* it. ' We've ridden side by side,' as the song says."

" So we have, Colly, so we have," roared the colonel, dashing at the port as it again passed up. " You know how I used to show them the way in Warwickshire— Ladbrooke Gorse, to wit ! "

" Ah, but Northamptonshire was the country you shone in most, wasn't it, thir ? " asked Fibby, determined not to be outdone by his detested rival.

" I believe you," replied the colonel, " I believe you. One doesn't like speaking of oneself," continued he, striking out with his right fin, " but I believe it's generally admitted that there never was a better man in the Pytchley than I was."

" They talk of you yet, sir ! " exclaimed Collop. " I've an uncle lives in that country."

" I make no doubt they do, I make no doubt they do," replied the colonel. " I firmly believe, if you were to go into the market-place at Northampton, and ask

who was the best man they ever had in the county, they
would exclaim, ' Blunt of the Heavysteeds ! ' "

An announcement that was received with the most
mirth-concealing applause.

" You *set* the squire, didn't you ? " asked Fibby, as
the noise subsided.

" I *did*," replied the colonel, with an emphasis, his
eyes glistening as he spoke—" I did. That was the last
time I was there," continued he, attacking the sherry
now in mistake for the port. " It was in the Harborough
country—met at Arthingworth—the man—I forget his
name—who lived there gave a spread. Took a thimbleful
of brandy — not a gill, certainly — half a tumblerful
p'r'aps," the colonel showing the liberal quantity on a
tumbler before him—" rode a famous horse I had called
Owen Swift—a horse I refused no end of money for—
immense field—Goodricke and a lot of the Melton men
down, the Pytchley men looking at the Melton men as
much as to say, ' What's brought you here ? ' and the
Melton men looking at the Pytchley men as much as to
say, ' What a rum-lookin' lot are you.' However, before
they got the question of looks settled—indeed, before
they'd got well clear of the premises—there was the most
aggravatin' tallyhoing that ever was heard from a whole
regiment of foot-people, and in an instant the Squire
was capping his hounds on to a great dog-fox. Well,
we all rose in our stirrups and prepared for play, for it
was clear there would be a tussle between the two hunts,
and though in no ways implicated, military men not being
expected to subscribe to hounds, I got Owen by the
head, and tickled him to the front. There, as I lay well
with the hounds—next to Jack Stevens, in fact,—I looked
back, and saw such an exhibition of industry—such
hitting, and holding, and ramming, and cramming, and
kicking, and scolding, and screeching. However, that
was no business of mine ; Owen kept me clear of the
crowd, and, as we got upon the great grazing-grounds,
he extended his stride, and seemed equal to anything.
Presently we came to lower ground, and I saw, by the
bluish-green of the grass, that there was water, and just
then the sun shone under the planks of a footbridge, as

it might be thus " (the colonel placing a knife and fork on each side of a plate), " showing that the path was liable to be flooded. ' Hold hard, one minute! ' exclaimed the Squire, holding up his hand, as the hounds, having overshot the scent, now spread like a rocket to recover it. ' Yooi, over he goes! ' screeched he, as they swept short to the left, and took it up again, full cry. The Squire then backed his horse, and crammed full tilt at the fence—a great high, ragged, rambling, briary place, with an old pollard willow hanging over. No go ; horse turned short round. At him again, same result. ' Let me try,' cried I, seeing we should soon have the whole field upon us. I took Owen back," continued the colonel, " about as far as the Squire had done, and giving him a taste of the Latchfords, crammed him at it full tilt, and *ab*solutely flew it like a bird."

" B-o-o-y Jove, how you must have crammed at it ! " exclaimed Collop, as if he had never heard the story before.

" I went at it like a cannon-ball ! " roared the colonel, ducking his bull head and putting his fins together, as if getting his horse by the head.

" I think I thee you," lisped the major.

" Biggest leap on record, isn't it ? " asked Collop, determined not to be outbid by the major.

" Mytton's leap over the flying higgler's tilt-cart, in the Tewkesbury-lane, was perhaps more marvellous ; but, for real sporting spirit, mine, I believe, is unsurpassed," replied he, giving his great chin a dry shave with his hand.

" You'd sell the orth for a good prithe after that, I imagine, thir," continued Fibs, leading the gallant officer onwards.

" Goodricke said to me, ' Blunt, I'll give you any money for that horse.' "

" And what did you say ? " asked several.

" I said, ' Goody, my boy, money won't buy him ! ' "

" Bravo, bravo ! " exclaimed several voices, Pippin muttering to Mattyfat, " The last time the colonel told the story, he said he got three hundred and a horse Goodricke gave two hundred for."

As, however, the colonel admitted that he had taken a thimbleful of brandy, he could not be expected always to tell the story the same way.

" What's the use of partin' with one's comforts ? " exclaimed the colonel, staring down at the now approving audience. " Couldn't do it !—couldn't, by Jove ! " continued he, lashing out with his left fin, and knocking the president's wine into his lap.

This caused a little interruption, and by the time the president had got himself dried, the mess allowance of wine was discovered to be done ; but the party seeming stanch, a fresh supply was ordered without reference to the fact. So they went on sipping and drinking and running their runs, or rather riding their ridings over again, and making magnificent arrangements for astonishing the Heartycheerites. At length they all passed the bottles, except the colonel, who, having finished them, and more than once, in the excitement and forgetfulness of the moment, applied to the water-bottle, whose contents he spluttered out like physic, he got himself raised, and, telling them to mind and not forget about the horses for the drag, bid them good night, and rolled off on the heels of a pair of terribly creaking high-lows.

Arrived at home, he found the ladies absorbed in the metamorphosis of some finery, and, after blinking for a while at the candles, to see that they were not burning four, he gave a hearty dive into his trouser pocket, and, scooping out the contents, laid it reef-ways on the table.

" There ! " exclaimed he, as he surveyed the dancing coin, " five half-crowns, two half-sovereigns, and a whole one, mixed up with threepence-halfpenny worth of copper, some shillings, sixpences, and fourpenny-pieces. There ! " repeated he, as he withdrew two cob-nuts, a piece of ginger, and a key that were mixed up with it, " g-g-go to Mrs Flounceys in the mor-mor-mornin', and get new b-b-bonnets, and I'll take you to see old Cheer's hounds throw off —get somethin' neat, but not—ga-gaudy, you know— red and y-y-yellow, or somethin' of that sort," he continued, sousing himself on to the old horse-hair sofa.

And before the ladies recovered from the astonishment into which his unwonted generosity had thrown them, he had commenced a melodious strain on that musical nightingale, his nose.

CHAPTER XV.

LORD HEARTYCHEER'S OPENING DAY.

THE amiably disposed reader will now have the kindness, by the hop, step and jump process, to arrive at the opening day with Lord Heartycheer's hounds.

Who shall describe the hunting costume of a non-hunting cavalry corps—the modern coats, medieval breeches, and ancient boots, or the modern boots, medieval breeches, and ancient coats?

The officers of the Heavysteeds were not even uniform in their uniforms; consequently, little could be expected from them out of it. They were not a hunting corps. We will just take a glance at a few of them.

The colonel, being the first to get into his "togs," as he called them, we will begin with him. His coat was above a quarter of a century old, and was made by a tailor at Dorchester when, as a stripling, he joined the Heavysteed Dragoons there. Through its subsequent patchings, enlargings, and alterings by the various regimental tailors, it still retained the character of its original cut. The collar, at first a soapy, but now a black-with-grease scarlet one, was right down upon the nape of the neck, while the closely-set-together waist buttons were halfway up his back. Two sword-like swallow-tails divided down a back that required no little stretch of the imagination to conceive they could ever have covered. Below the arms, "where it would never be seen," as the respective snips said when they put them in, palpable varieties of cloth appeared, chiefly the pick of cast-off uniforms; the colonel's creed being that the older and more battered a hunting-coat looked, the varminter and more appropriate it was. The coat had also been lengthened in front, with a view of bringing it in closer proximity with the drab smalls—if smalls, indeed, the capacious garments that girded up his loins could be called. These were met in turn by a pair of lack-lustre, rhinoceros-hide-looking Napoleons, his intractable calves having long declined tops. His waistcoat was of the scrimpy order, coeval with the coat—a washed-out buff step-collared stripe, with a much-frayed broad black binding, and forlorn pewtery-looking buttons. All the buttons were of the dull order in the middle, lighting up a little towards the sides, like so many moons in a haze.

Pippin dressed the old English gentleman. He had no taste for hunting, but a great one for dressing the character, and now appeared in the orthodox cut and costume of the order. From the subdued, not to say sombre character of the garments, it was not until after the first glance of recognition that one was sensible of the extreme care that had been bestowed upon the getting up. His cap came well down upon his close-cropped head ; he wore no gills, but a puddingy cream-coloured cravat, fastened with a gold fox's-head pin in the old diamond tie, which had the effect of showing off his swelling huntsman-like chops to advantage. He had a groomish-looking step-collared drab waistcoat, with dead gold buttons with a bright rim, which he also sported, in a larger size, on a roomy, round, slightly cut-away single-breasted scarlet, that looked as if it had undergone frequent wettings to get it sobered down to purple. A smart blue watch-riband, with a bunch of family-looking seals, dangled over his gosling-green cords, which were met by a pair of stout-soled mahogany tops ; dogskin gloves, painted wristbands, heavy spurs, and a hammer-headed whip, completed the equipment.

Mattyfat, on the other hand, was of the bright-coloured, highly-polished, satin-tie order of sportsmen, and looked as if he was got up for a ball. He sported a new dress-cut scarlet, a voluminous blue-flowered satin tie, secured by beadle-staff-looking pins ; bloodstone buttons adorned a canary-coloured vest, that was crossed diagonally by glittering chains, from the heavier one of which were gibbeted sundry miniature articles of utility—a pencil-càse, a make-believe pistol, watchkeys in great abundance, and some mysterious-looking lockets. Matty was chief lady-killer of the regiment. His delicate doe-skins now vied with the lustrous polish of his Napoleons. Old Fibs set all field propriety at defiance, for he absolutely sported a woolly white hat, a dressing-gown-looking old frock-coat with a blue collar, an old black satin waistcoat, while his iron-mouldy smalls were any colour but white. His tops, which had been intended for pink, had come out a bright orange colour. His wide-extending red moustache gave him the appearance of having caught the fox him-self, and stuck its brush below his nose.

The rest of the Heavysteedites were of the mixed order—some having good coats and shocking bad breeches, others having shocking bad coats and good breeches. We must, however, waive further description of them in favour of our Tom.

If the old stager takes more time to get into his old clothes the first day of the season, how much more must a youngster require who has never been in hunting-clothes before ? Above all, how much must he require if said clothes have been made in the country ? Our Tom, with a laudable regard for the interests of the bank, ordered his of tradesmen who kept their accounts there ; the consequence of which was that they were neither punctually delivered nor yet so easy as they might be. The boots, indeed, did not come till the morning, just as he sunk exhausted in a chair, after hauling on leathers that were sadly too tight for him. Then, as Tom eyed the knees, and thought how he should ever get them buttoned, the solemn tramp of a strange foot was heard ascending the stairs, and, in obedience to a " come in " that followed a slowly-delivered tip-tap, the door opened, and the phlegmatic Mr Corns appeared, with a green bag under his arm.

" Your servant, Mr Hall—Mr Thomas Hall, that's to say," said the aggravator, ducking his head, little dreaming of the blessings Tom had been invoking on his head, equalled only by those that were to follow his misfit.

The New Boots.

Wonderful is the audacity of a country bootmaker, and irrepressibly touching is the way a youngster perseveres with his first pair of tops.

"There, sir—now, sir—another try, sir, and I think we'll get it on, sir," exclaimed Corns, working away at the foot, in aid of Tom's hauling with a pair of handcutting steel hooks. "Now, sir, the foot's getting in, sir," continued Corns, giving the sole a hearty slap as the foot came to a dead lock at the instep. "S'pose you stand up, sir, and work your legs about a bit, sir," continued Corns, showing Tom how to do it.

"Work my leg about a bit!" exclaimed the now profusely perspiring Tom—"work my leg about a bit! Why, I can hardly move it."

"Oh, sir, stamp your foot, sir—stamp your foot; you'll soon get it on. It don't do to have them too easy at first, sir—must have them smart, sir—genteel, that's to say, sir."

And Tom takes a determined hold of the hooks.

"H-o-o-ray!" A desperate effort lands his foot in the boot, and gives him courage to attempt the other.

"I wish you health to wear your boots, sir—that's to say Mr Hall, sir—Mr Thomas Hall I mean to say," observed Corns, scratching his head, and eyeing the tight oppressive leather, looking as if it would burst from the oversized feet.

"I wish I *may* be able to wear them," replied Tom, waddling across the room, adding, "I can hardly walk in them."

"Oh, but they're not meant to walk in, Mr Hall, sir— that's to say, Mr Thomas Hall, sir; they're only meant for ridin' in, sir. Just knock your toe again the chimley-piece, sir, and you'll make them a deal easier, sir."

Tom did as he was told, and, after sundry lusty assaults, felt some little relaxation of the tightness. Having taken breath after his great exertion, mopped his perspiring brow, and washed the chalk powder from his hands, he now eagerly proceeded with his dressing.

Corns put on his spurs for him, buckling them outside instead of in, as Tom would have done, and giving the strap the orthodox Heartycheer lap over the buckle.

F

"You'd better copy my Lord Heartycheer in everything, sir—that's to say, Mr Hall—Mr Thomas Hall,"
observed Corns, scratching his head, as he eyed Tom's
rebellious calves beginning to bag over the tight tops.
Corns made for Lord Heartycheer's men.

Tom now adjusted a wide-extending sky-blue Joinville,
whose once round tie afforded ample exposure of his fat
throat. One would think that colds and sore throats
were banished from the category of illnesses, so reckless
and improvident are men in exposing their necks. A
shaggy, many-pocketed, brown waistcoat quickly followed
the Joinville, and then—oh! crowning triumph of the
whole! the joyous scarlet, a short, square, loose-fitting
jacket sort of coat, double stitched, back stitched, cross
stitched, with all the appliances of power and strength
peculiar to an old stage coachman's upper one.

And Tom, having taken a good front view, side view,
and back view of himself in the glass, receiving the
assurance of Corns that he was quite "the ticket," with
renewed wishes for health to wear his boots, proceeded
to waddle downstairs, to the imminent peril of his neck,
from his spurs catching against the steps. How he
astonished his beloved parents, now waiting for him at
the well-supplied breakfast-table.

Old Hall, as our readers may suppose, had not any
very defined ideas of the chase, his experience in that
line consisting solely in seeing certain indifferently-
mounted Fleecyborough gents, whose "paper" he would
not care to cash, parade the streets in their red or black
coats. Indeed, his commercial experience rather pre-
judiced him against hunting, and when, first, Cropper,
the horse-dealer, then Sticker, the surgeon, and, after
them, Seesaw and Slack, the opposition woolstaplers
(all of whom sported their scarlets either openly or on
the sly), appeared "successfully," as he called it, in the
'Gazette,' he chuckled and rubbed his hands, and jerked
his head, and fumbled his silver, and winked his eye,
and said to friends, "Well, thank goodness, I've never
either hunted or gammled." "Hunting and gammling,"
therefore, it is clear, he looked upon as synonymous,
and though he did not join the saint party, who wanted

to put down racing, he took good care never to put his name down to any of the stakes, and would stand with his nose on the dusty bank window-blinds, looking at those who were going, and thinking how much better they would be at home. Indeed so little did he know about hunting that, when Tom's scarlet came home, he thought it was the yeomanry uniform, and it was not until he saw the fox, with an "H" below, on the button which Tom had mounted, in anticipation of Lord Hearty-cheer making him a member of his hunt, that he found out his mistake.

"Well," mused he, with a shake of his head, as he eyed it gravely and demurely, "I *hope* there'll no harm come of it—I *hope* there won't; but you know as well as I do, Sally," addressing his wife, "that I've never either hunted or gammled—never either hunted or gammled," repeated he, letting fall the sleeve to brush a rising tear from his eye. And he almost repented having made our Tom a gent.

Not so Mrs Hall, who saw in Tom's rise the germ of future eminence; and when our fat friend rolled down from his bedroom in the glowing equipments of the chase, her exultation knew no bounds.

"Well, now he was a buck!—he was a beauty!—he was a love!" and she hugged and kissed him like a child.

The first transports over, Sarah the maid, and Martha the cook, and Jane the housemaid were severally summoned to the presence, and while laudations were yet in full flow, Mr Trueboy, the cashier, arrived for the keys of the bank safe. And while they were still fingering Tom, and feeling him and admiring him and turning him about, the notes of a cornet-a-piston, mingling with the noisy rattle of wheels, sounded in the market-place, and, turning into Newbold-street, a heavily-laden coach presently pulled up at their door with a dash.

"Who is it?" exclaimed Mrs Hall, rushing breathless to the window, which was nearly on a level with a car-dinal-like-hatted monster, enveloped in the party-coloured shawls and upper coats of a coachman. The roof was crowded with men in caps and men in hats, muffled in every variety of overcoat and wrapper, some smoking cigars, some flourishing hunting-whips, some dangling their booted legs over the lack-lustre panels of the vehicle.

It was a shady affair, on which even putty and paint, those best friends of dilapidation, were almost wasted. The history of that old drag, from the day when it rolled with a sound drum-like hum under the gateway of the London builders to take its place with the Benson Driving Club, through all its vicissitudes of town and country life, its choppings and changings, its swappings and sellings, its takings for debts, and givings for bets, down to the time when the grasping Sheriff of Middlesex seized it for taxes, when it was bought by the officers of the Heavysteeds for sixteen pounds, would form an instructive example of the mutability of earthly grandeur and the evanescence of four-in-handism. It had been yellow, and it had been blue, and it had been green, and it had been queen's colour, and it had been black with red wheels, and red with black wheels, and was now a rusty brown picked out with a dirty drab. It had had an earl's coronet on the panels, a baron's coronet, a red hand with three crests, next two crests, then a single one, after that a sporting device, two racehorses straining for a cup, followed by a ballet-girl, which the colonel had now had painted out, and a great wolf-like fox painted in. Coach, horses, and cargo were now quite of a piece. The horses were of the shabbiest, most unmatching order : Billy Roughun was only half-clipped, while old Major Pendennis stood knuckling as if he would lie down in the street. The harness was made up of three sets, one bridle having a unicorn on the blinder, another a greyhound, and a third a bull. Nevertheless, it was thought a very swell turn-out, and great was the excitement it caused as it rolled through the now coach-deserted streets of Fleecyborough to the music of the cornet-a-piston. Seeing it pull up at old Hall's was enough to turn the heads of half the young men in the town.

" Oh, it's the colonel ! it's the barrack drag ! " exclaimed our Tom, pushing past his mother ; and throwing up the sash, he elicited a round of view-halloas, " Tally-hos ! " " Who-whoops ! " and " Yea-yups ! " from the muffled passengers on the roof.

" I'll be ready in five minutes, colonel ! " exclaimed
Tom, speaking out of the window, like a candidate at an
election—" I'll be ready in five minutes, colonel : I
just want a cup of coffee and an egg."

" Time's hup ! " roared the colonel, flourishing a pig-
jobber-looking whip over his cardinal-like hat, adding,
" I'll give you your breakfast at Heartycheer's."

" Oh, but take something before you go !—take something in your pocket, whatever you do !—you'll be
starved ! you'll be hungered ! you'll be famished ! "
exclaimed Mrs Hall, darting at biscuits and buns and cakes
and dry toast and whatever came in her way, amidst
renewed clamour from the cornet-a-piston, and exclamations of " Now, Mr Slowman, look sharp ! " " Who-
whoop ! " " Tallyho ! " " Can't wait ! " " Harkaway ! "

" Well, I must go ! " exclaimed Tom, thrusting three
buns into one pocket, and half-a-dozen biscuits into the
other—" I must go ! " repeated he, tearing himself away
from his mother, who hugged him as if he was going to
have a turn at the Caffres instead of the foxes. Seizing
his hat he hurried downstairs, and out at the now crowded
street door.

" Room inside ! " roared the colonel, pointing downwards with his whip, as Tom appeared ; and while Mrs
Hall was congratulating herself that he would ride safe,
the draught caused by the opening of the coach-door
floated some lavender-coloured flounces past her eye,
carrying consternation to her heart. She felt as if Tom
was kidnapped. The coach door was quickly closed,
the colonel gathered his weather-bleached reins for a
start, and as Tom put his head out to nod his adieux,
Padder, who was passing to the office, exclaimed, " He
hoped they'd have a good run." And Trueboy, who
was watching the unwonted scene from the window,
responded with a groan, " He wished it mightn't make
a run upon the bank."

CHAPTER XVI.

THE HUNT BREAKFAST.

LORD HEARTYCHEER was a haughty man, proud as Lucifer, rich as Crœsus, keen as mustard. He was the head of a long line of Heartycheers, whose original ancestor came over with the Conqueror, though whether the ancestor rowed, or steered, or was sea-sick and sat still, is immaterial to our story. Suffice it to say that his lordship was so satisfied with his pedigree, that he would rather be a dead Heartycheer than a live anybody else. As a sportsman he was first-rate, and hounds had been kept at Heartycheer Castle time out of mind. The memory of man indeed scarcely ran to the time when his lordship didn't keep them. He had seen through many gallant sportsmen ; it is perhaps no exaggeration to say that he had seen through a dozen fields. So much for his sporting career ; now for his private one. Though his lordship was proud and haughty with the men— with all but his intimates, at least—he was a great patron of the fair sex, among whom he enjoyed a great reputation ior gallantry, though they all laughed and shook their heads when his name was mentioned, from the beautiful Mrs Ringdove, of Cupid Grove, who said he was a " *naughty* man," down to the buxom chambermaid at the Crown, who called him " a gay old gentleman." They all felt pleased and flattered by his attention : it stamped them as being handsomer than their neighbours. Indeed his name was a sort of byword throughout the country, and any unfortunate Caudle who was supposed to be sweet upon a Prettyman, was sure to be threatened with the Heartycheer retaliation.

There had been as great a succession of favourites at
the castle as there had been of sportsmen with his hounds.
His lordship, who was now well turned of seventy, used
to talk in his confidential moments of having sown his
" wild oats," and as being only waiting for the fair one's
husband (whoever he was talking to) to be summoned
to a better world to make her Lady Heartycheer. So
he kept half a dozen variously handsome women in
anxiety about him and their husbands ; the husbands,
we need hardly say, having the worse time of the two.
He, however, by no means confined his attentions to
the married ladies—he was too staunch a free-trader for
that,—and there wasn't a pretty girl in the country but
he knew all about her.

In this interesting pursuit he was ably assisted by his
huntsman, Dicky Thorndyke. Dicky had been with him
all his life, and thoroughly identified himself with his
master. Indeed he always spoke in the plural number.
If any one asked how his lordship was, Dicky would
reply, with a purse of his mouth, and a pleasant smile,
" Well, sir, I really think we are very well ; indeed I
think we are better than we have been for some time."
Though his lordship Dicky'd and Dicky Dyke'd him, it
was a freedom our huntsman allowed to none below the
rank of a baronet. Our friend, the prosy knight, tried
it on one day, when Dicky replied, " M-o-y name, sir,
is *Thorn*dyke," making a mighty mouthful of the thorn.

Better huntsmen there might be than Dicky, but none
so eminently qualified for the double pursuit of the fox
and the fair. Indeed as regards the fox, having a capital
pack of hounds, he early came to the conclusion that
if they couldn't smell which way the fox was gone, he
couldn't, and he never interfered with them as long as
they would stoop. The consequence of his non-inter-
vention was that he nailed up a considerable number of
noses. He looked like a nobleman's servant. In addition
to a comely well-conditioned person, he had a mild
placid expression of countenance, well befitting his delicate
duties. He had a great deal of tact and manner, too.
He didn't come blurting, open-mouthed, with an " I've
seen a devilish fine gal, my lord," or " Mrs Yarker's

husband's been whopping her again," but as he trotted
from cover to cover he would direct his lordship's attention
to some hound or some horse, or some object that would
enable him to draw up to his point.

" Old Conqueror's gettin' slow, my lord," he would say,
pointing to an old hound trotting along less stoutly than
the rest.

" The more's the pity," replies his lordship, throwing
the old favourite a bit of biscuit.

" Been a good 'un," observes Dicky, regarding him
affectionately, adding, " We've had more good hounds
from Cloverly Banks than any walk we have."

" What, he was from Cloverly, was he ? " asked his
lordship, remembering what he saw the last time he was
there.

" Yes," replied Dicky ; " we always have good 'uns
from there. They take so much care of them—never
clog them or tie them up. The gals are so good to them,
too. Cardinal's killed all their turkeys this year, and
they never so much as said a word."

" Ah ! I must ride over and see them, and make them
a present," replies his lordship.

And so, on the last day of cub-hunting, before the
season upon which we are now entering began, Dicky
pointed out a horse, with a " That's the horse, my lord,
I was a-telling you about last Tuesday that I was looking
at for us. I thought he would do to carry Will or Sam.
I didn't buy him on 'count of the splents," pointing to a
booted foreleg.

" Who's got him ? " asked his lordship, who knew how
to cap Dicky on the scent.

" A townsman—the man they call the Emperor of
Morocco." Then, sinking his voice, he added, in an
undertone, as he drew his horse nearer his lordship's,
" They say the emperor and her majesty have had another
breeze."

" What, *another ?* " exclaimed his lordship, who knew
what the first one was about.

" Yes, another," replied Dicky. " Last Sunday. But
p'r'aps you'll have the kindness not to mention it, as I
had it in confidence from their coachman."

And his lordship stored Dicky's hint up in his mind for future use. Indeed, for so great a man, it was wonderful what a quantity of gossip and scandal he collected.

Hunting a country undoubtedly gives gay old gentlemen great opportunities, for the meet brings forth all the youth and loveliness of a place ; while, under pretence of looking for his fox, a master of hounds may rummage anywhere from the cellar to the garret. And so people found, for what with setting out covers, looking at puppies, paying for poultry damage, complimenting preservers of foxes, and so on, there was no such thing as keeping Lord Heartycheer out of their houses.

And great grumbling his visits frequently occasioned, for he had a knack of making them on market-days, board of guardian days, petty-sessions days—days when the lords of the creation are necessarily absent, who ill-liked to see the imprints of his horse's hoofs stirring up their gravelled rings. But to the chase.

Our friend Colonel Blunt has already intimated that his lordship opened each season with a magnificent spread at Heartycheer Castle, where year after year he received, with almost regal grandeur, the homage and adulation of the country. A truce seemed to be declared over all his little " piccadillies," as Dicky Dyke called them, and people who had been loudest in proclaiming them, now cried " Shame ! " and said they didn't believe there was a word of truth in any of them.

Time would seem to run the reverse way with his lordship, for the older and greyer he got, the younger and more captivating the ladies declared him. Anxious mammas, who had reproved their ardent daughters for thinking of old men of five-and-thirty, openly encouraged his lordship's advances, assuring the dear girls that a man is never too old to marry.

He was a tall, slim, fresh-complexioned, handsome-featured man, blending the stately grandeur of the old school with a slight flourish of the French. His snow-white hair seemed almost out of keeping with his light youthful figure and the beaming radiance of his eagle eye. Having begun hunting during the last advent of mahogany tops, he had never wholly adopted the white ones, and

was now neither in the fashion nor out with rose-
coloured ones. Neither had he ever abandoned the white
cords, for whose milky purity he was always remarkable.
His new scarlet coat was of the single-breasted, slightly
sloped-away order, with a step-collared toilonette vest, a
starched striped cravat, with a small plaited frill to his
shirt.

And thus the reader will have the kindness to consider
our great lady-killing master of hounds attired for the
reception of company on this his—we know not what
number—opening day. His lordship, having breakfasted
in his sanctum, and passed his silk-stockinged, state-
liveried establishment in review, now proceeded to take
his usual post of reception, before the blazing entrance-
hall fire—a splendid hall beaming with ancestral honours
and trophies of the chase.

And here we should observe that the morality of the
country divided itself into three classes. First, the
desperately improper ones, who didn't care what people
said, and who boldly entered the castle, partaking of the
sumptuous fare, and calmly surveying the statues and
voluptuous paintings with which the beautiful rooms
and corridors were studded ; secondly, the more prudish
ones, such as old Miss Fozington, who would not even
enter the park, and merely took a drive " that way "
to take the chance of seeing the hounds, with which,
somehow or another, they generally fell in.

First among the forward ones on this occasion was our
superb friend the Empress of Morocco, who, despite a
tiff with the tanner about coming, drove up in her well-
built but badly-appointed barouche, gorgeous in purple,
ermine, and lace, with the slightest possible touch of rouge
on her plump beautiful cheeks. Often as Lord Heartycheer had greeted her, he thought he never saw her look
so bewitching, and he inwardly cursed the grinding of
wheels that preceded the announcement of Mrs and
Miss Marplotte. How low and courteous was the bow
that received them ! How different to the seizure of both
hands and earnest *empressement* that marked his addresses
to the beaming gazelle-like eyes of the empress ! The
Marplottes soon obeyed the obsequious flourish of the

well-drilled groom of the chamber, and passed onward to the banqueting-room. They were quickly followed by Mrs and the Miss Hoeys ; then came Captain and Mrs Horridbore ; after them the Beddingfields, then the Mountfields, then the Honeyballs ; after which there was a pause, and then a rush of hungry fox-hunters, ready for anything.

In less than twenty minutes from the first sitting down, the splendid dining-room rang with the popping of champagne-corks, the clatter of plates, and the joyous hilarity of unrestrained freedom. All went merry as a marriage-bell, till Captain Horridbore, who was to the Whig party what Sir Thomas Thimbleton was to the Tory, rose to propose the health of their noble host. Being one of those hungry hard-bitten radicals who come out great at elections and then merge into nothingness, he had the gift of the gab, and strung words together with amazing volubility. On this occasion he was so laudatory that one might almost have thought he was laughing at his lordship. The applause that followed the announcement of the name was the usual signal for his lordship to leave the post of reception before the entrance-hall fire and repair to acknowledge the compliment ; but it so happened that the Empress of Morocco, who, we forgot to say, had brought her little boy Freddy to see the " fine house," having made the tour of the reception-rooms, by the " greatest chance in the world " forced herself in the entrance-hall by the reverse door at which she had left it, and the coast being clear, all except a few footmen, who of course nobody cares about, his lordship waylaid her, to renew the attentions the Marplotte arrival inter-rupted. Having sent Freddy to look at the pretty pictures at the far end of the hall, she placed her beautiful foot on the broad fender, and slightly raising her velvet dress, as if to give her foot the benefit of the warmth, she was very soon whispering her domestic grievances into the ear of this fine old fox-hunting father confessor. There, as he stood looking into her eyes and imbibing her every word, listening to the Turkish despotism of the tyrannical tanner, and thinking how best to avenge her cause, the loud cheers of the health-drinkers burst unheeded on the scene, and it was not until Mr Snuffertray—the pompous butler—twice intimated the honour that had been done him, that his lordship awoke to the necessity of the occasion.

Offering the lovely empress his arm, he halloaed, " Here, e-lope! young 'un, e-lope! " ' as if speaking to a hound, and, followed by Freddy, they entered the banqueting-room in state.

What a commotion their appearance created.

" Brazen woman! " ejaculated Mrs Sowerby, half-choking herself with a chicken-bone.

" Would not have come if I'd known," muttered Mrs Mealymouth.

His lordship, of course, was quite taken by surprise at the unexpected compliment, and after expressing the embarrassment he felt, and the inadequacy of language to convey the sentiments of his heart, he branched off upon the subject of hunting, expatiating upon its advantages in a social point of view, its life-lengthening, health-giving properties, and its beneficial influence in promoting our breed of horses, which, however, he took the opportunity of observing were not so good as they used to be; adding that if he continued to have a difficulty in mounting himself, he should have to set to and breed a few—a declaration that was thought very plucky for a gay old gentleman turned of seventy.

And now, whilst his lordship is plying the empress with noyeau jelly, and Freddy with fruit, the slight crack of a whip, followed by a musical rate, is heard, and Dicky Thorndyke is seen in his new cap and coat, rising corkily in his stirrups, piloting the glad pack round the castle corner, followed by the whips, similarly attired.

" How are you, Dicky ? " " How are you, Thorndyke ? " " How are you, Dicky ? " bursts from the now crowded ring before the castle, as Dicky guides the pack on to the grass-plot, a salutation that Dicky acknowledges just as he thinks the speaker's intimacy with his lordship entitles him to Dicky or Thorndyke him.

Similar inquiries are now made of the whips, after which the gentlemen begin identifying the horses, and the ladies to lisp their admiration of the hounds. "*Such pretty creatures!*" "How many were there?" "All so much alike—wondered they could tell the difference!" And so on.

A diversion having been caused in the banqueting-room by the passing of the hounds, his lordship availed himself of the opportunity to withdraw with the Empress of Morocco, and having presently wrapped her up in her splendid Armenian cloak, and handed her to her carriage, he proceeded to mount a magnificent anything-you-like-to-call-it-worth white horse, to take his place in the centre of the hunting tableau before the castle. The hounds raised a glad cry, and dashed forward to meet him, while the men made aerial sweeps with their caps instead of reproving the ardour of the pack. His lordship bowed low and condescendingly to the second-class morality-mongers, whose sense of propriety would only allow of their partaking of refreshments at the door. The sherry and Maraschino, the Crême de Vanille and Parfait Amour, seemed to have exercised a mollifying influence on their prudery, and instead of the " Horrid bad mans ! " " Shocking old dogs ! " that generally accompanied his name, there were skilfully directed murmurs of " How well he looks ! " " What a handsome man ! " "Younger than ever ! " with a great disposition to catch his eye.

The day was bright and fair. A glittering flag floated proudly from the topmost tower ; while the expanding river, refreshened with November rains, swept impetuously through the park, a slight sprinkling of snow capped the summits of the far-off hills. Here, as his lordship sat at the receipt of custom, the compliments flying about him like bouquets round a favourite actress at a theatre, the notes of a cornet-a-piston suddenly sounded through the air, causing the steady pack to cock their ears, and all eyes to turn in the direction of the sound. Presently a heavily-laden coach emerged from behind a long screen of evergreens upon the open carriage-way through the park, exposing the weak leg-weary state of the horses, who with difficulty were kept at a trot, with the " Jip, jip, jippings," " Jag, jag, jaggings," " Crop, crop, cropp-ings," and double thongings of the driver.

" Who have we here ? " asked his astonished lordship
of Dicky Thorndyke.

" Don't know, my lord," replied Dicky, shading the
sun from his eyes, and straining in the direction of the
comers. " Player-folks, I should say, by their noise,"
added he. " No, my lord ; no. I see ; it's the cavalry
colonel—it's the cavalry colonel and his captains."

" Do I know them ? " asked his lordship, who made
it a rule never to speak to any one who was not properly
introduced.

" You'll know the colonel," replied Dicky. " Was
here some years back," adding, in an undertone, as he
leant forward in his saddle, " The corpulent captain
that used to be."

" I remember," replied his lordship, with a significant
jerk of his head. " Great, fat, vulgar fellow."

" Just so," said Dicky.

The corpulent captain had been one of his lordship's
horrors, and the recollection of his impudent brusque
gaucheries flashed upon his mind as he watched him
" Jip, jip, jipping," whip, whip, whipping, " Jag, jag,
jagging," and stamping on the splash-board, to get the
leg-weary screws to trot becomingly up to the door.
By the time he arrived, his lordship had got himself
screwed into the imperative mood—very stiff. A dead
silence followed the drawing up of the drag, all eyes being
on the watch to see how the party was received.

" How are ye, Heartycheer ? " roared the monster,
now slackening his reins, and casting a triumphant glance
over the scene.

His lordship made a slight bow..

" How are ye, Heartycheer ? " repeated he, in a still
louder key, nothing daunted.

His lordship now nearly kissed his horse's ears, so
deferential was his bow.

" Hope we haven't kept you waiting long," continued
the colonel, putting his clumsy whip into the socket.

" Precious little fear of that," thought Dicky Thorndyke, looking at his master with a laughing eye.

" Couldn't get our people started," continued the
colonel, standing up and looking over the crowded roof—

LORD HEARTYCHEER AND THE MONSTER.

" take such a deal of combin' and gettin' up some of these young fellers—waxin' their ringlets and corkin' their snouts; however," continued he, " let me introduce them to you now that I've got them here. This chap on my left," jerking his fin towards his white-hatted companion on the box, " you know, old Fibby ; came out of the ark with Noah—haw—haw—haw ; he—he—he ; ho—ho—ho ! The boy behind me on the roof is young Shuttleton, son of Mr Shuttleton, the great Manchester manufacturer—makes the Coburg cloth that looks so like merino—sixteenpence a yard. The man next him is Jaycock, a very promising officer, with great expectations from an uncle. This is Mattyfat, and that is Gape. No, not the beetle-browed one," continued the colonel, seeing his lordship's eagle eye fixed to bow to the wrong one—" not the beetle-browed one," repeated he, " the foxy-faced 'un next him." And so the gallant officer proceeded amidst much laughter to trot out the young gentlemen in front of the coach, just as the facetious Recorder trots out a newly-elected lord mayor before the barons of the Exchequer. When, however, he turned to deal with those behind, he found that they had taken fright at the examples made of their brethren, and cut off, so sousing himself down on his seat, he crossed his legs and proceeded to take a leisurely survey of the surrounding scene.

" And how have you been ? " roared he, addressing Lord Heartycheer in the most familiar way. " How have you been ? " repeated he, in the same tone, not getting an answer to his first inquiry.

" Pretty well, thank you, colonel," replied his lordship, with a smile at the unwonted familiarity.

" And how are you, Billy ? " said he, addressing Dicky Thorndyke. " Don't get any younger," continued he, returning to his lordship, not getting any answer from Billy.

" Few people do," replied his lordship tartly.

" Ah, but some people wear their years better than others," roared the colonel in reply. " You show age desperately—your hair's as white as snow."

" Indeed," replied his lordship, making him a very low bow.

"However," continued the colonel, nothing daunted by the frowns of all around, "you are a remarkable man of your years—a *very* remarkable man—few men of your age can get on to a horse, let alone go a-hunting." An observation that met with no reply and caused a momentary pause.

"Have seen your hounds look better, I think," continued the colonel, returning to the charge.

"*Indeed!*" exclaimed his lordship, boiling up. "I was just saying to *Mister* Thorndyke"—with a strong emphasis on the mister—"I was just saying to Mister Thorndyke that I thought *I* never saw them looking better."

"Ah, well," rejoined the colonel, slightly disconcerted, "I don't mean to say that the general wouldn't pass them, I mean to say that I don't mean to say they are not looking—healthy, wholesome, and so on—but I've seen them look better, I think—evener, I mean," added he, with a jerk of his right fin.

"Evener!" replied his lordship; "evener!" repeated he; "show me an uneven hound in the pack"—his lordship waving his hand as he spoke.

"Why, there's one!" roared the colonel, nettled at the challenge.

"Where?" asked his lordship.

"There!" roared the colonel, "under Billy's horse's nose."

"Why, man! *that's the terrier!*" exclaimed his lordship, to the infinite mirth of the meeting; and unable to bear with him any longer, he gave a nod to Dicky, who forthwith whistled the hounds together and moved briskly from the meet, leaving the colonel high and dry at the door.

CHAPTER XVII.

COLONEL BLUNT ENJOYS HIMSELF.

" WELL, that's cool," growled the colonel, as the hunting
cavalcade moved away from Heartycheer Castle door.
" That's cool," repeated he, " treating the Lieutenant-
Colonel of her Majesty's Regiment of Heavysteed Dragoons as if he was a postboy, leavin' him this way "—
the colonel looking down on his smoking steeds as he
spoke, with anything but a satisfied countenance.
" What are you going to do, colonel ? " exclaimed a
voice out of the coach window.
" Oh ! that's Jug," replied the colonel, recollecting
now that his coach was full inside and out—or, rather,
had been full inside and out, the outsiders having fled
and got their horses to join the hunt. " Oh ! that's
Jug," observed he.
" No, not Jug," replied the voice—" *Hall.*"
" Oh ! I meant Hall," replied the colonel, with a
chuck of his double chin, muttering to himself, " I knew
it was one of you. Do ! " continued he, raising his
voice, and coiling his whip-thong round the stick, " why,
I should say the best thing would be to go in and have
some breakfast."
" So say I," replied Hall, who was in no great hurry
for his first hunt.
" Stay, then, and I'll drive you to the door becomingly," continued the colonel, gathering up his reins,
whipping his horses, and moving the coach slowly on to
where a " gentleman's gentleman," and a couple of highly-
powdered, white-coated, crimson-breeched footmen were
lounging, and making their observations on the scene

G

outside. Having seen his lordship's reception of the
colonel and his party, the servants of course took their
cue from their master, and stood, with supercilious
smiles, watching the dirty incongruous-looking vehicle.

"Now, Johnny!" exclaimed the colonel, as none of
them seemed inclined to lend a hand—"now, Johnny,"
repeated he, "open the door, and let the ladies out ;
and you," continued he, addressing the gentleman out
of livery, "slip round to the stables, and tell Colonel
Blunt's groom his master's come"—the colonel thinking
the announcement of his rank would be sure to have a
beneficial influence in procuring attention.

The commanding tone of our man of war somewhat
threw the flunkies off their guard, or rather off their
impudence, for the man addressed as Johnny, but whose
real name was Peter, ceased twirling his napkin and
applied himself manfully to the coach door, while the
other footman lounged away to fulfil the duty assigned
to the hero of the gaudy plain clothes. Our fat friend,
Greasy Tom, as Angelena had now christened him, from
the profuse perspiration in which his tight tops kept
him, then popped out, and was presently protecting the
lavender-coloured flounces from the wheel. A confused
mass of ermine and satin then followed as best it could,
our Tom's gallantry not extending itself to mamma.

Though the colonel's munificence had not been mis-
applied, it had not exactly taken the direction he indicated,
for instead of red and yellow bonnets, Angelena shone
forth in a new brown and white glacé terry velvet, while
mamma had invested her share of the plunder in a dark
blue and white glacé, with coloured flowers in the cap.
While Angelena was nice and smart, Mrs Blunt was a
good deal of the twopenny head and farthing tail school,
the glossy freshness of the terry velvet bonnet contrasting
with the rather worn ermine tippet and cuffs, and the
stains on the satin below. Besides the stains and frays
on the dress, a critical eye might have detected some
darns on the instep of her ribbed silk stockings ; but
Angelena's were nice and well put on, showing her pretty
feet and ankles to advantage.

Such was the party that now alighted from the coach,

and stood at the castle door, on either side of our Tom ; who stood easing first one foot, and then the other, looking as if his leathers were ready to burst.

The soldier-groom at length arriving, munching his last mouthful of cold round of beef, relieved the colonel of the reins, who, desiring the man to see and get the horses well taken care of, proceeded to alight from the box, and divest himself of a dirty old drab Grosjean greatcoat, with large plate-like mother-of-pearl buttons, with black emblematical devîces, illustrating the Turf, the Chase, the Road, and the Ring.

" The hounds are just gone down to Thornington Spinney," observed the pompous Mr Snuffertray, the butler, who had now got waddled to the door, and saw that the colonel's under garments were significant of the chase—" the hounds are just gone down to Thornington Spinney," repeated he, thinking thus to get rid of them.

" Ah, that may all be," replied the colonel, with a nod of his bull-head—" that may all be ; we've come to draw your larder, not the Spinney," adding, as he put his overcoat into the coach, " which is the way to the cat-lap shop ? "

" The w-h-a-t, sir ? " drawled the astonished Mr Snuffertray.

" The cat-lap shop—the breakfast-room, to be sure," replied the colonel.

" Oh, this way, if you please, sir," replied the now enlightened Mr Snuffertray, extending his right arm, and motioning a gigantic footman, who was warming his pink silk calves at the hall fire, to take charge of the distinguished intruders.

The colonel then offered his right fin to Mrs Blunt, and went wad—wad—waddling across the stately hall, exclaiming over his left shoulder to Tom, who followed uneasily in his tight tops, with the tips of Angelena's fingers resting on his arm—

" Good shop, isn't it, Jug ? "

Without waiting for an answer, he waddled on to the open door of the late mirth-echoing dining-room.

The apartment was in the full glow of banqueting disorder—napkins lying here, napkins lying there, napkins

twisted into knots, napkins flaunting over chair-backs,
like drooping drapery. The whole force of plate-linen
and china had been brought to bear upon the entertainment, and very splendid everything was. The Heartycheer arms and crests and coronet glittered everywhere—
on the chair-backs, on the picture-frames, on the plate,
on the glass, on the china, and were even introduced
into the pattern of the long sixty-cover tablecloth.
Monsieur Crapaud, the cook, seemed to have vied with
Monsieur Frappe, the Swiss confectioner, in the novelty
and elegance of his dishes, while Brick, the baker, had
tortured flour into every variety of form. Pines and
grapes, the choicest fruits and flowers, mingled in elegant
designs in the epergnes and vases, were profusely scattered
down the centre of the table.

On the plate-loaded sideboard stood the splendid
Heartycheer testimonial, value five hundred guineas, the
spontaneous outburst of a country's gratitude, slightly
coerced by the tuft-hunting busybody who set it on foot.

" Well, this is somethin' like ! " exclaimed the colonel,
with glistening eyes, as he surveyed the disorderly but
still sumptuous banquet ; " this is better than hunting a
d——d stinking fox," added he, making for a chair
and sousing himself down. " Now, Hall, make yourself
at home," roared he ; " I told ye you'd light on your
legs comin' here. Eat as much as ever you like, for there's
nothin' to pay," diving into the breast of the turkey
before him with a carving-knife, and scoring himself
many slices.

" Take tea—coffee—cocoa—chocolate ? " asked a pert
footman, who now entered, in obedience to Mr Snuffertray's orders to go and see " those tigers didn't steal
anything "—"take chocolate, cocoa, coffee, tea," continued
he, running heel and flourishing his right hand towards
where the various beverages were encamped on different
parts of the table.

" I'll take chocolate, if it's hot," replied the colonel,
munching away at his turkey ; " only if it's *hot*, mind ! "
repeated he, following the man with his eyes to see how
it poured out. " Ah, that won't do ! " exclaimed he ;
" take it out and get it warmed ; and here, man ! "

continued he, diving into a napkin full of eggs, "get some hot what-d'ye-call-'ems?" holding up an egg as he spoke.

"What will you take, Angelena?" asked Tom, who, with unabated assiduity to the daughter, had left the old lady to take care of herself.

"I'll take tea," replied Angelena, untying her new bonnet-strings, and passing them behind her back—"I'll take tea," repeated she, adding, "What will you take?"

"I'll take tea, too," replied the complaisant youth, though his usual beverage was coffee.

The fair lady then took off her primrose-coloured kid gloves, displaying a more than ordinary profusion of rings on her taper fingers, and proceeded to concentrate the scattered tea-service in the vicinity of where they sat. Tom completed the movement by handing down a massive silver kettle, from whose lukewarm contents he replenished the already exhausted teapot.

"Lauk! it's nothing but water!" exclaimed Angelena, as she began to pour the slightly coloured beverage into a Sevres cup. What have we been about, Mister Tom, to make such a mess?"

"Oh! pour away," replied Tom—"pour away," repeated he, as Angelena stopped in her helping, adding, "I like it weak."

"Well, so do I, do you know," replied she. "Mr Hall and I won't ruin ourselves in tea," exclaimed she to mamma, showing her the light-coloured contents of the cup.

Mrs Blunt knit her brows, for she thought Angelena was going too fast.

Meanwhile, the colonel was "pegging away," as he called it, at all the good things within reach, to the astonishment of the servants, who kept dropping in to see the man-monster, just as they would to see an elephant at a show. He "at" everything that came in his way; Bayonne ham, Bologna sausage, blackberry jam, Minorca honey, quince marmalade, anchovy toast, Yorkshire pie, diluted with copious draughts of chocolate, which the footman favoured him with in his own good time.

"Well, I'll do!" at length exclaimed the colonel, throwing himself back in his chair; and, thrusting his fin ends into his corduroy breeches' pockets, he proceeded to suck his teeth and reconnoitre the room. His eye at length rested on a hunting picture opposite—"The Meet of Hounds"—in which everything was made subservient to the white-horse-mounted master in the middle.

"Why, that's old Heartycheer!" roared he, after a good stare, at length recognising the seat and scene of the morning. "Why, that's old Heartycheer," repeated he, adding, "What an old blockhead the man must be to stick himself up in that way."

"H-u-s-h, colonel; the servants will hear!" exclaimed Mrs Blunt, looking about, shocked at the speech, or rather at the loudness in which it was delivered.

"I don't care," replied he, looking very foolish; "I say it *is* a devilish good-looking horse." Then, turning to a group of footmen who were laughing at his fix, he exclaimed, pointing to the picture, "I say, isn't that the Duke of Wellington?"

"No, it's *my lord*," at length one of them replied, indignant at the original exclamation.

"Oh! my lord, is it?" rejoined the colonel, pretending enlightment—"my lord, is it? Could have swore it was the duke. Well," continued he, stretching for a glass, "have you any champagne in that bottle?" pointing towards one; "the ladies will be glad to drink his lordship's health," adding, in an undertone to his wife, "You may as well lunch, now that you are here."

If it hadn't been for the unfortunate speech about the picture, the colonel's inquiry would have produced a fresh bottle, as well for the credit of the house as for the servants' own rights as remainder men; as it was, however, they contented themselves with passing up a few bottle ends, and handing in some glasses, without any great regard to whether they had been used or not.

"Ah!" said the colonel, holding a bottle up to the light, "there's not much here—nor in this either," added he, taking up another. "You drink champagne, Hall?" continued he, addressing our friend across the table,

"Why, that's old Heartycheer!" roared he, after a good stare.

who was now busy pulling bon-bon crackers with Angelena
—" you drink champagne, Hall ? "

" When he can get it," replied Angelena, answering
for him.

" Oh ! get it—we'll get it fast enough," replied the
colonel ; then turning to a footman, who was still sounding
the bottles, he exclaimed, " I say, my man, tell the mess-
man—tell Mr What's-his-name, that Lieutenant-Colonel
Blunt, of her Majesty's Heavysteed Dragoons, and
friends, wish to do Lord Heartycheer the honour—I
mean to say, themselves the honour — of drinking his
lordship's health in a fresh bottle of champagne."

" Yes, sir," replied the man, walking deliberately away.

" Very old friend of mine, Lord Heartycheer," continued the colonel, speaking at the top of his voice for
the edification of the servants that were left—" knew
him when I was quartered here twenty years ago—
am sure he'd be quite shocked if he thought any friend
of mine wasn't made comfortable in his house."

Whatever impression the colonel might make upon
the *remanets*, he would not appear to have produced
much upon the one who had gone, for, lounging down
into Mr Snuffertray's room, who was reclining on a sofa,
reading the ' Post,' he said, with a laugh and a shrug
of his shoulders—

" Those Daniel Lamberts upstairs want a fresh bottle
of fizzey."

" Do they," observed Mr Snuffertray, deeply immersed
in his paper—" do they," repeated he, without looking
off. " Just put your hand into the hamper in the lamp-
closet, and take them up a bottle of the yellow seal."

The man did as he was bid, and presently returned
with the cork all ready for *débouchement*. Clean saucer-
like glasses having been supplied, and all hands now
grasping them, fiz—pop—bang went the cork, and up
foamed the creaming fluid.

" Ah ! thank ye—thank ye, that won't do ! " roared
the colonel, as its pale ginger-pop-like complexion shone
through the beautiful crystal. " Thank ye—thank ye,"
repeated he, setting down his half-filled glass with a
" none of your twopenny tipple here ! "

"Moets," replied the man, colouring brightly, lest the colonel should impound the bottle and show it to Lord Heartycheer.

"Moets be hanged!" responded the colonel; "reg'lar Vauxhall! British, every drop!"

"I assure you, sir, we get it from the very first merchants in London."

"Don't tell *me*—Lieutenant-Colonel Blunt of her Majesty's Heavysteed Dragoons—any such stuff. If that isn't gooseberry, real unadulterated gooseberry, I'll eat my hat!—I'll eat my coat!—I'll eat my weskit!— I'll eat your breeches, buckles and all. Look at it," continued he, holding up the pale-faced contents of the glass to the light—"look at it, and tell me if that's anything like any champagne—anything like what's in the other glasses?" pointing to the golden contents of some unfinished ones on the table.

Just then Mr Snuffertray, having been apprised of the disturbance the colonel was making, arrived in breathless haste with a bottle of the "other sort," this being some that Mr Snuffertray kept for the purpose of exchanging on occasions like the present. Motioning off the bottle and glass, and jerking his head for another glass to be supplied, Mr Snuffertray shot off the cork by the colonel's ear, who stood fire remarkably well, and proceeded to pour out its amber-coloured contents into the rose-and-shamrock-entwined wreathed glass.

"Ah, that's somethin' like, now!" exclaimed the colonel, eyeing the full roseate hue of the new bottle— "that's somethin' like, now," repeated he, holding his glass till it was as full as possible. "Your good health, Hall," said he, as the man stopped pouring. "Angelena," continued he, nodding to his daughter, "your good health," and with "my dear" to his wife, he drained off the contents. "That's good, now," said he, smacking his lips, and setting down the glass—"that's good, now," repeated he, eyeing the filling and gradual disappearance of the glasses of the rest of the party. "*Stay!*" roared he, as the man was walking away with the remainder of the bottle—"*stay!* we've omitted to drink his lordship's health—an omission I wouldn't be guilty of for all the world—a bumper it must be ; and if you manage well," continued he, addressing the butler, " you'll get what's left into these four glasses," the colonel holding up his own to be filled till the wine was again level with the edge. He then quaffed it off at a draught. " *Un*deniable stuff," exclaimed he, smacking his lips, and striking his great stomach as it descended— " undeniable stuff, but requires a little corrective of some sort, p'r'aps, to keep it all right," adding, " Have you any brandy ? "

" Oh, colonel, you are much better without brandy," exclaimed his wife, dreading the consequences.

" You be fiddled," growled he—" you be fiddled ; d'ye think I don't know what agrees with me better than you ? "

" He'll be fuddled," whispered Angelena to our Tom.

" What's in that bottle, my man ? " now asked the colonel, pointing with a dessert-fork to a queerly-shaped, highly-labelled black bottle a little way up the table.

" Huile de Venus," replied the man, reading from the painted label on the side.

" And what's that above that queer-looking thing like a mail-horn full of flowers ? " pointing to a pink glass vase in a light frosted-silver stand.

" Crême de Parfait Amour," spelt the man from the label.

" Perfect amour ! " responded the colonel ; " tell me, have you any perfect brandy ? "

" Plenty, sir," replied the men ; " old champagne brandy, choice old pale cognac, choice brown, and all."

" Ah ! give me choice brown," said he. " I'll make it pale myself—haw, haw, haw !—ho, ho, ho !—he, he, he ! Old soldier—up to the pale dodge—up to the pale dodge— haw, haw, haw ! "

Although there were all sorts of choice liqueurs in the room, the footman had to make another expedition to Mr Snuffertray, which gave Mrs Blunt an opportunity of attempting a diversion in favour of the hunt.

" Well, but you should be going to the dogs, shouldn't you ? " asked she. " The general—I mean his lordship— will be wanting you to keep the ground for him, or somethin' of that sort."

" Oh—ah—·yes," replied the colonel, scratching his bald head. " All in good time. I don't know, either— Cheer's a good chap, and all that sort of thing, and one's glad to countenance field sports in all their various ramifications, but hunting in the ' upper countries,' as Gentleman Smith calls them, spoils one for these d——d little cramped provincials," the colonel striking out with his right fin, as if he didn't want to be bothered about hunting.

" Well, but Mr Hall will want to go and show his nice red coat and new horse," observed the pertinacious Mrs Blunt.

" Mr Hall is very happy here," observed Angelena tartly ; " arn't you, Mr Hall ? " asked she, glancing one of her most bewitching smiles at our hero.

" Quite ! " exclaimed Tom, who really was extremely glad to exchange the dread vicissitudes of the chase for the pleasant tranquillity of the lady's smiles.

And she gave him another sweet look, with a gentle inclination of her head in acknowledgment of his coincidence in her views.

The door then opened.

" Ah, just a thimbleful, just a thimbleful ! " exclaimed the colonel, as the man now appeared with a taper-necked bottle on a massive silver salver, to which having added a very elegant but extremely diminutive Bohemian liqueur-glass, he stepped onwards to where the colonel sat.

" Oh, come," roared our friend in disgust when he saw the glass, " that *is* a child's measure—that *is* playin' with one's stomach with a vengeance. No, no, man," shouted he, " give me somethin' that I can get a taste out of, at all events."

" Perhaps you'll help yourself, sir," replied the man, placing the salver at his side.

" Ah, that's the best way," assented the now pacified colonel—" that's the best way—a man knows his own internals best. Now, give me one of those frosty-stomached gentlemen," pointing to some capacious tumblers flanking a beautiful cut and engraved water-jug. " Ah, that's somethin' like, now," said he, handling it. " I

hold a large glass to be an excellent thing. It doesn't
follow because one has it that one must necessarily fill
it," added he, as he poured out such a quantity as made
a very visible impression on the bottle.

Mrs Blunt sat in fear and trembling, dreading the
consequences, but not daring to interfere ; while Angelena
and Tom kept up a renewed fire with bon-bon crackers,
out of whose sentimental mottoes the fair one extracted
some very appropriate hints.

" Capital brandy ! " observed the colonel confidentially
to his wife ; adding, " Hadn't you better take a drop—
nothin' to pay, you know."

Mrs Blunt, however, declined, and knowing that
remonstrance was in vain when once he began, she sat
patiently by, watching the disappearance of the beverage
and the liberal replenishment of his glass, making mental
wagers with herself as to how many he would take.
As he warmed with his *eau-de-vie*, he waxed eloquent
on the subject of hunting, talked of John Warde, and
Osbaldeston, and Jack Musters, and the days when he
beat everybody—when no one could hold a candle to
him—running his runs, leaping his leaps, and selling his
horses over again, till a most skilfully-sounded gong,
beginning like the rumbling of distant thunder, and
gradually rising till it filled the whole castle with its
roar, acted the part of the merchants' ringing-out bell
on 'Change, and completely put a stop to his bragging.
He could scarcely hear himself speak, let alone any one
else. Finding it was of no use contending with the gong,
he hastily finished his glass, and buttoning his pockets
with a slap, to feel that his purse was inside, proceeded
to waddle into the entrance-hall, whence the sound
proceeded.

" What's the row ? " asked he of the gigantic footman
who was plying the gong with the muffler, making, if
possible, more noise than before.

" To drive the rats away," bellowed the man into the
colonel's ear.

" Drive the rats away !—one wouldn't think there
were any rats in a house like this," roared the colonel,
in opposition to the gong.

"Great many," shouted the man, as he thundered away.

"Did you say you wanted your carriage, sir?" asked the original gentleman's gentleman whom we found lounging at the castle door, now shuffling with a sort of half-impudent obsequiousness up to our friend.

"No, I didn't," responded the colonel; adding, "I don't care if I have it, though."

"Will order it round directly, sir," replied the man, hurrying away.

The gong still sounding, now rumbling in low tantalising murmurs as if done, and then swelling again into thunder, and the colonel, like most noisy men, being unable to bear any noise but his own, at length roared out, "Now, Johnny, have you had enough of your drum?"

Johnny thought not, and continued to rumble and roar, much to the colonel's annoyance, who kept shaking his head and kicking out his fins, and looking at him, wishing he had him in the barracks at home. The noise, indeed, was so absorbing as to overpower sundry pretty speeches of Angelena's as she roamed about the noble hall on the arm of our Tom. Mrs Blunt alone seemed grateful, inasmuch as it had roused the colonel from his brandy; she thought they would now get home safe, which she was by no means so certain of before, the colonel being a desperately rash man on the road when in liquor. We will finish our chapter by getting them under weigh.

The soldier-coachman-footman-groom, who had gone over with the colonel's hunter, as he called his little elephant-like horse, being unable to turn the vehicle out of the yard, his lordship's second coachman condescended to mount the box and bring it round.

"Thank'ee," exclaimed the colonel, as he stood on the steps of the Gothic-arched entrance-hall fumbling on his buckskin gloves as the carriage drew up. "Thank'ee," repeated he; "I'll do as much for you another time." That, or, "I'll remember you, my man," being all the return the colonel ever made for services.

"Well, now bundle in," said he to Mrs Blunt, as a spruce

footman stood with the coach door in his hand, making a sorry contrast between its threadbare red worsted-bound drab lining and his own smart scarlet and silver-laced white livery.

"I think I'll ride outside with you," observed the prudent mamma, in reply to the colonel's commands to "bundle in."

"Ride outside with me!" growled the colonel; "what's that for?"

"Got a little headache," replied the lady, touching her forehead.

"Ah, I twig," said he, in an undertone; "well, come, climb up, and mind you don't break your neck." "Then, Hall—I mean, Jug—no, I mean, Hall—Angelena and you'll go back inside, I s'pose, and mind you don't quarrel by the way—haw, haw, haw!—he, he, he!—ho, ho, ho!"

Tight-booted Tom gladly handed the fair lady in, Mrs Blunt scrambled up as best she could, while Tom squeezed himself through the narrow coach door, and the colonel having sorted his ribbons and fingered the crop of his whip, swung himself up in the old coachman style, and putting himself in posture on the box, exclaimed, "Let go their heads!" as if he had four of the friskiest horses in the world before him. Away they ground from Heartycheer Castle door, amidst the roar of the gong, the deputy coachman exclaiming to the footman, as they stood watching the departure—

"Well, that's as rum a lot as ever I seed in my life!"

CHAPTER XVIII.

LILY OF THE VALLEY, LATE RUMTOUCH.

"Has Jug—I mean to say Hall—offered?" asked the colonel of his wife, as, having shot down the incline from the castle, they got upon the plain sailing of level road in the park.

"Not that I know of," replied Mrs Blunt. "What makes you think so?"

"Oh! only from what she said at breakfast about the tea," replied the colonel, double-thonging his wheelers. "About their not ruining themselves in tea," added he.

"I think it was a mere slip of the tongue," replied Mrs Blunt.

"A slip of the tongue, was it?" rejoined the colonel, catching old Major Pendennis up short, who now made a slip with his groggy forelegs, and nearly came on his head. "Devilish awkward slip," repeated he, cropping the old horse about the ears; though whether he meant Angelena's or the horse's was not quite apparent.

They drove on for some time in silence.

"Well, I don't know that she'll make much of it," resumed he, flourishing his whip, and then laying the point of it scientifically into the near leader's flank. "I don't know that she'll make much of it," repeated he, attempting to pay the same compliment to the other, but with less success.

"Oh! I make no doubt he'll offer to her," replied mamma.

"Ay, ay, but offerin's one thing, and gettin's another," rejoined the colonel. "An offer, as we all know, is only a very short way on the road matrimonial."

" It's the first stage, at all events," replied his wife.

" Yes, and chokes off half the young men that venture," replied the colonel. " Well," continued he, cracking his whip, and springing his horses down a piece of sloping ground to which they now came, " we'll see—we'll see. Hall's a good feller—very good feller ; may be wiser men—don't say there're not—but he's quite wise enough for a man of his means, and I wish he only had them in possession."

" So do I," rejoined his wife ; " but it must come in time ; they've no one else to leave it to, and I make no doubt they'd make him a very good allowance."

" Ah, that's the rock we always split upon," observed the colonel, double-thonging his wheelers—" that's the rock we always split upon ; they always want me to come down with the dust too ; and, by Jove ! I can't—I've nothing to give—nothing whatever. They think, by jingo ! because I'm colonel of a crack cavalry corps, that I have money as well as men at command. However, we'll see. They say the old mechanic's rollin' in money— would skin a flea for its hide and tallow."

" He needn't mind about money for his son," observed Mrs Blunt.

" He will, for all that," replied the colonel, shaking his head, and dropping the double-thong heavily into his wheelers again, as if to revenge the father's mercenary spirit on the horses—" he will, for all that. The more these old thieves have, the more they want. It's a sort of disease," added he, trying to crop his wheelers, but missing them, and nearly losing his balance.

" Well, we can try, at all events," observed Mrs Blunt, as he got himself set straight again.

" Try by all means," assented her husband, flourishing the whip, to pretend that there had been nothing the matter—" try by all means ; there's no sayin' what you can do till you try. It'll be all smooth sailin' enough, I dare say, till we come to the lawyers, with their con-founded impittant inquisitive questions."

" But you might tell the old gentleman that you don't like that sort of interference, and as all you have will be your daughter's, and you suppose all he has will be his son's, you meet on equal terms, and there need be no parchments or inkwork in the matter."

"Humph!" mused the colonel, flourishing his whip and thinking the matter over, considering whether he, whose fortune consisted of his pay and a floating capital of gambling debts, could face the steady old three-columns-of-figures banker, and carry matters off with a high hand, talk of "love light as air," and so on. The colonel had been so often worsted by the lawyers, that he had little heart for engaging with them any more, though he thought his wife's suggestion worth considering. His great hopes, however, consisted in doing Tom in horses. He now directed his observations to that point.

"I wonder if Tom would like to buy Rumtouch," observed he, now laying the whip impartially—to the best of his ability at least—into all four horses.

"He couldn't ride her, could he?" asked Mrs Blunt, biting her lips, lest the colonel should upset them.

"Oh, I don't know," replied the colonel. "Angelena rides her; don't see why he shouldn't—stout, strong young man."

Rumtouch, rechristened by the colonel Lily of the Valley, as a more taking title, was the Arab-like, silver mane and tailed cream-colour introduced to the reader in the colonel's stable when Tom went to look at Captain Smallbeere's horse—my daughter's horse, in fact—the horse the colonel "couldn't bear the idea of parting with," though, like many others, she was only Angelena's till somebody else wanted her. It is observable that, though people do not like buying officers' horses, they have no objections to buying ladies' pads out of a regiment, and the colonel drove a briskish trade in that line.

Rumtouch, as we said before, was a beautifully-shaped animal, quite a fancy thing, with wonderful courage, action, and powers of endurance, but she had a little infirmity of temper that completely overbalanced all her good qualities. She was a gay deceiver. To look at, she was the most mild, placid, easy-going thing imaginable, seeming as if a child might ride her with a thread; and, indeed, in her tantrums, a thread was almost of as much use in her mouth as a bridle, for sometimes, when

Angelena and " Rumtouch," *alias* " Sweetbriar," " Carry-me-easy," " Queen of Trumps," " Heartsease," and other confidence-inspiring titles.

the creature was cantering leisurely along, apparently
in the best possible humour, giving pleasure to her rider,
and causing admiration in the beholder, she would stop
short as if shot, wheel round and away, when the rider
had the choice of letting her go, or pulling her back over
upon him.

She had mastered many men—and women too—
and been sold for many figures, varying with the intensity
of the conflict that caused the separation. Though she
never had regularly finished any one, yet many timid
and many confident horsemen and horsewomen had
thought it well to be rid of her. She had been sold under
all sorts of names—Sweetbriar, Carry-me-easy, Queen of
Trumps, Heartsease, and other confidence-inspiring titles.

Squire Leapingwell sold her to Mr Springwell, simply
because he had no further occasion for her—that is to
say, no further occasion for being run away with. Mr
Springwell, having been twice let down over her tail in
contentions at cross-roads, sold her to Mr Hubbock,
the union doctor, because she was up to more work than
he could give her. Mr Hubbock, having been made to
take a mud-cast of himself in road-scrapings, sold her to
Miss Martinshaw, because she was too good to put into
the cold stables and out-houses he had to frequent.
Miss Martinshaw, having been well run away with over
the open downs, and nearly landed in a gravel-pit, sold
her to her friend Miss Treslove ; who, having nearly had
her front teeth sent down her throat in a rear, strongly
recommended her to Mrs Sharp for her sons, who were
coming home for the holidays. The mare having soon
mastered all these, then passed into the hands of several
small dealers, getting lower at each change, till she finally
became the property of Lucifer Crowbar, a member of
a new fraternity that is now fast springing up over the
country. Lucifer bought her to travel by night through
a long tract of agricultural country, to pick up all the
poached game, stolen fowls, stolen pigeons, stolen anything that was left at his different houses of call, to be
by him conveyed to the railway station. Though he only
gave four pounds ten for her, he expected her to drive
as well as ride, in which expectation he was disappointed,

H

for she soon sent her heels through the front of his spring-cart ; and the stolen-property trade being an amazingly lucrative and increasing one in all countries, he soon found it utterly impossible to carry on his on horseback ; so, after half-riding Rumtouch, as he christened her, to death, he took her to Ripjade fair, where, though high in bone and low in flesh, the sagacious colonel quickly recognised many good points, and bought her for eleven pounds, with five shillings back. Though Lucifer passed " his word of honour as a gentleman " to the colonel that she was perfectly quiet and free from vice, he nevertheless assured a comrade that of all divils he had ever had to do with, she was the biggest ; adding, that not content with getting him off, she would stand and consider which eye she should kick out. This was the bargain the colonel bought, just before the regiment marched to Fleecyborough, where the mare arrived, with a fresh field for her now unblemished character.

Having recruited her from her over-exertions with Crowbar, and mashed her and fattened her, he put her into the riding-school, where she soon got into the routine of tractableness, and was pronounced quite fit for the fine hand and nerve of the fair Angelena. And indeed so the mare was, so long as she was in company with any horse she knew. It was only by herself she performed her vagaries. But the fair Angelena, not finding it convenient always to have her fat father at her side, had adopted a very ingenious method of management. She always had her fed at the place they rode to—consequently the mare was always going towards corn—and when she did show symptoms of restlessness or temper, she just humoured her, and played with her mouth in a light delicate way, instead of jagging and hauling at it as if it was made of india-rubber. So the mare passed for a very beautiful spirited animal, and rose greatly in value ; and though in the presence of a non-buying spectator the colonel would pretend he didn't want to sell her, yet he was always ready to do business at fifty, or as much more as he thought he could get. Indeed, Angelena, who could sell a horse almost as well as her father, had offered her to two or three greenhorns, whose parents, or whose prospects, or other entanglements, she thought prevented any idea of their taking her herself. Fifty pounds for a hack, however, is looked upon as a large price in the country, and she had remained " my daughter's mare " longer than any of her previous possessions.

Such was the valuable animal that the colonel now thought of pawning off on our Tom, and which Mrs Blunt thought his washball seat was hardly adapted to contend with, especially when the sudden halts and wheels about were taken into consideration.

" He couldn't ride her, could he ? " was the observation she made when the colonel suggested the idea.

" Oh, I don't know. Angelena rides her," replied he, flourishing his whip over his head and attempting to crack it like a French postilion.

At this unwonted music Major Pendennis began to kick, Billy Roughun started forward, shook his head, and seemed inclined to follow suit, while the bars tickling Goody-two-Shoes' hocks, caused him to squeal and wince, and the whole team seemed inclined to get clubbed. This brought the conversation to a somewhat abrupt conclusion ; so, leaving the colonel to right matters, we will see what our friends inside are about ; for which purpose we will begin a fresh chapter.

CHAPTER XIX.

A COURTSHIP MARRED.

ANGELENA, who was no advocate for long courtships, having decided that it was time to bring our Tom to book, proceeded to business as soon as she got him into the coach.

"Well, now, Mr Redcoat," said she, drawing up the glass on her side, "I dare say you wish you were tearing after that silly old man and his hounds?"

"No, indeed I don't!" exclaimed Tom, with great earnestness—"indeed I don't! I'm *quite* happy where I am!"

"Ah, that's flattery," replied Angelena archly; "you gentlemen are all such flatterers, there's no believing any one of you."

"Honour bright!" exclaimed Tom.

"Well, then, have you got your portrait pinted as you promised?" asked she.

A crimson blush declared the contrary.

"Ah, there, you see!" pouted she, for they were sitting opposite each other, "and yet you pretend——" she was going to say "to love me," but recollecting that she hadn't got him so far as that, she stopped short and let him make the running.

"Well, but, Angelena," exclaimed Tom, "hear me—hear me! I've been twice to Mr Ruddles to see about it, and he wasn't in."

"Oh, indeed!" replied she, brightening up, adding, "Well, and how were you going to be pinted?"

"In my uniform, as you said; only it's not ready yet," answered Tom.

"Why not in your hunting-dress? I'm sure you can't look better than you do now," replied she, looking him over, from his fat face down to his fat knees and bagging-over calves.

"Well, just as you like," replied the obedient Tom— "just as you like; I'm ready either way."

"No; it's as *you* like. It makes no difference to me," replied Angelena; "but I think it's a pity for men not to be pinted when they're young and——" Here she checked herself again, adding, "I mustn't say all I think."

Tom didn't like that. He thought it as good as said she meant to be Mrs Jug—the Honourable Mrs Jug— detested name! He sat silent, biting his substantial lips, thinking how else he could construe the speech. If he thought it possible she was making a cat's-paw of him, he would feign sickness and get out of the coach.

The fair flirt saw she had rather overshot the mark, and tried to hark back.

"It's odd," she said, "how well gentlemen look in red coats, and how ill snobs."

This rather cheered Tom, following the assertion that he couldn't look better than he did.

"And how will you be pinted—on horseback or on foot?" asked she.

"I don't know. Which would you think?"

"Oh! on horseback, I should say—on your beautiful brown."

"Well, I will," said Tom, readily assenting.

"Jumping a gite," suggested Angelena.

"Well," said Tom, wondering whether he was equal to the performance.

"You should have your hat in your hand, as if you were viewing the fox," continued Angelena.

"I don't know," paused Tom, thinking he couldn't manage it. His idea was that he would want one hand for the bridle, and the other for the pommel of the saddle.

"Oh yes," rejoined Angelena, "you must have your hat off—you must have your hat off; indeed, the artist would never be able to catch your fine commanding expression of countenance with your hat on," looking at Tom's vacant face, as if it was radiant with intellect.

"Suppose I was to be sitting on my horse, taking my hat off to you coming up," suggested Tom, thinking that would be easier than leaping the gate hat in hand.

"Well," replied Angelena, "I'll be cantering up on my beautiful cream-colour."

"That would do very nicely," observed Tom, thinking the pull was now in his favour as against Jug.

"We must have a ride together," exclaimed the accomplished tactician—"to-morrow, let us say. Sophy Fergey wants me to play pretty to her and Captain Mattyfat to the cottage by the windmill on Heatherblow Heath, and there's no reason why I should not have a beau as well as her."

"I shall be most proud," replied Tom, bowing before her, thinking he would beat Jug in a canter.

"You've seen my beautiful pop-pet-ty, haven't you?" asked she.

"Your what?" gaped Tom.

"My pop-pet-ty—my own delightful palfrey, my own Lily of the Valley."

"Oh yes," said Tom, "I saw her in the stables at the barracks."

"Such a love—such a dear—my pa is so kind—gives me everything I want—I might eat gold if I could. Ah! I've a *happy* home," sighed she, clasping her hands, and thinking, with upturned eyes, what she would give to be away from it, "and I'm very, *very* thankful," continued she, dropping hands slowly and reverently before her.

And Tom gaped in admiration of her piety, and thought whether he could make her as happy at his father's house in Newbold-street.

Angelena, who expected something better for this display, looked out of the window to give Tom time to brew up a bit of sentiment, but as none seeming inclined to come, she determined to change her tactics and endeavour to pique him.

"Mr Jug wanted to buy my beautiful Lily," observed she, flourishing a handkerchief redolent of otto of roses.

"Did he," replied Tom, nothing comforted by the information.

"Yes; he took a fancy to her one day out riding with me, and wanted pa to put a price upon her, but he wouldn't."

"Indeed," mused Tom.

"Mr Jug is very rich—at least will be," observed Angelena casually, "though he has nothing to do with tride. He's a grandson of old Lord Pitchers," continued she, as if Tom hadn't the same information as well from herself as from a score of other sources. A sprig of nobility was not so common in the Heavysteeds that they could afford to put the light of one under a bushel, though they sunk the fact of there being a whole row of little Jugs when it suited their purpose.

"I wonder you could refuse such a swell anything," observed our Tom.

"Oh, pa didn't refuse him exactly—he referred him to me. He said she was mine, and I might do as I liked."

"What, it was you, then, that refused him, was it?" asked Tom.

"Yes, it was *me*," replied Angelena.

"I wonder at that."

"Why do you wonder at it?"

"Oh, I don't know," replied Tom.

"Nay, you must know," replied Angelena winningly; "tell me why you wonder at it?" continued she, looking imploringly at our hero.

"Oh, I don't know," repeated Tom, half-afraid to say.

"Nay, that's not worthy of you, Mr Hall," observed Angelena pettishly, "making an assertion without a reason."

"Well, then, to tell you the truth," said Tom, screwing up his courage, "because they say——"

"What do they say?" asked Angelena, shaking with impatience.

"*That you are to be Mrs Jug,*" replied Tom, biting his lips after saying it.

"*Me* Mrs Jug!" exclaimed the artless innocent, throwing up her hands as if horrified at the idea—"*me* Mrs Jug!" repeated she. "Don't believe a word they

say, Mr Hall!" exclaimed the fair lady emphatically—
"don't believe a word they say about Mr Jug!—he is
nothing to me—he never was anything to me—he never
will be anything to me—I never had the *slightest* fancy
for him—his fortune, his title, have no attractions for
me."

This declaration comforted Tom exceedingly, for he
had had some frightful dreams, in which Jug appeared
in various forms—now as a bold dragoon, with his bright
sword gleaming ready for insertion in his stomach;
next, that Jug had him at twelve very short paces well
covered with his pistol; anon, that Angelena and the
dread cornet were kissing their hands to him from the
car of a balloon, with the words "Gretna Green" in
raised gilt letters on the panels; and now that they
were whisking away by northern express to the same
destination.

Hall was exceedingly comforted, for though he had
not got back the promise of marriage letter from dear
Jane Daiseyfield, it was so long since he had heard anything about her, that he made no doubt she had taken
up with some one else; at all events, he was quite ready
to risk an engagement with Angelena, who, apart from
her fifty thousand pounds, he looked upon as the most
interesting captivating creature he had ever beheld.

"Oh, my dearest, my sweetest Angelena!" exclaimed
he, seizing both her hands, and starting forward on his
seat to fall on his knees, when lo! the coach began to
rock, and, before he knew where he was, Angelena was
sprawling a-top of him. The colonel had upset them
at this most critical moment.

CHAPTER XX.

TOM BROUGHT TO THE SCRATCH.

THE catastrophe with which we closed our last chapter happened as follows : Colonel Blunt, who was at all times rather rash with the reins, was doubly so when under the influence of liquor ; and having got his horses well clubbed in going downhill, his difficulties were further increased by the cry of the hounds and the cheering of the men who presently crossed the road a little before him. Old Major Pendennis, who had a taste for the chase, though it had not been much indulged, first set the bars a-rattling, which, being responded to by his brother leader, Billy Roughun, there was such a milling and rearing and squealing and snatching as soon broke the pole, and landed the coach against the bank of a wide newly-cleaned ditch, shooting the ponderous colonel on to his head in the next field, with Mrs Blunt a little beyond him.,

The hounds had been running some fifteen or twenty minutes, with a breast-high scent over a stiffish country, settling all parties in their places with the regularity of a table of precedence. First came Bill Brick, the head whip, breaking the fences for Dicky Thorndyke, who was as pleased to ride second as first ; after him came Lord Heartycheer, going as straight as a line, followed by a groom in scarlet to keep off the crowd, his lordship's maxim being that the real danger in hunting consists in being ridden over, not in falling at your fences.

" Y-o-n-der they go ! " cried his lordship, flourishing his whip in the air, as he flew the hedge and wide ditch on to the Fleecyborough-road ; " y-o-n-der they go ! "

repeated he, eyeing the hounds settling to the scent on the pasture beyond. Just then his quick eye caught the prostrate vehicle on the road : " Ha—hem—haw—corpulent captain capsized ! " exclaimed he, glancing at the glorious confusion, as he gathered his horse for the off-the-road leap ; " haw—ha—hem ; sorry we can't offer him any assistance," added he, flying the fence into the next field. He then dropped his elbows, and rising in his stirrups, set to and hustled the white horse along as hard as ever he could lay legs to the ground, whooping and halloaing as if he was mad.

Fortunately, some of the field were less engrossed with the hunt than his lordship and the half-dozen composing his immediate tail ; indeed, some were very glad of an excuse to pull up ; and ere the second whip was out of sight, a crowd of dismounted horsemen had gathered round the vehicle, joining their clamorous directions with the kicking and struggling and groaning of the horses.

" Sit on their heads ! " shouted one ; " Cut the traces ! " cried another ; " Get the lady out ! " roared a third ; " Where's the colonel ? " asked a fourth ; " Catch my horse ! " exclaimed a fifth.

Lord Heartycheer's country being a good deal infested by sheep, as Dicky Thorndyke said, most of the gallant sportsmen carried knives to cut the nets, and Mr Shirker had scarcely seated himself on Major Pendennis' head, before a cry of " Now they're loose ! stand clear ! " was raised, and kicks and cuffs began to resound upon the horses' hides, making first one and then another rise like horses at Astley's ; when, after surveying the scene on their haunches, they regained all fours, and stood shaking themselves, and staring wildly round them.

Just at this juncture, and while the smoking steeds were scattered all about the road, Angelena emerged through the window in the arms of farmer Quickfall, and Tom came scrambling all-fours after her. The colonel, too, with Mrs Blunt, now appeared, at the white gate a little lower down—the colonel having sorely damaged his shoulder and cardinal-like hat, and Mrs

The end of the Coach Drive.

Blunt having completely crushed her new terry velvet bonnet. Great was the wrathful indignation of the colonel, now vented on Mrs Blunt for catching at the reins, now on Pendennis for kicking, now on Billy Roughun for swerving, now on the wheelers for jibbing, now on this person, now on that, but never a word against his own coachmanship! The coach was well embedded in the bank, the splinter-bar was broken to shivers, and the harness had been cut and mangled into a state of utter uselessness. Our Tom, too, shared in the common misfortune; for his tops, which had been sadly too tight for him all along, had now so swelled his fat calves that he could no longer bear them, and gladly availed himself of Quickfall's penknife to rip them open behind.

By the time our friends had got on their feet, and the actual damage ascertained, the assemblage had very greatly increased; and Dr Bolus, who led the roadsters, having at length arrived with his tail, and examined the colonel and assured him, with a shake of his head, that he must be very careful of his shoulder, it was arranged that our Tom should take Farmer Quickfall's dog-cart and drive to the barracks for the colonel's carriage. Quickfall's house, Hawthorn-hill, being close at hand, thither our party proceeded on foot, accompanied by the horses and cushions, leaving the old coach to be righted when they got some available harness. Mrs Quickfall, little used to such quality guests, insisted on ushering them into the best parlour, where they underwent the usual process of lighting a spluttering, smoking, green-wood fire, while there was a fine hot one burning in the kitchen. While Quickfall was out ordering the dog-cart, Angelena, who was the least damaged of the party, having fallen soft on our Tom and only deranged her ringlets, arranged, with great adroitness, to accompany Tom in it.   A lady so close upon an offer was not likely to be put off without an effort to recover the line. Fortunate indeed it was that she did accompany him, for our Tom, though a very enterprising youth, had never before tried his hand at driving a gig, and Quickfall's mare being rather fresh, he would assuredly have walked

into a waggon-load of turnips, had not Angelena caught
the reins at the moment. Tom then very prudently
resigned the command to her, and, without changing
her seat, the fair lady drove. On coming to rising ground,
she got the hot animal eased down into a walk, and
recommenced operations on Tom.

Never did Dicky Thorndyke make a more knowing
cast to recover a fox than she did to recover the line of
conversation the upset had interrupted. Like Dicky's
casts, it was wide and comprehensive, and made at a
good brisk pace. She began with the " pinting " again.
Well, now, he mustn't forget to be pinted. " Couldn't
he now, couldn't he go to Mr Ruddle's and make an
appointment ? Artists always pretended to be busy.
Dared say he had nothing to do—nothing, at least, that
he couldn't put aside for such a customer as you. He told
Mr Jug just the same thing—said he was so busy he
didn't know when he could appoint his first sitting. Mr
Jug just turned on his heel and said, ' Well, I don't care
about it ; it's my granddad, Lord Pitcher, who wants it.'
It wasn't, you know," said Angelena, confidentially to
Tom ; " the silly boy meant it for me "—a piece of
information that caused Tom to bite his lips. " ' It's
my granddad, Lord Pitcher, who wants it,' said he.
And would you believe it, as soon as Ruddle heard he was
the grandson of a lord, he immediately said he would
arrange it, and gave him his first sitting the next day.
He was pinted in full uniform, with his hair curled like
a cauliflower. Silly boy, he's so vain—thinks himself
handsome—thinks, because he'll be an honourable,
everybody must want him. No patience with such
conceited boys," added she, whipping the mare on, vexed
at Tom for not catching at the opening she had now given
him. " I think you'll wish now you'd gone with the
hounds," observed Angelena, as Tom began rubbing
the dry mud off his knees.

" No, indeed I don't," replied he ; " I'm quite happy
where I am."

" Stupid dolt," thought she, whipping the mare again ;
" that's what he said before." " What ! and saved
the upset ? " asked she.

" Oh, I don't care about an upset," replied Tom. No more he did, so long as he fell soft.

" But you'd have tried your fine new horse," observed she.

" Oh, I'll have plenty of opportunities of doing that," replied Tom ; " the season's only just beginning."

" A bad beginning for us," observed Angelena, " seeing the hounds upset the coach. I declare I haven't got over the fright yet," after a pause, as if she had been revolving the matter in her mind.

" Nor I either," replied Tom, who felt excessively for his tops ; indeed, the pain of his swelled calves, and the damage to his boots, which would wholly prevent the perambulation of the streets in his red coat, operated against a return of the enthusiasm the upset of the coach had interrupted.

After several more fruitless attempts to get up the steam of Tom's ardour again, they now rose Benningborough-hill, from whence Fleecyborough, with its railway station, its spiral churches, its tall-chimnied opposition gasometers, its barn-like opposition tanneries, and tower-ing town hall, burst conspicuous on the view.

" There's Fleecyborough, I believe," said Angelena, eyeing the white villas fringing the smoke of the blue-and-red town.

" So there is," replied Tom, thinking of his damaged tops, instead of expressing regret, or making any pleasant allusion to the quickness of time flying in pleasant com-pany, or anything of that sort.

Finding there was no chance of moving him to court-ship, Angelena got the mare well by the head, so as to time herself properly, and thus came at once to the point.

" By the way, Mr Talliho, what were you saying when we were upset ? "

" Saying—upset—upset—saying," stammered Tom.

" Yes, you know, about Jug—about my not being Mrs Jug."

" Oh, ah ! " replied Tom, blushing crimson ; " I was— I meant—I thought—I was glad——"

" Glad at what ? " snapped Angelena.

"Oh! ah! yes—glad that you were not going to be Mrs Jug—the Honourable Mrs Jug."

"But why were you glad?" asked she.

"Oh—why—to tell you the truth," replied Tom, screwing his hands together for the great effort, "because —simply because—I hoped—I ventured to hope—that you would be Mrs H."

Shriek!—screech!—shriek! went Angelena, as if horrified at the thought—shriek!—screech!—shriek! startling the mare and astonishing a ploughman who happened to be turning on an adjoining headland.

Fortunately, the loss of her presence of mind did not entail the loss of her command over the mare, whom she pulled up out of the undignified canter at which she went off, just as they met a Fleecyborough fly, with three Miss Gigglewells on the look-out for fatigued fox-hunters. How they stared! However, it was lost upon Tom. He was frightened. He feared he had offended the great heiress, and now saw the temerity of a man like him aspiring to the hand of a lady who had refused the son of a lord that-was-to-be. He wished himself well out of the gig.

"Oh, Mr Hall! oh, Mr Hall!" gasped Angelena, as she got the mare calmed into a trot, "you've— you've completely unnerved me—I—I—am not myself— indeed I'm not—you—you——"

"My dear Miss Blunt," exclaimed Tom, thinking the sooner he dropped Angelena-ing her the better, "my dear Miss Blunt——"

"Oh, don't Miss Blunt me!" exclaimed she, putting her little hand up as if in deprecation of the word— "don't Miss Blunt me—pray don't."

"Well, but, my dearest Angelena," resumed Tom, plucking up his courage again, "tell me how have I offended —how have I hurt you?"

"Oh, Mr Hall, you've taken me so by surprise—you can't *think* how you've astonished me."

Tom thought this was rather queer from a lady who seemed ready for an offer from the first.

"I'm sure I appreciate the compliment of your partiality," continued she, now driving very slowly; "I

do appreciate the compliment of your partiality, for I
believe it's disinterested—yes, I believe it's disinterested ;
but don't, pray don't think the worse of me for saying it—
but girls in my situation—girls, you know, without
brothers—heiresses, in fact,—are so liable to be persecuted by the unworthy, that, that—" and here her
voice faltered. " Oh ! what I would give for a brother ! "
" A husband would be a much better thing," observed
Tom, in his dry matter-of-fact way.
" Oh, Mr Hall, a congenial spirit—one in whom I could
confide—one whom I might look forward to for supplying
the place of my dear, dear father. It isn't wealth or
station I ambition—I wouldn't marry that little drunken
Jug if he had a million a month."
" He *is* a nasty little varmint," replied Tom, who
hated the very name of Jug.
" No, Mr Hall, no," continued Angelena ; " I believe
you are sincere — I believe I may trust in you — it's
not my money you——"
" Fourpence ! " exclaimed a voice from the Tiptin
turnpike-gate, through which she now drove without
dispensing the usual compliment—" fourpence ! " repeated a shirt-sleeved follower in a louder strain ; adding,
as he overtook the gig, " why don't you pay your pike,
you dirty bilks ? "
This inopportune interruption, combined with the
fretting of the mare while Tom fumbled for his pence,
completely threw Angelena off her point ; and as the
half-acre allotments and little sentry-box summer-housed
gardens of the outskirts now appeared, to be quickly
followed by the bad pavement of the town, she just got
the mare well in hand, and changing places with Tom,
drove smartly through the streets that cut off an angle
in the direction of the barracks, leaving a long train of
excitement and speculation among the natives, whom
the rattle of the wheels brought to the windows. Arrived
at the barracks, they found all stir and consternation.
Rumour with her hundred tongues had got there before
them, inflicting every possible injury on the gallant
colonel and his wife. Having ordered a servant to get
ready the mail-phaeton, and an orderly to return with

the dog-cart, the now nearly betrothed couple entered the colonel's house, in whose comfortable privacy our Tom closed the rivets of the bargain, swearing eternal fidelity to the fair lady, and telling her as much of his father's affairs as he could, computing him, of course, at the usual young gentleman's rate of ten thousand a year.

When Colonel and Mrs Blunt arrived, which, either from accident or design, they were in no great hurry to do, they found our Tom and Angelena comfortably seated on the old horse-hair sofa, Tom making a sandwich of the fair one's little hand between his own fat ones. The first transports of joy were well over, and Tom was regarding Angelena—the future partner of his life—very much as a man does a new horse, wondering whether she was as good as she looked ; indeed, if truth must be told, the idea had crossed his mind whether the little taper hand he then pressed would be equal to boxing his ears.

Hearing her mother's rustling satin coming first, Angelena just kept her hand where it was, and having satisfied herself that her mother saw it, she just slipped it out, adjusted her collar and gave her clothes a propriety shake, as the colonel appeared at the door.

At first, of course, their conversation was all about their injuries and miraculous escapes, with anathemas at the horses for their bad behaviour, and speculations as to the probable damage to the drag. These interesting topics being exhausted, the lovers then sat silent for a time, Angelena expecting our Tom would give tongue, and Tom thinking it was as much her business to do it as his, particularly in her own house. Although this was her ninth offer, she was just as eager to be into the thick of it as she was with the first one ; and mamma, who was well versed in her ways, saw she had a difficulty in containing herself. As Tom sat mute, now looking at her, now comparing his feet or eyeing his damaged tops and swelling calves, Angelena at length motioned her mother away ; and, after a few minutes spent in consultation, the colonel was summoned to the council. Of course, among themselves they dispensed with the usual forms of surprise—forms that, in nine cases out of ten, are pure hypocrisy, for no woman ever gets an offer without expecting it—and went at once to the point. "What should they do?" "Should they tell old Hall, or let Tom tell him; or carry it on as a sort of conditional engagement, to be ratified hereafter if both parties liked?" The ladies were all for trying to clench it at once, considering that Angelena—though a trifle older—was a most unexceptionable match for our Tom; while the colonel's experience and ulterior views made him rather incline to keep it on, lest he might kill the goose that lay them the golden eggs in the horse way. The ladies, however, prevailed. Mrs Blunt thought it was due from her to "say something," so, having exchanged her much damaged bonnet for a fly-away cap, full of poppies and wheat-ears, and arrayed her shoulders in a large profusely-worked collar, she emerged from the thinly-partitioned little room in which they had held their confab, and found Tom tying his damaged tops up with a little twine, leaving Angelena outside on her knees with her eye at the key-hole—a *surveillance* not very conducive to eloquence. After a good deal of hemming and hawing, and clearing of her throat, she gave two or three downwards sweeps to her gown, and seating herself beside Tom, on the sofa, thus addressed him, punctuating every three words with a "hem" or a cough, or both.

"Well, my dear—sir, my—darter has been telling—me the—compliment and honour, I may say, you have done her, which, I need hardly say, has taken the—colonel and me very much by—surprise, though we cannot but feel——grateful for the—preference you have shown; and though it must necessarily be a very—heinous and—painful separation, yet the colonel and I have such a high sense of your—integrity and excessive philanthropy—that, of course, we must yield to the——observances of nature, and wish you every——happiness that this——world can—supply."

Tom sat agape, for he had never been regularly over-hauled before, and did not know where to make the responses. After waiting a time, to see if he would rise, Mrs Blunt resumed as follows—

I

" My darter's young," she said, with a twinkle in her
eye, as if she would shortly shed a tear, "and inexperienced
in the ways of the world ; but I'm sure we're entrusting
her to a gen'l'man who will—appreciate her—talents
and excellencies, and preserve her in—affluence and—
independence."

" Yes," said Tom.

" It's an anxious moment, settlin' a young lady with
the pretensions of our darter," observed Mrs Blunt,
much to the satisfaction of the fair listener at the door,
who was afraid her mamma was going to omit touching
on that important point—" it's an anxious moment
settlin' a young lady with the pretensions of our darter,"
repeated she ; " for, of course, the—reputation of—riches
awakens the cupidity of the dangerous, and exposes a
gal to great persecution, not to say temptation ; but,
I must say, Angelena has always shown a discretion far
beyond her years, and no—parents ever had a more
satisfactory child. She might have made great matches—
great—lords, great—baronets ; but she has always shown
a disposition for the enjoyment of—intellectual society,
and the—tranquillity of country life. She's quite different
with you to what she's been with all her other admirers,"
added Mrs Blunt, looking smilingly on her fat son-in-law
to be.

" Indeed," said Tom, " I'm sure I'm very much flattered "—and he thought what a triumph he would have,
brushing past Jug, with Angelena on his arm.

And now the fair lady, thinking her mother had said
quite enough, and fearing she might commit herself,
rose from her knees, and after a prefatory glance at the
looking-glass, smoothing her glossy hair, she sidled
into the room, and announced that her dear papa thought
of going to bed. Mrs Blunt, auguring from this that he
was worse, lost no time in leaving our young friends
alone ; and Tom, being shortly after seized with the
qualms of hunger, and smelling nothing in the way of
dinner where he was, resolved to avail himself of a fly
that had just set down at the officers' quarters, and
drawn up to wait the chance of a fare. Hailing it from
the window, it was quickly at the door, and after a most

affectionate lover-like leavetaking, Tom jumped in with his packthread-tied tops, and, kissing his hand from the window, was presently whisked out of sight—he loved, and drove away—and, ere he was well clear of the gates, Jug was occupying his place on the sofa with Angelena, laughing at her other suitor.

CHAPTER XXI.

A MEETING OF THE FATHERS.

"Well, Tummus, and have you caught the fox?" asked old father Hall, as his muddied, tatter'd, booted son nearly upset him travelling from the cellar to the parlour with a bottle of port in each hand, a bottle of sherry under his arm—"well, Tummus, and have you caught the fox?" asked he, as he recovered his balance.

"No; but I've caught something better," replied Tom, grinning from ear to ear.

"Indeed!" exclaimed the old man. "I thought there was nothin' but foxes to catch out a-huntin'."

"Yes, but there is," replied Tom, full grin as before.

"What is it?" asked the old man, passing on into the parlour.

"Guess," said the son, following him.

"Can't," replied the father, after a pause.

"What do you think of an heiress?—a fifty thousand pounder?"

"Fifty thousand pounder!" gasped the old man. "Impossible, Tom."

"Fact, I assure you," said Tom, with a look of compassion.

"Wonderful," observed the old man, eyeing him intently.

"Wonderful! I don't see anything wonderful in it," replied Tom, recollecting Angelena's pretty compliments, and how irresistible Miss Sowerby and Jane Daiseyfield had found him.

"And who is it?" at length asked the old man, thinking it time to come to particulars.

" Guess," replied Tom again.

"Nay; I don't know," replied the banker, running all the monied people through his mind, and thinking who was likely to have such a sum as fifty thousand pounds, or anything like it. "Somebody you've met at the castle?" at length suggested he.

"No," replied Tom.

"No," repeated the father. "I don't know who it can be, then. Anybody I've ever seen?"

"Don't know," replied Tom; "not sure—p'r'aps you may. No; I think not."

"Can't think," replied the father.

"The lovely Miss Angelena Blunt!" proclaimed Tom, with victorious emphasis.

"Miss Angelena Blunt!" repeated old Hall, with terror-stricken looks—"Miss Angelena Blunt! What, do you mean the colonel's daughter?"

"The same," replied Tom; "most charming captivating creature."

"*Hem!*" mused old Hall.

His wife and he had had their misgivings about the lavender-coloured flounces, but little dreamt they were so near mischief.

"Ain't I a lucky fellow?" asked Tom, wondering that his father didn't hug him for joy.

"Sivin and four's elivin, and fourteen is twenty-five, and nine is thirty-four. If I throw cold water on it, it will only make him worse," mused he; "and twenty-five is fifty-nine. I'd better humour him. I s'pose she's a beauty, into the bargain?" observed he, having heard that she was not.

"Oh! she's lovely—she's angelic—she's perfectly divine!" exclaimed Tom, thinking over all her pretty speeches and prudent inquiries.

"Sivin and four's elivin, and ninety-one's a 'under'd and two. I'll sound him about the £ s. d.," thought Hall. "Fifty thousand punds, did you say she had?" asked he.

"Fifty thousand pounds," repeated Tom. "Fifty thousand solid substantial sovereigns," continued he, repeating Major Fib's information.

" It's a vast of money," observed the father, with a
shake of the head.

" It is," replied the son ; " but not more than such an
angel deserves."

" Oh, no," replied the father, who was not to be surfeited with money.

" It's near dinner, I s'pose," said Tom, seeing his father
reverting to the bottles, " so I'll go upstairs and change "—
the tightness of his nether garments making him wish
to be out of them.

He then went lobbing upstairs to his room ; and old
Hall, having hastily deposited the bottles in the cellaret,
went to communicate the dread intelligence to his wife
in the kitchen. Mrs Hall was horrified. Independently
of having set Tom out for a titled lady, she had had a
good look at Angelena while cheapening some Irish
poplins in Frippery & Co.'s back-shop, and had come to
the conclusion that she was nearer thirty than twenty.
The fifty thousand pounds she declared she looked upon
as purely imaginary ; nor did the prospect of having
the colonel to protect them from the " new Boney,"
as Mrs Hall called the now Prince President of the French,
reconcile her to the military connection. However, she
took her husband's advice not to appear to oppose the
match—nay, rather to approve it ; and dinner over,
the evening was spent in narrating the adventures of the
day, varied by reiterated explosions respecting Angelena's
beauty, and confidence in the abundance of her wealth.
So satisfied was Tom on this latter point, and so plausible
did the ladies' speeches appear, that the old people came
to the conclusion that there might be something in it ;
and if the " something " amounted to fifty, or even to
five-and-twenty thousand pounds, old Hall was inclined
for a deal. So, with his usual tumbler of toddy, the old
banker at length went to bed.

Morning brought no change of opinion on the subject ;
and, urged by his wife, our cautious friend decked himself
out in his best black coat and waistcoat, with knee-
breeches and black silk stockings, to pay a complimentary
fishing visit to the great commander at the barracks.
The sooner the thing was settled one way or another the

better, they both thought. Having breakfasted, and
seen the bank fairly open, and cautioned Trueboy against
the " paper " of certain weakly parties who he thought
might call, he stepped into Jack Flopperton's fly, and was
soon lilting and tilting over the irregularities of the
pavement, raising the speculations of the curious as to
whether he was going to a funeral or to a meeting of
creditors.

The colonel and Mrs Blunt had had their talk over
the matter, and it had occurred to them that such a
visit was likely ; so they had had the little room tidied,
the colonel's spare swords and weapons arranged in a
conspicuous way, and themselves got up in an extra-
elegant style. The colonel had anticipated a clean dress-
ing-gown by at least six weeks.

The grinding of the fly through the barrack-yard
attracted Mrs Blunt's attention, and looking out of the
window she saw, dangling over the door, such a fat hand
as could belong to none but Tom's father ; so, raising
a cry of " Here he is ! " the colonel soused himself into
the sofa, and Mrs Blunt, sweeping away a pair of his old
flannel drawers that she was darning, and the remains
of a bottle of stout, threw a painted crimson-and-black
cover over the table, and dealt a dirty old " Keepsake,"
a copy of ' Fistiana,' and an army list around it, as Hall
came heaving and puffing upstairs. The flounce of her
dress just swept through one door as the soldier-footman
announced " Mr Hall " at the other.

" Oh, Hall ! how are you ? " exclaimed the monster,
attempting to rise, and falling back like an over-fed
pig in its sty—" Hall, how are you ? " repeated he,
extending a fin, with an " excuse my rising, but the
fact is, I'm sufferin' from the effects of a fall—deuced
bad fall—nearly killed yesterday—upset on my coach—
stupid old man and his hounds—horses took fright—
pitched on my head—he just rode on—never asked if
I was killed. However, here I am, and I'm glad to see
you ; pray take a seat—arm-chair at your side—hope
Mrs Hall's well ? "

Having sidled himself into a seat, Hall crowned
one knee-cap with his broad-brimmed hat, and resting

his fat hand on the other, sat contemplating the colonel.

" You're the very man I want to see—you're the very man I want to see !—you can tell me all I want to know !" exclaimed he.

" Sivin and four's elivin, and nineteen is thirty, and twenty-four is fifty-four ; he's comin' to the point at once," thought Hall.

" You see, Brown—I mean, Hall—confound it, you're so like Brown that I never know the difference—hang'd if there isn't a resemblance throughout the whole of you Fleecyborough commercialists. Juggins is as like Huggins as ever he can stare ; Tiffin and Trotter might pass for brothers."

" They *are* brothers," replied the banker.

" What, was the father called Tiffin ? " asked the colonel.

" Trotter," replied the banker.

" Ah, then Tiffin changed his name, did he ?—for a fortin' most likely—mercenary dog. And that reminds me of what I was wantin' to ask you—to talk to you about. I've been in a devil of a stew these last few days. Every ' Times ' that I take up contains some marvellous story about gold—gold in the mud, gold in the clay, gold in bridges, gold everywhere ; and I want to know what's to be the value of gold ? I want to know whether gold's to be of any more worth, or one may just take and sow it broadcast over the land, or empty one's pockets of it among the little boys in the streets ? ' What shall I do with my money, in fact ? ' as I see staring me at the head of an advertisement."

" Sivin and four's elivin, and thirteen is twenty-four ; there's no doubt," replied Hall, slowly and deliberately— " there's no doubt that the abundance of any article has a tendency to lower its value ; but gold's not become a drug yet."

" Drug yet ! " exclaimed the colonel, striking out both fins—" drug yet ! Then you anticipate its becoming a drug, do you ? " added he, with a look of alarm.

" Sivin and four's elivin, and thirty-three is forty-four ; there's no manner of doubt there's a great deal of gold comin' into the country—the quantity from California was immense, and they're gettin' as much, if not more, in Australia. The Bank of England can't afford to pay three pund sixteen and a penny-halfpenny per ounce for gold, when others can buy it for three-four-six per ounce, seven and a half better than the standard."

" Ah, now," exclaimed the colonel, " you're gettin' into the mysteries of the currency, a thing I never could understand. I'm not a learned man—I'm not a mercenary man—I'm not a covetous man. I know that twelve-pence make a shillin', and that twenty shillin's make a pund ; but I want to know if a pun's to be only worth ten shillin's in futur', and if everything else is to fall in proportion ? "

" Sivin and four's elivin, and eighteen is twenty-nine ; the man has money, I think," mused Hall ; " and ninety-four is a 'under'd and twenty-three. I'll try and find out where it is." He then addressed himself to the colonel. " Money—that's to say Consols—will fall undoubtedly, colonel. If you reduce the interest on the national debt, say one per cent, you'll reduce the value of money one-third ; but land shares, and all other tangible available property, will rise."

" The devil they will ! " exclaimed the colonel. " Then do you mean to say the fundholder's to be robbed for the landowner ? "

" Sivin and four's elivin, and forty's fifty-one ; that touches him," thought Hall. " The monied interest has had a longish day, and not altogether a bad 'un," replied he, slowly and deliberately. " Much of our debt was contracted at sixty, and is now worth ninety-six and three-eighths, and it's about time the land had a turn."

" What ! you're a landowner, are you ? " asked the colonel.

" Sivin and four's elivin, and forty-nine's sixty, and fifty-four's a 'under'd and fourteen. Not exactly a landowner," replied our friend ; " somethin' akin to it, though."

" I twig," replied the colonel, with a knowing leer. " An *uncle*—an agricultural *uncle*, you mean to say. Haw, haw, haw ! ho, ho, ho ! he, he, he ! I dare say

there's a vast of land up the spout. You'll be grabbing
an estate some day, and setting up for a gentleman.
Fellers used to think when they got four silver side-
dishes they were gentlemen," continued the colonel ;
" but since those plated Brummagem things came up,
they've gone upon land—they think land's the thing.
You'll be setting your son up in an estate, at all events ? "
he added.

" Sivin and four's elivin, and two 'under'd and thirty's
two 'under'd and forty-one, and ninety's three 'under'd
and thirty-one," calculated Hall, getting up the steam.
" It was my son I was comin' to talk to you about,"
replied he—" my son and your darter," added he.

" Oh, faith, aye ! I'd forgotten all that in my anxiety
about my money," replied the colonel, in the most matter-
of-course off-hand way. " I dare say you and I will soon
settle that. We'll be much of the same mind. It's all
very well for boys and girls to philander, and bill and coo,
and make eyes at each other ; but experienced men of
the world, like you and I, know that it don't do for people
to marry too young. A man shouldn't marry before
he's thirty. Doesn't know his own mind—tires of a
woman—neglects her. Don't do—woman much better
single—girl with a fortin', at least. At the same time,
I assure you, both Mrs Colonel Blunt and I are sensible
of the compliment your son has paid our daughter. He's
a very fine young man, is Joseph—I mean Henry."

" *Tummus,*" interposed the parent.

" I beg your pardon, Thomas. I was thinking of
Buss's son ; his name's Joseph—a smooth-faced lookin'
sinner he is too—deep file for all that. But Thomas is
a good feller—very good feller—nice open-countenanced
feller, and fat. Don't like your whipping-post boys.
Now you and I," continued he, looking the banker over,
" are much what men ought to be—full limbed and
plump ; but the generality of the men nowadays are
mere lath and plaister, if I may use such an expression."

" Sivin and four's elivin, and ninety-nine's a 'under'd
and ten ; he's not such a bad old buffer after all," mused
Hall, as the colonel proceeded ; " looks as if he had money,
not being keen for the match. The room certainly isn't

well furnished," looking about him; "carpet doesn't half-cover the floor, and sofa looks like a job from Mrs Smoothley's in the Terrace-lane; curtains, too, are faded and dirty—but that may be whim, or the fortunes of war."

This reverie was interrupted by the colonel stamping with his iron-plated heel on the uncarpeted part of the floor, and exclaiming—

"You must take a little refreshment after your walk Hall; keen winter air must have given you an appetite. You don't hunt, I think, do you?"

"Never either hunted or gammled," replied the banker, with a shake of his head.

"Ah, well, you're a wise man," replied the colonel; adding, to a gigantic soldier-footman who now came settling himself into his tawdry coat, "bring a tray, Jasper, bring a tray."

"Thank'ee, colonel, nothing for me, I'm obleeged," interposed the man of money.

"Oh, but you must; indeed, you must," exclaimed the colonel. "This is the first time you've been in my little crib—wouldn't come to our ear-ache and stomach-ache—most brilliant thing of the season. Must break bread with us now—indeed, you must."

Jasper now returned, bearing a massive silver tray, with a richly-cut decanter of sherry, surrounded with little blown glass plates, containing finger-biscuits, saucer-cakes, currant buns, and other remnants of that notable feast, now fresh out of Mrs Blunt's bonnet-box.

"Get out the Cardigan, Jasper," said the colonel to the man, who forthwith produced a three-quarters-full black bottle, with the word "Brandy" in black letters on the ivory label.

"Ah, that's the stuff!" exclaimed the colonel, as the man placed it on the stand; "that's the stuff!" repeated he, his eyes glistening with delight. "Now, take a drop of this—just a thimbleful," continued he, seizing a tumbler, and filling it about half-full.

"Thank you, sir; thank you, sir—I'm very much obliged to you, sir," exclaimed Mr Hall, endeavouring to arrest the filling, "but I really——"

" You really must oblige me," interrupted the colonel ;
" this is the first time I have had the pleasure of seeing
you—at least, of seeing you here ; and though I've not
had the pleasure of dining with you yet, I shall have
very great satisfaction in doing so ; for you Fleecyborough folks, though there's not much style about you,
have a deal of good rough honest hospitality, which, in my
opinion, is a much better thing; and I don't know any
quarter in England where you get such undeniable mutton
—mutton that eats like mutton, instead of the nasty,
watery, stringy, turnipy stuff, neither mutton nor lamb,
that other countries are inundated with." The colonel
then filled himself an equally liberal glass, and, nodding
to his guest, was soon deep in its contents. " That's
good," said he, " very good," smacking his lips as he
placed the glass on the table.

" Very bad," thought Mrs Blunt, who was listening
at the door ; " I'm sure you'll be tipsy."

" Take a biscuit, or a bun, or some of these absurdities ? "
said the colonel, flourishing his hand over the tray.

" None, I'm much obleeged," replied the banker, who
thought they didn't look very fresh.

" Ah, well ; I dare say you're right," observed the
colonel. " Drinkin's better for the teeth than eatin',"
added he, draining the contents of his glass. He then
took, if possible, a more liberal measure than before.
" To resume our conversation," said he, glancing his
bloodshot eyes at the banker — " to resume our conversation about the young people. I think we understand each other—I think we understand each other.
I have, I assure you, the very greatest regard and consideration for my young friend Joe—I mean to say,
Tom ; there's no young man I have so high an opinion
of as I have of him—no young man that I would sooner
have as a son-in-law ; and if he continues of the same
mind, and all things were made pleasant, of course I
should not say no. But then, that must be all in good
time—all in good time ; must know each other—must
understand each other—must appreciate each other.
Young folks hardly out of their 'teens are not fit to enter
into the binding entanglements of matrimony—monthly

nurses, coral rattles, caudle, and cryin' children," the colonel kicking out his right fin as if undergoing persecution from a crying child already.

Hall followed the renewed debate, with the following mental commentary—

"Sivin and four's elivin, and a 'under'd and ninety's two 'under'd and one—wonder wot he's going to be at now ; and thirty's two 'under'd and thirty-one—wonder if *he* would make things pleasant ; and fourteen is two 'under'd and forty-five—she's a devilish deal older than that ; and forty's two 'under'd and eighty - five — a cryin' brat's a terrible nuisance ; Mrs Buss's bairn's always cryin'."

Text and commentary coming to a close, the plump diplomatists then sat staring, each wishing the other would come to the point.

"You don't get on with your beverage," at length observed the colonel, seeing his guest sat nursing his tumbler on his fat knee ; "would you like sherry, or gin, or shrub, or anything else ? "

"Thank ye, no, colonel ; it's very good, but rather strong," replied Hall, taking a sip, and setting down the glass.

"Oh, brandy can hurt no one," replied the colonel ; "brandy can hurt no one—most wholesome beverage there is—recommended by the faculty," continued he, draining his tumbler again, and replenishing it plentifully. "Your good health, Hall," said he, holding it up, and addressing the banker ; "your good health—Mrs Hall's good health, my friend Tom's good health. I like a feller like you," said he, smacking his lips, as he set down the glass— "a man without any gammon or blandishment, who comes to the point at once, instead of hummin' and hawin', and beatin' about the bush, as some aggrivatin' fellers do."

"Sivin and four's elivin, and forty-five is fifty-six— he's humbuggin' now," thought Hall ; "what does he mean by blandishment ? "

"You and I are gettin' on in years," continued the colonel, "and shall both be damping off before long, and our objects, I've no doubt, are the same—to see

our children comfortably settled while we live; and
should anything come of this youthful—romantic attach-
ment, I've no doubt you'll come down devilish handsome—
turn some of your dibs into land, and buy them a good
substantial family house, with greenhouse and granaries
and gardens and all complete, so that they may increase
and multiply in comfort."

"Sivin and four's elivin, and five 'under'd and nine
is five 'under'd and twenty—he's coming to the point in
style," thought Hall. "How would it suit *you*, colonel,
to get out of your money, and invest it in land?" asked
he.

"Confounded old beggar has me there," growled the
colonel to himself. "Why, I don't know," replied he,
"it might be a temptation; or as we *are* castle-building,
you and I, s'pose we say—if the thing takes place—we
each put down—what shall I say?—twenty, or five-and-
twenty thousand?"

"Sivin and four's elivin, and three 'under'd and four
is three 'under'd and fifteen—that's to the point, at all
events," mused Hall. "Well," said he, taking up his hat,
and stretching it incontinently on his knee—"well,"
repeated he, "I'm not prepared to say that I wouldn't.
But then, again," continued he, after a little more mental
arithmetic, "it would fall much heavier on me than it
would on you."

"How so?" asked the colonel, chuckling at the idea
of any one supposing him worth five-and-twenty thousand
pounds.

"Why, this way, you see," said Hall, still stretching
away at his hat; "my money's employed in business,
yielding me from 15 to 20 per cent."

"The devil it is!" exclaimed the colonel; "and yet
you only allow 2 per cent to depositors, and talk of
reducing that. Well, hang me," added he, slapping
his thigh, "but I've always said bankers, brewers, and
bakers are the biggest rogues under the sun!"

"Indeed," smiled the banker, amused at his host's
vehemence; "mine's a successful business, because it's
well attended to—you never see me huntin', or gammlin',
or drivin' coaches and four." Our friend looking earnestly

at the colonel, as if he had paid him off for his rude speech. " But what I was goin' to say, colonel, is this : my money being so well employed, and yours so ill, wouldn't it be better, before the great influx of gold sends down the funds, for you to sell out and buy an estate ? "

" Well, I don't know but it might," replied the colonel, with an air of indifference. " I'll consult my lawyers on the point—no man dare blow his nose without consulting his lawyer, you know ; haw, haw, haw ! "

" Well, then," observed Hall, after a long pause and a sideways stretch of his hat, " I s'pose that's as far as we can go this mornin' ? "

" I s'pose it is," replied the colonel, " unless you'll take another go of brandy—plenty in the bottle," added he, nodding towards it.

" Thank'ee, no more, colonel, I am obleeged," moving his chair as if about to rise ; when a thought struck him. " You're in the funds, I think you say—Consols, I s'pose ? "

" Consols," nodded the colonel.

" In your own name, of course ? " observed the banker, with an air of indifference.

" In my own name," repeated the colonel.

The man of metal then rose to depart.

" Well, then, Brown—that's to say, Hall," observed the colonel, scrambling off the sofa and grasping his hand, " I'm much obliged by the friendly nature of this visit. Damnation ! I like an honest open-countenanced feller, without guile or blandishment, who comes to the point like a man. I little thought, when I called to ask you to our ear-ache and stomach-ache, that we should ever come to anything like this ; but I'm sure, if the young people, after a rational acquaintance, feel the same way towards each other that they do now, that we, out of our great abundance, will make them very comfortable," the colonel dashing his fat paw across his blear eyes as if to check a rising tear as he spoke.

Hall returned the warmth of the colonel's grasp, and then, with a " Your servant, colonel," rolled out of the room, nearly tumbling over Jasper, who was kneeling with his ear at the key-hole.

Arrived at the bank, Hall drew out his daily letter of advice to his London correspondents, Messrs Bullock & Hulker, enclosing a slip of paper, with the following written in pencil—

"Please get Mr Ferret to find out the amount of stock standing in the name of Lieutenant-Colonel Thomas Blunt, of the Heavysteed Dragoons. I have a particular reason for wishing to know. T. H."

CHAPTER XXII.

ANOTHER HORSE DEAL.

THE betrothed ones now take a ride together; Tom on his hundred-and-twenty-guinea horse, Angelena on the redoubtable Rumtouch, now called Lily-of-the-Valley. Miss Sophia Ferguson—the Sophy Fergey of Angelena's approbation—had established a violent flirtation with Captain Mattyfat, of the Heavysteeds; and old Ferguson, a most respectable J.P., but not at all a "war's alarm or spear and shield"-ish sort of man—indeed a man with rather a horror of the military than otherwise—had what he called "put his foot upon it." As, however, there is a difference between scotching and killing, the worthy man had only driven Matty, as they called him, from the house to seek out-door relief; and Angelena, ever anxious to promote sport—on the reciprocity principle, of course—was relieving officer to the couple. Many people can manage poor-law unions better than they can their own houses. Angelena could afford the generous sympathies; for, independently of Mattyfat being one of many, and therefore quite unsuitable for her, Sophy was short and dumpy, and neither in looks, style, manner, nor vivacity, anything of a rival for her.

Mattyfat was anything but fat, being more like a pair of tongs on a horse than a man; and Smothergoose, the poulterer, seeing the fair ladies with their respective beaux riding out together, observed that they were "paired like rabbits—a good 'un and a bad 'un." But we anticipate.

Each board of guardians' day Sophy availed herself of her father's absence to ride towards Fleecyborough;

K

and somehow or other, almost at the same spot, she met her darling Angelena, with her own beloved captain and Jug, or (on this occasion) Hall, riding on either side of her. How surprised and delighted they always were !— Well, who *would* have thought it ? So nice ! so unexpected ! Why it was only last week that they met there. Then, riding four abreast till they met a coal cart, they fell into double line—Angelena and our Tom contemplating the wasp-waisted captain and the *embonpoint* of the fair Sophy from behind.

Angelena was in full feather. On the strength of the great match she was about to make, she had treated herself—or rather, for the present, Downeyfelt, the hatter, had treated her—to a smart brown Garibaldi, with a rich black plume, while her London-made riding-habit set off her smart figure in advantageous contrast to the country-made thing of her companion's.

Lily-of-the-Valley had been most carefully groomed, and shone forth beautifully sleek. Indeed, as she was destined this day to make an impression, she had been exercised over the very ground they were now going, and regaled with a feed of corn and chopped carrots at the miller's, of which she evidently entertained a lively recollection ; for, instead of stopping, and starting, and trying to bolt down Endive-lane, or up Brocoli-bank, she stepped placidly on, playing merrily with the bit of the fancy packthread reined, pink silk-fronted bridle, while Angelena patted her and coaxed her and entwined her light whip in her flowing silvery mane.

" Isn't this a charming creature ? " asked Angelena, leaning forward and patting her mare's arch neck. " I do think she's the most perfect creature that ever wore a bridle."

" Yes," said Tom, regarding both rider and mare with an eye of ownership.

" Will you ride me a race," asked Angelena, gathering her reins for a start, " to the white house on the hill, there ? " nodding to one about half a mile off.

" Not this morning, I think," replied Tom ; " not this morning. The fact is, I've no seat in these things," alluding to his wide-patterned woollen trousers.

" Nor in any other, I should think," thought Angelena, looking at his rolling seat.

Just then Lily-of-the-Valley cocked her neat ears, and a gold-laced cap was seen bobbing above the irregular fence on the left.

" Good mornin', fair lady ! Good mornin', Mithter Hall ! " lisped Major Fibs, greeting each with a military salute, as he emerged from the narrow intricacies of Lavender-lane. " This is indeed an unexpected pleasure," continued he, sidling his horse up to them. " I had just gone out for a tholitary thaunter, little expectin' the gratificathion that awaited me."

" Indeed ! " smiled Angelena, struck with his fine natural talent for lying.

" Hope I don't intrude," observed the major, with a knowing look at the lady, and a bend of his head towards Tom.

" Oh, not at all," replied Angelena ; " most happy to see you. I was just asking Mr Hall to ride me a race."

" What a beautiful animal that is ! " observed the major, eyeing Lily-of-the-Valley stepping easily along.

" Isn't she ? " exclaimed Angelena, leaning forward, and patting her again.

" Goes nearer and thafer than any orth I ever thaw in my life," observed the major ; " thows that lofty break-my-knee-against-my-tooth-acthon's not eththenthal to thafety."

" She never makes a mistake," replied Angelena, " though you can scarcely put a sixpence between her foot and the ground."

" What a tharmin' cover 'ack she would make ! " observed he to Tom.

" She would look well with a red coat on her," replied Tom.

The sound of a strange voice attracting the foremost lovers' attention, they now reined in their steeds, to exchange compliments with the new-comer as he advanced. The party were just on the entrance of Heatherblow Heath ; and, by a dexterous cavalry manœuvre, the major drew into line next Sophy, with Tom outside on his left. Mattyfat was thus placed between his lady-love and Angelena, who occupied the same position on the right that Tom did on the left. Having further separated Tom, so as to get him out of earshot of Angelena, after a few complimentary observations on his horse, and remarks on the state of the weather for hunting, he asked Tom, in a mysterious undertone, if he knew whether the colonel had heard from the Dook.

"The what?" asked Tom, who was not quick of comprehension.

"The Dook—old Wellington," replied the major, as Tom still kept staring.

"No," replied Tom, "I didn't know that he had written to him."

"Didn't you!" exclaimed the major, with well-feigned surprise. "Haven't you heard that the colonel's written to ask the Dook to the wedding—to give Miss Angelena away, in fact?"

"No," replied Tom, staring with astonishment at the idea of such an honour, and wondering what his mother would say.

"Oh yes; the Dook and the colonel are very thick, you know," observed the major—"doothed thick, I may say—and I've no doubt the gallant F.M. will come down most handsomely with the necklaces and things. A thousand's about his mark, but I shouldn't be at all thurprithed if he was to make it two in your case."

"Indeed!" gasped Tom, with astonishment.

"You'd better not menthon the letter, p'r'aps," observed the major, "as the colonel hasn't told you of it himself."

"No," said Tom, as all people do say, whether they intend to keep their promises or not.

The confab was interrupted by the ladies challenging the gentlemen to a brush over the heath, whose springy sward seemed to have imparted elasticity to their horses' legs. Sophy's mealy-legged bay and Lily-of-the-Valley were off in a canter before the gentlemen had gathered their reins, and Tom's brown, starting forward to follow their example, nearly unshipped our friend.

"Near go!" exclaimed the major, as Tom, after

sundry uncertain efforts, at length got shuffled back
into the saddle.

" 'Deed was it ! " replied our friend, adding his former
excuse, " The fact is, I have no seat in these nasty
slacks."

" Well, let us puth on," said the major, settling himself
into a charging seat, and riding as if he had swallowed
the poker.

Tom prepared to obey ; but although his horse was
generally as dull and tractable as a circus horse, it found
that it had a rider who might be disposed of, and with
a sideway sort of prance began ducking its head, and
dashing out its forelegs it went bounding and hopping
among the gorse bushes, sometimes bounding when Tom
expected it to hop, sometimes hopping when he expected
it to bound, and sometimes walking in preference to either ;
causing our Tom to show much daylight, to the infinite
amusement of the party, and repeated exhortations from
Angelena to " stick to the shopboard whatever he did ! "

" Ah," observed the major, as Tom at last got the
animal reined in, and his own equilibrium re-established,
" he's not used to hacking, that orth ; he's a nithe
animal—a very nithe animal, but hunting's his forte,
not hacking."

" Exactly so," replied Tom, glad of an excuse for his
inglorious display.

" That palfrey of Miss Angelena's is the model of a
hack," observed the major, nodding towards it.

" So it seems," said Tom ; " very quiet—very easy,
too, I should think. This animal is rather rough—stots
me off the saddle, and when I pull the curb he stops
so short that he's like to shoot me over his head."

" Ah, that's merely from confined space for action.
If you had that orth once fairly away with 'ounds, there'd
be no further occathon for pulling or holding ; you
might give him his head, and sit as if you were in an
arm-chair."

" Indeed," said Tom, thinking that hunting must be
much easier work than hacking. He then took a richly-
flowered bandana out of his queer little coat-pocket,
and proceeded to mop his profusely perspiring brow.

"Misther Hall covets your beautiful cream-colour, Miss Angelena," observed the major, sidling up to her.

"Well, he must have her, I suppose," replied she resignedly, after a pause, fearing she had offended her fat friend by laughing at him.

"Not until after Wednesday, though, Tom," continued she, addressing him direct as he now came up; "not until after Wednesday," repeated she.

"Oh, thank you," replied Tom; "but I mustn't rob you of your pet."

"Oh, after Wednesday you shall be welcome to her," adding, in an undertone, "I couldn't refuse *you* anything."

"You're going to see the hounds on Wednesday, then, I thuppose?" observed the major. "Where are they Wednesday—Merryfield?"

"No—Merryfield, Monday," replied Angelena; "Silverspring Firs, Wednesday."

"Ah, Thilverspring Firs, Wednesday, so it is; not a bad country—best about here by far. Do you hunt Wednesday?" asked he of our friend.

"Oh yes," replied Tom, with a matter-of-course sort of air, adding, "Do you?"

"Why, no, I think not," replied the major—"I think not. The fact is, I don't much fancy old Cheer."

The fact was, old Cheer didn't much fancy him; and these sort of likings and dislikings are generally reciprocal.

"I don't like your stiff-necked, overbearing, private ethablithments. Cheer may be a very good feller, but he's not one of my thort."

"Nor mine," assented Tom, who liked to give an opinion, though he knew nothing at all about his lordship.

"All private packs are objectionable," continued the major; "nothin' like a thubscripthon for keeping masters of hounds in order. Why, this old buffer rides as if the country was made for him, and no one else; won't let a man come near a fence till he's over."

"And does he cram along?" asked Tom.

"Oh, he'll ride," replied the major—"he'll ride; but where's the merit of riding such horses as he has? He began life as a rider; and though he's so old that he ought to be ashamed to be seen out of his grave, he thinks he has a character to keep up, and is just as jealous as a beginner."

" You don't say so ! " said Tom, who only knew jealousy of another sort. That observation put him upon the tack. " He's a great man among the ladies, isn't he ? "

" Oh, the old fool, he's always philandering with some one—thinks himself captivating—forgets that he's near a hundred," lisped the major.

" But he's a fine-looking old man," observed Angelena, who was lenient where age—gentlemen's age, at least— was concerned.

" The man's well enough," sneered the major, " if he wasn't such a confounded disagreeable old jackass, so jealous of his riding, so conceited of his looks ; he's as jealous as a woman, and as vain as a girl," added he, spurring his horse.

The start the major's horse gave set them all a-doing, and Tom was presently stotting and bumping and crying " Who-ay, who-ay," to his horse, and jagging its mouth, while Angelena's light hand guided her fractious brute as if the characters of the animals were changed.

This enabled the major to expatiate afresh on Rum-touch's beauty, her merits, her action, and powers of endurance ; and though Tom was pretty much of George the Third's opinion, who used to say, " Hang all presents that eat," he began to think she might be cheap—at all events, not dear—in a gift. As yet Tom had not compassed the fact that a horse was not like a carriage, that only requires washing, greasing, and certain little attentions of that sort to make it go from year's end to year's end ; and he didn't see the use of keeping two horses where one would do. Still, as the major insisted that he must have a cover-hack, and that, of all colours, cream colour was the most becoming for a red coat, he was not indisposed to submit ; particularly as, in the ' Times ' City article of the day before, he had read the old stereotyped line, " Corn ruled dull, with the turn in favour of the buyer."

During the remainder of the ride he regarded the mare with an eye of ownership, and we are almost ashamed to

say, bethought him of dismounting Angelena, and riding
the cream-colour to the meet on the Silverspring Firs day.
That, however, he saw required a little diplomacy; and
before he had time to broach the subject the gift horse
assumed a new aspect.

Arrived at the barracks, after separating from Sophy
at the place where they so accidentally met, and Tom
having resigned his horse to the care of the soldier-groom
who came to take Angelena's, he followed the fair one upstairs to the drawing-room, where they found the colonel
and Adjutant Collop hard at work at a game of dominoes.
Collop, though too good a judge to think of beating the
colonel, more especially as they were only playing for
sixpences, nevertheless ran him pretty hard, which
elated the colonel; and Angelena, taking advantage of
his exultation, proceeded, with due exhortations "not to
be angry," to tell him what she had done with her valuable
—or rather invaluable—mare.

"Ah, well," said the colonel; "well," considered he,
shaking the sixpences up in his hand, to see that they were
all good, "very kind of you, my dear—very kind—just
like you, though—always say you're the kindest-hearted
creature that ever lived—would give your last sixpence
away. You've given Mr Hall a most excellent animal—
very kind of you—very good of you—very pretty of you.
She's an excellent animal, Hall; you'll say so when you've
ridden her—never saw a finer-actioned, finer-tempered
animal. Isn't she, Collywobbles?"

"Wonderful animal," replied the adjutant, who had
had the pleasure of a slide over her tail in a rear.

"But I thought you were going to see the hounds
throw off at the Firs upon her," observed the colonel,
after a pause.

"So I am," replied Angelena—"so I am; Mr Hall is
not to have her till after that."

"Ah, well," said the colonel, "that may do—that
may do. I don't know, either," continued he, after a
pause, and a dry shave of his great double chin—"better
have no obligation perhaps—better have no obligation.
I'll tell you how we'll manage it. Obligations are disagreeable to gentlemen—should always be avoided.

There shall be no obligation in this matter. You,"
addressing Tom, "shall give Angelena a cheque—for,
say, a hundred—just for form's sake, you know. It
will be returned to you afterwards—and then mare and
money will be both yours."

"Oh," exclaimed Tom, who was by no means keen
about it, and knew that both his father and Trueboy
would say he had better learn to ride one horse before
he got two—besides having no authority to draw on
the bank—"oh," exclaimed he, "I—I—I wouldn't rob
Angelena of her mare for the world. I—I—I——"

"My dear fellow," interposed the colonel, "you're
most welcome to the mare, I'm sure—most welcome.
I wouldn't be any obstacle to carrying out my daughter's
wishes for the world ; all I mean to say is that obligations
are disagreeable, and, where possible, ought to be avoided.
Now, you know, of course, whatever is Angelena's in due
time becomes yours, and what I propose is a mere temporary arrangement, so that there may be no obligation
in the meantime—you understand—eh ? " looking earnestly at him.

Tom didn't understand, but he said " yes " all the
same, which sealed the fate of the transaction.

"Just you, then," said the colonel to Collop, "write
out a cheque on Hall & Co. for a hundred—a hundred
guineas, say—guineas sounds better than punds—and
Mr Hall will sign it. You haven't a blank cheque on you,
I s'pose ? " turning to Tom.

"No," replied Tom.

"No matter," rejoined the colonel—" no matter ; a bit
of letter-paper will do quite as well. You'll find some inside
' Fistiana ' there," nodding at a little book-shelf against
the wall—" obliged to hide it, to keep it from the
servants. There," added he, as the paper fell out,
"now, Collop, take a pen and write a cheque on Hall
& Co.—great man that Co.—is in partnership with
almost everybody—haw, haw, haw !—ho, ho, ho !—
he, he, he ! "

"He, he, he !—haw, haw, haw !—ho, ho, ho ! " chuckled
the obsequious adjutant, as he took a pen and did as
directed.

"Now, Tom, sign that," said the colonel, as Collop ceased writing, "and give it to Angelena. When she's Mrs Hall, you'll get it back; meanwhile, there'll be no obligation, you know."

And Tom complied with the matter of form.

155

CHAPTER XXIII.

LORD HEARTYCHEER AT SILVERSPRING FIRS.

"SHALL have a large field to-day, I'm thinkin', my
lord," observed Dicky Thorndyke, replacing his cap on
his grizzly head, after the sky-scraping he gave it as his
lordship cantered up on his way to cover with the hounds.

"What makes you think so?" asked his lordship,
riding gently in among the glad pack.

"Several horses on," replied Dicky, pointing with his
whip to the imprints on the side of the road ; "and I
was in Fleecyborough yesterday, and heard there were
a good many elegant extracts going from there."

"Indeed!" mused his lordship, who didn't like the
townspeople.

"The Colonel's daughter—Miss what-d'ye-call-her's—
comin'," observed Dicky, rising corkily in his stirrups,
as he always did when he had anything particular to
communicate.

"Indeed!" said his lordship, seeing Dicky was making
one of his usual casts. "Is she as fat as her father?"
asked he.

"Fat! bless you, no," replied Dicky, his eyes sparkling
as he spoke—"fat, no ; nice, slim, spicy lass as ever you
seed."

"Indeed!" smiled his lordship, brightening up as
Dicky's object began to disclose itself.

"Rides like a fairy," added Dicky, shooting his right
arm forward, as if using a sling.

"You don't say so!" observed his lordship, who
liked anything game.

"Fact, I assure you," said Dicky, with a knowing

jerk of his head. " They say they'll back her to beat most any man in our hunt."

" The deuce they do ! " exclaimed his lordship ; " I should like to see her take the shine out of some of them uncommonly——"

" That saucy Mr Healey, for instance," suggested Dicky, with a touch of his cap.

" Ay, or that Mr Beale ; he's as bumptious a beggar as any we have," observed his lordship.

" So he is," said Dicky, with another touch of his cap ; " Brassey too's a beggar," added he.

" Head-and-shoulders Brown's as bad as any of them," observed his lordship, admiring his own pink tops, and thinking of the mahogany ones of his horror.

" So he is," said Dicky tartly ; " pity he has no neck that he might break it."

His lordship then reverted to Angelena.

" Is Miss Blunt pretty ? " asked he.

" Nice-lookin'," replied Dicky—" nice-lookin' ; not zactly what you call a beauty, but a smart well-set-up gal," Dicky holding himself up, and sticking in his back as he spoke ; " much such a gal as little Lucy Larkspur, in fact."

" Indeed ! " replied his lordship, who had patronised Lucy extensively at one time.

" They say Miss—what-d'ye-call-her—Blunt's goin' to marry the fat boy at Fleecyborough," observed Dicky.

" What, the banker's cub ? " asked his lordship.

" The same," observed Dicky, with a rap of his fore-finger against his cap-peak.

" Well, there'll be plenty of means," said his lordship.

" Plenty," said Dicky, " plenty ; but the lad's a lout."

" She'll lick him into shape, p'r'aps," replied his lordship.

" Here she is," whispered Dicky, as the brown Garibaldi now appeared above the hedge on the left. Lily-of-the-Valley slightly rearing on being reined in to let the hounds pass, Tom and the lady emerged from Rushworth-lane into the high-road the hounds were travelling.

Although his lordship, as we said before, made it a rule never to speak to any sportsman who was not properly introduced, he relaxed it in favour of the ladies—if they were good-looking, at least—and introduced himself, or let Dicky introduce them, if that useful functionary had established a previous acquaintance. His lordship, having known the colonel as the corpulent captain, who had reintroduced himself in the free-and-easy way described in a previous chapter, was at no loss on this occasion ; and seeing at a glance that Angelena answered very accurately to Dicky's description, he cleared himself of the hounds, and putting his horse on a few paces up Rushworth-lane, with loftily-raised hat and low bent head, proceeded deferentially to greet her.

The unexpected and gratifying compliment, coupled with the excitement of the scene and the bracing freshness of the morning air, imparted a glow to the fair one's cheeks, and made her look quite lovely.

" I was *very* sorry, Miss Blunt, to hear of your father, the colonel's, accident, when he was good enough to come to see my hounds the other day. I hope he is quite recovered ? "

" Oh, thank you, he's a great deal better, my lord," replied Angelena, with a sweet smile, that disclosed a beautiful set of pearly teeth, with playful dimples hovering on either cheek. " He's a great deal better, I thank you, my lord," repeated she.

" I'm afraid he would think me very rude—very unfeeling indeed," observed his lordship, having now turned his horse round, and, with Angelena, regained the hounds, who had rather hung back for him, " never sending to inquire after him ; but the fact is I never heard of the accident until this morning, and that by the merest chance in the world."

" Indeed ! " smiled Angelena ; " I thought everybody had heard of our roll."

" Well, one would have thought so," replied his lordship, raising his white eyebrows, with a shrug of his shoulders— " one would have thought so. I suppose everybody had heard of it except your humble servant. I was just rating Mister Thorndyke for not telling me of it," added he, raising his voice at Dicky's back, to get him to help him on with his story.

" Yes, my lord, yes," replied Dicky, looking round

and weaving away at his cap. " The fact is, my lord, if you recollect, you were going to dine at my Lord Lofty-chin's, and left us as soon as we broke up our fox ; and I never saw your lordship again till the Thursday, when I concluded, in course, your lordship know'd all about it."

" Ah ! exactly so," said Lord Heartycheer ; " that was the way of it, I believe. However, Miss Blunt, you'll perhaps have the kindness to explain to the colonel how it was, and say I should have made a *point* of coming over personally if I had known, which I shall now take the earliest opportunity of doing."

" Most happy to see you, I'm sure," smiled Angelena, more delighted than ever at the turn things were taking. Who knew but Lilla might be a lady ?

" Won't you introduce me to your brother ? " asked his lordship, glancing at our fat friend, sitting, mouth open, like a sack on his horse, lost in astonishment at the greatness of his intended's acquaintance. " Won't you introduce me to your brother ? " repeated his lordship.

" Oh, my brother ! he's not my *brother !* " laughed the fair flirt ; " he's my—he-he-he ! " going off again in a giggle. " Mr Hall, Lord Heartycheer wants to know you," observed she, touching Tom slightly with her light riding-whip ; whereupon, off went his lordship's hat, which Tom imitated with as much grace as could be expected from the lessons of a cheap dancing-master.

" Fond of hunting, Mr Hall ? " asked his lordship, in a sort of lofty-actioned tone of supercilious condescension.

" Very, my lord," replied Tom, thinking that would be the ticket.

" Hope you'll not have the usual luck of a new coat," observed his lordship, eyeing Tom's country-made thing, and wondering at his impudence in mounting his button.

" Hope not," muttered Tom, wondering that they should " nip for new " out hunting. He now wished he had taken Padder's advice, and steeped the laps in water.

While all this was going on, the crowd was increasing behind ; and ere the hounds reached Silverspring Firs— a clump of trees on a perennially green mound on a

gently rising hill on the outskirts of a fine country—the
field had swelled into more than usual Heartycheer-
hound dimensions ; gentlemen were still coming up on
hacks and in dog-carts, the latter discarding their dingy-
coloured wraps, and joining the scarlet-coated throng
who encircled the pack, while the usual " Good-mornings ! "
" Where are you from ? " " Who's got a cigar to spare ? "
" Where shall we send the hacks to ? " " Who's seen my
horse ? " passed current in the outer circle.

At length, all things being adjusted, and his lordship
having exchanged his hundred-guinea chestnut hack for
a three-hundred-guinea black hunter, and spoken to such
of the field as he deigned to recognise, gave the signal
to Dicky Dyke, who forthwith whistled his hounds
together, and, preceded by the first whip, wormed his
way politely through the crowd, " by your leave "-ing to
gentlemen, and exchanging civilities with farmers and
others who were not exactly adapted for capping. "Good-
morning, Mr Heathfield—and how are you, sir ? " "Allow
me the pleasure of shaking hands with you, Mr Lightbody," tendering an ungloved right hand ; "hope Mrs
Lightbody, and all the little Lightbodys, are well " (this
to a man who generally sent him a goose). " Well, Mr
Barlow, have you got your gate mended ? " (this to a
man who had been kicking up a row about a gate the
second whip had broken). " Now, Mr Hubbard, you've
got the kicker out again " (this to a man who wouldn't
like to buy Dicky at his own price).

Dicky, we may here observe, was an aristocrat in
his way. He didn't take tips—sovereigns or small coin
tips, at least. " Oh, thank you, sir, no," he would say,
bowing with the greatest blandness—" thank you, sir, no ;
you are very kind—very good, and I fully appreciate
the compliment intended by the offer ; but my lord is
very gracious, and his salary is abundantly adequate
to my limited wants—no occasion for anything of the sort,"
he would add, as the yellow boys went back to the offerer's
pocket. Five-pound notes he treated differently—perhaps
he didn't look upon them as the current coin of the realm,
and Dicky just bowed as he crumpled them up in his
hand and stowed them away in his waistcoat-pocket,

as if he meant to light his pipe with them at his leisure.

A quick eye, coupled with long experience in the field, had enabled Dicky to discriminate between the metallic and paper currency men, and we believe there is no instance on record of his mistaking one for the other. Fish, game, poultry, sucking-pigs, fruit, wine, cheese, we may add, were acceptable from any one—Mrs Dyke was open to groceries, and things of that sort ; flattery didn't come amiss to her—she had been a beauty, and hadn't forgotten it. But to our sport.

The head of the cavalcade being thus formed by the pack, his lordship, after leaving a liberal space between the second whip and himself, bowed affably to the fair equestrian, and, motioning her to advance, reined his horse up beside her and proceeded ; while the hatted groom in scarlet and the dark-clad second horseman interposed a barrier between the giggling, nudging, winking, well-done-old-boy-ing crowd behind them. Thus they turned up Lovecastle-lane, the field lengthening like the sea-serpent as it proceeded.

"It's a fine day," observed his lordship, looking up at the now sunbright sky.

"Very," replied Angelena ; adding, "when I first looked out this morning I thought it was going to rine."

"What, you were up early, were you ? " asked his lordship ; adding, "are you fond of hunting ? "

"Oh, I don't *hunt!*—I don't hunt, I only go to see them throw off," replied Angelena, who rather reproached herself with having lost Tom Softly of Nettleworth, in consequence of beating him across country.

"I'd go till I came to a difficulty at all events," observed his lordship, who wanted to test Dicky Thorndyke's report—"I'd go till I came to a difficulty, at all events ; the country's easy, and my lad can ride you through it, if you are afraid of jumping."

"Oh, of course I'll go till I'm stopped," replied Angelena, recovering her courage ; adding, "I'd rather ride over than open a gate, any day."

"Well done you," said his lordship to himself, looking back to see where he had the "crammers" of his country ;

and in the line he saw the caps of Jacky Nalder and Billy Dent and Major Ryle bobbing up and down, and the knowing " shallow " of Mr Woodcock stealing a march on the soft inside the adjoining field. Brassey, too, he thought he saw ; and farther back the frog-on-a-washing-block-figure of the detested head-and-shoulders Brown. " I'd give a guinea—I'd give a five-pound note—I'd give fifty pounds to have the conceit taken out of some of you fellows by a woman," thought his lordship, eyeing the cavalcade.

He then resumed his attentions to Angelena, complimenting her graceful seat, her quiet way of handling her lovely horse, and the becoming plume in her brown Garibaldi. He said he felt greatly flattered by her coming out, and he pulled up his gills, and fingered his frill, and flourished and simpered and smirked, just as he simpered and smirked at the close of the last century. Angelena, on her part, was all eyes and vivacity. Thus in the full glow and excitement of newly-formed acquaintance they arrived at the cover, a well-fenced gorse of some two or three acres in extent, with cross-rides situated in the middle of a large undulating pasture, surrounded by others of similar extent.

" Now, gentlemen," cried Mr Thorndyke, rising in his stirrups, and facing the approaching field—" now, gentlemen, my lord will take it as a 'tickler favour if you'll all stand at the high corner of the cover," pointing to it with his whip.

" I s'pose you mean to say you'll give us a tickler if we do," observed Mr Bowman.

" I'll do my best, sir," replied Dicky, with a slight bow and a touch of his cap ; for Mr Bowman occasionally complimented him with a brace of pheasants or a hare.

" And you fut people," continued Dicky, addressing the panting pedestrians, " you do the same, and don't halloa the fox, whatever you do, or you may head him back into the mouths of the hounds." So saying, Dicky passed through the bridle-gate into the cover, and, cap in hand, was presently " Yoicking " and cheering the hounds. " Yoicks, wind him ! yoicks, rout him out !

Have at him, all of ye!" with a loud reverberating
crack of his whip, enough to awaken a fox in a trance.

All hands clustered at the appointed corner, at a respectful distance from my lord; some watching the hounds
trying for the fox inside, others watching the "old fox,"
as they called his lordship, "trying it on" outside.

"Do you know the country, Mr Hall?" asked his
lordship of our fat friend, who, having emancipated
himself from the crowd, where he had heard some unpleasant jokes cut on the fair Angelena and her prospects,
now appeared to join his prize.

"No, I don't," replied Tom, pouting at this repeated
poaching of the aristocracy on his preserves—Jug, to
wit.

"Ah well," replied his lordship, chuckling at his bear-
ishness, "that spire you see in the distance is Heyday
Church; those hills on the left are Fairmead Downs;
that wood—found, by Jove!" exclaimed he, taking off
his hat, as a great banging bright-brown fox darted
across the junction of the rides, and dived into the green
gorse beyond.

Hoop! hoop! hoop! Screech—screech—screech went
many voices. Tweet—tweet—tweet went the shrill
horn, and in an instant there was such a charge of impetuous hounds to the spot, as left no doubt in Tom's
mind that the fox would instantly be torn to pieces.

The joys and fears that found expression in other
men's faces, therefore, were not reflected in his own;
and while others were buttoning their coats, anchoring
their hats, adjusting their caps, disposing of cigar-ends,
prophesying points, and gathering their reins, Tom
sat with an expression of vacancy strangely at variance
with those of all around. There was no great fun in
hunting, he thought—further than wearing a red coat,
at least.

Angelena, on the other hand, was all joy and excitement—all agog at the sight of the fox, all delight at his
lordship's affability, all dread lest Lily-of-the-Valley
should play any of her rum-touchish fantastic tricks,
and bring her headlong to grief.

Hopes, doubts, and fears were speedily dispelled by

the appearance of a cap in the air at the low end of the cover, and in another instant a gallant fox was seen going stealthily away over the grass, his ears well laid back, listening to the confused din and uproar behind. Twang—twang—twang went the shrill horn, as Dicky blew his way to the place. An avalanche of hounds instantly answered.

"One moment," cried his lordship, who always saw his hounds well settled to the scent before he began to ride. "One moment," repeated he, eyeing the line the fox was taking. "Ah, he's away for Vickenford Glen, and we shall have a rare gallop," added he, settling himself into his saddle, and getting his horse short by the head. "Follow me, my dear," to Angelena.

His lordship's being a well-regulated hunt—none of your equality scrambles, where might makes right— not a soul moved until he set the example ; when Paxton, the head groom, having fenced Angelena and his noble master off from the field, his lordship stuck spurs to his horse, and, with Angelena following him, reached the low end of the cover, just as the last hounds crashed over the fence, responsive to Sam, the second whip's melodious cheer and hurried cry of "On, on—on, on !"

"Come, Tom, come !" cried Angelena, seeing our plump youth fighting with his horse, with every probability of being overwhelmed by the now pressing crowd, who were little inclined to listen to Paxton's exclamations of "Room ! room ! room !" for any one but his master. "Come, Tom ! Tom !" repeated she, as an outburst of melody from the now clustering pack drowned all voices but their own. Away they swept like the wind. The ground was in capital order for riding, as well as for holding a scent, and the hounds settled to it with a closeness and energy that bespoke mischief. The long pasture which the fox traversed diagonally, as if to give our friends as much of it as possible, opened upon another of nearly equal extent ; and his lordship, bearing a little to the right, to avail himself of the well-accustomed bridle-gate, left a fine ragged fence open to those who never miss a leap. First to go at it, full grin, was head-and-shoulders Brown, who, getting his great raking chestnut well by the head, dropped the Latchfords freely into him, and giving him a rib-roasting refresher with his flail of a whip, was presently up in the air and over.

"Curse that Brown," grinned his lordship, as Paxton held back the gate, and Brassey and Beale and Billy Dent all appeared in line, ready to follow Brown. "Curse that Brown," repeated his lordship, as Brassey bounded over the bullfinch, adding, as he saw his late flying laps subside, "I believe you'd ride into a red-hot fiery furnace if Brown went first. Forrard on!" screeched he, pointing to the still flying pack with his whip, as if the hunting alone occupied his attention. "Forrard on!" repeated he, muttering to himself, "we'll take the conceit out of some of you before we're done." He then smiled on his fair friend, whose horse lay close on his quarter.

So they passed through Everley fields, over Wick-common, and sunk the hill at the back of Mr Beanland's farm at Wilford. The enclosures now gradually became less, and Dicky Dyke got Billy Brick, the first whip, to the front, as he said, because Brick was handy at opening gates ; but, in reality, because the vale fences were bad to break.

"Now," said Lord Heartycheer to our fair friend, who still kept gallantly beside him, much to the horror of Hall, who was lobbing behind, his features endangered by the throwing up of his horse's head to escape his heavy hand—"now," said his lordship, "if you are afraid of crossing the vale, my man," alluding to Paxton, "shall ride you by Wetherfield Mill, and so past Stub-wick to Corsham, which seems his point."

"Oh, no," replied Angelena, bending forward on her horse, and adjusting her much-splashed habit, "I think I can manage it, if there's nothing very frightful."

"There's the Liffey," said his lordship, "and it's rather full ; otherwise the fencing is practicable enough."

"Well, I must just go till I'm stopped," replied she, thinking it wouldn't do to part company with his lordship if she could help it.

"You're a game one!" exclaimed he, spurring on to the now slightly pace-slackening pack.

" Angelena ! (puff) Angelena ! (gasp) Angelena ! "
(wheeze) cried Tom, now running down with perspiration,
" let's go ho—ho—ho—home. This brute of mine's
pu—pu—pulling my very ar—ar—arms off."

" Oh, never say die ! " cried Angelena ; " give him his
head—give him his head—he'll go quiet enough."

" I dare s—s—s—say," replied Tom, still hauling
away, " and then he'll run off with me."

" Not a bit of it," exclaimed she, reining in her steed,
obedient to Dicky Dyke's upraised hand, the hounds
having overrun the scent on the Donnington-road, and
come to a momentary check. Then head-and-shoulders
Brown and Brassey and Beale and Billy Dent, all the
ramming cramming cocks, cluster behind Paxton, mopping
their brows and relating their feats. A hat in the air
from a man on a cornstack quickly breaks up the council,
and clapping spurs to his horse, with a slight twang of
his horn, Dicky gallops off to the spot—his activity
being great when the " eyes of England " were upon him.
Before the hounds reach the stack the galvanic battery
of scent arrests their progress, and dropping their sterns,
they perfectly fly up the adjoining hedgerow.

" Across the vale for a hundred ! " is the cry, followed
by certain observations about water, and brandy-and-
water being pleasanter.

" Told you so," said his lordship to Angelena, as he
gathered up his reins.

" Room ! room ! " cries Paxton, flourishing his whip,
as the over-eager ones, forgetful of their allegiance,
press too closely upon the lordly one, and reluctant
Tom is again impelled forward by the rude impetuosity
of his horse.

" Drop your hand, Tom ! drop your hand ! " cries
Angelena, eyeing the lathered half-frantic steed, fighting
and tearing to free itself from the unwonted oppression
of the curb.

" Your *friend* is not much of a horseman, I think,"
observed his lordship quietly, as they galloped on together.

" Not much," replied Angelena, laughing at the figure
Tom was cutting, his horse's legs going one way and his
head another.

" Rot this hunting ! " growled Tom to himself, thinking
what a licking he would give the horse if he only had
him quietly tied by the head in a stable.

Away they all go up Crowfield-lane, and again brave
the enclosures at Marygate, the fox now giving most
unequivocal symptoms of crossing the Vale, with little
hopes of any alleviation from a heading.

At the end of five minutes' pretty easy fencing, "Crash !
war' horse ! war' horse ! Vigilant ! " is heard at the
narrow corner of a field, where flattering hope led the
anxious ones to expect there would be a gate, and Dicky
Dyke is seen hovering from a high bank into the adjoining
enclosure.

" Jump wide," cries he, looking back at the great
bullrushy ditch included in the performance.

His lordship gathers the black well together, and
lands him beautifully on the top. Another instant, and
he far outspans the treacherous ground beyond.

" Hold hard ! " exclaims he, pulling his horse round
to stop the fair Angelena ; but ere the words are out
of his mouth, she is coming clean off the bank too. "Well
done you," shouts he ; adding to himself, as he scans
her bright eye and unruffled composure, " Dash it, old
Dicky was right."

A brown horse's head, with a whipt strawberry-cream
mouth, is now seen bobbing above the bank ; presently
a pair of black legs are added to the view, and voices
are heard exhorting the rider to get on, while others
are imprecating him for stopping the way. It is Tom and
his horse, at variance still ; the horse wanting to be over,
Tom wanting to be back. The horse, however, has it.
With a deep grunt, for he is nearly pumped out, he lands
on the bank, and, as Tom keeps tight hold of his head,
both Angelena and Lord Heartycheer, who are looking
back, expect to see him down, with Paxton or head-and-
shoulders Brown, or some of the field, a-top of him :
somehow or other the horse sees the ditch, and with
another desperate effort, lands in a clumsy, floundering,
sidelong sort of way just beyond it ; but Tom, whose
seat at best is very uncertain, loses his balance, and,

A VERY UNCERTAIN SEAT.

after an ineffectual hug of the neck, drops, sack-like, upon the ground.

" I must go back ! " exclaimed Angelena, turning pale on seeing that her fat man didn't move.

" Oh, no ! " shouted his lordship vehemently ; " my groom will set him upright. See, he's at him already," continued he, looking back at Paxton throwing himself off his horse and clutching Tom up in his arms.

Sam, the second whip, having caught the horse, joined the group at the same instant ; and Paxton, having done all that was needful, left Tom to the attention of Woodcock and Bowman and Ryle and others, who had had enough to awaken their sympathies, and make them glad of an excuse to pull up, especially now that water seemed inevitable. Paxton then remounted his horse and galloped on to his lordship, whom he assured that Tom was " nothin' the worse—only a little shook—more frightened nor hurt," he thought. And Angelena thought that was very likely the case.

The field was now much reduced ; but among those that remained his lordship distinctly recognised the unwelcome features of Brassey and head-and-shoulders Brown.

" Forrard on ! " was still the cry ; and looking back, he thought he saw evidence that the pace had told in the diminished stride of their horses. He would give, he didn't know what, for Angelena to beat them. Her horse seemed equal to doing it too.

" Yonder he goes ! " cried his lordship, who had a wonderful knack of viewing foxes—" yonder he goes ! " continued he, riding with his hat in the air, showing his venerable white head—an exhilarating sight to gentlemen beginning to flag, though his keen-eyed lordship's " yonder " might be in the next field, or on the next farm, or rounding the base of the distant hill, or even rolling over the summit of it.

On this occasion the " yonder " was on the bright-green margin of the swiftly-flowing Liffey, on whose banks Reynard was shaking himself after his swim, preparatory to setting his head for the main earths at

Thornbury Scar, still distant some three or four miles—
nothing on paper, but a good way to ride, taking the rough
and smooth of the way, and the distance our friends had
come, into consideration.

" I fear you'll get wet," observed his lordship to
Angelena, as he eyed Billy Brick dropping from the rugged
bank into the smoothly-eddying current, and raising
his legs like shafts on either side of his horse's neck.

" Oh, never mind," replied Angelena, preparing to
tuck up her habit and follow.

" Stop ! " cried Dicky Dyke, pulling up to listen, with
his hand in the air—" stop ! There's a bridge just above,
and they are running that way."

So saying he wheeled about, and scuttled away as hard
as ever his horse could lay legs to the ground ; for he rode
like a trump when he knew there was nothing in the way.

All the rest had made for the bridge at starting, pre-
ferring that the fox should save his life by field than
that they should lose theirs by flood ; and Paxton had
some difficulty in getting them to make way as our line
riders came up.

The shirkers looked savage at Angelena. Head-and-
shoulders Brown thought she would be much better at
home ; Brassey hated to see women out hunting ; while
Jacky Nalder observed it was " pretty clear what she was
after." Altogether, they were not complimentary. It is
fortunate that people do not hear all the kind things
that are said of them in this world.

Just as our party reached the bridge the hounds came
bristling out of the fields on to the road, and, from the
way old Flourisher feathered down the hedgerow, it
almost looked as if the fox had recrossed the water by the
bridge. The pause that a highway generally occasions
was shortened by Billy Brick's unmistakable view-halloa,
which drew Dicky's horn from its case and sent him blowing
and hurrying, with the pack at his horse's heels. Brick
had met the fox full in the face and nearly stared him
out of countenance, and now stood cap in hand, sweeping
it in the direction he had gone. The still stout-running
pack dashed at the place, and, taking up the scent, went
off nearly mute.

Lord Heartycheer, who had got his second horse in capital order at the bridge, furnished an excuse for Jacky Nalder and another to sit still and say that "when second horses appeared, it was time for one-horse men to shut up." It was not a case admitting of delay, for at the pace the hounds were going—all over grass also— if a man didn't buckle to at once, he was hopelessly left in the lurch. Head-and-shoulders Brown and Brassey would fain have declined too, particularly Brassey, whose horse's shabby tail was shaking like a pepper-box, had it not been for the " hussy in the habit," as he called Angelena. A hammer-and-pincers trot, however, was all they could raise, and most gratefully the noise fell on Lord Heartycheer's ear. They'll soon be *hors de combat* thought he.

" *For*rard on ! " cheered his lordship, rising in his stirrups, and pointing to the still racing pack, as Angelena again stole up beside him : " *for*rard on ! " repeated he, adding as he looked at the now white-embossed cream colour, " that's a gallant little mare, to be sure."

" Isn't she ? " smiled Angelena, patting Lily-of-the-Valley's thin neck.

" And a gallant little rider," added his lordship, squeezing Angelena's arm.

He then set himself back in his saddle, and charged a dark bullfinch as if he meant to carry it into the next county. The mare, lying close on his quarter, got Angelena through before it shut up like a rat-trap.

" That's good ! " cried his lordship, seeing she was safe, without missing the plume from her hat, which the jealous hedge had retained. " That's good," repeated he, hustling and spurring his fresh horse over the springy turf ; adding to himself, " it *is* a satisfaction, after being persecuted by those bragging beggars, and their bragging fathers before them, to see them beat—*dis-re*-putably beat—by a woman ! " added he, again looking back to where Brown was hitting and holding, and Brassey vociferating, " Get out of the way !—*get* out of the way ! and, damn it, let me try ! "

" Try, ay ! " laughed his lordship, " you may try " ; adding, as he saw Paxton's scarlet coat coming up behind them, " I hope he'll not be fool enough to help them."

Paxton wasn't fool enough; for, knowing that he was taken out hunting, which he didn't like, solely for the purpose of keeping these people off his lordship, he thought he couldn't do better than let them stay where they were, especially as he would have to take the leap in turn; so dropping his whip-thong as he advanced, he proceeded to pitch into the head-and-shoulders horse, whose master had now dismounted, in hopes of getting him to lead.

While this was going on behind, Billy Brick, who had again appeared in the extraordinary way that whippers-in sometimes do, was suddenly seen capping the now thrown-up hounds in a contrary direction to what they had just been running; and looking out, his lordship saw the fox threading the hedgerow of the next field.

" Here he is! " cried his lordship, pointing him out to Angelena; and a sod-coped wall being all that intervened between the fox and them, they over it together, just as Frolicsome turned him; and the whole pack, breaking from scent to view, rolled him up amongst them in the middle of a large pasture. " Who-hoop! " shrieked his lordship, throwing himself off his gallant grey, and diving into the thick of the pack for the prize. " Who-hoop! " screeched he, in wilder tone, fighting the pack for possession. " Whip off his brush, and give them him before those beggars come up," cried he to Billy Brick, who now came to the rescue; which Billy having done, and his lordship having plentifully smeared his delicate white cords with blood, up went the fox, and in an instant his head, now flourished triumphantly by Sorcerer, was all that remained to be seen.

" *That's grand!* " exclaimed his lordship, jumping round in ecstasies to Angelena—" that's *grand!* " repeated he, seeing the coast was still clear.

" By Jove! " added he, " you've lost your fine feather; what a pity! However, never mind; we'll put in the brush instead." So saying, his lordship dived into his fine frill shirt—for he was a dandy of the old school— and producing a splendid diamond pin, such as a jeweller would ask at least a hundred for, and perhaps allow five-and-twenty as a favour, and running the brush into the Garibaldi band, pinned it up to the crown with the lustrous trinket.

" Now," said he, squeezing her ungloved hand affection-ately, " you are yourself again ; that matches your hat beautifully—wear it on your way home, and keep the pin for my sake." So saying, his lordship kissed her little hand, and remounting his horse, proceeded to parade her back through the country.

CHAPTER XXIV.

MR WOODCOCK, DEALER IN CRIPPLES.

BUT for Bowman, Woodcock, Ryle, and others, who felt it incumbent on them to make Tom hurt in order to excuse themselves for pulling up, there is no saying but our hero would have remounted after his fall and attempted to rescue his fair flame from the gallant old Lothario, who was witching her through the country as it were to the music of his hounds. These worthies, however, would not hear of such a thing. They were certain Tom was hurt—couldn't *be* but hurt. " No bones broken," Woodcock thought, " but very much shook," he added, as he felt Tom's shoulder and collar-bone and arm and elbow, and dived into his fat sides for his ribs. " No, the best thing he could do was to go home," they all agreed, and after straining their eyes in the direction of the diminishing field till the hounds disappeared, and the horsemen looked like so many dots dribbling along, they turned their pumped and lathered horses to the grateful influence of the westerly breeze. It was a fine run, they all agreed, though if the fox reached Bramblewreck Woods, which seemed his point, they had just seen as much as anybody could—nothing but labour and sorrow, tearing up and down the deep rides, pulling their horses' legs off in the holding clay ; and so they reported to Mr Jollynoggin, the landlord of the Barley Mow, where they pulled up to have a nip of ale apiece, and Jollynoggin swallowing the story with great apparent ease, they proceeded to tell subsequent inquirers they met on the road all, how, and about the run.

Bowman, who was rather near the wind in money

matters, and not altogether without hopes of making a successful assault on old Hall's coffers, especially if assisted by our enterprising friend, Tom, set-to to ply him with what he thought would be most agreeable to his vanity. Alluding to the run, he said, " Tom certainly deserved better luck, for he had ridden most gallantly, and all things considered, he thought he never saw an awkward horse more neatly handled." This pleased Tom, who, so far from being surprised at his fall, was only astonished he had managed to stick on so long ; and not being sufficiently initiated in the mysteries of hunting to appreciate the difference between tumbling off and a fall, he began to think he had done something rather clever than otherwise. In this he was a good deal confirmed by the deferential tone in which Bowman addressed him, and the inquiring way he asked his opinion of his lordship's hounds, observing, with a glance at Tom's pink, that doubtless he had seen many packs ; Tom didn't care to say that this was his first day out with any—any foxhounds, at least—so he contented himself with saying that he " didn't think they were much amiss."

This gave Major Ryle an opportunity of launching out against Dicky Thorndyke, who had incurred the major's serious displeasure by sundry excursions after his pretty parlour-maid, whom Dicky was very anxious to entice away into Lord Heartycheer's establishment. The major now denounced Dicky as a pottering old muff, and declared that Billy Brick, the first whip, was worth a hundred and fifty of him, either as a horseman, a huntsman, or a man. Bowman, on the other hand, was rather a Thorndyke-ite ; for Dicky distinguished him from the ordinary black-coated herd by something between a cap and a bow, and Bowman's vindication of Dicky brought out much good or bad riding and hunting criticism that served our Tom a good turn. Bowman expatiated on the way Dicky rode to save his horse—how he picked his country, avoiding ridge and furrow, deep ground and turnip-fields, never pressing on his hounds even in chase. The major retorted that Dicky was so slow at his fences that it was better to take a fresh place than wait till he was over ; which produced a declaration that it was

only certain fences he rode slowly at, bidding Ryle observe
how Dicky went at places where he thought there was a
broad ditch—above all, at brooks with rotten banks—
those terrible stoppers in all countries. They then discussed Dicky's prowess at timber-jumping, at which
even Ryle admitted him to be an adept ; but still he came
back to the old point that either as a horseman, a huntsman, or a man, Billy Brick was worth a hundred and
fifty of him.

The liberal width of the Mountfield road now presenting
grass on either side, the heretofore silent Mr Woodcock
managed to get our Tom edged off to his side, and pinning
him next the fence, essayed to see if he could do anything
for himself in a small way. Not that he thought he could
accomplish anything at the bank, where it was well known
his paper wouldn't fly ; but there was no reason why
the venerable nag he bestrode might not be advantageously
transferred to Tom's stud, either in the way of an out-
and-out sale, or in that still more hopeful speculation—
because admitting of repetition—a swap, with something
to boot. This antediluvian " had-been " was a fine,
shapely, racing-like bay, in capital condition ; for Woodcock, being a chemist, and a one-horse man to boot,
had plenty of time and ingredients for physicking and
nursing and coddling the old cripples it was his custom
to keep—or rather not to keep longer than he could help.
He went altogether upon age ; nothing that wasn't past
mark of mouth would do for him, though somehow,
after they got into his stable, they rejuvenated, and
horses that went in nineteen or twenty came out nine or
ten. " Seasoned horse—nice season'd horse," Woodcock
would say, with a knowing jerk of his head, over the
counter, to a nibbling greenhorn sounding him about
price ; that horse should be in Lord Heartycheer's stud ;
no business in my stable—rich man's horse. Why, Sir—
Sir John Green gave two hundred and fifty guineas—two
hundred and fifty guineas, sir, for that horse." And
so he had, very likely, but a long time since.

Woodcock had an acquaintance among grooms through
the intervention of valets, he having a brother a valet
in a pretty good situation, where he was, of course,

improving his opportunity after the usual manner of the brotherhood ; and whenever a good-looking nearly worn-out horse was about to be cast he got early intelligence ; and competition having about ceased with the extinction of stage-coaches, Woodcock picked up screws very cheap, almost at his own price—ten, fifteen, twenty pounds, perhaps—though this latter price he looked upon as bordering on the fanciful. Twelve or fourteen was about his mark—say three fives and a sov. back. That was the price of the valuable animal he now bestrode, who in turn had been a hunter, a racer, a steeple-chaser, and yet condescended to go in a phaeton. Neither his withers nor his quarters, however, discovered any signs of the degrading occupation. Indeed, his teeth were the only real tell-tale feature about him ; for though he was weak and washy and tender in the sinews and queer in the feet, still he had all the outward and visible signs of a noble animal, with a fine cock-pheasant-like bloom on his close-lying bay coat. He retained a good deal of the flash and enthusiasm of the chase ; indeed, we believe the spirit was willing, though the flesh was weak ; and to see him in the excitement of getting away—his ears cocked, his head erect, his tail distended, and his sunken eye still lighting with its former fire—a stranger to him and his master would conceive a very favourable opinion of the animal. Woodcock was a varmint-looking fellow too, dressed in a low-crowned hat, a short brown jacket, stout cords that had seen much service, and boots of so dark a hue as to make it difficult to say where the tops began and the bottoms ended—tops that the deepest-dyed Meltonian would find it difficult to emulate.

Woodcock was a regular once-a-week man, and oftener if he had a customer in view and could get his cripple out. To this end he rode very carefully, always looking out for easy ground and soft footing, and never taking an unnecessary leap unless there was somebody looking— that somebody, of course, being a hoped-for customer. Like all people, however, who cheat in horses, or indeed in anything else—unless they have a large field such as London to practice in—Woodcock had about got through the circle of country flats ; and when any one, in reply to the often-put inquiry of " Do you know of a horse that could suit me ? " answered, " Yes, Mr Woodcock, the chemist of Fleecyborough, has one," the rejoinder was pretty sure to be " No, no ; no Woodcocks for me, thank'ee." Such being Woodcock's position with regard to old stagers, it was doubly incumbent on him to make the most of a new one ; and when he heard that the officers at the barracks had sold young Mr Hall a horse, he felt as though he had been defrauded of his rights.

Having, as already stated, got Tom on to the soft on his side of the road, he dropped his reins on his now sweat-dried hunter's neck, and with the slightest possible pressure of the leg got him into a striding walk, that looked like action and confidence combined. Thus he kept him about half a length in advance of Tom, playing his arms loosely like a jockey, and ever and anon casting a sheep's eye back to see if Tom was looking. Our friend was not easily attracted, for what with admiring his coat, sticking out his legs to examine his tops, and wondering when his fall-dirtied leathers would dry, coupled with catching at his tripping horse's head, he had about as much to do as he could manage. Mr Woodcock, feeling that time was precious, varied the performance by touching his horse with the spur, which caused him to grunt and hoist up behind.

" What, he's a kicker is he ? " asked Tom, giving him a wider berth.

" Oh no, sir, no," replied Woodcock, " nothin' of the sort, sir—nothin' of the sort—quietest critter alive."

" What was he doing then ? " asked Tom.

" Oh, it was just my ticklin' him with the spur," replied Woodcock, doing it again, when up went the hind-quarters as before. " It's a trick he'd been taught in the racin' stable, I think," added he, patting his arch neck.

" Racing stables ! " replied Tom ; " what, is he a racehorse ? "

" Racehorse !—yes," exclaimed Woodcock. " This horse," added he, taking a rein in each hand and staring energetically—" this horse is thoroughbred—thoroughbred as Eclipse. He's by Jacob the First, dam Jude by

Squirrel, grand-dam Maid of the Mill, the dam of Hearts of Oak and Spinning Jenny by Little Boy Blue, great grand-dam Peppermint by Big John, great great grand-dam " something else, and so on, through an amazing length of imaginary pedigree—a species of weaving at which Mr Woodcock was very handy. Tom Hall sat agape, for he had never heard of a horse with such an ancestry.

" This nag could beat anything out to-day," observed Woodcock, now turning himself sideways in his saddle and slapping the horse's hard sides. " He's quite a contradiction to the usual prejudice that thoroughbreds are shy of thorn fences ; for I really believe he likes them better nor any other—if, indeed, he has a partiality for one more than another—for indeed he's equally good at all sorts. It doesn't make a penny'sworth of difference to him what you put him at. Post and rail, in and out, stone walls, banks with blind ditches, brooks, bullfinches with yawners on both sides—all alike to him. He's the most perfect hunter ever man crossed." So saying, he gave the horse another hearty slap on the side as if in confirmation of what he was saying. " That's not an unlikely-looking nag of yours," observed he, now turning his attention to Tom's horse. " I've seen many a worse-shaped animal nor that," added he, with a knowing jerk of his head.

" No, he's not a bad horse," replied Tom ; " far from it."

" Not 'zactly the horse for you, p'r'aps," continued Woodcock, again reverting to his own—" at least, I think he's hardly up to your weight ; you'll ride pretty heavy—thirteen or fourteen stun, p'r'aps ? "

" About it," replied Tom, who had no very definite idea on the point.

" Ah well, that horse shouldn't carry more nor ten—ten or eleven, at most," continued Woodcock, scrutinising him attentively. " He's a nice, well-girthed, well-ribbed, well-put-together horse, but he's small below the knee, and there's where a hunter should have substance. He'll be givin' you an awkward fall some day," said he, drawing a long face, and giving an ominous shake of the head.

M

Scarcely were the words out of Woodcock's mouth ere the horse struck against a hassocky tuft of grass, and nearly blundered on to his nose. Nothing but the pommel of the saddle saved Tom another roll.

" Hold up his head, his tail's high enough ! " exclaimed Major Ryle, as horse and rider floundered along in doubtful result.

" Ah, that's just what I expected, sir," observed Woodcock condolingly, as Tom at length got shuffled back into the saddle—" that's just what I expected, sir. It's a pity—a great pity—for he's a pretty horse—a very pretty horse—but he's not fit to carry you, sir ; indeed he's not, sir. You'll have an accident, as sure as fate, sir, if you persist in riding him."

Tom looked frightened.

" I'd get out of him before he does you an ill turn," observed Woodcock. " Think what a thing it would be if he was to brick your neck—you, with your manifold money, messuages, and tenements without end ! "

Tom did think what a go it would be if such a calamity were to befall him.

" You'd have no difficulty in gettin' shot of him," continued Woodcock, " 'cause he's a neat, creditable, gentlemanly-lookin' horse ; but, ' handsome is that handsome does,' is my motto ; and it matters little whether you brick your neck off a cow or off Flyin' Childers himself, so long as you do brick it."

" True," observed Hall, feeling his now much-deranged white Joinville, as if to see that his neck was right.

Woodcock was in hopes of something more encouraging ; but after riding on for some time in silence, and seeing they were approaching Major Ryle's lion-headed gates, which would probably throw Bowman upon them for the rest of the way, he observed, after a good stare at Hall's horse—

" I really think that horse of yours might carry me. He's up to my weight, I should say. P'r'aps you wouldn't have any objection to sellin' of him ? "

Tom, who was most heartily disgusted with his purchase, hadn't the slightest objection to selling him— indeed, would gladly be out of him, even at a trifling sacrifice, though, of course, as a true chip of the old block, he wasn't going to commit himself by saying so.

" Oh," replied he, in an easy indifferent sort of way, " I wouldn't mind selling him if I could get my price."

" You'll p'r'aps be wantin' a good deal ? " suggested Woodcock.

" Why, I gave a good deal for him ; and, of course, one doesn't invest capital without expecting a return— at least we don't at our bank," replied Tom.

" True," rejoined Woodcock ; " but horses are often the 'ception to the rule—few gents get what they give."

" Ah, that's because they want the money, or don't know how to manage matters," replied Tom, who thought himself rather a knowing hand. " However," continued he, thinking to do the man whom nobody had ever done, " I'll take a hundred and fifty for him, if you know any one who'll give it."

" A hundred and fifty—a hundred and fifty," mused Woodcock, sucking his lips, and looking the horse atten- tively over, apparently not much appalled by the mag- nitude of the sum. " How old is he ? "

" Oh, I s'pose eight or nine," replied Tom—" eight or nine—just in his prime—just in his prime—seasoned hunter, you know—seasoned hunter."

" Well, I don't say he's not worth it," replied Wood- cock obligingly—" I don't say he's not worth it ; indeed, considering what this one cost," alluding to his own, " he may be cheap of the money."

This was satisfactory to Tom, and looking as if he hadn't paid too dear for his whistle. Still, Tom did not lead on in the accommodating sort of way that Woodcock could have wished, and our persevering friend had to make all the running himself.

" Perhaps you wouldn't mind makin' a swap ? " at length observed he, seeing how near they were getting to the major's gates.

" Why, no, I wouldn't," drawled Tom, " provided I could get something to suit better—something a little stronger, p'r'aps."

That was encouraging, and Woodcock proceeded to follow up his advantage.

"How would this do for you, now ? " asked he, putting the question boldly, as he threw forward his arms, as if to show his perfect confidence in the sure-footed bay.

Tom eyed the horse attentively, looking at him as all men do at their neighbours' horses, with a feeling of covetousness—thinking how well he would look upon him.

" Is he a good fencer ? " at length asked he.

" Oh, capital fencer," replied Woodcock, sucking and smacking his lips, as if the very thought of his leaping was syrup to him ; " capital leaper—grand fencer. Didn't you see him clear the hog-backed stile, with the foot-plank over the big rotten ditch, just now, at the back of Willey Rogerson's pea-stacks, just after we crossed Mr Cocksfoot's hard corn ? "

Tom had not, being too intent on sticking to his own shopboard to have time to notice the performances of others.

" Well, he did," rejoined Mr Woodcock, again sucking his breath—" he did, and after Brassey and another, too, had refused. Up he came, as cool and collected as possible, and took it like winking."

" Indeed ! " said Hall, who now began to appreciate the difference between an easy and an awkward fencer. Not but that Tom would make any horse awkward, only he did not think so himself. His idea was that the bridle was equally meant to hold on by as the saddle. " This horse is a good leaper," observed Tom, thinking it was time he was saying something handsome for his.

" Is he ? " said Woodcock cheerfully, as if quite ready to take Tom's word for it ; " just let us trot on a bit," continued he, " and see his action," though in reality he wanted to shoot away from Bowman, who would soon be on their hands, to the serious detriment of a deal.

Tom did as requested, but though his horse had a good deal more go in him than Woodcock's, the latter contrived, by judicious handling, pressing, and feeling, to make his step out in a way that quite outpaced Tom's. As Woodcock came to where the strip of grass ran out to nothing on the road, he pulled up, with an apparent effort, though in reality the weakly horse was but too glad to obey the bit, and looking back at Tom, who was still labouring along—the farther he went, the farther he was left behind—Woodcock exclaimed, "Well, mine has the foot of yours, at all events, in trotting."

"Ra-a-a-ther," ejaculated Tom, pulling and hauling away at his horse's mouth, adding, "But mine can go when he's fr-r-esh."

"He's done nothing to tire him to-day," observed Woodcock.

"Oh, but I rode him to co-o-ver like blazes," observed Tom, still fearing to trust his horse with his head.

This was true, for Lily-of-the-Valley was very impetuous with Angelena at starting, and she had thought it best to let her go, and a smart canter was the consequence.

"Well now, shall we have a deal?" asked Woodcock briskly, thinking the trot had given his horse a decided advantage over Tom's.

"What will you give me to boot?" asked Tom, determined to begin on the safe side, however he might end.

"*Give!*" exclaimed Woodcock, opening wide his mouth and exhibiting an irregular set of tobacco-stained teeth —"*give!*" repeated he, breaking into a horse-laugh; "it's what will you give, I should think," replied he.

"Suppose we try them at evens?" suggested Tom, who in his heart fancied Woodcock's horse, as well on account of his looks as because he seemed easy to ride.

Woodcock shook his head ominously.

They then rode on together for some time in silence, Tom pondering whether he should offer a sum or ask Woodcock to name one; while the wily chemist kept eyeing Tom's vacant countenance, and looking over his shoulder to see where he had Bowman.

"Well, what will you take?" at last asked Tom.

"What will I take?" repeated Woodcock, sucking away at his lips as if every thought of the horse was luscious—"what will I take?" continued he, as if the idea of price had never entered his mind. "Well," said he, "I'll tell you in two words"—a phrase that generally means anything but what it professes—"I'll tell you in two words," repeated he. "I reckon your horse is not altogether an unsuitable horse for me, though I think he's an unsuitable horse for you. In the fust place, you see, he's under your weight, and there can't be a more grievous, direful, aggravatin' fault for a hunter than being under your weight. There can't be a more disastrous lamentable bedevilment than, in the middle of a good run, to find your horse gradually sinkin' beneath you, till at last he sticks out his neck with a throat-rattle, and comes to a dead standstill in the middle of a field. What a thing for a gent in a scarlet coat, and all complete as you are, to have to drive his horse home before him, or give a countryman a shillin', or may be eighteenpence, for gettin' him into the nearest stable. No, sir, no ; take my word for it, if you want to hunt comfortably and creditably, you must have a horse rather over than under your weight ; so that, when hounds are apparently slipping away, you may feel that you can take a liberty with him with im- punity ; or when they are drawin' homewards—which they all do, confound them ! when the master's not out, which, however, is not often the case with the old cock at the Castle—but, I say, when hounds are drawin' home- wards, the contrary way, in course, to where you live, you may say, ' Oh, hang it, I'll go, my horse wants work ' ; or, ' Hang it, I'll go, this horse never tires,' instead of saying, ' Well, Mr Woodcock,' or, ' Well, Mr Bowman, I s'pose we must shut up—we must be toddlin' homewards ; don't do for us to run the risk of bein' benighted.' So that I may conscientiously say, that a gent like you, with ample means and a bank to back him, doesn't do himself ordinary justice who rides anything but perfect horses— horses that are equal to more than his weight, and can do everything that my lord's or anybody else's horse can do, and do it comfortably to the rider, instead of fretting, and fuming, and fighting, and going tail first at his fences, as some aggravatin' animals do, instead of fust lookin' and then poppin' over, as this horse does," our friend patting the bay as if extremely fond of him. " Now," continued he, as Tom made no response at this interval, " I'm not a man wots always runnin' down other people's horses, and praisin' of my own—far from it ; neither am I a man wot always has the best horse in England under him ; on the contrary, I've been bit as often as most men. But I don't

Woodcock tries a Deal.

hold with some that, because I've been bit, I've to bite others. Oh no! that's not the way—fair dealin's a jewel. I'd as soon think of sellin' a man oxalic acid for Epsom salts, as I would of sellin' him a bad horse as a good un—one as I *know'd* to be bad, howsomever," added he, looking intently at our friend.

" Ah well," observed Tom, with a chuck of the chin, " that's not the point. The point I want to know is, what you'll take to change horses with me ? "

" I'll tell you in two words," rejoined Woodcock again. " This horse stands me, one way and another, in a vast of money. I didn't get him a clean out-and-out bargain, you see—so much money down on the nail ; but there were a good many pecooliar circumstances attending the purchase of him ? In the fust place, the man I got him on owed me a good deal of money, and knowing that he was very near the wind, I thought I had better make a little concession, and get as well out of him as I could. Then, in the second place, there was a long unadjusted account between Mr Monkseaton, the great wholesale chemist in Cripplegate, and myself ; and Monkseaton and the late owner—that's to say, Mr Bowers—being first cousins—Bowers's father and Monkseaton's mother being brother and sister—it was arranged that Monkseaton, you know, should transfer my debt along with another man's, of the name of Sparks, for which I was jointly liable along with Mr Splinters, the cabinetmaker of Baconfield, into Bowers's name. And then I had a grey horse, called the Little Clipper—you may have heard tell of him—a very remarkable horse for water-jumping. He was by the Big Clipper—a dark chestnut horse, free from white, full fifteen three, on short legs, with immense bone and sub-stance, great muscular power, fine symmetry and temper, perfectly sound, and free from blemish ; and I had an old rattle-trap of a dog-cart, that might be worth to a man that wanted one, p'r'aps, five pounds ; and then Bowers had a cow that had gone wrong in her milkin', and we agreed——"

" Oh, never mind what you agreed," interrupted Tom, seeing the story was likely to be interminable ; " can't you tell me what you'll take to change with me—a clean offhand swap—and sink the cows and the rest of the quadrupeds ? "

" Well," replied Woodcock, " I'll tell you what I'll take—I'll tell you what I'll take. I'll take twenty pounds."

" Twenty pounds ! " repeated Tom, who had been speculating on all sorts of sums during Woodcock's exordium.

" It's givin' of him away," observed Woodcock.

Tom sat silent.

" Well, what d'ye say ? " at length asked Woodcock.

" I'll consider of it," replied Tom, as Fibs's aphorism, " Buy in haste, repent at leisure," occurred to his mind.

" Nay, never think twice about a twenty-pund matter ! " exclaimed Woodcock.

" ' Buy in haste, repent at leisure,' " observed Tom sententiously.

" Well," replied Woodcock, rather disgusted at having given himself so much trouble, " you know best, sir—you know best. Only, if you happen to have an accident with that horse of yours, you'll have nobody to blame but yourself."

This observation told upon Tom, who was desperately afraid of breaking his neck, and had all the horrors of horsemanship fresh in his mind.

" I'll consider of it, and let you know in a day or two," said he, adding, " I don't think it's unlikely that I may —but, however, we'll see."

" Well, p'r'aps you'll let me know by Saturday, at all events ? " rejoined Woodcock ; " for Mr Gazebrooke is after him, and is to call on Monday."

" I will," said Tom, thinking whether he should clench the matter at once.

Just then Bowman stole up, and the skilful chemist immediately turned the conversation upon some bullocks in the adjoining pasture ; and so the trio proceeded on their ways homeward, Woodcock never as much as hinting that Tom and he had been trying to have a deal.

CHAPTER XXV.

COLONEL AND MRS BLUNT DISCUSS PROSPECTS.

COLONEL BLUNT, though he liked the looks of the diamond pin, and valued it at fifty pounds, was not so elated at Angelena's success with Lord Heartycheer as her mamma ; indeed, he regarded the acquaintance as rather unpropitious. His lordship's reputation for gallantry was too notorious, and his adventures too numerous, to admit of a reasonable supposition that such a long career of unbridled libertinism would terminate in a match with his enterprising daughter ; while he foresaw that any interruption of the Hall courtship might be prejudicial to the fate of the hundred-pound cheque, which the colonel meant to cash at the first opportunity. He therefore listened with anything but complacency—at all events, with anything but expressions of approbation—to Mrs Blunt's recapitulation of Angelena's feats and triumphs ; how she had beat the field ; how she had delighted Lord Heartycheer with her riding, who had set her as far as the blacksmith's, at the cross-roads at Liphook, and charged her with his best compliments to them, and expressed an ardent hope that they would soon pay him a visit at the castle.

"Well," growled the colonel when he heard all that— "well, his lordship's very good—very complimentary ; very good house to stay at, and all that sort of thing ; but I shouldn't like to have Hall ill-used. Good young man, Hall—no near relation of Solomon's, perhaps, but still a good young man, with good prospects ; not bad connections either. I wouldn't have her throw Tom over for the chance of a coronet. Coronets are queer things to catch, very queer things. Heartycheer's a queer feller, very queer feller. No, I wouldn't have Tom thrown over on any account."

" Oh, but there's no occasion for anything of the sort," replied the diplomatic Mrs Blunt ; " only you know there's nothing settled—definitely settled, at least—with old Mr Hall, and showing a desirable rival might have the effect of quickening their movements."

" True," responded the colonel—" true, there is that to be said—there is that to be said ; and, so far as that goes, his lordship may, perhaps, be profitably used ; but after all is said and done, I should say Tom was the best, the likeliest chance of the two."

" No harm in having two strings to her bow," replied Mrs Blunt, who was used to sending young gentlemen to the right-about.

" No," replied the colonel thoughtfully, " perhaps not. Only mind the old sayin' about two stools, you know."

" Oh, there's no fear of her letting Tom slip," observed Mrs Blunt, who had a high opinion of her daughter's dexterity in love affairs.

" Well, but I wouldn't be too sure," observed the colonel ; " these young fellows are slippery. I question Hall be over and above pleased at Angey ridin' away, and leavin' him when he fell."

" Perhaps not," replied mamma, who thought her daughter had been rather indiscreet in so doing.

" I think I'd best go down in the mornin' if he doesn't come up here, and inquire how he is," observed the colonel after a pause.

" It might be well," rejoined his wife, who lived in perpetual dread of the incursions of her own sex, well knowing that such an unwonted prize as Tom Hall would be fought for even up to the very church door ; and so, having settled matters, the colonel waddled off on his heels to the mess, leaving Angelena to entertain her mamma over their tea with the further detail of her hunting adventures, hopes, and aspirations.

CHAPTER XXVI.

TOM THE DAY AFTER.

WORDS cannot describe how Tom Hall ached after his hunt; he felt as if every part of his person had been pommelled. He could hardly bear to turn over in bed. Hunting, he thought, was very severe exercise, and what no man ought to take too much of. Indeed, he was not sure that he would be wanting much more of it—very homœopathic doses, at all events. The consequence of all this was that he had his breakfast in bed, where he lay ruminating over the previous day's proceedings, re-calling the impetuosity of his horse, the unfeeling desertion of Angelena, and Mr Woodcock's polite offer. Angelena, it is true, occupied the most of his thoughts. He thought she should have turned back, and seen that he had not broken his back, or any of the other compartments of his person; and he could hardly reconcile her conduct to his ideas of lover-like etiquette and deportment. To be sure, in his shilling's-worth of the " Chase," in Murray's ' Reading for the Rail,' he read how, when Dick Christian went under water in the Whissendine, and one man exclaimed, " He'll be drowned! " another replied, " Shouldn't wonder! but the pace was *too good* to inquire." But Tom didn't think there was any occa-sion for Angelena to emulate the indifference of these Leicestershire worthies. Then she was riding his mare too, and ought to have stuck to him instead of to Lord Heartycheer; and considering how fractious the mare had been at starting, Tom would not have been sorry to hear that Angelena had ridden her to death. Just as he was in the midst of a speculation as to whether the

colonel would be as good as his word in not presenting
the cheque, and wondering whether Trueboy would cash
it without referring to him, the whole house shook with
the most riotous knocking at the street door—the exact
duplicate of the clamour that announced Colonel and
Mrs Blunt's arrival, to ask "Hall and Co." to the ear-
ache and stomach-ache. It was, indeed, the colonel, in
undress uniform, mounted on one of his elephantine
chargers, attended by a soldier on foot, in a shell-jacket
—the same man who on the former occasion had enacted
the part of a gold-laced-hatted footman behind the mail
phaeton. The sound startled every one—from Trueboy,
who was weighing sovereigns in the bank, to Sarah the
maid, who was making her bed in the garret.

"Now take this horse home!" roared the colonel at
the top of his voice as the pounding ceased; "and tell
Major Fibs to ride old Cherry as far as the Flaxholme
turnpike gate and back, and try if he can fall in with
Peter Seive about the oats—those nasty things he sent;
tell him I wouldn't have them at no price—not, not even
in a gift; and now knock again," continued he, still
speaking as loud as he could, adding, "The people must
be asleep, or dead, or drunk, or somethin'," as he stared
from his horse up to the windows, from whence sundry
cap-strings whisked in sudden perturbation. The soldier
made a second assault, if possible more furious than the
first, which drew all the street to the windows, and caused
Sarah to rush downstairs in a state of agitation bordering
on frenzy. Seizing the door handle, she threw wide the
portal as if she expected to see Louis Napoleon at least
outside.

"Well, Jane, and how are you?" asked the colonel
from his horse, staring full in her face; for she was rather
good-looking, and the hurry and excitement had imparted
a bloom to her cheeks.

"Nicely, thank ye, sir," replied Sarah, dropping a
curtsey.

"Are your old people—I mean to say, your young
gentleman—Mister—Mister Peter, no, not Peter—Joseph
—no, not Joseph——"

"Sivin and four's elivin, and five is sixteen—that's a

reg'lar piece of impittance," growled old Hall from the inner recess of his bank. He sat on a high stool at a desk, with his London correspondents' (Bullock and Hulker's) letter of that morning before him, containing on a small slip of paper the following memorandum : " Our Mr Ferret cannot make out that there is any stock standing in the name you mention," being their answer to our banker's request that they would ascertain what money the colonel had in the funds. " Sivin and four's elivin, and five is sixteen—that's a reg'lar piece of im- pittance," growled Hall, as the well-known voice sounded through the low bank, and right into the dingy hole he called his parlour. " *Old* people, indeed ! " muttered he ; " and then callin' ' Tummus, Joseph ! '—knows his name's Tummus just as well as I do."

While " sivin and four " was accompanying the colonel's inquiry with the foregoing commentary, Sarah had helped our gallant friend to her young master's Christian name, and also informed him that Mr Thomas was in bed, which produced an exclamation from the father-in-law- to-be that he hoped his young friend was not hurt ; and without more ado the colonel proceeded to unpack him- self from his miniature dray horse, and handing him to the soldier, without another word of inquiry of Sarah, proceeded to waddle into the house.

CHAPTER XXVII.

ADVICE FROM THE COLONEL.

MRS HALL being busy arranging her domestic affairs in the kitchen—making mince for Christmas pies, if the truth must be known—and " sivin-and-four " never showing to callers, company callers at least, our friend the colonel had ample time for making a mental inventory of the furniture of their drawing-room, which he did, commencing with the old, well-indented, high-backed chairs, with black horse-hair seats, which he valued at four and sixpence each, going on to the old red merino damask curtains, which he felt a difficulty in putting a price upon, not being able to guess the quantity in the baggy hangings, though he fixed thirty shillings as the value of the round, eagle-topped mirror, and thought the brass fender and fire-irons might fetch five-and-twenty shillings at a sale.

" Confound it," said he to himself, " what a screw-drivin', skinflintin', usurious appearance everything has in this house ; one could almost fancy the walls and crannies filled with coin, and the very ceilin' swaggin' with the weight of iron chests. What a nasty shabby rug too," continued he, kicking at the corner of a much-worn, drab, worsted-worked rug, with a green cat lapping out of a pink saucer in the middle, considered a perfect triumph of art at the time it was done. " The carpet, too, 's uncommon mean—a reg'lar Scot, I do believe," continued he, stooping to examine it, adding, as he eyed the grey drugget above, " I wonder whether it's covered to keep it clean or to hide the frays ? "

While the colonel was in the act of turning the drugget

back with his foot, Mrs Hall noiselessly entered the room and stood behind him.

"Ah! my dear Mrs Brown—I mean, Mrs Buss—that's to say, Mrs Hall—I'm so glad to see ye," exclaimed he, seizing her hand—"I'm so glad to see ye you can't think; lookin' so well, too—I declare it does one good to see such a buxom body as you. I'd just dropt a sixpence," continued he, looking at the disordered drugget; "but, however, never mind; let the girl have it—let the girl have it; she'll find it when she sweeps the room."

"Oh, but we'll find it, colonel," replied Mrs Hall, preparing to search for it.

"Couldn't think of such a thing!—couldn't, by Jove!" exclaimed he, raising her up, and backing her towards a roomy arm-chair, into which the lady now subsided.

"Well, mum," said the colonel, settling himself into another at her side, "I'm sorry to hear my young friend Joe—no, not Joe——"

"Tummus," interposed Mrs Hall.

"Ah! true," responded the colonel—"Thomas. I was thinking of that ugly lad of Tucker's; his name's Joe—Joseph, at least—Joseph Tucker, not Tommy Tucker, as I tell him it ought to be—haw, haw, haw. Well, mum," repeated he, "I'm sorry to hear my young friend Thomas has had a fall out a-huntin', very sorry indeed to hear of it, so is Mrs Blunt and my daughter; couldn't sleep, none of us, for thinkin' of it; and they have sent me down with their kindest compliments, and all that sort of thing, to inquire how he is."

"Thank'ee, colonel, thank'ee," replied Mrs Hall, smoothing her apron. "Tummus is—is—very well, I thank you, colonel. He was rather a little fatigued last night, but—but——"

While all this was going on, Tom, who had been startled with the clamorous knocking at the street door, with infinite labour, for he was both stiff and sore, had managed to lift his legs into his trousers, and excusing his downy chin its usual beard-growing scrape, had made a hasty toilet, in order to catch the colonel before his departure. He now came hobbling, and holding on by the banister, downstairs.

" My dear Hall, how are you ? " exclaimed the colonel,
rising from his chair with a desperate effort, like a cow
in a lair, as our young friend now opened the door and
came shuffling into the room. " My dear Hall, how are
you ? " repeated the colonel, advancing, and getting him
by both hands, and looking earnestly in his face.

" Why, I'm—I'm rather stiff—sore, that's to say,"
replied Tom, wriggling and rubbing himself.

" Don't wonder at it ! " exclaimed the colonel at the
top of his voice—" don't wonder at it ; enough to make
any man stiff and sore ; you had a desp'rate day—
desp'rate day, indeed. Angelena came home all trashed
and draggled to death. I was very angry with her for
perseverin'. Women have no business tearin' across
country ; very well to go and see the hounds throw
off, but they should stop as soon as they find—at all
events, they should never think of followin' when they
drop into a quick thing—a burst, in fact. Besides, as I
told her, she was ridin' your horse, and had no business
to take the shine out of her in that way. Indeed, if the
mare hadn't been the very best bit of horse-flesh that
ever was foaled, she never could have got to the end,
for Angelena's no horsewoman, poor thing—not a bit of
one. Her mother tells her she has only one fault—that
of having far too much money ; but I tell her she has
another—that of being a very indifferent horsewoman—
haw, haw, haw—he, he, he—ho, ho, ho. However,"
checking his risible faculties, " I'm deuced glad to see
you all safe and sound ; falls are nasty things, very
nasty things—fall one ever so softly. And how did your
horse please you ? " asked the colonel.

" Nastiest beast I ever rode in my life," replied Tom,
who, though he had not ridden a great many, could still
find fault ; " nastiest beast I ever rode in my life,"
repeated he, thinking of the way the brute threw up its
head to the danger of his ivories and the detriment of his
features.

" What, was he fractious or violent, or what ? " asked
the colonel.

" Oh, everything that he oughtn't to be," replied Tom.
" He bored, and he pulled, and he fumed, and he fretted,

and he rushed at his fences, and would go his own way. Altogether, I think I never saw such an animal."

" Indeed ! " exclaimed the colonel, with well-feigned astonishment ; " you surprise me."

" He surprised me, I can tell you," replied Tom, " for I understood he was a perfect hunter—a horse that I had nothin' to do but sit still on."

" What a pity ! " ejaculated Mrs Hall, who feared that her son had been done.

" Well, I'm sorry for it," observed the colonel after a pause—" very sorry for it—very sorry indeed. Not that I have anything to reproach myself with in the matter, for if you remember, I by no means encouraged you to think of this horse ; but Fibbey will be sorry to hear of it, for he gave himself a good deal of trouble about it, and flattered himself he had mounted you unexceptionally—most unexceptionally. Indeed, I heard him tell old Quittor, the vet., that he thought if he could buy you such another, you'd be the best mounted man in the country."

" Indeed ! " shuddered Tom at the thought.

" Fact, I assure you," replied the colonel, with a jerk of his bull-head ; " and Fibbey's reckoned one of the best judges of horse-flesh in her Majesty's service. There's no man whose judgment I'd sooner buy a horse on as his."

" Perhaps there's a difference between a soldierin' horse and a huntin' horse," observed Mrs Hall.

" Mum, this *was* a huntin' horse," replied the colonel ; " considered one of the best huntin' horses in the Royal Hunt—that's the Queen's."

" Indeed," replied Mrs Hall, smoothing out her apron again.

" Captain Smallbeere's was the horse for you," observed the colonel in the coolest manner possible, just as if the captain's horse and the one Tom bought were really different animals instead of being one and the same— the same, at least, except in as far as clipping and squaring the tail made any difference. " I always thought Captain Smallbeere's horse was the horse for you," repeated the colonel, scrutinising his expectant son-in-law's vacant

N

countenance, to try if he could discover whether he had any inkling of the deception that had been practised upon him.

" He couldn't have suited me worse," replied Tom, lifting one fat leg with difficulty on to the other, adding, " I declare I feel just as if I had been possed in a washin'-tub."

" I dare say you do," replied the colonel ; " just as if you'd been kicked all round about the town."

" Precisely so," said Tom, feeling his back.

" But that's not all attributable to the horse," observed the colonel ; " all people are more or less stiff after the first day's huntin'."

" Are they ? " said Tom, thinking he might perhaps get over it.

" It's severe exercise," observed the colonel—" very severe exercise."

" I'm sure I can't think what pleasure there is in such work," observed Mrs Hall.

" Oh why, mum, it's a British amusement," replied the colonel ; " it's a manly sport too, and brings people better acquainted that would otherwise be strangers. There's no better introduction for a young man of figur' and fortin', like your son, than at the cover-side."

" But if he breaks his neck ? " exclaimed Mrs Hall.

" Oh, mum, there's no fear of that—none at all," replied Colonel Blunt. " He's made an unlucky hit at first, but that's what almost everybody does. Few people get themselves suited at first ; but the world's very wide, mum, and men with money need never be dismounted—need never ride unsuitable horses."

" Tummus gave a great deal for this quadruped," sighed Mrs Hall.

" Did he ? " replied the colonel, pretending not to know—" did he ? Major Fibs never said what he gave, but I presume he would never think of puttin' your son on a cheap 'un. However, though he don't suit Thomas, he may suit some one else, and he's a horse that will be easily disposed of."

" Mr Woodcock has offered to change with me," observed Tom, " for one of his."

" Mr Woodcock — Jemmy Woodcock," replied the
colonel ; " very nice gentleman—deep dog, for all he
wears a shallow hat ; have nothin' to do with him."

" Why not ? " asked Tom.

" Biggest rogue goin'," replied the colonel ; " would
cheat his own father."

" Shockin' man ! " exclaimed Mrs Hall.

" Horrid feller," assented the colonel ; " have nothin'
to do with him."

" He wasn't a bad-like horse," observed Tom, who
was rather taken with the animal.

" What, a ginger chestnut ? " asked the colonel.

" No ; a bay," replied Tom.

" A bay," repeated the colonel—" a bay. Ah, he *has*
got a bay, I believe, now ; swapped away the chestnut
for it."

" What's the matter with him ? " asked Tom.

" Old as the hills," replied the colonel ; " teeth as long
as my arm," striking out his right fin as he spoke.

" Lor, what a curious animal ! " exclaimed Mrs Hall.
" It must be very ugly."

" Why no, he's not an ugly beast," replied the colonel ;
" but he's *passé*—done his work, had his day, you know."

" Well, but he'll be steady," observed Tom.

" Steady enough, I dare say," replied the colonel—
" too steady, p'r'aps ; for he'd knock up at the end of
five minnits. No ; take my advice—or, rather, Sam
Slick's advice—my young friend : never buy a crack
horse ; they've always done too much."

The discussion was here interrupted by the appearance
of Sarah with a couple of bulbous-shaped decanters on a
tray, garnished at intervals with biscuits, plain and currant
cakes, and saucers of almonds and raisins—being as close
an imitation of the tray the colonel set before old Hall
the day he called at the barracks as Mrs Hall's memory
and resources enabled her to extemporise.

And now, while our fat friend is helping himself to the
port and sherry and doing the honours of the table in
relief of his stiff son-in-law, we will take a peep at the
banker as he sits in his " little den."

CHAPTER XXVIII.

MR HALL AND THE COLONEL.

THOUGH little addicted to morning callers, and in a general way not at all likely to make an exception in favour of the colonel, the man of money was yet so " aggravated " at the imposition attempted to be practised upon him by the colonel with regard to his money in the funds, coupled with the unceremonious, not to say impertinent, way he had spoken of him and his wife as " old people," that the spirit moved Hall to go upstairs and give the colonel battle on the spot, " then and there," as he said.

" Sivin and four's elivin, and four's fifteen—I've half a mind to slip upstairs and see what that great man-mountain's about," said he to himself. " Sivin and four's elivin, and eight is nineteen—I think I could sound him without lettin' out I know it's all my eye about his wealth. Sivin and four's elivin, and twenty-five is thirty-six—he must be a very bad man, tellin' such wholesale false-hoods in hopes of entrappin' our Tummus into marryin' his darter. Sivin and four's elivin, and forty-five is fifty-six —it's very fortinate Tummus has a father to keep him right, or there's no sayin' what such a bad old buffer might get him to do. Sivin and four's elivin, and ninety-nine's a 'undr'd and ten—I really should like to put the old man to the blush. Sivin and four's elivin, and a 'undr'd and four is a 'undr'd and fifteen—wonder if sol-diers ever blush. In one's own house one couldn't get far wrong takin' the bull by the horns. Not like the barracks, where he might call out the drummers and fiddlers, and give one a trimmin' ; but in one's own house there can't

be much fear. Sivin and four's elivin, and a 'undr'd and
ninety is two 'undr'd and one — I'll risk it, at all
events."

So saying, he put the London banker's note saying
Ferret the broker did not find any stock in Colonel Blunt's
name into his desk, and halloaing to Trueboy, the cashier,
that he was going upstairs for a few minutes if anybody
wanted him, he disappeared through an almost invisible
door in the dingy-coloured wall.

"Ah, here's little Podgy himself!" exclaimed the
colonel, setting down the decanter, after helping himself
to a second bumper of sherry, as our friend, having
noiselessly opened the old-fashioned black door, now
stood with it in his hand surveying the scene. "Come
in, old boy, come in," continued the colonel, in the most
patronising way, extending a red-ended fin for the banker
to shake.

"Your servant, colonel," replied the man of figures
with a stiff bow, shying the fist as he made for a seat
beside his wife.

"Yours," replied the colonel, ducking his bull-head
and drinking off his wine.

"Well, Tummus, my dear, how are you after your
hunt ? " asked the fond father, surveying his fat son.

"Middlin'," replied Tom, shuffling about on his seat.

"Hard work huntin'," observed the father. "Can't
think what pleasure people can see in such work," observed
the banker—"tearin' across fields, now that there are
such good roads in all directions. I'm sure my highway
rate comes to near tenpence in the pund, and one ought
to have somethin' for that."

"Why, as to the matter of huntin'," observed the
colonel, as he took another turn at the decanter, "your
good lady and I were just talkin' the matter over, and I
say that it's all very well and proper in moderation—
taken medicinally, as I may say, to cure bile, indigestion,
and so forth. Nay, as a provocative to appetite, it has
some sterlin' recommendations. Moreover, as I was
tellin' your wife, it's a good introduction for a young
man, and will get him to houses that he mightn't otherwise visit at ; and wearin' a red coat has its attractions."

" Well, but it's *dangerous*," observed old Hall with a stamp of his heel.

" That depends upon how you take it," replied the colonel, " and what sort of horses you ride. If you ride rips, you are pretty sure to come to grief ; if you ride good uns, you'll most likely go scot-free all your life, just as old Heartycheer has done. So, with your permission, we'll drink ' The Chase,' " continued he, tossing off his glass, and replenishing it plentifully as before.

The trio then sat silent for a time, the colonel considering what excuse he could frame for taking another glass, old Hall thinking how he should lead up to the question of the Consols.

The spirit moved the colonel to speak first.

" Well, and how's your bank ? " asked he, turning short upon his host.

" Sivin and four's elivin, and forty-one is fifty-two— what an impittant question," mused our friend. " Middlin', thank'ee, colonel," replied the man of wealth, rubbing his finger-nails together.

" What ! you're not goin' smash, are ye ? " exclaimed the colonel.

" Sivin and four's elivin, and fifty-nine is seventy— what a cool hand," thought our friend, fixing his watery grey eyes intently on his interrogator. " No, not smash," replied our friend, now filing away with his forefinger on his chin ; " not *smash !* " repeated he with an emphasis ; " but there's a redundancy of money, and not much employment for it."

" Hand a little of it here, then," said the colonel, holding out his great red fist.

" Sivin and four's elivin, and twenty-five is thirty-six, and forty is seventy-six—I think I'll get an openin' now," mused Hall.

" Oh, *you* don't want money, colonel," replied the banker in a tone of irony—"*you* don't want money, colonel."

" Don't I ? " rejoined our friend. " You just give me the run of your safe, or whatever you call your money-box, and see whether or no."

" Sivin and four's elivin, and ninety-nine is a 'undr'd
and ten—the man's forgettin' himself," thought Mr
Hall ; " I'll pin him to the pint."

" Well, but the dividends are a comin' due, and you'll
soon be in full feather again," observed he.

" Dividends ! Rot the dividends ! What have I to do
with dividends, think'ee ? " asked the colonel.

" Sivin and four's elivin, and a 'undr'd and sivinty's a
'undr'd and eighty-one—wot an unconscionable old
scoundrel it must be," mused Hall, staring intently in the
colonel's great apple face. " Sivin and four's elivin, and
three 'undr'd and forty-one is three 'undr'd and fifty-two
—the old rascal told me as plain as he could speak that he
was in the funds. I'll put it to him point-blank. Well,
but," said Hall, placing a hand on each knee, and speaking
slowly and deliberately, as he stared the colonel full in
the face, " I thought you told me you were in the
funds ? "

" Funds, did I ? " replied the colonel, now suddenly
recollecting himself ; " funds ? " repeated he, hesitating,
and looking redder than usual.

" Funds, yes ! " repeated Hall ; " that day at the
barracks, you remember."

" Oh, ar—true," replied the colonel, with an air of
sudden enlightenment—" oh, ar—true, the day we were
talkin' about settlements, and so on. And so I am,"
resumed the colonel confidently ; " in the Consols, at
least. We always, not bein' up to snuff in your money-
changin' phraseology, call them Consols, not funds—
Consols, or consolations—haw, haw, haw—he, he, he—
ho, ho, ho," the colonel attempting to carry his former
confusion off with a laugh.

Old Hall, however, was not to be done that way.

" Well, then, you *are* in the funds ? " observed he,
reverting to the point.

" Funds, yes—Consols, that's to say—Three per Cents,
in fact ; not your Bank Stock, or Long Annuities, or
Short Annuities, or Spanish Passives, or rubbish of that
sort—*Consols*," repeated he, with an emphasis on the
word.

" Sivin and four's elivin, and nine is twenty—now I

have you," mused Hall. "Well, then, that comes to what I said at first," resumed the banker ; "the dividends are due next month, and you'll be full of cash."

"No doubt," rejoined the colonel—"no doubt ; flush —very flush," continued he, slapping his thigh.

"Sivin and four's elivin, and ninety-nine's a 'undr'd and ten—now I'll pin you," mused Hall, looking at his wife, with a sparkle in his eye that as good as said, "See how I'll work him."

"We can receive your dividends for you here," observed the banker, "which may save you trouble."

"Can you?" exclaimed the colonel, rather taken aback at the trap into which he had fallen. "Can you?" repeated he ; "you're very kind—very good ; it may be an accommodation, 'specially if you don't nip too much off for your trouble."

"Oh no," replied the banker ; "we'll do it at the usual figur'—rather under than over."

"Ah well, that's kind of you," observed the colonel— "that's kind of you," adding, "You're not such a Jew as you look."

"There'll be the power-of-attorney, of course," observed the banker in an offhand sort of way.

"Will there?" mused the colonel, thinking it would require a very strong one to raise his stock.

"Shall I order one, then?" asked the banker.

"Why, yes ; I think you may," drawled the colonel thoughtfully, chuckling at the idea.

"We should require to know the exact amount," observed the banker ; "p'r'aps you could furnish that information as you go through the bank."

"I dare say I could," said the colonel ; "let me see, as the blind man said—twenty thousand bought in thirty-two—no, thirty-three,—Scraper's mortgage paid off in thirty-nine—ten thousand bought in forty somethin', I forget the year—and——"

"Sivin and four's elivin, and forty-two is fifty-three, and ninety's a 'undr'd and forty-three—I really wish I mayn't have been a-doin' the man injustice," mused Hall, as the colonel proceeded with his narration.

The pleasing delusion was, however, speedily dispelled
by the colonel exclaiming—

" But how will it be ? You see the stock don't stand
in my name."

" Sivin and four's elivin, and a 'undr'd and three is a
'undr'd and fourteen—now he's a-goin' to jib," mused
Hall ; " and fourteen's a 'undr'd and twenty-eight—
told me as plain as he could speak that the money was
in his own name—and twenty-four's a 'undr'd and fifty-
two—I don't believe he has anything of the sort—a reg'lar
take in—hasn't a rap, I dare say."

" I thought you said the stock was in your own name ? "
responded the now bristling banker.

" Did I ? " replied the colonel in a careless tone—
" did I ? Then I must have made a mistake. Hang it,
you're such a matter-of-fact fellow—one doesn't expect
to be swor to the accuracy of every particklar word one
utters. If a man says he has fifty or sixty thousand
punds, he means to say he has the use of it. It doesn't
mean that he has it in his trunk, or in his cupboard ;
or that he can go and kick it about the country—make
ducks and drakes on't, as they say."

" Of course not," replied Hall—" of course not ; only
when a man—a gent I mean," added he, correcting
himself—" takes on matters o' business with men o'
business, men o' business must keep gents right ; nothin'
more," added he apologetically.

" Well, true enough," rejoined the colonel, now pretending to be pacified—" true enough ; only one doesn't like
to be always talkin' by book—always ridin' the high
stool of 'rithmetic. I'm not one of your learned ex-
emplifications of polite humanity. I'm not a man to
send to a literary and philosophical society to illustrate
a problem on the globes. I don't expect Packinton to
send me to negotiate a commercial treaty with the King
of the Cannibal Islands, or any other great potentate ;
but for a question involving high honourable feelin',
combined with military etiquette and the tactics of
Addiscombe, with the flourish of the Eglinton tournament,
though I say it who shouldn't, there's no man more

honourably, more creditably, recognised than Lieutenant-
Colonel Blunt of her Majesty's Regiment of Heavysteed
Dragoons," the colonel bowing and striking out his right
fin as he finished.

"Sivin and four's elivin, and forty-sivin is fifty-eight
—that's all balderdash," mused Hall. "I very much
doubt his havin' anything of the sort. However, I'll at
him again," continued he, trying to catch the now wine-
watching eye of the colonel.

"Well, but if we can be of any service in gettin' your
money down here after it's received in London, we shall
be very happy," continued the pertinacious banker.

"Thank'ee," said the colonel—"thank'ee; p'r'aps we
may trouble you that way. Only it passes through so
many hands before we get it that I don't know it will be
much better for yours."

"In Chancery, p'r'aps?" suggested old Hall.

"No, not Chancery," replied the colonel, making
another attack on the bottle—"not Chancery, but devilish
tight tied up for all that. If my whole regiment had it
in the centre, with field-pieces at each side, it couldn't
be safer. Don't know how many lawyers there are for
trustees, and they make work for themselves and each
other in the most marvellous way. Take my advice, my
young friend," continued he, addressing our Tom, "and
never have a lawyer for a trustee."

"Sivin and four's elivin, and forty-three is fifty-four
—that really looks as if the man has money," mused
old Hall, again wavering in his opinion. "Sivin and
four's elivin, and sivin is eighteen—I'll take another
ventur'."

"It'll be Mrs Blunt's money, p'r'aps," observed Hall,
"as it's so tight tied up?"

"Mrs Blunt's money it is," rejoined the colonel confidently—"Mrs Blunt's money it is. She has it for life,
and when she damps off, it goes to my daughter."

"Sivin and four's elivin, and nine's twenty—that's
more like the thing," mused Hall.

"But you'll have a life interest, too, I s'pose?" observed the banker.

"No, I haven't," replied the colonel, with an air of

indifference ; "no, I haven't," repeated he ; "goes to my daughter at once."

"Sivin and four's elivin, and twenty's thirty-one— that's all in favour of her husband," thought Hall. "Sivin and four's elivin, and seventeen's twenty-eight—been a runaway match, p'r'aps," thought he.

"Mrs Blunt was an heiress, I presume ? " observed Hall, addressing the colonel.

"Heiress—great heiress," assented the colonel, casting a sheep's eye at the decanter. "Another glass," thought he, "will just leave this old screw a pint for his dinner." So saying, he proceeded to help himself. "Mrs Blunt married me for my looks," said he as he sipped away at its contents. "I believe I may say, without vanity, that I was one of the handsomest men in the army. Mrs Blunt took a fancy to me, and I tell her I loved her for what she had ; and if she'd had twice as much, I'd have loved her twice as well——" the colonel haw, haw, hawing —he, he, heing—ho, ho, hoing—amid exclamations of—

"Oh, fie, colonel ! I wouldn't have thought that of you ! " from Mrs Hall.

"Well, but, however, I must be off," continued the colonel, not liking the cross-examination to which he had been subjected. "I've paid you a longish mornin' visit, but your company's so agreeable (disagreeable, he thought) that there's no tearin' oneself away "—casting an anxious eye at the sherry, which he would fain have finished. "I like you Fleecyboroughites ; there's a deal more warmth and cheerability about you than there is about your fine, languishin' die-away duchesses, who really seem as if life was a bore to them, and who, if they ask you to dine, give you nothin' to eat, and send the footmen to sweep you out with the coffee things, just as you think you are goin' to get somethin' to drink. But the best friends must part," continued the colonel, setting down his glass, and hoisting himself up with an effort ; "I've a deal to do—must go and inspect our corn. That Mister Peter Seive of yours, I fear he's what they call a rogue in grain ; he's sent in a lot of forage that would disgrace a poultry-yard. Quartermaster Diddle says he never saw such stuff—never," muttered the colonel to himself, "unless it was accompanied by a fat turkey, a haunch of mutton, or somethin' of that sort, to make it pass—the proper appendages, in short."

"Well, mum, I must bid you good-mornin'," continued he, advancing and seizing Mrs Hall's retiring hand—"I must bid you good-mornin' mum," shaking it severely.

"Good-mornin' to you, sir," continued he, turning short round on Hall, waiting to see whether he would be more affable than he was on his entry.

But Hall was not a hand-shaking sort of man at all, at least not without due consideration, which the colonel's movements did not allow time for; so with a "Your servant, colonel," and an awkward thrust out behind, old Hall saw him pass on to his son.

"And now," continued he, addressing our Tom, slipping a little three-cornered highly musked *billet-doux* into his hand, as he turned his broad back on the old people, "I'm very glad, indeed, to see you all safe and sound; we really had a very uncomfortable anxious night on your account—fearin' all sorts of unpleasant-nesses, not to say bedevilments. However, I'll tell them you are all right; and," added he, dropping his voice, "if you feel any little inconvenience from the saddle, diachylon plaister's the best thing; get a whole sheet for a shillin' at Rhubarb and Surfeit's, round the market-place corner." So saying, the colonel struck out his right fin, and, getting under weigh, hobbled off on his heels, making the old passage and rickety staircase creak with his weight as he descended. Tom, having accom-panied his father-in-law to the second landing, where he transferred him to Sarah the maid, now stood eagerly imbibing the contents of the note. The exact words are immaterial; suffice it to say that Tom speedily regained his bedroom, where, having hastily revised his toilet, he set off for Mr Ruddle, the portrait painter's.

CHAPTER XXIX.

IN AN ARTIST'S STUDIO.

RUDDLE was a great artist, at least in his own estimation. He didn't begin life as an artist, unless, indeed, modelling ornaments for confectioners' cakes can be viewed in that light. However, he didn't stay long with the confectioner —one Mr Queencake of Basinghall-street. Mr Queencake had a daughter, Alicia, on whom Ruddle cast a favourable eye, which the master-man resented as a piece of unpardonable impudence. He therefore picked a hole with poor Ruddle about a pan of preserves, and presently got rid of him. Ruddle, being surfeited with sweets—though not of the "sweet" he wanted—hung about town for some time ; but Queencake, being more than a match for him, shifted his daughter from London to Gravesend, and from Gravesend to Margate, and from Margate to Herne Bay, and from Herne Bay back to Basinghall-street, till poor Ruddle's finances were exhausted in following her. He then gave up the pursuit, being partly reconciled, perhaps, to his loss by meeting a very elegant young creature, half Dutch, half English, aboard a two-penny steamer.

This was in the heyday of railway times, when everybody with a "touch of larnin'," as the country-people call it, could get employment either as secretaries or directors, or in surveying or pretending to survey lines, laying down plans, drawing prospectuses, checking estimates, conferring with engineers, down to folding, sealing, and delivering letters ; and Ruddle carried on a very brisk trade for a time. He was a director of several imaginary lines, and having married his new *inamorata* on the strength of his prospects, he set her up a very pretty pea-green and straw-coloured cab phaeton, with a buttony boy to pick up her bag. He adorned himself with rings and brooches, and presented himself with a substantial large tasselled cane. The crash, however, soon after came, and boy and cab phaeton and cane were all swept away, leaving Mr and Mrs Ruddle high and dry on the strand. We meant to be allegorical there, but he really was left in the Strand, that being the locality in which he had established his quarters. He then tried his hand at confectionery, and set up a shop in Mayfair, relying upon Mrs Ruddle's charms for attracting attention. Here, to a certain extent, he was right, though whether it was that the charms were so powerful as to take away appetite, or the cakes were so bad as not to be eatable, certain it is that the profits were so small as not to be appreciable; and when the landlord, Mr Grinder, walked in for his rent, Captain Mainchance walked off the charmer, leaving poor Ruddle to put up the shutters. He was, however, now free again, and felt so equal to anything that he didn't know what to turn his hand to. At length he came to Fleecyborough, where he had an uncle, one Mr Stencil, a painter and glazier, with whom, having an unlimited run of the paint-pot, he soon began to vary the monotony of door and window priming and painting, by producing sundry surprising horses and other animals, that drew amazing custom to the public-houses at which they were put up.

The natives commended, nay, were astonished at his performances, and Stencil's back-shop became the *rendez-vous* of all the critics and connoisseurs of Fleecyborough, who assembled of an evening to glorify Ruddle's perform-ance, and stimulate him to deeds of immortality. We don't know what wasn't predicted of him, and Ruddle, notwithstanding the humiliations to which he had been subjected, being a most thoroughly self-sufficient dog, inhaled their adulation with the air of a professor.

There being nothing in the shape of a man but what is acceptable to some woman or another, Jacky Ruddle, as they called him, was soon besieged by the most *exigeante* of the fair, which greatly contributed to his self-com-

placency ; and as, first, Miss Catchside, and then Miss
Balsam, and next Miss Fairfield, followed by the buxom
widow, Mrs Winnington, respectively besieged him, driving the recollection of the frail fair one out of his mind,
he began to reduce the impressions they respectively
created to canvas, which greatly increased his reputation,
and soon caused him to give up sign-painting altogether.
The ladies then came trooping to have their portraits
painted—some in silk, some in satin ; some in wreaths,
some in turbans ; some with fans, some with bouquets in
their hands ; but all smiling, and looking very " What-
do - you - think - of - me - ish." Good, strong, bold, hard-
featured, tea-boardy, stiff-ringleted things they were,
with just that provoking degree of resemblance that
enables a spectator to say, " Ah, I suppose that's meant
for Miss Nightingale " ; or, " That's not unlike Mrs
Crossfinch." His men, however, were worse, for they
generally looked as if they were drunk, and going to be
sick. Still, as this was not apparent until they were
finished, Ruddle always acquired great credit as they
proceeded ; and as the roughly-chalked outline gradually
advanced into coat, waistcoat, and cravat, with a face
above, the fame of the progressing and outstripping-all-
other pictures increased. It was not until they were
finished and hung up that their defects became fully
apparent. Still Ruddle was not dear in his charges—
two pound ten for kit-kats, and five pounds for full-
lengths, with miniatures on card or ivory at " from one
pound and upwards," as he ambiguously worded it.
Sooner, however, than lose a sitter, Ruddle would take
payment in kind—paint a tailor for a coat, an innkeeper
for a dozen or two of wine, a butcher for his quarter's
bill, and so on—a moderation that was all the more com-
mendable, inasmuch as he was without opposition.

The reader will now have the kindness to consider
Ruddle as having discarded his painter's apron, and
taken a first floor in Angel-court, with the privilege of
displaying a gilt case full of specimens in Market-street,
one of the most frequented thoroughfares in the good
town of Fleecyborough. They will also have the kindness
to consider us arrived at the period of time when our

friend Tom goes to be " pinted," in accordance with the oft-repeated recommendation, not to say injunctions, of Angelena.

Ruddle was dividing his time between the fat shoulders of Miss Rumbolde, who had been sitting for her portrait preparatory to her marriage with Mr Muffins, the baker, and a plate of boiled beef and peas-pudding from Tosswell's eating-house hard by, when the laboured ascent of our Tom on the uncarpeted staircase caused Ruddle to pause and listen to the sound.

" That's a strange foot," said Ruddle, dashing his long light hair off a moderately high forehead, and taking a hasty glance at himself in a cracked looking-glass, behind a red screen, as he pulled a dirty dickey above a blue-and-white striped Joinville.

" Rap, tap, tap," went Tom at the door.

" Come in ! " cried Ruddle, whipping the half-finished plate of beef on to a chair behind the screen, and buckling his loose jean blouse about his waist.

" Your humble servant, Mr Hall," said he, with a most reverent salaam.

" Yours," replied Tom in an offhand sort of way, looking at the various finished and progressing portraits and artistic lumber scattered around ; " I've come to see about being painted."

" If you please, sir," replied Ruddle, handing Tom a roomy rush-bottomed chair.

" Thank'ee, I'd rather stand," replied Tom, who wasn't at all comfortable after his walk, or rather limp.

" A full-length, will you, sir ? " said Ruddle, jumping to a conclusion.

" Oh, I don't know about that," replied Tom ; " I mean to say, I'll stand while I talk."

" If you please, sir," said Ruddle, again bowing very low.

" Well, how do you think I should be taken ? " asked Tom.

" Taken," said Ruddle, stroking his imperial'd chin, and scrutinising Tom's fat vacant face with a laughing blue eye. " Taken," repeated he, adding, " You have a commanding presence, sir ; yes, sir, a very commanding

presence. Excuse me for saying of it, but if you hadn't
been a rich man, sir, you'd have been anything you turn'd
your attention to—a general, a judge, a rear-admiral, an
extraordinary master in the High Court of Chancery—
anything, in short. Never saw so finely developed a
head—quite a study for the classic authors."

" *Hem!* " mused Hall, who was not at all averse to
compliments.

" It'll do me good to paint such a gent as you, sir,"
continued Ruddle ; " yes, sir, it will do me good, sir,"
repeated he, wondering how much he could charge our
hero. This consideration brought him back to the question how he would be taken. " You are in my Lord
Lavender's Hussars, if I mistake not ? " observed the
polite confectioner ; " I suppose you will be taken in
your uniform, with your horse—your charger—by your
side ? "

" W-h-y, I don't know," drawled Tom, thinking of
Angelena's injunctions—" I don't know. I was thinking
of my hunting-dress ; how would that do ? "

" Very becoming, sir," observed Ruddle—" very becoming. Scarlet looks well on canvas. Of course, you'd
have a favourite horse introduced ? " added Ruddle,
wishing to make the picture as full as possible.

" How would it do to paint me jumping a gate ? "
asked Tom.

" Very fine attitude," replied Ruddle ; " very—on a
white horse, *a la* Abraham Cooper, R.A. ; respectable
artist Abraham—done some goodish things. Or you might
have a hunting scene altogether, with hounds and horses all
grouped in the centre—such as Grant's meet of the Queen's
stag-hounds on Ascot 'eath ; respectable artist Grant—
done some passable things. Landseer's not without
merit. Indeed, there are some of the London gents who,
in particular departments, are not altogether to be
despised ; the worst of them is, they are not general
artists—not universal geniuses. Lee can paint a river,
Pickersgill a portrait, Landseer a Scotch terrier, and so
on ; but they are not men-of-all-work. Put them down
here and they'd be lost, totally lost. No ; they may
do well enough in London, but they wouldn't succeed in

the country. It's only real merit that can get on here.
I've no doubt they'd make me President of the Academy
if I would go to London, but I won't. Would send them
a pictor, p'r'aps, if they'd hang it in a proper place ; and
why shouldn't it be a pictor of you, sir ? And that reminds
me, sir, of the pint we were discussing, sir—how you
should be taken. I really think, sir, a fullish subject, sir,
would be the most satisfactory memorial—the most
nationally interesting ; of course, you would be the
centre-piece — the Lord Chesterfield of the pictor ; and
you might have all your sporting chums around you, one
asking you how you are, another admiring your horse,
a third offering you a pinch of snuff, a fourth a cigar,
a fifth a sugar-plum, and so on ; or you might be on foot,
like Count D'Orsay in Grant's pictor, resting on your
whip-stick, with a liberal allowance of turned-back wrist-
band ; or we might have you going full chivy after the
fox, or——"

"How would it do to have me jumping a gate ? "
interrupted Tom.

"Nothing could be better," replied Ruddle—"nothing
could be better, or more natural."

"It wouldn't be absolutely necessary for me to be
jumping a gate in order for you to paint me that way,
would it ? " asked Tom, who had no idea of doing anything of the sort.

"Oh, by no means," replied Mr Ruddle—"by no
means ; imagination, sir—inspiration will do all that,"
tapping his forehead with his forefinger.

"Well, then," said Tom, who, like his father, always
wanted an estimate, "what do you think you could do
it for ? "

"Do it for—do it for," repeated Ruddle in an offhand
sort of way—"do it for," continued he, looking up at the
ceiling. "Oh, sir, we shall not quarrel about that, sir—
we shall not quarrel about that, sir."

"Well, but I should like to know," replied Tom, who
knew that that sort of answer generally led to a wrangle
—"I should like to know—to have an idea, at least. I
don't mean to tie you to a shillin' or two ; but still I
should like an idea, you know."

" Oh, why," said Ruddle. " I could either take it at
so much per head or so much per dozen, if you chose a
full pictor ; but the fact is, I don't look so much to
the matter of emolument as the credit and renown of
painting such a gent as yourself," the obsequious pastrycook bowing as he spoke. " Now if you want a grand
national work," continued he, again taking up the running,
as our friend Tom stood mute, " a real, stunning, super-
lative pictor, that will grace the walls of the Royal
Academy, and engrave after, I would say, by all manner
of means, have a full one—either a military piece, with
your regiment under arms, or marchin' with their colours
flying and band playing, bringing all the pretty gals to
the winders,—or a hound piece—hunting piece, as they
call them—with yourself and all the swells of the hunt
countin' the dogs, or lookin' at the fox before they set
him off ; or you might have it, as I said before, all goin'
helter-skelter, in a devil-take-the-hindermost sort of way,
over hedges, ditches, rails, gates, whatever comes in the
way, yourself on a white barb, say, going what they call
like a brick ; or you might just have a single figure—
yourself on a favourite horse, speakin' to your servant,
or adjustin' your stirrup ; or, again, you might be in the
private individual style—quite plain and genteel—brown
coat and a red velvet vest, with a gold curb chain to
your watch, like this portrait of Mr Simpkinson, the gent
who's a-makin' love to Miss Tiler," continued Ruddle,
pulling out a kit-kat of a very stiffly-curled gentleman,
whose unfinished dress was assuming those colours ; " or
you might be in bottle-green, with a black satin weskit,
or an embroidered weskit, or any sort of weskit. In
fact, I feel, sir, that I could produce a great work, sir
—a very great work," continued Ruddle, eyeing Tom
intently—" a work that would adorn the walls of the
Royal Academy, and transmit our names to a grateful
posterity. I feel that I could take the shine out of all
those conceited A.'s and R.A.'s, who think there's nobody
like them. I feel, sir, that in painting you, sir, I could
combine the expression of Raphael with the fire of Michael
Angelo and the warmth of Titian, and put Reynolds and
Lawrence and all of the moderns to the blush," friend

Ruddle fairly blowing himself with the sublimity of this last effort, and now standing balancing the portrait of Mr Simpkinson on one corner, as if he was going to spin it.

"Well," said Tom, as the delicacy of Simpkinson's position recalled the peculiarities of his own and the injunctions of Angelena, " I think I'll be taken on horseback, leapin' a gate."

"A full pictor, that's to say," rejoined Mr Ruddle, making a last effort to get a good order—" a full pictor, yourself leadin', the rest followin' ? "

" No, just myself," replied Tom, not seeing the fun of immortalising Woodcock, head-and-shoulders Brown, or any of the Fleecyborough worthies who might desire it— " no, just myself," repeated he firmly.

" I'm afraid it would hardly make what I call a historical subject," replied Ruddle, staring intently in Tom's face, " without some adjuncts—horses or dogs, or somethin' to show you are huntin'."

"Well, but my red coat will show that," replied Tom.

"True," assented Ruddle, biting his lips ; "practically speakin', it will, but, artistically speakin', it will not. You see, you may be what they call larkin'— cuttin' across country for fun. There should be a few hounds or somethin' introduced to show the real nature of your profession, your occupation, or calling."

" Well," replied Tom after a pause, " as far as a couple of hounds or so go, I wouldn't mind, but I can't stand— I mean to say, I don't want a full picture ; the fact is," continued he, dropping his voice, " it's for a lady."

" *I twig*," replied Ruddle with a wink of his eye.

" You'll not mention it, of course," observed Hall.

"Mum's the word with me," rejoined Ruddle, sealing his lips with his forefinger.

"You must do your best," observed Tom.

" I'll surpass myself, if possible," asserted Ruddle. " I'll throw Lawrence and Reynolds, and Watson Gordon and Grant, and all the incompetents far, far in the shade," Ruddle holding up his dirty right hand as if they were all flying before him.

" And what will it be ? " again asked Tom.

" Oh—why, sir—if it's for a lady, sir, the lady, sir, shall set the price, sir."

" *Hem !* " mused Hall, wondering how that would cut.

" I'm a-doin' a gent on those terms already," observed Ruddle, diving behind the red screen and producing a portrait of little Jug—Jug in full-dress uniform, a richly gold-laced coat, with kerseymere shorts and white silk stockings.

That was a sickener for Tom. There was no mistaking the little pig-eyed, spindle-shanked cornet any more than there was who he was getting " pinted " for.

" This is the gent—the right honourable gent—that's a-courtin' the great heiress at the barracks," observed Ruddle, dusting Jug over with a bandana, and biting his lips as he suddenly recollected to have heard that young Mr Hall was doing the same.

Tom glanced an angry glance at his detested rival, and telling Ruddle he would call again to arrange a sitting, rolled off downstairs, shaking his head and muttering something about " Cat's-paw," " Not stand it," " Too old to be done," and so on.

Having purchased a sheet of diachylon plaister—as a first step, we presume, towards a sitting—he returned home, when his thoughts were suddenly diverted by the receipt of a smart-sealed note, headed with an embossed hare hunt, inviting him to partake of the pleasures of a puss hunt with the well-known Major Guineafowle's harriers—a character to whom we shall have great pleasure in introducing our readers.

CHAPTER XXX.

MAJOR GUINEAFOWLE was a great man—a very great man; indeed, most of our characters are great men somehow or another. The major, however, was a great man in a small compass; and here we may remark on the admirable dispensations of Providence, that whenever a man is troubled with an extra deal of consequence, it is generally put into a small body. But for this the world could never get along. All the roads and thoroughfares would be stopped and choked if great, gigantic lifeguardsmen fellows went strutting and fuming about like the little bantam-cocks of creation. But to the major. Though it would be difficult to say on what particular point our little great man was greatest, there were few upon which he was greater than that of being a master of hounds—" five-and-twenty years master of hounds, *without a subscription,*" as he emphatically adds, puffing out his cheeks, and diving into his pockets. And, certainly, " five-and-twenty years master of hounds, without a subscription," sounds well in these poverty-stricken, money-scraping times. Five-and-twenty years master of hounds, without a subscription, shows that a man is a keen, steady-going sportsman, clearly above the wants and exigencies of this most necessitous world. When, in addition, a family man—a grown-up family man, too—a double-barrelled family man, indeed, dispenses with a subscription, there is every reason to think that, in the language of servitude, " money is no object." So it was with Major Guineafowle.

He had buried his first wife, who, though quite a suit-

able match for him at the time he married her (he having
then recently failed as a wine merchant, and set up as
an auctioneer at Tewkesbury), was, perhaps, rather below
the advanced position he subsequently attained by the
unexpected descent of the Carol Hill Green estate, in
Mangelwurzelshire, which also obtained for him the
majority of the militia—an honour that very materially
added to his consequence, " Major Guineafowle, Master
of Hounds, of Carol Hill Green," sounding much better
than " Mr Guineafowle, auctioneer and appraiser, High-
street, Tewkesbury." His dear wife having left him three
daughters, all fair, rather reddish-haired girls—Mrs
Guineafowle being white and our major rather gingery,—
and our friend being then quite in the " morning of life,"
as the quack doctors say, resolved to send the girls to
school, and in due time to have another venture in the
lucky-bag—passing for a bachelor or otherwise, as circumstances might favour. Accordingly he placed the
girls at the elegant Miss Birchtwig's " seminary for a
select number of pupils," at Maida Hall, London, where,
for fifty guineas per annum, and about as much more
for extras, with " three months' payment always in
advance," they were to be taught everything ; and while
Miss Birchtwig was fulfilling her part of the contract,
the major mounted a dead gold button with a great
border, and the letters " C.H.G.H." (Carol Hill Green
Hunt) in bright, on a green cut-away coat, with a buff
vest, and proceeded to disport himself at the watering-
places. Like a wise man, he did not take a servant from
home with him, but picked up the first likely-looking
one he fell in with, when, arraying him in his livery—
green and gold—with a cockade in his hat, he gave him
such a dose of his consequence—" moy hounds, and moy
horses, and moy country, and moy regiment "—and so
on, that the man was glad of a let-off at the saddler's,
blacksmith's, and other importance-propagating places.
The result was that the major very soon grew into consequence, and wherever he went he was always pointed out
by those who take a pleasure in the sports of the field,
and indeed by some who do not, but who like to be
thought knowing, as the " great Major Guineafowle, the

master of hounds," or the "great Major Guineafowle, the gent who hunted Mangelwurzelshire." The major, too, used to aid the delusion and gratify his own curiosity by lounging into the shops, under pretence of buying a knot of whipcord, a set of spur-leathers, or some trifle of that sort, when he would worm out all the secrets of everybody and everybody's establishment—how many daughters Mrs Longhead had, whether there were any sons, why Mrs Meggison didn't live with her husband, what Mrs Winship gave her coachman, and how many suits Miss O'Flaherty's footman had. The wages of everybody, too, he knew; and altogether there was scarcely anything that didn't seem to be worth the major's cognisance. The curiosity, however, was not all on his side, for many were the questions raised and observations made upon our sportingly dressed, consequential little cock. Mrs Mantrappe thought it a pity he should be so devoted to hunting; Mrs Mouser heard he was very rich; Mrs Soberfield supposed he was a "great catch"; while Jack Lawless asserted that he had the finest pack of hounds in the world.

Thus our bachelor-widower friend passed about from watering-place to bathing-place, and from bathing-place back to watering-place, always as the great Major Guineafowle, always talking about "moy hounds," and "moy horses," and "moy huntsman," but always keeping his weather-eye open for an heiress or a widow. Several good finds he had, and several smart bursts he ran, always, however, ending in trouble and disappointment. The inquisitive ferreting women invariably turned up the daughters, and then all the big talk about "moy hounds," and "moy horses," and "moy huntsman," went for nothing. Mrs Doublefile, who, while he passed for a bachelor, didn't think him a day too old for their Sarah Jane, then discovered that he was a nasty made-up old fellow, who she wouldn't let her daughter think of on any account. Mrs Grinner, who had hounded her daughter on with all the vehemence of a petticoat, then *pirouetted*, and said, "It would be a pretty thing for her beautiful Bridget to go and tackle with a nasty, ugly, old fogey-like Guineafowle, with a ready-made family." The major had been so often repulsed that he began to lose heart, especially as he felt that each fresh defeat only increased his difficulties, women's tongues, as he said, being bad to muzzle. He almost began to wish he had gone on the honest tack.

At length the famous Rumbleford Wells befriended him. To it there came, just as the major had inflated himself to his fullest extent and mastered everybody's affairs in the place—what Colonel Filer gave his coachman, what Mr Gobleton his cook, and why Miss Mantle's maid was leaving—to it there came, we say, just as the major was thinking of packing up his portmanteau and going, the once capital but then slightly waning beauty, Miss Longmaide, with her fortune of sixty thousand pounds.

Miss Longmaide had overstood her market, and would gladly have recalled some of the earlier suitors whom, in the arrogance of youthful beauty, she had rejected. Her serenity was at this time more than usually ruffled by the last of these—the charming Captain Balmeybucke of the Royal Gentle Zephyrs, having come in for a large fortune, and married the " dear confidante " who strongly advised Miss Longmaide not to have him. Under such circumstances a woman is very pregnable, and the major was just the man for the occasion. He was in the Imperial Hotel yard as her green travelling chariot came jingling in (for this, of course, was before railway times), and soon learnt, through the usual course of hotel communication, all, how, and about her. He paused and drew breath as he pondered on the vastness of her wealth— sixty thousand pounds—sixty, not fifty, which made it look more real—but he presently recovered his equanimity, and felt he was equal to it whatever it was. He thought it seemed the very thing. Here was a lady no longer in her *première jeunesse*—a lady too, apparently, all in her own disposal, without being environed by troublesome busybodies whose sole object seemed to be the suppression of matrimony. The major had undergone much persecution, and seen much service in the wars of Cupid —more than he was ever likely to see in the militia, if he lived to be a thousand. He determined, however, to have another *coup*—the last—the very last, as he always said when he buckled on his armour. He therefore altered his plans, and took his lodgings on for another week.

This being in the days of bags, when every lady carried one, there was never any difficulty about an introduction, a lady having nothing to do but drop her bag in the library, or other approved lounge, when down would go the gentleman for it. Sometimes a couple would cannon with their heads, which made it all the more interesting. On this occasion, however, the major had it all to himself. Miss Longmaide visited Creamlaid and Satinwove's library at an earlier hour than the *beau monde* frequented it, and found the major busy as usual with the ' Morning Post,' reading the fashionable parties, the Duchess of So-and-So's ; stud sales—" Messrs Tattersall will, &c., the entire stud of Mr Doneup, who is declining hunting " —and so on. She had marked the little man from her window ; indeed, had met him strutting in the street the day before, when, though she thought him a queerish-looking, cod's-head-and-shoulders little man, still the glowing account her maid gave of his worth and his wealth, his hounds, and his horses—above all, of his exalted position, made her look complacently on him, instead of " eyes right "-ing as she passed.

Moreover, Miss Longmaide was tall and stately, and the major little, which, perhaps, made them incline to each other. She now came rustling into the library, extremely well got up in a close-fitting black satin dress and a white chip bonnet with a graceful white feather reclining over the left side. There being a couple of steps up to the library door, and this being before the nasty draggle-tail days, she slightly raised her dress as she ascended, showing very symmetrical *bien chaussé* feet and ankles. She passed her lavender-colour gloved hand down her Madonna-like dressed hair, and in lowering her arm dropped her bespangled reticule at the little major's feet. " Old Flexible Back," as they called him, from his great bowing capabilities, pounced upon it like a hawk, and in an instant was restoring it, with a profusion of grimaces, to the smiling beaming-eyed owner. They then struck up an acquaintance ; and watering-place courtships always proceeding with railway rapidity, at

the end of a week—during which time the major plied
her well with "moy horses," and "moy kennels," and
"moy hounds kept without a subscription "—Miss Longmaide, whose Bath and Cheltenham experience had made
her familiar with the Duke of Beaufort's and Lord Fitz-
hardinge's establishments, concluded he must be very
rich ; and having her affections well in hand, despairing
of ever supplying the place of the elegant charmer she had
lost, she thought might just as well share the honours and
attentions that our major represented were so freely
lavished on himself. Indeed, we believe the gallant officer
and liberal sportsman might have brought the affair to
an earlier termination, had he not thought it prudent—
due to himself, as he said—to get his lawyers, Keenhand
and Blunderby of Tokenhouse-yard, to " cast their eyes "
over the will of the late Marmaduke Longmaide of Slumpington Grove, in the county of Somerset, under whom
she claimed. These worthies, who did all the major's
amatory business gratis, on the understanding that they
were to have his settlement when he married again—a
chance that they thought rather long in coming—reported
that Marmaduke had died "seised and possessed " of
several capital estates—to wit, of Slumpington and
Squashington, in the county of Somerset ; Scratchington,
in the county of Salop ; and Rushington, in the county
of Kent ; together with a colliery or coal-mine near Leeds,
in the county of York—all of which he devised to trustees
in trust for his daughters, Blanch, Clementina, Rosamund,
and Priscilla, our fair lady, in equal shares and propor-
tions. They further reported that, with regard to the
Slumpington and Squashington estates, their client, Mr
Heavybille of Glastonbury, knew them well, and reported
that they were not only very large, but capable of great
improvement—an assertion that may be safely hazarded
of three-fourths of the estates in the kingdom ; and
altogether Keenhand and Blunderby, though they " didn't
advise," thought it " very promising."

The major turned the thing quickly over with his mental
hay-rake, and though he felt it would have been better,
more satisfactory, if the excellent Marmaduke had had
his money in the funds, so that it might have been seen

at a glance what each daughter was worth, yet when
he came to reflect on the honours of land-ownership,
with the perils and dangers of protracted courtships, the
repulses he had suffered—repulses more galling and
humiliating than anything Sir Harry Smith [1] has since
encountered at the Cape—he thought it wouldn't do to
haggle about it. In this view he was confirmed by re-
calling the particulars of the mishaps of some of his
former adventures—how Miss Willowtree had jilted him
at the last moment in favour of the captain of Heavy
Dragoons, because, she said, he had been too inquisitive
about her fortune, and she didn't want any man to marry
her for her money ; how the rich widow, Mrs Quickly,
would have taken him offhand if he had only had the
courage to close with her at once, instead of waiting to
ascertain the value of her Bridgewater Canal shares,
thereby affording time for her too assiduous friends to
find out about his daughters. Worse than all, he thought
with horror of the long lawyer's bill that accompanied
the return of his proposals for a marriage with the eldest
daughter of Mr Butternail, the retired cheesemonger,
whom the major thought would only have been too glad
to have a gentleman of his *calibre*—a major and a master
of hounds—for a son-in-law. These and many more
mortifications flashed across his mind as he sat before the
mirror making his morning toilet, taking an alternate
scrape of his chin and a glance at Keenhand and Blunderby's letter. He remarked with a sigh that his once
gingery whiskers were getting rather grey, and the roof
of his round head was not so well thatched as it used to
be ; that Time's graver was biting furrowing lines deep
in his once fat face ; while Backstrap, the trouser-maker,
had asked permission to pass the measure round his
waist the last order he gave him—clearly intimating that
he thought he was getting *ray*ther stout.

The consequence of all this meditation and experience
was that the major determined to risk it ; and making
an elaborate toilet—a cream-coloured cravat, whose
diamond-pattern'd tie was secured with a gold pointer

[1] Major-General Sir Harry Smith, Governor of Cape Colony, 1847-
1852.

pin, a step-collar'd canary-coloured kerseymere vest, with
a new light-green cut-away with velvet collar and " moy
hunt " buttons, above fawn-coloured doeskin trousers
and patent leather boots, his whiskers well trimmed, so
as to show as much ginger and as little grey as possible,
and his hair brushed out to the greatest advantage, he
stuck his punt-hat jauntily on one side, and sluicing his
blue bird's-eye kerchief with lavender-water, he drew on
a white doeskin glove, and, whisking the other in his right
hand, set off on his sixteenth crusade.

Arrived at the Imperial Hotel, he was received by
Timothy Tenpence, the head waiter, who, with a profusion of bows—" marked respect," as the major said—
passed him on to Miss Longmaide's pretty maid, Emma
Springfield, into whose little hand the major, with admirable tact and judgment, at an early day had managed,
with no great difficulty perhaps, to insinuate a sovereign ;
and Emma had made it her business to ply her mistress
with all the pleasant importance-giving stories she could
raise relative to our gallant master of hounds.

Emma smiled as she saw how smart the major was,
knowing full well what was coming ; indeed, she thought
him rather slow, and had lost half a dozen kisses to Alder-
man Portsoken's " gentleman," whose master was staying
in the house, that " Old Ginger Heckle," as they called
the major, would offer on the Tuesday, this being Thursday.
However, the kisses were neither here nor there ; so with
an arch smile, as she answered the major's observation
about the weather—asking if her mistress was at home
being now quite out of the question—she ushered him
into the sitting-room, where the fair lady was already
arranged with her company work to receive him. Emma
then withdrew ; and passing gently into the adjoining
bedroom, which was only separated from the sitting-
room by folding doors, with the aid of the keyhole, she
saw and heard everything, just as well as if she had been
in the room.

He commenced with that steady old friend to stupidity,
the weather, expatiating on its favourableness to agricultural purposes, which led him to hope for an early
harvest, which would enable him to begin hunting early,

which was very desirable for masters of hounds, as it
enabled them to get their packs in good order before the
great influx of sportsmen arrived, who were sometimes
rather unreasonable in their expectations, and did not
make allowance for the difficulties masters had to contend
with. Indeed, he sometimes wondered that gentlemen
could be found willing to make the great pecuniary and
other sacrifices necessary for their maintenance, for nobody
knew what keeping hounds was but those who tried ;
that Lord Petre's observation to Delmé Ratcliffe, that a
master of hounds would never have his hand out of his
pocket, and must always have a guinea in it, was most
correct ; and so he went maundering on, the fair lady
contrasting his matter-of-fact egotism with the im-
passioned languishings of Captain Balmeybucke, who
worshipped her eyes, and worshipped her nose, and worshipped her lips, and worshipped her teeth, and worshipped
her hand, and worshipped her feet, and worshipped everything belonging to her.

Indeed, the gallant master of hounds dwelt so long on
the scent that Emma Springfield began to wish he might
get done before the servants' dinner-bell rang, and she
couldn't help wondering her mistress didn't give him a
lift. Emma was a dashing little girl with her own suitors,
and always brought them to book within the third day.
However, the major went towl—towl—towling on, never,
as he would say, with a burning, but still with a good
holding scent, but making apparently very little progress.
At length the lady, looking up from the broad-bordered
kerchief she was hemming, touched a chord to which the
major's heart responded. Gentle reader, that word was
—TURNIPS !

A gardener's waggon was passing with a load, and
Miss Longmaide observed on its height. The major
went off at a tangent. He grew turnips, the finest in the
country ; indeed, whatever he did, or had, or grew, or
bought, was always the best, the very best, far better
than anybody else's. He grew turnips, the finest, the
very finest in the country ; nobody could hold a candle
to him in that line. He had some beautiful turnip-land
at Carol Hill Green, worth three-pound-ten an acre of any-

body's money. " Three-pound-ten an acre," he repeated, sucking his breath, as if he were kissing the land. Indeed, if Emma's eye hadn't been to the door, she'd have thought he was kissing her mistress. However, that was shortly to come. From the merits of the turnip-land the major proceeded to expatiate on the beauties of "his place," Carol Hill Green : its lovely situation, its splendid avenue of ancient elms, its healthy climate, its glassy lake, its conservatories, its pleasure-grounds, its mossy slopes and purling brook—topics much more interesting and intelligible to the fair lady than either hounds or turnips. She therefore chimed in with the subject, getting up a good cry, asking many particulars about the roses, of which the major assured her he had every sort under the sun, feeling confident he could get them at short notice should circumstances favour their requirement. From the roses, the lady led him with considerable adroitness to enter upon a description of the gardens of the neighbouring gentry ; whence she speedily diverged to their houses, and was assured by the major that he had the run of them all—could do what he liked with the owners of every one of them, all of whom looked up to him with the greatest respect, and arranged their parties in the winter to suit the meets of his hounds. Altogether he made himself out to be a very great man, and Miss Longmaide, being heartily tired of single blessedness, and despairing of ever cobbling up her feelings to what they were before the Balmeybucke catastrophe, decided that she might just as well invest herself with our consequential friend, and receive whatever honours and attentions he could spare from himself. She therefore encouraged him to proceed, helping him on just as he would his hounds with a failing scent.

Miss Longmaide, who had had nearly as much experience in matrimonial matters as the major, hung her head when he came to what the old Chancery lawyers used to call the " charging part," but, being a bad hand at blushing, she gave her chair a slight wheel, so as to get her back to the light, when, clearing her sweet voice with a prefatory *hem*, she proceeded to recapitulate her acknowledgments of the compliment the major had paid her, punctu-

ating them with hems and coughs. It " was, indeed, so
unexpected that it had taken her quite by surprise.
Though their acquaintance had only been of short dura-
tion, she might admit—candidly state, perhaps—that he
was not indifferent to her " ; whereupon she attempted
to conceal her face in the company-kerchief, which the
gallant major resisting, a slight scuffle ensued ; whereupon Emma, rising from her knees, with a mental ejacula-
tion of " Wot a couple of old fools ! " proceeded to tell
all she had seen downstairs, and in less than an hour the
news was all over the town.

The proceedings, however, did not terminate with
what Emma saw, for Miss Longmaide, having had several
most promising offers, most undeniable proposals, all of
which melted like snow before the fiery search of the two
scrutinising lawyers, although the turnips and master-
ship of hounds inspired her with considerable confidence
in this case, still she thought it would be well to get some
more definite ideas of the major's circumstances, were
it only to enable her to make the most of him on the
fine-scented, rose-coloured note-paper she had already
prepared to write to her friends upon. After the first
transports of joy were over, and little Flexible Back had
again subsided in his seat, now drawn close to our fair
friend's, she began, in a very pretty simpering way, to
banter him on his boldness in engaging with a lady he
knew nothing about, intimating that she thought it only
fair to give him such information as she could supply
without the aid of her lawyers, Messrs Roaster and Pinner,
to whom she begged to refer him for the remainder. But
the gallant major, knowing full well that if he went to
Roaster and Pinner's they would not only roast and
pin him as to his own affairs, but very likely give him
the sack into the bargain, protested most vehemently
against such a proceeding, vowing that he didn't care a
farthing about money ; that he'd be too happy to take
her without a copper ; that he was above all mercenary
considerations, as might be inferred from the fact of his
keeping a pack of hounds without a subscription ; and
he went on at such a rate that Emma, who had now
returned to her post, declared she never heard such a

man, and expressed her belief that he could "talk a table off its legs." Miss Longmaide remonstrated, but the major was staunch. He would have nothing to do with Roaster and Pinner, or any confounded parchment-faced lawyer, who, he said, were fit for nothing but spoiling sport, adding that he would like to rub half of them over with aniseed, and run them down with his hounds. To be sure, when he had driven Miss Longmaide off the lawyer line, as he thought, and got calmed down a little, he showed a disposition to exchange Carol Hill Green information for that appertaining to her property ; but he'd have " no pen, ink, and paper work—no schedules, no rent-rolls, no balance-sheets, no bankers' books. It should be the very soul and essence of honour and confidence on both sides."

So he kept steadily to this point, urging on the match with the greatest importunity, and refreshing the little maid with another sovereign. Circumstances favoured our friend. Miss Longmaide attributed the loss of the divine Captain Balmeybucke a good deal to the interference of her over-zealous friends, who persuaded her that the contingency which had since arisen was one of those remote possibilities it would never do to marry upon ; and she began to suspect that her friends, as they called themselves, were leagued together to prevent her marrying, in order that they might share her money among them. The idea of this she couldn't endure ; and though the gallant major was as unlike any of her former lovers as anything could possibly be, still she believed him to be a worthy, warm-hearted, disinterested man, most ardently attached to her, and with whom she made no doubt she could live in comfort and respectability. So she faltered " yes " to the major, and further yielded to his urgent solicitations of an immediate marriage. Another sovereign to the maid overcame all difficulty about dresses, and Rumbleford Wells rose in repute by the match.

Great was the day when the little major, in the full uniform of the Mangelwurzelshire Militia, strutted up the flags of St Bride's Church, looking so arrogantly bumptious that if he hadn't been going to be tamed by

P

matrimony, he ought to have been taken before a justice and bound over to keep the peace. He strutted, and sidled, and fumed, like a turkey-cock at the sight of a red coat. But if he went in great, how much greater did he come out ! with the tall, elegant, Italian-complexioned angel leaning on his arm, thinking, perhaps, of some one far different to the pocket Adonis who now guided her steps ; while amidst the merry peal of the bells, the shouts of the populace, and the silvery showers of the shillings, the little major hugged himself with his astonishing Waterloo-like victory. He had, indeed, accomplished wonders, and felt revenged for all the slights and snubbings of former times. So *hoo*ray ! for Rouge and Noir, as Miss Jaundice called the happy couple, as they stepped into their travelling carriage and four. Crack go the whips, round go the wheels, and back the white favours stream.

What a pity to leave such a charming theme, to return to the dull realities of life ! However, we must do it.·

We are free to admit that there was a little disappointment on the part of the lady when she arrived at Carol Hill Green, for instead of approaching through a long avenue of venerable elms, as the bridegroom represented, the chaise suddenly stopped ere she was fully aware they had entered the grounds, the dozen or two trees, of which the straight avenue was composed, being all passed ; neither was the mansion very imposing. Indeed, had it not been for the determined stop of the carriage, she would have thought the tidy, little, whitewashed house they stood before was the lodge. However, like a wise woman, she kept her opinions to herself, feeling, perhaps, that the disappointment would be reciprocal when the major came to find how the colliery or coal-mine near Leeds, in the county of York, kept down the rents of the Slumpington and Squashington estates in the county of Somerset, of Scratchington in the county of Salop, and of Rushington in the county of Kent.

The existence of the daughters was an after-find, and perhaps our readers will allow us to dispose of that discovery as one of those catastrophes that are more easily imagined than described. Still there was the consequence of the hounds to console the lady ; and perhaps our sporting friends will do us the favour of accompanying us to the kennel. Kennel, did we say ? There was no kennel—only an old root-house, with a bench in it. The following was the rise and progress of " moy establishment " :—

When Carol Hill Green descended on the auctioneer there was then in the neighbourhood a small trencher-fed pack, called the " Jolly Rummagers," from the independent way they scrimmaged over everybody's land, and which had got into sad disrepute, as well for their trespasses as for their propensity to mutton. In fact, they were under sentence of capital punishment, when it occurred to the butchers, bakers, publicans, beershop-keepers, and people they belonged to that it would be a good thing if they could get the major (then Mr Guinea-fowle) to head them, which would give them respectability and greater liberty over the land. Accordingly they waited upon our friend, and represented to him the great advantage these hounds were of to the country in a public (house) point of view ; expatiated on their anxiety to promote the sports and amusements of the people, than which there could be nothing more legitimate or more truly national than the noble pastime of the chase ; and they concluded by informing our friend that if he would only consent to lend them his name—let the hounds be called his, in fact—they would indemnify him against all costs, charges, damages, and expenses whatsoever. Honour on such easy terms not falling to the lot of man every day, the auctioneer, after due consideration, acceded to their proposal, and forthwith the hounds became his. He then struck the fine gilt button, and established a uniform—green, with a red waistcoat and white breeches,—and proceeded to qualify for his high office by reading all the books he could borrow on the subject.

Before taxing time, however, came round most of the worthies had vanished, and our friend was left sole master of the establishment. They were now Mr Guineafowle's hounds, in every sense of the word. Many men, with no more taste for hunting than our friend, would have revived the old sentence of extermination ; but our Guineafowle, having tasted the sweets of office, didn't like to lose it so soon. He therefore agreed, among his own and some of the neighbouring farmers, that if they would keep the hounds, he would pay the tax ; and that his groom - cow - keeper - gardener, Jonathan Falconer, should collect them the evening before hunting, and distribute them after.

This was thought very handsome of our friend, seeing that each hound would cost him sixteen shillings, and there were seven or eight couple of them. To be sure, as between the public and the tax-gatherer, there was always a slight discrepancy ; the major, when on his high horse, at market-tables and other public places, talking of them as a full pack, five-and-thirty or forty couple ; while to the tax-gatherer he used to say, with an airified toss of his head, that there were only a few couple that he kept out of charity, and he wished he was rid of them altogether. Indeed, he once went so far as to try to pass them off as fox-hounds, in order to escape the then certificate duty, alleging that they only condescended to hare in the absence of fox ; but this the surveyor wouldn't stand, and our master didn't think it prudent to risk an appeal.

A very severe contest having taken place for Mangel-wurzelshire shortly after our friend's accession to the Carol Hill Green estate, in which he particularly distinguished himself by voting for the Whig candidate, after promising, and canvassing with, the Tory, he was rewarded by the majority of the militia, in lieu of being placed on the commission of the peace, as he wished, the justices of his petty-sessional division vowing they would all resign if he was. However, he got his majority ; and then the hounds were Major Guineafowle's, and Jonathan Falconer got a cockade and a gold band for his hat.

Many of our sporting readers, we dare say, will remember " Major Guineafowle's, the Carol Hill Hounds," figuring in the papers along with the packs of dukes and other great men, making quite as great a figure on paper as any of them. A pack is a pack, in the eyes of the

uninitiated, just as a child thinks a cherry is a cherry
when it eats a baking one. The major got leave over
more land, too, though Lord Heartycheer—at the earnest
solicitation of whose steward, Mr Smoothley, our friend
had voted as he did—said, in his usual haughty way
when applied to, that "though the man undoubtedly
ought to have something for disgracing himself, he didn't
know that letting him maraud over a country was the
right sort of payment."

His lordship's natural fox-hunter's contempt for a
hare-hunter had been greatly heightened by hearing
from Dicky Dyke that the major classed their establishments together, and talked of Heartycheer and "oi"
hunting the country.

Very telling, however, the major's talk was when the
first batch of daughters were emancipated from Miss
Birchtwig's, and began twisting and twirling about to
the music of the watering-place bands, the major still
haunting the scenes of his early career—still talking about
"moy horses, and moy country, and moy hounds kept
without a subscription."

Offers came pouring in apace, each suppliant feeling
satisfied that a five-and-twenty, or four-and-twenty, or
three-and-twenty years' (as the case might be) master of
hounds "without a subscription" could want nothing
but amiable well-disposed young men for his incompar-
able daughters, and that was a character they all could
sustain—at least, for a time. Mrs Guineafowle, being
anxious to get the first brood off before her own beauties
were ready to appear, favoured all-comers, bringing men
to book with amazing rapidity, and never letting one off
without a thorough sifting. She took possessions, rever-
sions, remainders, and contingencies into consideration,
with all the acuteness of an assurance-office keeper.
Having been done herself, she was not going to let any
one do her. If the unfortunate passed the ordeal of her
inquiries—the Commons of the Guineafowle constitution
—he was passed on to the Lords in the person of our
great little major, now "five-and-twenty years master of
hounds without a subscription."

Then the major, having got up as much consequence as a newly made sergeant, would receive the smirking simpering simpleton with an awfully stiff bow, and, motioning him into a chair, would invite him to unbosom himself—just as a dentist invites a patient to open his mouth.

"Of course," Guineafowle would say, with a puff of his cheeks and a dive into the bottom of his pockets, as he stuck out his little legs before him—"of course I don't want you to go into elaborate detail—acreage and all that. What I want is *merely* a general outline of your p-r-o-r-perty and means of living, so that I may be able to judge whether you have the means of maintaining my daughter in the elegant luxury and comforts to which she has been accustomed. The lawyers will look to the detail of the matter, see that things are all right and on the square," with which comfortable assurance Guinea would again inflate his cheeks and—"pause for an answer."

Bless us, how that ominous speech used to scatter and annihilate the hopes and aspirations of signs, and glances, and squeezes, and supper-dances! Guinea knew how to wield the terrors of Roasters and Pinners, and had been done too often himself to let any one do him. But to be brief: the consequence of all this was that men whom our master of hounds without a subscription thought good enough for his daughters did not think the daughters good enough for them—at least, not unless he came down with a good many guineas, which he always most peremptorily refused to do, doubtless considering it honour and glory enough for any one to marry the daughter of a master of hounds without a subscription, the owner, as he used to insinuate, of Slumpington and Squashington, and all the other places.

Guineafowle had bowed out so many insinuating young men, who, snatching up their hats as they rushed through the entrance-hall, felt quite shocked and grieved that there should be such a mercenary spirit in the world, that Mrs Guinea was about tired of passing bills for her lord and master to reject; and the young ladies themselves had resolved just to accept offers without falling in love, until such times as there was a possibility of the suitors passing the upper house. This, however, they did not do, and Mrs Guineafowle saw with concern her own dark-haired, dark-eyed beauties now treading on the heels of the light-haired angels of the former marriage.

Miss Birchtwig had returned Laura, the eldest of the three dark ones, whom, like the street orange-women, she only counted as two, making up, perhaps, in extras what she took off the other end—Miss Birchtwig, we say, had " finished and polished " Laura, and returned her with such a glowing description of her virtues, that any one reading it would immediately exclaim, " Why, this Maida Hill establishment must be a real manufactory for angels ! " Laura was " obliging, enchanting, engaging, endearing, and so remarkably attentive to the instructions of her music, dancing, drawing, French, and Italian masters, that they all regretted her departure." Indeed, she had endeared herself to every one, while Miss Birch-twig doubted not that having had to come in contact with some whose tempers were not quite in unison with her own, would have a beneficial result in exercising her patience—much such a circular as she sent to the parents of all the " select number of pupils," leaving them, of course, to believe as much of it as they liked, according to their individual capacity for gammon. Best of all, Laura was a perfect beauty ; an elegant sylph-like figure, with raven-black hair, a clear Italian complexion, and the largest, deepest, Lola-Montes-like blue eyes, with flashing fringes, that ever were seen. The whole country rang with her beauty. Dicky Thorndyke's report of her to Lord Heartycheer was so encouraging that his lordship, who had always kept that " pompous, pot-hunting hum-bug "—as he profanely called Major Guineafowle—at a distance, observed, with a pout of his lips and a hoist of his snow-white eyebrows, that he " didn't know that there would be any great harm in letting Captain Guinea-pig towl over Barkinside Moor, and so up to their covers at Snipeton and Firle."

And now, after this wide hare-hunting circumbendibus,

made for the purpose of introducing our distinguished friend, we again break off at the major's invitation to Tom Hall to partake of a hare-hunt, leaving our fair friends to put whatever charitable construction they like on his motive.

So ends this terrible long chapter.

CHAPTER XXXI.

THE CAROL HILL GREEN ESTABLISHMENT.

THE note of which we have spoken was not sent to Tom
Hall without very deep and mature consideration. It
had formed the subject of very anxious deliberation
between Major and Mrs Guineafowle; the former oppos-
ing his wife's urgent precipitancy, on the ground that they
were not prepared for company ; the latter insisting on the
necessity of immediate action, because of the certainty
of such an undoubted prize as our Tom being quickly
caught up. She knew what a run there would be after
him, she said, and how all the designing women would
be spreading their nets and snares to catch him. The
fact of Tom breaking out in the character of a sportsman
seemed to favour their design, and Mrs Guineafowle
congratulated herself upon not having let the major
give up his hounds, as he had often and often threatened
to do. The result of the debate was that the major
wrote the aforesaid note, quite in the sporting strain,
inviting our friend to come over and hunt with his hounds,
and partake of whatever might happen to be going on,
adding that he could put him up a couple of horses, and
hoped he would stay as long as he liked : quite the hail-
fellow-well-met sort of note. This style was thought
better than requesting the honour of his company on
such a day, to stay till such a day, inasmuch as, though
they would get up all the steam of pomp and circumstance they could raise, it would enable them to put any
deficiency to the rough-and-ready score of the sportsman.
In truth, it was rather an anxious time for our friends ;
for with an advance in family expense there had been a

decline in amount of income ; the rents of the Squashington and Slumpington estates, as indeed their names
would imply, having been seriously affected by the repeal
of the corn laws ; while the colliery, or coal-mine, near
Leeds in the county of York, still did nothing towards
their assistance. The consequence was that the major,
who had been an ardent repealer, and, like some other
intemperate men, had denounced the class of which he
was an unworthy member, began to sing extremely small,
and complain that he had been robbed and plundered for
the million, who had got far more than they ought to
have. He threatened most vehemently to give up his
hounds. This Mrs Guineafowle still opposed, feeling
assured that he would be nothing without them ; and
knowing how attractive they had been to herself, she
was anxious that her daughters should now participate
in the benefit. It was only the tax on eight couple—
twelve pound sixteen a year—and an occasional lap at
the pig-pail the night before hunting. It was worth all
that to see them figuring in the newspapers, even though
the knowing editors did class them as harriers.

Though a trencher-fed pack is generally a troublesome
affair, there being generally some one or other of the
worthies in mischief, either worrying sheep or lambs or
poultry, or hunting on their own account among the
standing corn, yet, upon the whole, the major's were as
well conducted as any.

For this they were mainly indebted to the exertions of
their neighbour, Mr, or, as he was commonly called, Billy
Bedlington, of Cakeham Manor, a ponderous twenty-
stone farmer—not an agriculturist, but a farmer—a man
who farmed to make money, who paid great attention
as well to the hounds' breeding as to their morals. He
it was who crossed them judiciously, drafting the skirters,
and babblers, and nickers, and choppers, and cunning
ones, keeping none but true nose-to-the-ground hunters,
that wouldn't go a yard without a scent, his maxim being
to keep no cats that didn't catch mice. Billy was ably
assisted by our old friend, Jonathan Falconer, who had
grown not only grey but snow-white in the service of the
major.

Jonathan Falconer was one of a class of servants now nearly extinct—an honest, industrious, painstaking man —who was always doing something, and could turn his hand to anything, never standing upon this not being his work or that not being his place. He did not begin life as a huntsman, or, indeed, as anything else in particular ; and, we dare say, if the major had taken a yacht instead of a pack of hounds, Jonathan would have turned his hand to the sea-service just as readily as he did to the land. In the major's establishment he filled many offices, being huntsman, coachman, groom, gardener, game and cow-keeper, and occasionally second footman. The major, when on his high horse at his dear watering-places, and so on, used to talk as if he had a man in each of these departments ; and even at home, when talking before those whom he thought were not up to the ins and outs of his establishment, this man-of-all-work was called Jonathan in the house, and Falconer in the field, as if for all the world he were two men.

The real domestic staff, at the period of which we are writing, consisted of one Joshua Cramlington, a tall, knock-kneed stripling, who outgrew his clothes, and whose protruding hands and receding knees now showed how far advanced was the quarter. He was an awkward careless boy, always breaking and spoiling things, whom no drilling would ever make into a servant. The major, who always dealt in cubs of this description, used to console himself for their awkward *gaucheries* with the reflection that they were cheap, and by getting them young, he attached them to his person ; while, he said, they would make fine figure footmen as they grew up and got furnished. When, however, they did grow up and get furnished, they invariably took themselves off, and the major had to catch another, and go through the process of teaching and attaching again. Cramlington was, however, perhaps the most hopeless article the major had ever had to do with, being as stupid and mischievous a lad as ever came out of a workhouse. His extreme cheapness—£8 the first year, and £10 the second—was completely counteracted by the enormity of his appetite and the amount of his breakage.

The sporting reader will perhaps observe that, amid the great multiplicity of real or imaginary servants, there has been no mention whatever of that usual appendage to a pack of hounds, a whipper-in. The censorious will perhaps imagine that the major had none, or, perhaps, that he filled that department himself, or was indebted to the exertions of any chance sportsman for turning the hounds to Jonathan Falconer ; but there they would be wrong—the major had a whipper-in, though he didn't do to talk about, being, in fact, neither more nor less than a great, tailless, Smithfield cur, that ran at the erring pack just as he would at a flock of sheep. At a word—almost a look—from Jonathan Falconer, Bluecap—as they called him, from his colour—would rush from his horse's heels, and " at " the pack with a zeal that made them uncommonly glad to fly to Falconer—for protection. It was a cheap and ingenious device ; and if it had been ingenious without being cheap, possibly the major might have proclaimed it ; as it was, however, he was content with knowing it himself, and let others find it out that liked. " Moy whipper-in," therefore, was never mentioned.

We will now take a look at our Tom, for which purpose we will begin a fresh chapter.

CHAPTER XXXII.

TOM'S AFFECTIONS IN DANGER.

" SIVIN and four's elivin, and fourteen is twenty-five—
I've heard of Major Guineafowle ; that's to say, I know
the name. He's one of your huntin', gammlin' chaps,"
replied old Hall, in answer to his son's inquiry if he knew
anything of him. " Ah ! " continued he, running his
memory through the light reading of his ledger, " his
name was to Longwind's bills in 1849, and a precious
deal of trouble we had with it—was forced to put it into
Grinder's hands afore we could get the money."

" He keeps a pack of hounds," observed Tom, exhibiting
the fine hunt-embossed note—men, with winding horns,
riding among a porpoisey pack along the top.

" I know he does," replied Hall, taking it ; " see 'em
in the papers constant—at least, every now and then ;
and that's what surprised me that he didn't take up the
bill. But these huntin', gammlin' chaps are all queer—
never know where you have them—always outrunnin'
the constable, as Grinder says."

This was rather a damper ; and there is no saying
but Tom would have listened to his father's suggestions
had he not been suffering under the united influence of
Angelena's coquetry and Laura's loveliness.

Ruddles' " this is the gent—the right honourable gent
that's a-courtin' of the great heiress at the barracks,"
still sounded in Tom's ears, while Laura had drawn her
languishing, love-killing eyes slowly over his face and
down his fat person as she lolled becomingly in the old
barouche before Diaper and Dimity's door. She had
given him just such a look as Miss Longmaide gave the

major the first time they met at Rumbleford Wells—a look that neither said "what an object you are!" nor yet "what a beauty you are!" but just a medium look of approbation, inviting, as it were, a further acquaintance.

Tom, who always loved best the last eyes that beamed upon him, was so struck with Laura's beauty that he took three turns up and down before the carriage ere he went to the Salutation Inn to ask the ostler whose carriage that was with all the fine things on the panel, the major having come out uncommonly strong with two crests, the Longmaide and his own, and supporters, two guinea-hens, with a many-quartered coat of arms, made entirely out of his own head, surmounted with red-and-white petti-coats, entwined with bell-pulls in great abundance. Jona-than Falconer, too, wore a three-rows-of-curls coachman's wig under his gold-laced cockaded hat, an appendage that Jonathan complained gave him cold when he ex-changed it for his hunting-cap. However, "pride feels no pain" being one of the maxims of the major, he adhered to the wig, consoling Jonathan with liquorice, and assuring him that it was the weather and not the wig that gave him cold; that he had cold himself, just the same, and he didn't wear a wig.

This sort of finery being unusual in the country, and the major's carriage haunting the streets of Rattlinghope rather than Fleecyborough, caused considerable com-motion, especially with such a beauty as Laura inside, and such dashing green-and-yellow rosettes flowing at the well-shaped but rather light-carcassed hunter-carriage-horses' heads. Shuttleton, and Jaycock, and Gape, and Pippin, and several others of the Jolly Heavysteeders, had been ringing their spurs on the flags, and ogling the fair inmates of the carriage as it jingled from Miss Flouncey's to Mrs Sarcenet's, and from Mrs Sarcenet's to Miss Cheap-stitche's, and from Miss Cheapstitche's to Mrs Skein's, for an ounce of Lady Betty worsted, and from the Lady Betty worsted-shop back to Miss Flouncey's again. Whether Laura had looked benignly on *them*, too, is not to the purpose of our story, seeing that Tom was not there, and assuredly she looked pleasantly on him. That look, or rather that series of looks, were now counteracting old Hall's advice.

"Well, but he" (meaning the major) "must have money," observed Tom, "for he keeps a pack of hounds, and I've heard that old Heartycheer's cost him three or four thousand a year."

"Sivin and four's elivin, and twenty's thirty-one—if they do, he must be a very bad old man," replied Hall. "Sivin and four's elivin, and thirteen is twenty-four—no wonder the major couldn't take up the bill. Sivin and four's elivin, and forty-one is fifty-two—these huntin', gammlin' chaps are none on 'em to be trusted," mused Hall, inwardly determining to get rid of head-and-shoulders Brown's account, which was oftener on the wrong side than the right.

And so old Hall talked against the invitation.

Mrs Hall thought better of the major than her husband did, or rather, having had a good look at Laura as she passed the carriage on her way to Brisket the butcher, she thought she was not only a great deal younger but a great deal better-looking than Angelena, whom, she inwardly hoped, Laura might extinguish; consequently she favoured the expedition, and undertook to get all Tom's flash shirts and ties ready against the day, by which time she had no doubt he would have recovered from the unpleasant effects of the day with Lord Hearty-cheer's hounds. So, after many pros and cons, our Tom wrote to the major saying that he would have great pleasure in availing himself of his polite invitation—an answer that reconducts us to Carol Hill Green.

CHAPTER XXXIII.

THE GUINEAFOWLES ORGANISE A DINNER.

THE receipt of Tom's note changed the spirit of speculation in which our friends were indulging into that of bustling active preparation. The major, as we said before, ever since the repeal of the corn laws, had been reducing his expenditure, and in place of maintaining, had been letting things go downhill a little. The consequence was that, what with the natural wear and tear of that consuming animal, a house, aided by the spoilage and breakage of such boys as Cramlington, now that it became necessary to smarten up a little, it was found that there was a very serious deficiency in glass, china, crockery—all perishable articles, in fact ; the very lamp-shades that Cramlington displayed so conspicuously on his shelves were found to be broken on the far side, though, as the major had not taken stock on the departure of his predecessor, John Snuffles, of course Cramlington declared they were so when he came. Of tumblers and decanters there was a woeful deficiency, while the stock of wine-glasses was scarcely worth speaking of. Altogether the major found things in a very dilapidated state ; though, as Cramlington stood out that they were just as they were when he came, the major could only anathematise Snuffles, and determine to look sharper after Cramlington and Co. in future.

Though it was so near Christmas, and his credit by no means first-rate, sundry little documents being in course of preparation at Rattlinghope, headed with the ominous words, " to bill delivered," the major was forced to try his luck at Fleecyborough for such things as couldn't be dispensed with, thereby suffering severely in carriage for his want of credit at home. However, he hoped it was all for the best, and that the expenditure would tend to the capture of our most desirable young friend, Mr Hall. So the major took heart, and dashed off his order just as if he was full of money.

Mrs Guineafowle, too, knowing the influence that the first daughter marrying well has on the fortunes of her sisters, was most anxious that Laura should have every advantage ; so, step-mother-like, she intimated to the fair-haired daughters of the first marriage that, having had their " opportunities," they must not interfere with Laura.

Well knowing, too, how even the greatest beauty may be improved by dress, Mrs Guineafowle spared no expense in getting Laura up becomingly. Miss Birchtwig, of course, had a first-rate London milliner—namely, her cousin, Miss Freemantle, calling herself Mademoiselle de Freemantle, of the Rue de la Paix, Paris, and South Audley-street, London—with whom she always recommended her young friends to leave their measures, in case they chanced to want anything smart when they got into the country ; and from this eminent artist was procured, at the usual short notice of ladies, a beautiful light-blue silk dress, with trimming *en tablier* down the front, composed of a dozen very narrow silk flounces, embroidered in chain stitch. The body was made tight, setting off to advantage Laura's beautiful figure, with, of course, amply fly-away sleeves for sweeping things off tables and draggling into teacups and soup-plates.

Dresses being at length arranged, dinners occupied their united attention. The major and Mrs Guineafowle were most anxious that they should be of the most elegant description, partaking as much of the character of one recently given by the Duke of Gormanstone as Miss Nettleworth, the Gormanstone Castle toady, had been able to recollect and narrate to Mrs Guineafowle.

Gormanstone Castle, we may observe, was the stronghold of the Tory—a heaven from which our major was expelled when he ratted over to the Whigs.

After due deliberation and counting of the cost, it

was determined that the major should write off to Shell
and Tortoise for as much of their turtle-soup as would
serve two parties of ten, which the major did, promising
to send a post-office order for the amount, but omitting
to furnish a reference, thinking, perhaps, his signature,
with " Major, Mangelwurzelshire Militia," attached, would
be sufficient ; but Shell and Tortoise, not reverencing
military rank as they undoubtedly ought, after the lapse
of some days sent a bill, intimating that the soup would
be forwarded when the money came. This threw our
friends completely out ; for, independently of the fine
dashing style of leading off a dinner with turtle-soup, the
Shell-and-Tortoise procrastination prevented their making
other arrangements, and in lieu thereof they were obliged
to put up with mutton-broth—a much better thing, by
the way, when well made, than spurious turtle-soup.

Misfortunes, however, never come singly ; and Mr
Clearwell, the stupendous landlord of the Duke's Head
at Rattlinghope, who had always acted butler at Carol
Hill Green on state occasions, having become afflicted
with the usual innkeepers' malady, *delirium tremens*,
wrote, or rather scratched, to say he couldn't possibly
come ; so that the execution of affairs devolved on Joshua
Cramlington, assisted by Jonathan Falconer.

The major used to have an arrangement with Clearwell, who was a fine, stately, important-looking personage,
for enacting the character of butler, whereby he flattered
himself he not only imposed upon strangers but got his
raw lads a little useful drilling. When on his high horse,
especially at watering-places, he used to talk of " moy
butler getting fat," and " moy butler having nothing to
do," and " moy butler acting the gentleman."

Clearwell's defection greatly afflicted our friend, for,
independently of the imposing appearance of this magnificent man, revolving noiselessly about the little dining-
room, scarcely elevating his voice above a whisper,
Cramlington was so totally undrilled that even among
themselves he was continually making the stupidest mistakes, which made the major dread his appearance in
public.

However, there was no help for it ; so the major just

ordered a rehearsal, making Joshua arrange the table for a party of ten, with the Italian-patterned T. Cox Savory electro-plated covers and corner-dishes, showing him how to raise the former, without giving the next sitter a shower-bath, and how to hand the latter about on the palm of his hand, without upsetting them into a helper's lap. The major, too, established a code of signals —a forefinger to his nose indicating when Cramlington was to bring in the champagne, a piece of bread stuck up on end when he was to hand round the sherry. There had been no asking to take wine at the duke's, and, of course, our friends must follow the fashion, be it ever so absurd and unsociable. That observation, however, reminds us that we may say a few words about the Carol Hill Green guests.

Deep and anxious were the deliberations who they should have to meet our distinguished friend. They must be people whom Tom would think stylish, and yet people who would not interfere with their plans. As it was a dead set at our Tom, of course they were most anxious to make it appear otherwise. The major, indeed, would shudder at the idea of asking young men to his house in the hopes of getting them for his daughters, while Mrs Guineafowle was equally disinterested in theory, only determined not to lose a chance in reality. They hugged themselves with the reflection of having such an excellent excuse as the hounds for asking Tom over.

Well, who should they have to meet him ? Sir George and Lady Happyhit were their cock acquaintance, and had no daughter old enough to interfere with their plans ; but they were hitey-titey, prior-engagement, or " expect-ing-a-friend-from-London " sort of people, who never came if they could help it. Still, asking them enabled the major to say, in his usual offhand way, " We asked the Happyhits to come, but unfortunately they were engaged," and so on. Accordingly they sent a hunt-embossed note, requesting the honour of Sir George and Lady Happyhit's company at dinner, and enclosing a hunt-embossed card of two days' meets of Major Guinea-fowle's, the Carol Hill Green hounds—one at Hester-combe House, the other at Loxley Mount, each morning at half-past ten. They also asked Mr and Mrs Dominic Smith, and Mr, Mrs, and Miss Brandenburg Brown, thinking that out of so large a venture they were sure to get as many, if not more, than they wanted. Indeed, they made so sure of the Browns that they asked young Smoothley, the curate, who was supposed to be looking after Miss Brown, to meet them. Here, however, they were all wrong again ; for the Browns expected company at home, and had booked Mr Smoothley themselves, the Smiths were going away, while Sir George and Lady Happyhit merely presented their compliments, and were sorry they were prevented the honour, &c. What a nuisance ! what a bore ! It surely was the most un- sociable neighbourhood in the world ; and then they had to set to and cast over their acquaintance again. The Carboys had no carriage, and would not like to hire one ; the Owens were hardly good enough for a state occasion ; and Mrs Manfield was so disagreeable, with her great staring daughters, that they had firmly resolved never to have them any more. Worse than all, time was running short, and people who heard that others had been asked would not be likely now to accept, and so book themselves as second-class guests. They thought over several people, both far and near—the Fieldings, the Thompsons, the Passmores, the Lockseys, the Braceys, the Flappers, and the Figginses ; but there were objec- tions of some sort or another to the whole of them. Instead of having two parties of ten, they did not seem likely to get one. Billy Bedlington was always to be had at short notice, but turtle-soup would be wasted on such a monster as that. It then occurred to Mrs Guineafowle that the mention of turtle-soup, so unusual a thing in their quiet circle, might have a beneficial effect in drawing company, and the major forthwith penned a " Dear sir " epistle to the Rev. Mr Pantile, saying he would esteen it a favour if he would come and give his opinion on some he expected from London, adding that he hoped Mrs and Miss Pantile would accompany him.

Pantile was a learned man, full of Herodotus, Thucy- dides, and Demosthenes, who thoroughly despised hunting and all belonging to it. But for the mention of the turtle-soup, he would have refused to dine with such a hare-hunting squireen as Guineafowle. As it was, he pretended to yield, at the suggestion of Mrs Pantile, that it was his duty as a Christian minister to go and endeavour to reclaim Guineafowle from the wild atrocities and in-humanities of the chase, and implant nobler and loftier principles in his bosom. Mrs Pantile liked a run out as well as anybody, and knew how to tickle her Solomon into going. Miss Pantile, too, was all for going from home whenever she could, and strongly supported her mother's views ; for though plain, she had an irreproachable hand and arm, and played beautifully on the harp.

After so many refusals, it was a god-send to Guineafowle to get an acceptance, and he followed up his luck by asking another divine, the Rev. Arthur Pinkerton, to come and pass judgment on the soup also. Pinkerton, however, hearing that Pantile, whom he hated, was coming, declined ; and, as a last resource, Guineafowle summoned the great Billy Bedlington, intimating that as Mr Pantile was coming, it would be well to avoid the sub-ject of hunting. And Billy, who could talk of little else, wondered that there should be such a creature in the world as a man who didn't like to hear about hunting, and inwardly promised himself considerable amusement from the interview. So he told his hind to give " t'ard meer " an easy day in the plough, as he should be wanting her in the Whitechapel at night.

CHAPTER XXXIV.

TERRIBLE is the trouble of unaccustomed party-making —desperate when you want to make a dash with inefficient forces. Our gallant friend felt the full force of the situation, and never appreciated Clearwell at his full value before. Our major could have raised a regiment of militia with less trouble than this party gave him, and drilled and trained them with more ease than he could drill and train Joshua Cramlington.

Though they had had three rehearsals, he could not get the stupid boy to understand that the punch was only to be handed round after the turtle-soup. Jos would have it in at all intervals, thinking, no doubt, that it was much better stuff than wine. Our host never despaired of the turtle-soup until the Shell and Tortoise bill arrived, which it did close upon dinner, having taken a jaunt to some other town beginning with an R. Then, indeed, he was horrified. Pantile, too, coming expressly to eat it ! He denounced Shell and Tortoise from the bottom of his heart.

But to our spread. The major having finished the third rehearsal, and especially charged Joshua Cramlington to be on the alert, and not to forget any of the injunctions he had laid upon him, dismissed him to run his arms and legs through his green-and-yellow livery, while he went and got himself up for the reception.

Resolved upon doing the thing in style, and having read in the papers how the Duke of Wellington received Prince Albert at the door of Apsley House on the anniversary of the battle of Waterloo, he went and squeezed

his little pot-belly into the now very tight militia
uniform in which he achieved his great victory over
the beautiful Miss Longmaide, inwardly hoping that
it would lead to a similar beneficial result in Tom
Hall's case.

Then as he stood before the glass, examining first one
grizzly cheek and then the other, his hair now partaking
more of the silver-grey than the ginger-heckle, a luggage-
loaded fly was seen crawling up the avenue, and, girding
on his sword, our friend nearly broke his neck by tripping
over it as he hurried downstairs. Fortunately, the nearly
exhausted horse gave him time to recover his equilibrium,
and as the door opened responsive to the porch bell-pull,
our flexible-backed major, *chapeau bras* in hand, stepped
courteously forward, making a series of those remarkable
salaams that never were equalled save by old Vauxhall
Simpson of glorious memory.

Our Tom, who was gaping out of the fly-window at
the white-winged, white-bodied, little house, in the
manner of an appraiser, or a person with a design upon
it, was startled at the apparition that suddenly disclosed
itself ; while the fly-man stood with his hand on the
door, unable to make out what it meant.

The flexible-back having at length subsided, and the
major having motioned the man to open the door, out
rolled Tom, in a pair of the widest red-checked, snuff-
brown, tweed trousers that ever were seen, a light grey
jacket, with scarcely any laps, a stout, double-breasted,
white corduroy vest, and a wide-extending, once-round,·
buff joinville—looking as if his stomach was sensible of
cold, but his fat throat impervious to it.

" Proud of the honour of seeing you at my humble
hunting-box," bowed the major, tendering Tom a hand.
" Hope, if I can't put you up as sumptuously as I could
wish, I shall be able to make amends by the sport I shall
show you with my hounds ; and if you will honour us
with a visit at either Slumpington or Squashington, in
the county of Somerset, we shall be able to do by you
as we could wish."

Whereat our Tom grinned, being partly struck by the
magnificence of the major, and partly occupied in think-

ing what the gates had been in coming, so that he might not be imposed upon by the fly-man.

The clatter of the major's sword in the passage and the pompous prosiness of his greetings acted as warnings to the inmates of the little drawing-room on the right, causing them to hurry their aprons and things out of sight, and arrange themselves in company postures ; Mrs Guineafowle in the centre, supported by Laura, in her beautiful Freemantle dress, on her right, with the three other girls, in various coloured rather shabby merinos, on the left.

The major, lord-chamberlain like, then appeared, backing and bowing our Tom into the presence, introducing him to his intended and the family circle generally. And if the truth must be told, Laura thought Tom rather stout ; while the sour-grapes sisters declared they never saw such a man, and they pitied poor Laura excessively. However, they all chimed into a forced conversation, chiefly about the weather, which was unusually open, leading into speculation as to its probable features at Christmas. The major helped the cry on by expatiating on the splendid season his hounds had had ; something quite unusual, as indeed all his seasons were. " Never had a better season," he said, " and he had kept hounds now five-and-twenty years—five-and-twenty years—a long time—very long time—though not so long as his brother master, Heartycheer, had done," the memory of man not running to the time when Heartycheer took them.

Then the major asked if Tom's horses were come, and was glad to find he had only one, which he thought would save the bin ; and then he asked whether Tom would take anything before dinner, observing " that they dined at six, which he thought was a better hour than seven in winter. After a hard day's hunting he was always quite ready for his dinner at six, for he never took anything out with him, except it might be a biscuit, or a bun, cr something of the sort, which he often brought back, the excitement of the chase completely absorbing his faculties, and making him insensible of hunger, thirst, danger, everything," kicking his sword behind him as he spoke, to prevent its tripping him up again.

The gallant man was proceeding in this strain when
Cramlington came sneaking into the room, announcing
to Mrs Guineafowle, in such an undertone as enabled
every one to hear, that " cook wanted her " ; whereupon
Mrs Guineafowle knit her brow and disappeared, wondering whether the cat had got the fish, or the soot had come
down the chimney, or the cook was overcome with the
heat of the fire or the strength of the brandy, or which
of the hundred-and-one ills of party-making had befallen
her. The Amphitryon reader will readily conjecture that
the non-arrival of the turtle-soup was the cause : Jonathan
Falconer had returned for the third time from the station
without it, and the mis-sent Shell and Tortoise letter
arriving simultaneously with Jonathan, extinguished the
last ray of hope. " What a go ! " as the major said when
he read it. There was nothing for it but to substitute
the mutton-broth ; and then, oh dear ! what would
Pantile say ? There surely never was anything so unlucky.
If the major could have got at Shell and Tortoise, he
would have run his sword down the throat of one and his
scabbard down the other.

The fly-man then sent to say he was " ready to go "
(Guineafowle's house not affording entertainment either
for man or horse) ; and just as Tom had settled his
demands, his newly caught groom, Jack Tights, arrived
with his horse. John was a slangy, saucy Londoner, who
could dress himself, or dress his master, or dress a hook,
or dress a mutton-chop—indeed, dress anything except
a horse. He called himself " groom and valet," and was
up to all the bad practices of both services. He had been
in many good places, but, like all these characterless
fellows, the experience of adversity was totally lost upon
him, and no sooner did he get a fresh place than he
seemed to be trying how soon he could get out of it again.
His last master had dismissed him for making his horses'
corn into brandy-and-water. His real name was Branfoote—John Branfoote—but he had ridden several steeple-
chases—" Aristocratics," of course—as Captain de Rose-
ville. He had acquired the name of " Tights " from
having his clothes made so tight that it was a marvel
how he ever got into them. He was a nephew of Greedy

Sam's, the ostler at the Salutation Inn, who had strongly recommended him to our Tom as the " very man for him " ; and Tights, being hard upon starvation, had not let the chance slip. He had now got himself into a complete new rig-out at Tom's expense—a flat, indeed a rather *retroussé* brimmed hat with a cockade, a tremendously long-backed, short-lapped, tight, grey coat, with an equally long-striped waistcoat, leathers that would do nothing for his legs after their accompanying stomach had had the run of old Hall's kitchen for a month, and roast-chestnut-coloured topboots, with very long-necked spurs. Such was the gentleman who came working his arms into the little Guineafowle stableyard, with his horse knee-capped and head-stalled, in proper marching order.

" Ah, that's you, is it ? " observed Tom, recognising them through the gathering gloom of a winter's evening. " How's the horse ? " asked he.

" All is serene, sir ! " replied Tights, with a sort of military salute, throwing himself jockeyways off his horse.

" All is what ? " muttered Tom, who had not got the last London phrase.

" Well," said Tom, following Tights into the stable, " I shall want you to dress me in half an hour or so."

" By all means, sir," replied Tights, who had been imbibing on the road, and was obligingly drunk.

" Your things, and my things, and the stable things are somewhere," observed Tom, whose fly-load of luggage had not been all for himself, though he had certainly brought as many clothes as would serve a moderate man a month.

" All is serene," repeated Tights, lurching up to the horse's head.

Tom, puzzled at the phrase, then returned to the family circle in the parlour, where his quantity of luggage was undergoing discussion, raising the important speculation how long he was going to stay.

" I hope you find everything right and comfortable for your horse," observed Guineafowle, as Tom entered, adding, " I wish, though, you had brought a couple with you, as then we might have hoped for the favour of a

Tights.

longer visit ; for really it's due to oneself to get as much hunting as ever one can before Christmas."

" It is," assented Tom, who had just as much taste for the thing as Guineafowle. " However," said he, " I have a very excellent groom—a Melton man—who tells me he has a most wonderful recipe, by means of which he can bring a horse out every day in the week."

" Indeed," stared Guineafowle, observing, " it must be a very valuable recipe ; he must be a very surprising man."

" It's an invention of his own," continued Tom in an offhand sort of way. " The Melton men offered him no end of money for it, but he wouldn't sell—preferred dispensing it himself."

" Indeed ! " said Guineafowle. " What is the principle of it ? "

" Don't know," replied Tom—" don't know ; it's some decoction of herbs, mixed with spirit—rum, I think. But he makes it at midnight, and won't let any one come near, let alone see what it is."

Tights kept bad hours, and when found fault with used to declare that he was busy with his chemistry.

After some more forced discussion about the wonderful discovery, during which Mrs Guineafowle re-entered, showing by her anxious face that there was something wrong, our host proposed showing Tom his room—the best lofty four-poster, of course, with the usual indications of a lady's eye—where the redoubtable Tights was laying out such a multifarious wardrobe—such coats, such waistcoats, such cravats, such trousers, so many pairs of boots—that the major thought any deficiency of horse-flesh was amply compensated by the quantity of clothes. Having stirred the fire, lighted the composites, and told Tom dinner would be ready in half an hour or so, the major retired to hear of the soup calamity, and indulge in the denunciations against Shell and Tortoise we have already mentioned. Our gallant friend then proceeded to release himself from the bondage of his tight uniform, and instal himself in his green dress hunt-coat with bright buttons, velvet collar, and silk facings, and a roll-collared white waistcoat, with a yellow

silk under one. Dressing was the order of the day throughout the house. Tinkle, tinkle went the bells ; hot water
here, hot water there. One miss wanted her shoes,
another wanted her comb ; and the whisking commotion
of petticoats sounded up and downstairs and throughout
the little house. Our Tom went to work anxiously, and,
after no end of tryings-on and takings-off, alterings, and
changings, and pinchings, and tyings, and twistings, he
at length accomplished a toilet that stood the test of the
mirror ; for, being an ugly dog, of course he was corre-
spondingly vain—that is to say, in the inverse ratio,
ugly dog, great vanity.

And Tights, as he now retired from valeting him, met
Harriet, the joint-stock lady's-maid, as she emerged
from her young mistress's room, and in reply to her inquiry
what all the crumpled cravats dangling over his arm
were about, answered, with the most pompous throati-
ness—

"*F-a-i-l-yars! f-a-i-l-yars!*"

The sound of Pantile's phaeton wheels grinding under
his window aroused Tom from admiration of himself,
and caused him to put the finishing stroke to the performance by a copious dash of essence of Rondeletia into
his cambric pocket-handkerchief. He then gave his
ivory-backed brushes a final flourish through his light
hair, and, descending the little staircase, he re-entered
the parlour just as the Pantiles were subsiding into seats,
after the grinnings, and smirkings, and bowings, and curt-
seyings of coming were over. They then resumed the
operation, and Mrs Pantile's quick eye now seeing at a
glance what Laura's beautiful blue silk, chain-stitch
embroidered, flounced dress was for, by a skilful manœuvre
took a chair nearer the fire, leaving a vacant one between
the pretty blue and the silver-grey silk of mamma for
our Tom.

The major, seeing the petticoat movement, observed,
as he finished introducing Tom, that Mr Hall was a
brother sportsman who had come to have a little hunting
with his hounds ; and Mrs Pantile, who was a tolerably
skilled mouser, said to herself, as she eyed Laura, glancing
alternately at our Tom and then at her own pink tulle

drappé, " Believe as much of that as we like " ; and as
she was talking earnestly to Mrs Guineafowle about the
weather, thinking all the time what a shame it was dressing Laura out in that way instead of in a neat book-
muslin, like her sisters, the door opened, and, to Pantile's
horror, the great Billy Bedlington came sweeping the
ceiling with his head. Pan hated Billy, and Billy didn't
like Pan. Moreover, Pan thought Billy wasn't exactly
the sort of man to have to meet them, and therefore
gave Billy a very cool reception, and closed in, instead of
making room for him, at the fire.

Nor did matters mend when, on the announcement of
dinner, Tom stuck to Laura instead of offering his arm
to Miss Pantile, who consequently fell a prey to the
giant ; and Pantile, who was watching how things went
as he took Mrs Guineafowle out, doubted, if he had
known, whether even the turtle-soup could have induced
him to come. Judge then of his dismay when, after
enunciating an elaborate grace, Joshua Cramlington gave
the orthodox flourish to the tureen-cover, and the major
began apologising for the substitution of mutton-broth !
Pantile inwardly didn't believe a word about the turtle-
soup. It was just one of the major's cheap flashes that
he was always indulging in ; and he began cross-question-
ing him most severely how the thing could have happened ?
—who wrote ?—who took the letter to the post ?—whether
it was legibly directed ?—and, as a climax, who he sent to ?

This was rather a clencher, for if the major answered
" Shell and Tortoise," the murder would be out, and his
splendour thought nothing of ; so, after a moment's
hesitation—recollecting where Lord Heartycheer got his
—he boldly answered, " Painter, in Leadenhall-street."

" Indeed," replied Pantile, thinking he had heard the
name.

" Have dealt with him for twenty years," asserted the
major, " and this is the first time he ever disappointed me."

" Very unfortunate," observed Pantile, wondering he
had never heard of the major's turtle-soup parties before ;
and presently Joshua Cramlington, as if by way of adding
insult to injury, placed a green glass of punch under
Pantile's nose, when an exclamation from the major of

" No ! no ! you stupid dog ! " so startled Jos that he spilt the contents over his mistress's turban and silver-grey silk. Great then was the hubbub, and mopping, and napkining, and declaring that it wasn't of the slightest consequence, though Jos knew it would be a very different story on the morrow. However, that stopped the further supply of the punch ; and when he got the tray into the kitchen, Tights, who was making himself agreeable to the cook, moved that, as they couldn't drink it in the parlour, they should have it in the hall ; and filling glasses round, he tossed off a bumper to a better acquaintance with them all.

Mrs Hogslard and he had been speculating whether the fine London dresses would be likely to catch his young master, and affording each other such insights into their respective families as servants are in the habit of doing. There is very little that servants don't know, as any master or mistress will find if they make an unexpected descent into their receiving-rooms at meal or unexpected times. But to our story.

Cramlington's glass of punch, hastily swallowed after sundry bottle ends, coupled with the hurry of waiting and the anxieties of office, got into his head, and he nearly let the best chain-bordered porcelain down as he entered with the second course, giving Mrs Guineafowle and all parties interested in its welfare the creeps. The major looked unutterable things ; but the drink was more potent than the major's eye, and our host sat trembling as he saw the lad blinking and winking at the candles, and every now and then making a false dart at the dishes. The major always insisting upon having everything handed round by the servants, the dinner made very little progress, and Jonathan Falconer, never having " led," was of little or no use. The major sighed for the days of Clearwell, who made all things go as if of themselves. The lad presently got stupid.

The sherry signal and the champagne signal were equally disregarded, and as the major, of course, could not be so unfashionable as ask any one to take wine, the guests were soon high and dry. The boy had been round once with the sherry, making some very bad shots at the glasses, then filling bumpers, and dribbling the wine plentifully over people's hands. " Get some champagne ! " at length snapped the major, as the guests being now helped to the contents of the dishes, Joshua stood winking and blinking, and disregarding the signal.

Jos then disappeared, and finding Tights in his old quarters in the kitchen, they took another glass of punch together ; then diving into the foot-bath in the sink, where he had the wine cooling, he hurried away with a bottle. It being the finest sparkling, not to say frisky, 42s. a dozen stuff, made at the well-known champagne and foreign liqueur distillery in Lambeth, the major had especially charged Jos on no account whatever to cut the string until he had the wine in the room, well knowing that if it once got away there would be no stopping it ; and this injunction suiting the *laches* of which Jos had just been guilty, he now frantically seized a knife off the sideboard, and cutting the string as he stood behind his master's chair, *pop ! bang !* went the cork against the opposite wall, and w-h-i-s-h went the foaming fluid right into the major's hair ! What a commotion there was ! If the major had been played upon by a fire-engine, he couldn't have been wetter, while Jos, in the agony of the moment, put his thumb over the bottle-top, causing it to spirt sideways into Mrs Pantile's face.

" Get out of my sight ! Get out of the room ! Get out of the house ! " screamed the little major, rising from his chair, seizing the still fizzing bubbling bottle with one hand and Joshua with the other, whom he kicked and cuffed into the passage, while the remanents rose and offered such consolation to Mrs Pantile as a lady in a new black-watered—now, alas ! champagned—silk required. Great was the mopping and rubbing and patting and drying again.

At length, having done all they could, the guests resumed their seats, and Mrs Guineafowle sent Jonathan Falconer to get Harriet to come in and wait. This she did so ably that when the major returned, after locking Cramlington up in his bedroom and changing his own wet upper garments, he found Pantile leading the charge against men-servants in general, vowing they were nothing

like women for waiting—an opinion in which Billy Bedlington heartily concurred, adding that he would match
his Mary against any two men that ever were seen. But
though the major wouldn't admit this, attributing Pantile's preference a good deal to jealousy because he only
kept a tea-tray groom himself, he candidly admitted that
Cramlington was not quite the thing, muttering something about his " old butler, Clearwell—never used to
have any trouble "—observations that were meant more
for Tom Hall's ear than Pantile's, who was evidently on
the alert for a cavil.

However, now that they had got rid of the chill of
etiquette, and people began to reach and ask each other
for what they wanted, dinner progressed more pleasantly.
They got what they wanted to eat at the time they
wanted and not after, while Harriet subdued a bottle
of champagne very skilfully, and doled it out to Guineafowle's satisfaction. As yet he could not accord his guests
the privilege of helping themselves. The " Duke " had
had the wine handed round, and so must he. By the
time the second—but what ought to have been the third
—bottle was disposed of, and the chopped cheese had
circulated, people began to be more at their ease, especially
as they heard, by Cramlington's kickings and roarings
at the door, that the dangerous boy was in safe custody.
So the cloth was drawn, the wine and dessert set on, and
the room presently vacated by the servants. Our friends
then began to be more sociable, and to take the events
of the evening more philosophically. Pantile was the
least agreeable of the party. In the first place, he didn't
fancy being made a cat's-paw of, helping Guinea to
capture Hall ; in the second place, he had been done
out of a day's coal-leading with his horse by having to
come there to serve, as he thought, on a turtle-soup jury ;
and in the third place, he thought they had no business
to ask Billy Bedlington to meet them. Thinking to have
a cut at his pretentious host through Billy, he attacked
the latter about his hunting as soon as the ladies withdrew.

" Well, Mr William Bedlington," drawled he—for he
did not care to come the familiar " Billy "—" well, Mr.
William Bedlington, I see you still pursue the chase."

"Whiles, Mr Pantile, whiles," replied Billy, sucking away at an orange.

"Well, but don't you think you might employ your time more profitably, more beneficially, than scampering about the country after a poor timid hare ? "

"No, I don't, Mr Pantile," replied Billy firmly.

"Life was given us for a nobler purpose, surely ! " exclaimed Pantile.

"P'r'aps it may," replied Billy carelessly.

"Besides," added Pantile, "a man of your size and weight can never hope to ride up to hounds as he ought."

"P'r'aps not," replied Billy ; "but ar can glower at 'em all the same."

"Glower at 'em all the same," snapped Pantile, as Hall and Guineafowle began tittering at Billy's cool treatment of the classic. "But where's the pleasure— where's the excitement of glowering ? I thought the great enjoyment of hunting consisted in braving and surmounting the dangers and obstacles of nature."

"Ah," said Billy, "that'll be your steeplechase gents, and chaps wot want to break their necks. I go to see hounds work, not to crack my crown."

The major here tried to turn the conversation by passing the wine, and engaging Tom Hall on the military tack, expatiating on the splendour of Lord Lavender's Hussars, and hoping their regiments might be embodied together ; but Pantile, who had got up a petition against the militia, would not chime in, and, the first opportunity, was nagging at Billy Bedlington again.

"Well now, Mr William Bedlington," resumed he in his usual sneering, drawling tone, " I don't understand the pleasure of a man who can't follow the hounds going out to hunt."

"Well, Mr Pantile, that's possible enough," replied Billy, taking a back hand at the port—" that's possible enough ; but you might as well say that no one has any business at a race that can't ride one, as that no one has any business at a hunt unless he can ride to tread on the hounds' tails."

"I don't see that, Mr William Bedlington," replied Pantile, rubbing his hook nose for an idea.

R

" I do," replied Billy, now taking a back hand at the sherry.

" I don't," rejoined Pantile, looking very irate.

The major then again tried to turn the conversation by inquiring if Mr Pantile had succeeded in getting the old land hay he wanted, which led to a discussion on the price of straw, and the difficulty of getting any, all the tenants being restricted from selling, which Pan thought a foolish rule, and Guinea a wise one ; and finding that they had got on a disputed point, the major made another effort to turn the conversation by dilating on the un-punctuality of their foot-messenger with the letters, but Pantile, who had been meditating another cut on Billy, availed himself of the break to make it.

" You still have your great brown horse, I see, Mr William Bedlington," observed he.

" I have," replied Billy, with an emphasis, adding, " You did wrong not to buy him." Billy and the parson had had a hard deal, and only parted for fifty shillings.

" Well, but they say he's spavined," observed Pantile.

" Do they ? " replied Billy, adding, " As much spavined as I am."

" They say he's not good in the shafts," observed Pantile.

" Good in anything ! " exclaimed Billy, adding, " That horse can draw anything."

" Can he draw an inference ? " asked Pantile.

" He can draw a ton and a half," replied Bedlington, with a shake of his head, drawing his acre of buff waist-coat from under the table as he rose to depart. And the major, who accompanied him to the door, in order to have a few words with him about the next morning's meet, reported on his return that it was a fine starlight night, which induced the Pantiles to stay, in order that the fine hand and arm might do a little execution on the harp ; the consequence of which delay was, that it rained dogs and cats the greater part of their way home.

And Pantile declared that no power on earth should ever induce him to dine with that humbug again, and the Guineafowles unanimously agreed that the Pantiles were the most disagreeable people under the sun.

CHAPTER XXXV.

A NEW IDOL.

OUR Tom went to bed with a desperate heart-ache ; he thought he had never seen such a beauty as Laura, and how he should ever get on without her he couldn't for the life of him imagine. Angelena wasn't to be compared to her, and already he began to regard that volatile lady with other than feelings of affection.

Then the fifty thousand pounds flashed across his mind and caused him to ponder. Pooh ! he didn't believe she had it ; at all events, it wouldn't be hers for nobody knew when, and Laura was worth half a hundred of her without a halfpenny. Then it occurred to him that Laura would have money—that the major wouldn't keep hounds if he wasn't rich ; and as to his father's objection about Longwind's bill, Tom didn't see any reason why the major should take up Longwind's bill, so long as there was any chance of Longwind taking it up himself. Tom thought it showed caution rather than poverty, and liked the major the better for it.

Then it occurred to Tom that his friend Padder, who was learned in the law, being in the second year of his clerkship with Mr Habendum, had told him that heiresses' fortunes always went to their own children ; and if that was the case, Laura would be a catch, if not as great, at all events—beauty and all taken into consideration—as desirable as Angelena. Then the name of Squashington and Slumpington occurred to Tom's mind in the accommodating way that things do turn up in aid of Cupid's endeavours, and Tom began to doubt whether Laura mightn't be a better spec than Angelena. He now re-

collected to have heard old Trueboy, the cashier, and
his father discussing a city article of the ' Times,' stating
that it would take little more than fifteen years of the
existing production of gold to cause an alteration in the
relations of property of 50 per cent ; and if Angelena's
fifty thousand solid substantial sovereigns, as Major Fibs
described them, went down one-half, and Squashington
and Slumpington went up in like manner, why, then,
Laura would be the best chance of the two. Of course,
Tom, in these speculations, made no allowance for Laura's
sisters' shares, who were still at Miss Birchtwig's. Indeed,
how could he, seeing he did not know of their existence ?
though Tights had been fully informed by Mrs Hogslard,
if the punch had not driven the information out of his
head. Mrs Lard—as Tights called her—and he had not
quite made up their minds whether they should favour
the Guineafowle speculation or not, and Tights thought
he had got the length of his master's foot to a nicety.

The house clock here struck one, and Tom reverenced
the sound on account of the lady. He wondered whether
she was lying awake thinking of him. What a darling
she was ! How sweetly she smiled, and showed her
beautiful teeth as she bade him good-night, holding out
her little ungloved hand ! He would have her, come what
would. He didn't care a copper about his engagement
to Angelena ; it was quite clear she would throw him
over, if she could get any one better—why shouldn't he
do the same by her ? Jug's, the detested Jug's portrait
again presented itself to his mind, with Ruddle's " This
is the gent—the right honourable gent that's a-courtin'
of the great heiress at the barracks." Hang her ! he'd
be done with her. What business had she to ride away
with old Heartycheer, leaving him doubled up like a
gibus hat ? She didn't know but he might have been
killed.

Two o'clock found our friend in a profuse perspiration.
He had fallen asleep, and dreamt that the colonel had
called him out, and he couldn't get rid of the idea. In
his mind's eye he was being hurried on to the box of a
fly alongside of Major Fibs, while an enormous mountain
of a man, enveloped in a military cloak, assisted by the

shoulder of the fly-man, had at length succeeded in squeezing sideways into the fly, carrying a brace of ominous-
looking articles in blue bathing-dresses, whose shape too
evidently showed they were pistols. Tom was terrified,
for he had no taste for fighting ; and though he awoke
to the consciousness that it was only a dream, he felt
most forcibly that the dream might be the precursor of
reality. He thought he had better not try any tricks
on with Angelena ; and then how his heart wrung him to
think that he must give up all thoughts of the lovely,
angelic, blue-eyed beauty, who now seemed more necessary to his existence than ever ! He felt as if he had been
kidnapped.

Sleep again befriended him, and he dreamt that old
Trueboy, the bank cashier, had negotiated a compromise
with the colonel ; after giving him all the five-pound
notes in the drawer, was now shovelling the sovereigns over
the counter with a copper shovel, for him to put in a sack
which seemed to have no bottom ; for the more Trueboy
shovelled over, the more the colonel seemed to want,
till Tom, dreading the result of the operation on the
bank funds, shrieked out, " That's enough ! that's
enough ! " in a voice that completely startled himself
and sounded throughout the house. After this exploit
he slept again until aroused by Tights with his tops and
hot water.

There was unusual commotion in the house, caused
as well by the unwonted company-making as by the
preparations for the hunt and the overnight inebriety
of Mrs Hogslard, the cook. Tights and she had made a
night of it with the punch and her private bottle of spirits ;
and now, when she ought to have been up and doing,
she was tossing and tumbling about in bed with a desperate
headache. Mrs Hogslard was one of those wretched
country cooks whom everybody has had and no one
keeps ; and in a country office she was a perfect prodigy
of information concerning peoples' establishments. She
could sit behind Mrs Chatterbox, the registry office
woman's screen, and tell tales that were enough to horrify
a hearer, lest his own establishment should be laid bare
the same way—what masters prowled about the kitchens

and places where they had no business ; what mistresses
were " nasty covetous bodies," and stinted for beer or
butter, or locked their tea-caddies, and didn't allow
meat luncheons or hot suppers ; what butlers agreed with
the housekeepers, and what didn't ; who were supposed
to have false keys, and who to have been false to the
lady's-maid; from which valuable information Mrs Chatterbox—herself an old cook—would draw such deductions
as enabled her to place the intelligent " ladies and gentlemen," as she called the servants, who honoured her with
their custom, most advantageously. In return for all
this, Mrs Chatterbox used to mention Mrs Hogslard,
casually, to parties who applied in the middle of a term,
as a person " wot thoroughly understood cooking, and
had lived in most respectable families," leaving it to the
inquirers to find out why it was that so experienced a
person was out of place. And this suited Mrs Hogslard
almost as well as regular service, for she made harvest
wages, and had greater indulgences as a stranger than
she would as one of the establishment.

She had been a fortnight at the major's, and not having
had a chance of any of the house drink before, had been
unable to resist temptation, especially when instigated
by so interesting a companion as Tights.

Breakfast, however, being a much less formidable meal
than dinner, and one which most women can assist in
preparing, things were pretty forward by the time our
master of hounds had got himself into his best boots and
breeches, and arranged the loosely-tied blue silk scarf
under his buff vest, that he thought contrasted so well
with it and his green hunt-buttoned coat.

Our Tom, aided by Tights, made what he thought a
most killing toilet. After half a dozen *failyars*, he at
length accomplished a wide-extending, cream-coloured
Joinville above a pink, racehorse patterned shirt with
gold foxhead studs. He had got his thick thighs into
leathers ; while Tights, who was much given to buying
recipes (with his master's money, of course), had tried
his last guinea's worth on Tom's tops, and made them
a red-hot colour.

" Why, what an extraordinary colour you've got my

boots!" exclaimed Tom, as Tights withdrew the napkin with which they were covered.

"All is serene, sir," replied Tights, hissing as he dusted them over with the napkin—"all is serene, sir," repeated he, setting them down; "the Melton gents would give any money for such tops, but I wish they may get them, that's all."

Tom was bad to please in the matter of coats. He wanted to put on his pink, but Tights wouldn't hear of such a thing, alleging that it would be the ruin of both their reputations if such a thing was known at Melton.

"Nobody ever hunted with currant-jelly dogs," as he profanely called the major's hounds, "in pink."

The major himself wore green, as Tights knew; for he had been seeing how he looked in the major's coat, as he found it lying on the back kitchen table. Tom then proposed breakfasting in pink, and changing after, but this Tights also strenuously resisted, on the plea that it would look disrespectful to the major, first showing in scarlet, as if Tom thought he kept foxhounds, and then changing; and Tom, having a high opinion of Tights' judgment, was at last reluctantly obliged to content himself with laying the scarlet over a chair-back, and leaving the door open for all passers-by to see. Having then tried on a dark-brown duffle, and a red-brown, and a pepper-salt duffle, and a black saxony jacket, all with most liberal sleeves, at length chose the red-brown duffle as the gayest of the whole. When he got down he found the beautiful subject of his dreams ready to receive him, though, by some strange circumstance, none of the others were down. Perhaps Laura had had the first turn of the maid, who certainly had done her full justice, making her beautiful hair shine like the raven's wing, while the blue Freemantle dress stood imposingly out in a way that none but spic-and-span new things will stand. Tom was quite enchanted, and stood gaping for utterance as, having again given him her hand on wishing him good-morning, Laura proceeded to draw on a pair of new primrose-coloured kid gloves.

If Tom hadn't been a slowcoach he would have been far on the road to an offer ere Mrs Guineafowle made her

appearance with the keys. As it was, having to travel
his ponderosity through the weather, prognosticating the
severity that was to come from the mildness that had
prevailed, and travelling onwards through the mess that
frost makes of a flower garden, he had only got as far as
the approaching New Year's ball at Fleecyborough when
mamma appeared, followed by her light-haired step-
daughters at intervals, the major, who had been holding
a court-martial on Cramlington for his overnight de-
linquencies, bringing up the rear. Cramlington presently
came sneaking in with the urn and the viands, and breakfast commenced.

The major was the first to throw up, not because he
was so keen that he couldn't eat any breakfast on a
hunting morning, but because he had another project
in view, which, as he wasn't sure it would come off as he
wished, he did not like to announce, but for which he
wished to reserve a little appetite in case it should. So
he presently began trifling with his breakfast, looking
about him and wondering whether our Tom and the
smart girl on his right would make a match of it, or
rather whether the smart lady would be able to capture
our Tom. Laura, too, trifled with hers, being apparently
more intent on getting Tom what he wanted than ad-
ministering to her own gratification. One of Miss Birchtwig's urgent injunctions to her finishing pupils was,
never to eat much before gentlemen. Our Tom, considering his interesting position, the disturbed night he
had passed, and the disagreeable amusement he was about
to partake of, played a pretty good knife and fork, and
it was not until he had paid his respects to all the solids,
hot as well as cold, and made a considerable impression
on the sweets, that the musical notes of the major's gold
repeater awoke him to a sense of his dreadful situation.
He was going to hunt !—to hunt with a man who was
keener, he believed, if possible, than Lord Heartycheer ;
and the day with Lord Heartycheer had made him
wriggle about ever since, just as if his trousers were stuck
full of pins. Tom would have given anything for a frost,
but there was no such luck for him. Hunt he must, and
appear fond of it too. So, without more ado, he drained

his cup, and screwed up his courage like a man going
to a dentist's. Just then Tights appeared before the
window with the redoubtable horse, and the ladies rose
en masse to admire it—" such a love ! such a beauty ! "
—though they could only see his head and tail for the
sheet in which Tights had him enveloped.

" Y-e-a-yup ! " now exclaimed Tom from the steps of
the door, where he stood drawing on a pair of clean
doeskins—an exclamation that caused Tights to curtail
his circuit and hurry up with the horse.

" And how is he ? " asked Tom, with an air of un-
concern, though he would have given something to have
been getting off—getting off all safe, at least—instead of
getting on—" how is he ? " asked he.

" All is serene, sir," replied the slangy Londoner in a
tone of confident familiarity, as he cast a roguish eye over
his master's vacant face.

" All is serene," replied Tom, comforted by the assurance, which he interpreted into an intimation that the
horse had had the fiery edge taken off him—iced, perhaps,
as Lord Alvanley recommended Gunter to have done by
his hot one—" all is serene," repeated Tom to himself as
he dived at the stirrup, and at last getting his foot in,
with a vigorous hoist succeeded in landing in the saddle.
He then looked to the windows, and, catching Laura's
eye, received the sweetest of sweet smiles, while Mrs
Guineafowle whispered in her ear, " How well he looks
on horseback ! " And Tights, who now stood with the
sheet over his arm watching his master's departure, said
to himself, " If you can ride, I'm werry much mistaken."

CHAPTER XXXVI.

HIGH LIFE BELOW STAIRS.

HESTERCOMBE HOUSE, a tumble-down old family mansion
about five miles from Major Guineafowle's, the property
of the Duke of Gormanstone, was occupied by a gentleman
farmer, who—low be it spoken—had formerly been butler
in the family, and married the very pious housekeeper,
Miss, or, as she called herself, Mrs Holdsworthy. The
duchess, who had the upper hand, thought she could
not better mark her approbation of the very respectable
couple than by placing them upon one of the duke's farms
at a very moderate rent. Mrs Holdsworthy had been
fourteen years in the duke's service—a long time as
servants go—and having early impressed the duchess
with a sense of her extreme rectitude, she had had a
fine time of it ever since. In the accomplishment of this
most desirable end, she had been greatly aided by an
apparently very trivial, but in reality a very telling,
assistant in the shape of a large earthenware medallion,
with the words " FEAR THE LORD " upon it, which, immediately on her arrival at the castle, she suspended above
the mantelpiece of her comfortably furnished sitting-
room. This struck the duchess amazingly. She thought
she never saw anything so nice, so pretty, so proper and
becoming, and she instructed all the servants to show
Mrs Holdsworthy, who was " a very superior person,"
every respect and attention.

This was a grand thing for our housekeeper, for if
ever servants do tell of each other, except out of spite,
or when they know what they tell has been or will be
found out, this would effectually have stopped their

mouths, and Mrs Holdsworthy might have carried off half the things in the castle without ever a word being said. Not that she was at all abstemious, but she did her "spiriting so gently," and was so prudent withal that nothing but whispers ever arose. If she ever committed herself by taking anything that could be identified, she kept it long on the premises, in case it should ever be asked for ; and in one or two instances, when the duchess was inquisitive about things that had been thus put away, Mrs Holdsworthy produced them with such a sanctified self-satisfied smile that the duchess's conscience reproached her for having ever harboured the shadow of suspicion against so immaculate, so invaluable a person, and forthwith a new silk gown or a becoming shawl would atone for the impropriety.

Mrs Holdsworthy, who was a stately, commanding-looking person, kept all the inferior servants completely at arms' length—none but the second-table ones were ever honoured with her condescension. Of these, Mr Hermitage, the equally stately butler, was long first favourite, and they very soon came to terms, and agreed that as soon as they made what they thought a sufficiency, they would marry, and retire on their fortune. In due time, the amount being realised, the duchess heard with unfeigned regret of Mrs Holdsworthy's intended "change of state," though, of course, she could not be so selfish as wish to keep her to herself ; she so loaded her with presents that what with her fourteen years' "puttings away," our housekeeper had very little occasion to break into the savings bank accumulations for other than the more solid unstealable articles of furniture.

When she left the castle, which she did in her own proper *voiture*—a fe-*a*-ton, as she called it—she felt an inward satisfaction that though she had never let any one cheat their Graces, she had never missed a chance of doing so herself. She had mountains of linen—" old rags," as she called them when she put them away, but very good linen now that it reappeared after its slumber in her boxes ; china that was supposed long to have passed into that mausoleum of departed crockery, the ash-hole ; carpets, and curtains, and hangings, and covers, and brown holland, and house-flannel, and curtain-holders, and old blinds, and old screens, and old fans, and old books, and things that had been so long withdrawn from sight as to be entirely forgotten. Nothing had ever come amiss to her ; and by judicious tithing of the mattresses and feather-beds, she was enabled to furnish four very comfortable ones for herself. This had all been done by instalments, and carried out the same way by a pious niece, whom she used to have to instruct in the way she should go, and to whom, being then fit for service, she gave the " FEAR THE LORD " medal when she married.

Hermitage, too, had acted well his part ; for though he did not sport a medal, yet his great intimacy with her who did operated in his favour, and often caused the duke to attribute discrepancies in the wine account to the treachery of his own memory. So, what with his com-mission on tradesmen's bills—at least 10 per cent—presents from competitors, together with his wages—which latter, indeed, he looked upon much as a lawyer looks upon a retaining fee, or a policeman his pay—he managed to feather his nest too.

Hestercombe House, with a hundred and twenty acres, chiefly grass and turnip land, just then coming vacant, they were installed therein at such a moderate rent as would have ruined a much more active man than Mr Hermitage. He was quite a gentleman farmer, rose at eight, breakfasted at nine, and, after spelling through a second-hand copy of the ' Post '—for, like the duke, he was a Tory—he would sally forth, Norfolk spud in hand, crowned with a " drab rustic," a green cut-away coat with basket buttons, white cords, and drab gaiters, to see what his people had been about. Very pompous and consequential he was, demanding the most humble obsequiousness from the unaccustomed " chaws," who always called him the squire, though the wags christened him " Lord Hestercombe." That being done, his lordship returned to dinner, after which he would drive Lady Hestercombe out in the chay, for which purpose a draught would be laid idle.

During the winter he was a great patron of the major

and his hounds, and went blundering about the country after them on a short-tailed machiner, flattening the fences like a clod-crusher. Once or twice during the season the hounds met before Hestercombe House, on which occasion there was an elegant *déjeuner*, with the comedy of ' High Life Below Stairs ' enacted by Lord and Lady Hestercombe.

The consequence of all this was that the farm didn't answer, and from a very clean well-conditioned one, which it was when they entered, it soon became a wild, foul, weed-run place. The fallows were as green as grass, the turnips were never half weeded, while, under the old plea of ploughing them out and laying them down better, one after another he got all the old pastures turned into tillage. Mr Easymind, the agent, found it was no use remonstrating, for if Hermitage couldn't get what he wanted out of him, forthwith Mrs Hermitage ordered her fe-*a*-ton, and drove off to the dear duchess. Then in went the plough, and out went the grass ; and if ever it was attempted to be laid down again, it was only with weeds. Letting farmers plough out old pastures, on the plea of laying them down better, is very much like persevering in the game of thimble-rig, each move making the field and the player worse.

Although, of course, the major was not the greatest of the Hermitage acquaintance, still he was the greatest in the " reciprocity " line ; for, though Pantile occasionally called at Hestercombe House—as much, perhaps, to say he had called as anything else—he never took any refreshment, and always gave the Hermitages to understand it was a mere duty visit, which they need not return. Guinea, therefore, was the greatest acquaintance ; and very grateful they were for his condescension. They made as much fuss about Guinea as Guinea would make about the duke, if his grace had honoured him with a visit. Very pleasant it is, this sliding-scale of condescension, whereby we all, however humble, may hope to come in for some one's admiration. Still the Hermitages were exclusive.

Dicky Dyke, instigated by his " good lady," no doubt, had made overtures for a visiting acquaintance, which they indignantly rejected, stating their surprise at a mere livery servant thinking of such a thing.

" Things were come to a pretty pass," Mrs Hermitage said. But to our breakfast.

The cunning Guinea had made the meet at Hestercombe House for the purpose of letting Tom Hall see the estimation in which he was held ; and one of the injunctions he laid on Billy Bidlington, as he saw him to his dog-cart after dinner, was to go Hestercombe House-wards home, and tell old Hermitage that young Mr Hall, the banker's son, would be out. Now there wasn't a name in the country so prized as that of " Hall " ; for old " Sivin-and-four " issued his own notes ; and Christmas, with its disagreeable concomitants then coming on, made people regard the greasy thumb-marked old things with additional affection. Indeed, the very name of Hall acted beneficially on Hermitage, for he had about got to the end of his tether, and couldn't see his way to any more money. Rent, of course, he gave himself no uneasiness about ; but he was behindhand with his labourers' wages, and certain malcontents in the township had begun to be inquisitive about the application of the highway rates, just as if highway rates were not the special emolument of the party undertaking the collection of them, and seeing to the couping of the field-stones into the cart-ruts !

Hermitage, therefore, rejoiced at the interruption that brought him from his nightcap of brandy-and-water to the door, at what, to a dun, he would have called an unseasonable hour of the night ; and Billy, having delivered his message, and declined all further nourishment, Hermitage hurried back to tell his " missis " what awaited them. She had been getting things up on a medium scale of gentility, for she wasn't sure that repetitions to the same audience—Bolus, the doctor ; Waddleton, the retired flax-dresser ; Bushel, the corn-factor ; Ribs, the butcher ; Felt, the hatter ; Buckle, the saddler ; and others of a like calibre—did them any good.

Mr Hall coming made it quite a different case, and she was up betimes in the morning, looking out the best ducal " rag " of a tablecloth, with napkins, or rags of napkins, to match, and set Hermitage to polish up the

richly-chased, Louis-Quatorze-T.-Cox-Savory-plated tea
and coffee service that Mr Epergne, the silversmith, had
presented them with on their marriage, over and above
the 10 per cent Hermitage had on Epergne's bill. Very
busy and bustling Mr and Mrs Hermitage were, far
busier than ever they were at the duke's, where they used
to command instead of work.

And now, leaving them for a while toasting, and cake-
making, and buttering, and bread-slicing, and ham-
cutting, and egg-picking, and jelly-ejecting, and preserve-
opening, we will suppose our friend Tom and the major
jogging along to the meet—the major with a horn at the
saddle of his carriage-horse hunter, all spruce and *cap-a-pie*.

"We must go in and see old Hermitage and his good
lady," observed the major, as if the idea had suddenly
struck him. "Excellent man, the Hermit ; wife seen a
great deal of good society—quite tip-top, indeed—very
intimate with the duchess," the major sinking the how,
and treating it as a question of equality, or, at all events,
of visiting.

"With all my heart," replied Tom, who was glad of a
reprieve, however short, from the hunt ; not that his
horse was troubling him much, for, independently of his
naturally soft sluggish disposition, Tights had him put
on a very reduced allowance of corn, having arranged
with one of those pony-keeping, light-cart-owning scamps,
with which most countries are infested, to take whatever
Tights could spare, or rather "prig." The horse was,
therefore, far from fractious, quite a different animal to
what he was on the Silverspring Firs day, and Tom and
the major trotted along very pleasantly, admiring their
breeches and taking care of their boots.

"Ah, here we are," at length exclaimed the major,
as an old stone-roofed, mullion-windowed mansion, with
massive chimneys, now peered above the trees, and
Jonathan Falconer was seen with a slightly formed circle
round his little hounds in the last remaining grass field
before the house. It was a sad picture of desolation. The
carriage ring had long been obliterated, and large docks,
thistles, and coltsfoot grew up to the polished steps of
the portico. The entertaining rooms in front had long

been dismantled, but a peep through the partially hoarded window disclosed the marble chimney-pieces and crimson-and-gold paper of the dining-room, now bagging and mouldering about the damp walls. It had been a good and hospitable mansion once—too good and hospitable, perhaps—but the names of the feasters were almost forgotten.

The Hermitages only occupied the kitchen and back part, Mrs Hermitage making what used to be the breakfast-room into a parlour. She was always " going " to furnish the once gold-papered drawing-room, but she never made any progress that way, having now no castle to draw upon for the needful. They attributed the deficiency to the repeal of the corn laws, though we question that an eighty-shilling fixed duty would have enabled our friend to furnish out of the profits of his farm. However, it served as an excuse, it never doing for a man to blame himself for his misfortunes.

No one, to see Mrs Hermitage, would imagine for a moment that she had ever been anything but a would-be fine lady, so thoroughly unoccupied and disengaged was she. It was capital to see a woman who had been up before daybreak, putting out this, putting away that, opening out this, shutting up that, and who, at the last moment, was making bread and butter and scolding her solitary farm-servant, all at once whip off her apron and throw herself into a *chaise longue* (stuffed, we are sorry to say, with Gormanstone Castle hair), and subside, ' Post ' in hand, into the elegant unconcerned lady of fashion. Indeed, she pretended to blink and be taken by surprise, as her white-breeched husband came ushering our great master of hounds, followed by his hoped-for son-in-law, into the little parlour, whose crackling wood-and-coal fire threw a cheerful radiance over the pictures, fans, and stolen finery around.

" Oh, Major Guineafowle ! is it you ? " exclaimed she, recovering her vision, and tendering him a turpentiney gloved hand. " I declare I quite forgot it was a hunting morning, though," simpered she, sighing, as she placed the ' Post ' behind a china monster on the mantelpiece, " I've been so dreadfully shocked at this 'orrid business of poor Lady Florence Mayfield's that I haven't been myself since I read it. Poor thing ! to think of her making such a match ; knew her so well—nice, mild, modest, unassuming thing. However, I 'ope this will be a lesson to all mammas, how they let these nasty, intriguing, for-eignering chaps come about their daughters—just as if there weren't English music-masters, and plenty too, without them. But won't you introduce me to your friend ? " continued she, sighing heavily again as she looked at our Tom, who all this while had been standing, mouth open, lost in astonishment at the great society he was getting into.

" I was going to do so," bowed old Flexible Back, who had held Tom by the button for this purpose.

" Any relation of Sir Binjimin 'All's ? " asked she, half of Tom and half of the major.

" No, I believe not," replied the major ; " Mr Hall, great banker at Fleecyborough," the major in turn now making the best of our Tom.

" Come, let's have breakfast ! " growled Hermitage, giving the little hand-bell a hearty flourish, as if to drown his wife's loquacity, who, he feared, might mar a little project he had conceived for getting our Tom to assist a bit of his infirm paper through the bank. " *Breakfast !* " repeated he, as the perspiring damsel answered the summons ; and Mrs Hermitage, motioning our friends to be seated, observed with a sigh, as she stroked down her dyed-green satin, that they would have had breakfast in the large room if she had known they'd been coming. But Hermitage, knowing it was no use trying the gammoning tack on before Guinea, who was in the same line of busi-ness himself, handed a piece of biscuit out of his green coat-pocket to his wife, as a polite intimation to hold her tongue. Meanwhile, Tom, not feeling quite at home in such exalted society—a lady whose nerves were un-strung by the elopement of an earl's daughter,—began to fidget about the room, pretending to stare at the knick-knacks, ornaments, and pictures, that were profusely scattered around, Mrs Hermitage being now under no fear of any of the castle people coming at this early hour and catching them.

S

" Ah ! that's a portrait of dear Lady Gertrude,"
observed she, as Tom halted before a coloured lithograph
of a pretty girl feeding chickens out of a basket, with a
lamb in a blue ribbon by her side. " That's a portrait
of dear Lady Gertrude," repeated Mrs Hermitage with a
sigh, for she was a great sigher. " Poor thing, I really
think I must have it removed," observed she to her
husband, " for the sight of her recalls such painful recollections. Poor thing ; did you know her, sir ? " to our
Tom, who was thinking she was not nearly so pretty as
Laura.

" No," replied Tom, who did not aspire to such distinction.

" Made an unhappy match, poor thing," sighed Mrs
Hermitage ; " married Captain Rainbow, the great lady-
killer—dessay you've 'erd of him. I strongly advised her
off, but girls will be girls, Mr 'All," sighed the lady, as she
adjusted a profusion of mosaic manacles up her fly-
away sleeves.

" And how's the duchess ? " asked the major, as if they
were all as thick as thieves.

" The duchess is pretty well—at least, as well as ever
she is at this time of year," replied the lady ; " subject
to a little cold and irritation of the mucous membrane ;
and that reminds me, my dear," added she, turning to
her ponderous badly booted husband, " I shall want the
fe-*a*-ton to-morrow or next day to drive over to the
castle," adding to the major, " she takes it unkind when
one doesn't go over, though the days are so short that
it's not very convenient, though I always say when one's
in one's cage (carriage), it doesn't make much matter
whether one goes five miles or ten " ; and as she was
proceeding in this strain—rather raising than lowering
the steam of her flash—our friend again dived into his
pocket, and handed her a larger piece of biscuit than
before. She took the hint this time, knowing she would
" catch it " if she didn't, and again addressed herself to
our Tom, who had brought himself to bear upon the
portrait of another young lady in crayons, with the name
Matilda below.

" That's a sweet pretty face, Mr 'All, isn't it ? " asked

the lady, advancing towards it ; "that's a very charmin' person—Lady Matilda Overton, wife of the sixth Lord Overton of Overton Castle—only a baron, but a very good sort of man—wish I could say as much for the 'usband of this one " (pointing to a companion picture)— "this is Lady Overton's sister—Lady Jane Baconface ; married Sir John Baconface—never had a 'appy day since ; poor thing—uses her shamefully. I'm sure I often and often shed tears for her, poor thing," said Mrs Hermitage, emitting a deep sigh as she spoke.

The further discussion of the aristocracy was here interrupted by the bouncing in of a great buxom-looking dairymaid in a wide-sleeved silk gown (one of Mrs Hermitage's cast-offs, given in part wages), with a trayful of the good things that Mrs Hermitage and she had been preparing ; and after kicking the door to behind her, she proceeded to clatter them about on the table, just as she would clatter the plates of cabbage and bacon at the chaws' dinner—a noise that enabled Mrs Hermitage to apologise to Tom in an undertone for the "absence of their man, who was busy in the stable—the depressed state of the agricultural interest not allowing of their keeping a reg'lar flunkey."

And Guineafowle, seeing how nobly they had responded to his notice, began cackling and complimenting his host and hostess on the display, observing "that they must be expecting the Duke and Duchess of Gormonstone, or some great guns of that sort. They surely would never think of making such a spread for a mere master of hounds like himself " ; and receiving the assurance that it was all in honour of him, he set his flexible back a-going so briskly that it looked as if it would never settle again ; but when it did subside, and he got himself into a chair on the right of his elegant hostess, he set-to upon the provender in a way that looked very like having saved his own breakfast at home. Tom, too, did pretty well, considering he had taken as much as he meant for that meal at Carol Hill Green, and that he was desperately in love also. Those little episodes of life, however, never interfered with our Tom's appetite.

The meal was now interrupted by the clatter of a

horse, and the passing of a man in a macintosh and ante-gropolos boots, on a badly shaped, badly clipped, mouse-coloured hack.

" Oh, here's old Bolus ! " exclaimed Hermitage, beckoning him in through the window ; " good man—very respectable man," added he, propitiating his guests in his favour.

" Quite agree with you—quite agree with you," bowed old Flexible Back nearly into his cup—" very respectable man—very useful man in a country ; people can get on much better without lawyers than they can without doctors."

" And here's another man we can do badly without—Ribs, the butcher," exclaimed Hermitage, as that fat, round-faced, rosy-gilled functionary came shuffling past on a flea-bitten grey.

Having hanked their horses on at the door, in the independent way these worthies dispose of their quadrupeds, they now came rolling into the house, as if it was an inn or their own.

" What'll you drink ? " asked Ribs as they stamped along the passage.

" Thank you, I'm not dry," replied the doctor mildly.

" Hoot, ye brute beast ! d'ye nabbut drink when yeer dry ? " growled the butcher.

The doctor, like most country doctors, was humble and meek, for he had a terrible rival in Mr Digitalis, the union one, who charged less than himself ; but Ribs, who was well-to-do in the world, and, moreover, had Hermitage deep in his books, was quite the hail-fellow-well-met, nodded to Guineafowle, and joked Hermitage about his farming, observing that he must grow his turnips for pickling instead of for feeding cattle upon—they were so small. Guineafowle, on his part, not owing Ribs anything, and caring very little whether he came out with his hounds or not, took him very coolly, expending any little condescension he had to spare from Mrs Hermitage upon the doctor. To the lady he was most complimentary and attentive ; so much so, indeed, that it was well Mrs Guineafowle was not coming her *quondam* maid Emma Springfield over him through the keyhole.

He praised Mrs Hermitage's looks, and praised her dress, and praised her figure, and admired her multitudinous armlets, and spoke well of everything on the table, from the muddy coffee to the folding of the coroneted napkins, which, he said, were got up in a style infinitely superior to the work of the generality of servants of the present day. Mrs Hermitage, not liking this near approach to the " shop," especially before Ribs, who served the castle, and might tell of the coronets, turned the conversation by asking our Tom if he had been at any of her Majesty's balls the last season, which very much flattered our friend that he should be even thought of for anything of the sort. Finding he had not, she expatiated on their surpassing splendour, strongly recommending him not to miss an opportunity, and even hinting that she could get him to the palace.

Hermitage, too, availed himself of the change of partners for drawing Guinea into a discussion on the corn laws, and the impossibility of farmers going on without a very great reduction of rent—a proposition that did not altogether suit our distinguished friend ; for though he was quite ready to admit that he had been robbed and plundered by the million, and that things had gone quite contrary to what he anticipated when he ratted from the Tories, yet, as a now liberal landlord, he was not for taking more on himself than he could help.

Hermitage, however, was urgent and importunate, hoping, perhaps, to enlist Ribs, who was now at the blue-bottled spirit-stand on the side-table, in his favour ; but Guinea, not relishing the discussion, took advantage of the movement in the room for looking out of the end window on his hounds ; and observing that punctuality was the politeness of princes, he made a series of most condescending salaams to Mrs Hermitage as he shook her by the hand, and sallied forth.

CHAPTER XXXVII.

A DAY WITH THE MAJOR'S HARRIERS.

OUR Tom and the major having remounted their horses and simpered their adieux to Mrs Hermitage, waving her lace-fringed kerchief at the breakfast-room window, now sought the patient Jonathan Falconer, who was moving his little hounds to and fro and round about the dockeney thistly pasture, wondering whenever his master and Co. would come. Since our friends entered the house the field had increased by Mr Seton, the self-taught veterinary surgeon, mounted on a woe-begone, iron-marked, white Rosinante, that looked for all the world as if he kept it to try experiments upon ; by Mr Dweller, the auctioneer, who, having ferreted out Guinea's early career, had the impudence to talk of him—over his cups, of course—as a brother chip—" one of us " ; by Mr Ginger, the horse-coper, on a finely shaped antediluvian brown, that he complimented by calling " the colt." Mr Drumhead and Mr Ribgrass, the cattle-jobbers, too, had turned up in their baggy drab overalls and sack-like macintoshes, just as if they had been seduced from the road by the sight of the hounds, though in reality they had both started from home with the intention of having a hunt, it being observable that hare-hunting is a good deal pursued on the sly, few people going out, or professing to go out, for a regular day, but pretending to cut in for a game of romps, just as they would for a rubber of whist at a card party. Mr Vernal, the market-gardener, too, was there ; also Mr Elbows, the architect's apprentice, with a long tin plan-case under his arm ; and Mr Tapper, Mr Sweater's clerk, who had come that way round with a writ in his

pocket to serve on Giles Sloper, the farmer. Altogether
there were fifteen or sixteen horse, pony, or rat men—
an unusually large field for the major—and their united
cavalry might be worth fifty or five-and-fifty pounds.
The major, with our Tom on his right, now approached
them, and having acknowledged Falconer's hoist of the
cap, proceeded to pay his respects to the field.   The
day being fine, and the news having spread that the great
Mr Hall, the banker's son, would be out, half the neighbouring village of Codgerley had come down to have a
look at the reality of a name that was so familiar on their
five-pound notes, just as one would go to have a look at
Mr Matthew Marshall of the Bank of England if he would
be kind enough to parade himself at Charing Cross.

Very gratifying to the major must have been the
respect our Tom saw him receive, as well from horse as
foot. How gracious and condescending old Flexible Back
was in return. How he sky-scraped and bowed and bent
forward to the raisings and touchings of hats, the curtsey-
ings and good-mornings of the petticoats ! No election
candidate, primed by the subtlest " Gents, one, &c.,"
ever so thoroughly identified himself with a constituency
as did our major with the good people around. He had
a word to say to every one, and said it neatly too, instead
of blundering like Colonel Blunt, calling Mrs Stack Mrs
Hen, or Mr Broadcast Mr Turnipfly, but sent each shot
right home to the bull's-eye, showing how infinitely
superior—in tact at least—the militia are to the regulars.
Being a great man for cheap favours, and never for-
getting any he had conferred, he had now a favourable
opportunity for calling them over, which he proceeded
to do as soon as his punt-hat got settled on his head,
after replying to the salutes of Seton, and Ginger, and
Drumhead, and Ribgrass, and Vernal, and Tapper, and
Elbows, and his profane brother, Dweller, who, it might
be observed, was the most humble and subservient of the
whole.

" Well, Mr Vernal," said the major, resting his whip
on his thigh like a field-marshal's baton, " I hope you
got the Italian ryegrass seed I sent you safe ? "

" Thank you, major ; yes, I did," replied Vernal,

who had long ago acknowledged the receipt in writing,
and expressed his obligations for the quarter of a bushel
on three several occasions.

"Glad of it," replied the major pompously ; "hope
it will do you a vast of good." Then turning to Seton,
he said, " Well, Seton, how are you ?—child keeps better,
I hope ? " The major had given the child, who had a
sore hand, an outdoor ticket for the infirmary a year and
a half before.

" Nicely, thank ye, major," replied Seton, with another
touch of his greasy hat ; but, without waiting for an
answer, our friend had passed on to Drumhead, to whom
he had once sent word that some stray cattle had got
into his field.

"How's Mr Drumhead ? " asked he. " Hope he's
well." Then, without waiting for an answer from him
either, he proceeded, " Hope you've had no more trespass
—monstrous disagreeable thing trespass—no knowing
what complaints stray cattle may have, is there, Seton ?
By the way," continued he, now addressing Mr Ribgrass,
" you once admired my gooseberries—shall be most
happy to give you some cuttings " ; and so the major
went on through the field, finishing off with the ladies,
who he coupled with their cats, kittens, and children.

But it is time we had a look at the hounds. Here
they are : two, four, six, eight, nine—nine couple and
a half of by no means bad-looking little wrigglers. A
happy medium between the old psalm-singing potterers
of former days, that a hare seemed really to think were
playing with her until all of a sudden they got her by
the back, and the flying, dwarf foxhound hare bursters
of modern times.

" And how do you like my hounds ? " asked the major,
pointing them out to Tom, adding, " There's as neat a
pack of hounds as any in England—in the world, perhaps
—bred with the greatest care and attention—regardless
of expense. I'm quite of the great Lord Chesterfield's
opinion, that what's worth doing at all, is worth doing
well, and I've always said I wouldn't keep hounds if I
couldn't keep them well. This is my six-and-twentieth
season—six-and-twentieth season," repeated he. " Long

time—very long time to keep hounds without a subscription—believe Heartycheer and oi have kept hounds
longer without subscriptions than any two men in the
kingdom. There's a lot of game 'uns," said he, as the
lively little animals began baying and frolicking under
Falconer's horse's nose. " Move them on a little, Falconer
—move them on a little, and let Mr Hall see them—Mr
Hall understands hunting—no man better. Now, there,"
continued the major, " are a pack of what I humbly say
hounds ought to be. Only a short pack out to-day—a
good many lame ones—obliged to economise at the
beginning of the season—but there are hounds here that
would do credit to any pack—the great Sir John Dashwood
King's himself, who was reckoned the great improver of
harriers, introducing the present pushing breed in lieu of
the tedious exactness of the old psalm-singing sort. The
late Lord Sondes of Rockingham Castle gave Sir John
seven hundred guineas for his hounds—a large price—
but they were worth it, and so are any well-established
pack, such as his or moine," the major wishing any one
would offer him half, or a quarter the money, and let
him be done with them altogether.

This, to Tom, as good as a Greek lecture, was here
interrupted by a fustian-clad, poacherified-looking scamp,
with a red cotton kerchief twisted carelessly round his
scraggy neck, stepping up to our master, with a touch
of his foxskin cap, and muttering something, which
caused our friend to exclaim, " Oh, ah—you're the man
who took Violet to Mr Bluffield's the day she was kicked,"
observed Guineafowle aloud, now diving into the right-
hand pocket of his white cords, and fishing something
out (a fourpenny-piece), which he slipped in an un-
ostentatious sort of way into the ready hand of the
applicant, observing, in an undertone to Hall, as he
turned his horse away—

" How true Lord Petre's observation to Delmé Radcliffe was, that a master of hounds will never have his
hand out of his pocket, and must always have a guinea in."

" It's a vast to give for a job of that sort," observed
Tom, who thought a shilling would have been enough.

" Keeps things pleasant," replied Guineafowle, raising

his eyebrows, and pouting his lips — " keeps things
pleasant," repeated he. " There's no hunting a country
with any degree of comfort unless you are liberal with
your money. A guinea's badly saved if you're to be
talked of as a shabby fellow," added he, with a curl of
his nose and a toss of his head.

" He must have plenty of money," thought our Tom,
and thereupon the Laura funds rose considerably.

" You remember the story of old Hanbury and the
Hertfordshire farmer, don't you ? " asked the proposed
papa-in-law.

" No," replied Tom.

" Oh yes—in Radcliffe's ' Noble Science,' " rejoined
the major, who thought everybody must be as well read
in that work as himself.

Tom stared, and shook his head, never having heard
of it.

" I'll tell it you, then," said the major, seating himself
consequentially in his saddle. " Old Hanbury, you know,
was a great brewer in London, and hunted Hertfordshire
many years—as many as I've done this country, and more
p'r'aps—with a subscription, though ; and he used to
send the farmers who walked him pups, or received
damage from the foxes, presents of porter—' Hanbury's
Entire,' as it is called—which kept all things right. However, one year the porter was forgotten, and the worthy
master received the following anonymous reminder—

> " How can you expect the foxes to thrive,
> When they have no porter to keep them alive ? "

A story that was received by our Tom with all the honours.

The great Billy Bedlington now appeared at the field
gate, having been round his farm to see all things straight ;
and the major, knowing that Billy would soon read the
riot act if he was kept waiting, pulled out his watch, and
observed that it was time to throw off.

" But first," said he, addressing the foot-people, who
were preparing to strike across the fields for the well-
accustomed pasture, " let me entreat of you to be quiet
and orderly. No person can be more truly happy to

contribute in any shape or way to your gratification or amusement. I'm not one of your stiff-backed aristocrats who think the world was made for none but themselves ; on the contrary, I feel great pleasure in seeing you all out with my hounds, but you must be aware that mobbing and shouting and disorderly conduct only tends to mar your own sport and diversion, and——"

An oration that was cut short by the mob bustling away, one long unshaved monster exclaiming—

"Ay, ay, 'ard man, we knaw arle that—better gie us a trifle to drink."

The major then giving old Falconer a nod, that worthy whistled his little animals together, and moved towards the gate, followed by the major, with our Tom on his right, to whom he began expatiating on the merits of the horse his huntsman was riding—said huntsman looking as little like the overnight footman as did the horse look like the carriage-horse Tom had seen in company with the one the major was on, drawing the fair cargo in the streets of Fleecyborough.

Billy Bedlington having moved his elephantine horse a little from the gate, to allow the hounds to pass, now took the vacant place on the major's left, and mutual salutations being exchanged, with inquiries how Billy got home, the major proceeded to consult him where they should try first.

"Oh why, I should say Mr Hermitage's aquatic plants —that he calls turnips—would be as likely a place as any this mornin'," replied Billy.

"The ship are in there, sir," observed Falconer, with a touch of his cap.

"Sheep are in, are they," repeated Billy, adding, "Then go to Rushmede Bottoms."

"Rushmede Bottoms!" exclaimed the major ; and forthwith Jonathan Falconer's shoulders began bobbing responsive to the order, and with a "Come along, hounds, come along," he turned down Blobbington-lane, along which there was presently a fine splashing and floundering, and stone-scattering and noise.

"Gee!" cried one sportsman to his horse ; "Hee!" cried another ; "Hold up!" roared a third ; "Rot ye!"

exclaimed a fourth, cropping and sticking his solitary
spur into his bran-fed beggar's side, " ye're not tired
already ? "

Then came Mr Hermitage, astride a wretched fiddle-
case-headed, collar-marked, mealy bay, sticking his legs
out as though he meant to catch all the gate-posts in the
country.

When the stringing cavalcade reached Rushmede
Bottoms, the peculiarities of the chase began to mani-
fest themselves, for instead of being marshalled in a
corner, with standing-still orders, till the wild beast got
away, each man was invited to exert himself in whipping
it out of the gorse-bushes and rushy patches with which
the pastures abounded, while the foot-people, now breaking rails and pulling out hedge-stakes, scattered far and
wide on similar errands. The major acted more as super-
intendent-general and *cicerone* to our Tom, in which office
he was assisted by Hermitage, the two pointing out to
Tom the various points and remarkable features of the
country, and expatiating on the marvellous runs they
had seen from Skyline Clumps, Heathery Grove, and
Loosefish Hill. Just as the major was in the middle of
one of his yarns, the hero of the fourpenny-piece held up
his fur cap, and the field started convulsively, as if about
to encounter a lion.

" Put her away without a view ! " exclaimed the
major authoritatively, and as Falconer drew his hounds
one way, and the man of the cap went the other, many
of the gallant sportsmen sat in nervous trepidation, some
of them wishing they hadn't come, others that it was
well over. Our Tom, thanks to Tights' curtailment of
his horse's corn, had been a good deal more comfortable
than he was on the Silverspring Firs day, with Lord
Heartycheer's hounds, but now that the fatal moment
for action had arrived, the agonies of his former enjoyment rushed back upon his recollection with horrid vivid-
ness, and he would have given something to have been
getting off his horse at the end. However, there was no
help for it ; and with twinkling eyes he watched the
knowing poacher's extended staff and stealthy stride as
he crouched for pussy's form. He pokes the place, Tom

" Put her away without a view ! "

and field expecting to see her start away like an arrow
from the bow. Wrong for once ! There's nothing in,
and roars of laughter announce the fact.
" What a go ! " shouts Drumhead.
" What a sell ! " exclaims Dweller.
" Stupid feller ! " roars Tom in considerable relief,
adding, " You're a pretty feller to find a hare."
Find or no find, the gentleman in question was one of
the best hands in the country, and as any gamekeeper
within a circle of ten miles could testify.

This *contretemps*, however, having got all heads up, and
the bottoms being pretty well tried, at least all the parts
ever used by a hare, our major drew his horn from his
saddle, and tweet-tweet-tweeted to some of the wide-
ranging beauties at a distance.

The forces being collected, a council of war was now
held as to where they should go next, each man advocating
a visit to his neighbour's farm. Drumhead was sure
they would find immediately at Ribgrass's ; Ribgrass
assured them there hadn't been such a thing as a hare
seen upon his farm since September, and proposed instead
that they should go to Mr Dweller's, at Noddington,
where they had such capital sport last time. Dweller,
who had a nice crop of turnips that he didn't want
mashed, to say nothing of a good take of seeds that he
didn't think would be improved by the antics of such
cavalry as he now saw around him, advised that Mr
Heavycrop's, at Beanlands, would be more likely ; but
Heavycrop having already intimated that they came
rayther too often, and moreover wanted some oat money
of Guineafowle, which it wasn't quite convenient for
Guinea to pay, our master thought, perhaps, they had
better not go—alleging " that it wasn't right, as Heavy
wasn't out." In truth, the major, though extremely
popular according to his own account, hadn't it all his
own way as he wished it to be inferred. In this dilemma,
Bleaberry Common was suggested, and produced a burst
of assent from the farmers present—Tapper, Seton, Elbows,
and suchlike, of course, not caring whose land they went
upon. Bleaberry Common was then the word, and forthwith Falconer's cap and shoulders resumed the place in

front of the crowd that they had occupied down Blobbington-lane. Bump, bump, splash, splash—whip, spur, hec,
gee, hec—the field followed as before. All were now in
high spirits, for going to Bleaberry Common was like all
putting into the lucky bag to take their chance, instead of
being invidiously singled out for a trampling match, the
hare being as likely to select one man's land as another's.
So our friends spread themselves industriously over the
common, flopping and hissing, and shoo-shooing at everything that came in their way. Still no puss responded
to their noises, and Tapper and Vernal had both looked
at their watches to see if their time wasn't "hup," and
Drumhead feared he "must be goin'," when a terrific
yell, as if some gentleman had suddenly encountered the
devil, startled the field, and, looking ahead, a hare was
seen going away at a pace that looked as if she would
never be caught.

"Hoop! hoop! hoop!—screech! screech!—yell!—
tallyho!" mingled with the twang of Jonathan's horn,
and the shrill tweet of the major's rent the air; and, as
these noises gradually died out, the musical notes of the
little hounds rose and swelled on the breeze like the
melody of musical glasses. They clustered like a swarm
of bees.

"There!" exclaimed the major, pointing them out to
our now trembling Tom, as the hounds bustled away
with the scent—"there," repeated he, "ar'n't they like
a lot of gallant fellows, who, when they engage in an
undertaking, determine to share its fatigue and dangers
equally amongst them?"—a piece of Beckfordism that
was lost on Tom, who was fully occupied with his horse.

"Hold hard! and let Mr Hall take his place!" exclaimed the major to Tapper and Elbows, who were
having a trial of speed with their hack-horses, regardless
of the hounds. "Hold hard!" repeated he, frowning at
them, as he hustled with Tom in before them.

The common being open, and the hare having run the
full length of it, our friends had some pleasant plain
sailing at starting—a most favourable thing for steadying
the nerves for future exploits—and they rode and rode
as if raspers and rivers were nothing in their way. As

they reached the end, however, and a sod boundary fence, with a line of furze along the top, obtruded its ungainly dimensions, there was a good deal of *pas* yielding politeness, and scientific explanation as to why the hare shouldn't cross it, and it was not until old Stormer popped into the enclosure beyond, and proclaimed it with his wonted energy, that our friends became sensible of the awful predicament they were in. There they were, with a fence nearly five feet high before them, with nobody knew what on the far side.

"Don't be in a hurry!" exclaimed the major—"don't be in a hurry," repeated he, as if quite ready to take it when necessary, only wanting to be convinced that the hare was on—a fact that was soon placed beyond all doubt by the pack scrambling to Stormer's proclamation, and peeling onward with the scent. "Forrard" went Warbler and Bustler, and Wanton and Frolic, and Ringwood and Clearer, and Fortune and Twister, and Lovely and Countess, and Skilful and Tickler, and Towler and Lilter—all the merry little minstrels to the veteran's summons.

Jonathan Falconer having expressly stipulated, when he agreed to be huntsman, that he was never to be called upon to leap, and no one seeming inclined to volunteer, our major, though it went sore against the grain, was compelled, in the presence of Tom, to attempt the dread barrier; so, getting his old screw by the head, he ran him at it in an irresolute sort of way, exclaiming, as he brandished his whip, "Yooi, over he goes!"

But it was no such thing. The old horse, running his nose against the gorse, wheeled short round, nearly unshipping Guinea, and the coast being now clear, the lately despised Tapper, cramming his spurs well into his sides, ran his tit at it full tilt, and in an instant Tapper and tit and writ were floundering among the sods.

"That's your sort!" roared Ribgrass, crushing onward, regardless of Tapper's danger, and his big horse, setting his great flat foot upon the writ, sent it for ever out of sight, to the temporary advantage of Sloper.

The major followed Ribgrass, loudly denouncing Tapper's mischief; and the lately pent-up field being

now released, pushed on after the streaming pack. Being
now on Mr Muttonfield's farm, with a line of gates full in
view, there was a rare display of spurring, and cropping,
and kicking, and spread-eagling, as each man pressed on
to his utmost. How they hurried and scuttled along !

At the end of seven minutes and a half, which to some
seemed an hour, the hounds come to a momentary check,
having slightly overrun the scent, and our friend Blue
Cap, the tailless cur to whom we owe an apology for our
apparent neglect, now leaves Falconer's horse's heels,
and rushing round the hounds as he would round a flock
of sheep, sends them flying to our huntsman's halloo,
who, holding them on towards the gate where " fur cap "
has pricked her, they presently strike the scent, and go
away like a pocketful of marbles. But who is so fortunate
as to see this second burst, almost as terrible as the first ?
Our memory supplies, and we think we can name them
all. If we look at the left, we shall see Major Guineafowle's punt hat and green arms working away like a
shuttle-weaver's, closely followed by Hall, with his brown
horse in a white lather ; behind whom, and rough-casting
the next man with mud as he goes, come Dweller, Elbows,
and Drumhead. On the right are Vernal and Hermitage,
going at a very " galloping dreary done " sort of pace,
while the clatter and pother farther off proceeds from
Billy Bedlington pounding up Knockington-lane, followed by Seton, Ribgrass, Bolus, Ribs, and Tommy
Coulter's young man, on a horse fresh out of the harrows.
In the distance the game Tapper may be seen persevering
on foot, leading his back-sinew-sprung horse, and trying
to coax one of Messrs Remnant and Ribbon's genteel
young men, who has slightly deviated from his course
with patterns of mourning for Lady Snuffles, out of his
hack horse in exchange.

And the mention of mourning reminds us that we ought
to be winding up with a kill, " no chase," as Nimrod
truly says, " being complete without one."

The hare dies within a stone's-throw of the Barley-
Mow beer-shop, on the Gillinghurst-road—a most convenient spot for our sportsman,—the pack pouncing upon
her in the middle of a large grass field, where she had

"TAPPER AND TIT AND WRIT FLOUNDERING AMONG THE SODS."

" clapped," as they call it, every hound getting a snatch
at her haunch, and some a mouthful of fur. Major Guineafowle, jumping and dancing about with her over his head,
would be a subject worthy of Leech himself. Falconer's
who-whoop reverberated in the beer-shop, and brought
out the landlord, with a lurcher at his heels, and a pipe
in his mouth. Every man present is ecstatic with delight.
" Give me the scut ! " cries one. " Give me a foot ! "
cries another. At length, all being satisfied in that line,
poor puss is disembowelled, and Tapper arrives just in
time to have his pasty face besmeared with her blood,
to the infinite mirth of the field.

" What superb hounds ! " now exclaims Tom Hall,
looking them over, quite delighted with his own performance.

" Ar'n't they ? " replied the major, eyeing Falconer as
he deposits the hare in the case.

" They talk about my Lord Heartycheer," continued
he, shrugging his shoulders, and tossing a sneer on one
side—" they talk about my Lord Heartycheer and the
great doings of his pack, but for regular continuous sport
I'd back mine against them—and they don't cost half
what his do," added he in a confidential tone to our Tom.

Amidst most hearty good-byes and adieux, the bulk of
the field then sheered off to the beer-shop, and the major
and Tom turned their heads towards home, all highly
delighted with what they had done.

T

CHAPTER XXXVIII.

LORD HEARTYCHEER GOES A-ROVING.

" WHICH is my best way to Fleecyborough ? " asked
Lord Heartycheer of Dicky Dyke, after the usual kennel
spell, the first non-hunting day after the Silverspring
Firs one. " Which is my best way to Fleecyborough ? "

" That 'pends upon which end of the town your lordship
wants to be at," replied Dicky, with a purse of his mouth
and a knowing twinkle of his little blue eyes. " If you
want to be at the corn-market end, your lordship must go
by Jerico Green and up Spicer-lane ; but if you want to
be at the cattle-market——"

" The barrack end," interrupted his lordship, knowing
it was no use humbugging Dicky.

" The barrack end," replied Dicky, drawing his breath
and sucking his lips—" the barrack end," repeated he,
thinking his lordship must steer clear of the Emperor of
Morocco's, in Fish-street, and get there as quietly and
unobserved as possible. " Why, I should say," continued
he, lifting his ideas as he would his hounds, " I should
say you must strike across Lingey open fields, keeping
Thorneyburn to the right, and skirtin' our cover at
Marshlaw ; then pass the windmill that stands a little to
the left of Mr Draggletaile's large white house, with a
quarry at the back, and that lets you into the high-road,
when you'll have the barracks right afore ye, without
ever goin' into the town or settin' foot on the pavement."

" That'll do," replied his lordship, adopting the idea,
adding, " Then just you see Peter, and tell him the way,
so that he may know it in case I forget."

" By all means," assented Dicky, with a touch of his

hat, as he opened the kennel door for his lordship to depart, adding to himself, as he watched him cantering up the avenue home, " Dash my buttons, but you're a game 'un ! *Seventy* years of age !—seventy years of age, 'cordin' to the census paper."

Next day but one, a couple of remarkably neat thorough-bred brown hacks were going the rounds before Hearty-cheer Castle door, in charge of a very diminutive groom, whose youth caused him to be selected for secret service ; and as if to keep up the delusion he was attired in an undress livery, dark coat and waistcoat, cream-coloured leathers, and rose-tinted tops, with a belt round his waist, and a cockade in his hat—a dress that even in London any club bow-window lounger could appropriate to the owner at a glance, and people in the country can never mistake for any but his. However, that was what his lordship called going " incog " ; and after the horses had made some half-dozen rounds of the spacious gravel ring, a quick clapping of hands, followed by the word " *Sharp !* " from an uncovered gentleman's gentleman, who suddenly appeared at the door, caused the tiger to bustle up to the steps with the horses, just as a couple of gigantic footmen threw back the portals, as if Daniel Lambert or the Durham ox were about to emerge instead of his slim antiquated lordship. He was got up with uncommon care—gay and various in his colours. A spic-and-span new black hat crowned his silvery white hair ; a wildly tied light-blue gauze Joinville coquetted with his smally pleated shirt-frill, protruding through his canary-coloured vest, which was buttoned with blood-stone buttons, and traversed with chains and watch appendage gewgaws. He wore a light-blue velvet-collared dress-coat, with burnished gold club buttons (an earl's coronet above a flying fox), and his faultless fawn-coloured leathers fell in creaseless easy lines upon his taper feet. His brown paper measure has long occupied the " H." post of honour in Anderson's back-shop. His lordship was of the Anglesey school of dressers, and was quite as great as his great original.

Thus caparisoned, with a light gold-mounted riding-whip in his primrose-kidded right hand, the gay old gentleman put his patent-leathered toe into the stirrup, and, vaulting into the saddle, ambled away like a lad going to see his first love, followed by the youthful tiger with his tongue in his cheek at the winking and nudging and laughing of the footmen. So his incognito lordship flourished through the country, drawing down the animadversions of some, and the speculations of others, as to "where the 'shockin' old rascal' was going?" But as they neither scowled nor menaced him as he passed, but, on the contrary, smiled as they touched or took off their hats to him, he flattered himself that he was considered a very respectable dignified nobleman. So he tit-upped away as gay as a lark, thinking that no one knew what he was after.

The world was well-aired ere the tramp of the noble lord's horses on the wood pavement at the barrack-gates caused the stalwart sentries to stand and stare, and the shirt-sleeved soldiers to pause in their brushing and pipe-claying operations. Mattyfat and Gape were hanging listlessly out of a window, smoking and basking in the wintry sun preparatory to lady-killing in the town ; while Stalker and Pippin, and Whopper and Spill, and others, lolled and strolled about the messroom, talking of their overnight host, his claret, and daughters, in the listless sort of way of idle wine-headachy gentlemen in general.

His lordship, who recollected the "country" as soon as they got within the gates, spurred on at a canter for the colonel's house in the corner, and reining up his steed, beckoned the lad to dismount and make for the bell on the right of the door. Scarce had the quick-footed youth applied his hand to the brass nob ere Jasper, the gigantic footman, looked down like Jack the Giant-Killer upon him, and at the same instant a rich clear voice broke out in accompaniment of a piano, putting it quite out of Jasper's power to say that his young mistress wasn't at home. In truth, she had just decked herself out in a beautiful, almost new, drab and pink shot watered silk dress, with very wide sleeves, and Irish point ones underneath, and a high chemisette of the same material, secured with French diamond studs down the front, to receive young Mr Downeylipe, son of Sir John Downeylipe, Bart., who had just joined the regiment, and on whom she purposed trying the strength of her charms.

Great was her surprise when, as she sat on her music-stool with her dress all becomingly spread out behind her, Jasper creaked up and announced Lord Heartycheer instead of the name of the newly caught cornet.

" Oh, my lord ! " exclaimed she in a perfect ecstasy of delight, " this is so kind—so unexpected—so——" And thereupon, fearing she was going too far, she applied her kerchief to her lips, while the gallant old beau pressed his own lips to the other little hand, as, half-kneeling, he humbled himself before her. And Mrs Blunt, who commanded the scene from a convenient crack in the wainscotted partition, wondered how so gallant a beginning would end.

" Won't your lordship be seated ? " asked Angelena, as the spicy old cock still kept his hold of her hand—" won't you be seated ? " repeated she, motioning him towards a cane-bottomed chair, beside which stood another quite convenient.

" How's my friend the colonel ? " asked his lordship, conducting Angelena towards the proffered resting-place.

" Pa's pretty well, I'm much obliged," replied she, seating herself. " Very well, I may say," added she, arranging her dress, and wondering whether her mother was watching.

" And Mrs Blunt ? " bowed his lordship, depositing his hat by his own chair.

" Ma's pretty well, too, I thank you," replied the fair lady, passing her little beringed hand down her Madonna-dressed brown hair.

" At home ? " asked his lordship in a tone of indifference.

" No, they're out driving, I'm sorry to say," faltered Angelena, dreading lest the colonel, who was playing skittles behind the riding-school, should make a sudden irruption for some bottled porter.

" Well done you," smiled mamma, thinking how worthy Angelena was of a chance.

" Indeed," simpered the old buck, preparing to make play. " Well, and how's the little mare ? None the worse, I hope, for her canter the other day ? "

"Oh dear, no," replied the fair lady; "all the better."

"And her lovely mistress—I needn't ask how she is after it," continued the old peer, grasping Angelena's arm incontinently as he spoke.

"Oh, her mistress is quite well," simpered the lady, with a slight flourish of her cambric.

"All the better, too, I hope, for the little gallop," suggested the gay old gentleman.

"Indeed, I think I am," replied Angelena gaily, adding, "I always do feel better after a ride."

"That's right!" exclaimed the old man, his eagle eye lighting up with youthful enthusiasm. "'Gad! I think that's the neatest—the very neatest—cleverest—the very cleverest—handsomest—the very handsomest—little creature I ever set eyes on. 'Gad! I've thought, I've dreamt, I've talked of nothing but the beautiful maid and her beautiful mare ever since," continued his lordship, now feeling her arm a little lower down.

"She's a sweet little thing," observed Angelena.

"The maid, I suppose you mean?" observed his lordship gallantly.

"No, the mare," replied Angelena.

"Both!" exclaimed his lordship—"both! 'Gad! I was telling Mr Thorndyke I'd give him a *carte blanche* to buy me such a one."

"Indeed," mused Angelena, thinking her papa would accommodate him. Then she recollected he had sold the mare to Tom Hall. By a curious coincidence, his lordship's rapid thoughts now wandered to that gentleman; and as Angelena was thinking whether she could not get off the Hall bargain, he exclaimed—

"And how's your young friend, Mister—Mister—Mister —the plump brawny youth, as Somerville would say, who came out hunting with you, you know?"

"Oh, Mister Hall—Tom Hall—my father's friend. Upon my word, to tell you the truth," said she, raising her eyebrows, and speaking in a confidential energetic tone—"to tell you the truth, I've never seen him from that day to this."

"Indeed!" replied his lordship, raising his white ones

in return, with an accompaniment of the shoulders—
" indeed ! I thought he'd been your intended."

" *Intended !* " shrieked Angelena—" intended ! Oh,
heavens, no ! He's just as much my intended as you
are."

" Humph ! " smiled his lordship, wondering whether
that was artlessness or design.

" Well, but he's a useful young man—a useful young
man, and should be encouraged—should be encouraged,"
observed his lordship. " These young men are very
convenient at times—very convenient at times," added
he with a knowing leer.

" I do make a convenience of him," replied Angelena,
sotto voce ; " he's a good-natured goose."

" He seems so," said his lordship—" he seems so ; not
much of a horseman—I should say, not much of a horseman."

" Horseman ! " exclaimed Angelena. " I shouldn't like
to be his horse, I know."

" Nor I," replied his lordship—" nor I ; he fell off,
absolutely fell off—made a regular voluntary," added he,
with a slap of his fawn-coloured knee, as if such a thing
as falling off was perfectly unheard of.

" Just the sort of man to do it," laughed Angelena.

" Just," assented his lordship gaily—" just," repeated
he. He then sat silent for a second or two, eyeing Angelena
intently—her hair, her eyes, her teeth, her nose, her
complexion, her hand, her foot, her figure. " That's a
lovely dress ! " exclaimed he, taking hold of the stiff shot
silk ; " very lovely dress."

" Glad you like it," smiled Angelena.

" Charmed with it—perfectly charmed with it ! "
reiterated his lordship, adding, in an undertone, " either
with it or the wearer."

" Oh, you flatter, my lord," simpered the fair flirt.

" Not a bit of it ! Last man in the world to do anything of the sort ! " exclaimed his lordship, throwing
out his hands ; " but I've an eye for beauty notwithstanding, and yours, I must say, is of the transcendent
order. But let me see," continued he—" let me see,"
repeated he, pinching and eyeing the dress more intently ;

" it's two colours—two colours, I declare ; 'gad it's two
colours if not three, ' added he, now turning it to the
light.

" It's what they call a shot silk," observed Angelena.

" Shot silk, is it ? " repeated his lordship—" shot silk ;
well, I must say, it's very pretty—very pretty, indeed ;
but your elegant, sylph-like figure would set off anything,"
added he, relinquishing his hold, as he recollected that he
ought to be getting to his point.

" Well, now, my darling, when will you come out with
us again ? " asked his lordship hurriedly, as a stentorian
voice halloaed out, after a heavy thump at the back
door, " PORTER—TWO BOTTLES ! " which his lordship
knew could proceed from none but the ex-corpulent captain, now our corpulent colonel.

" Out again ? " shuddered Angelena, biting her lips,
dreading lest her parent should come in and spoil the
finest chance she ever had in her life. " Out again ? "
repeated she, as the flurry of petticoats from the other
side of the wainscotted partition was followed by a
gentle but protracted " H-u-s-sh ! " from the top of the
stairs.

She now pictured to herself her mamma with her
finger on her lip, and her astonished papa beating a hasty
retreat.

" Yes—out with us again ? " repeated his lordship,
pretending not to notice the interruption.

" Oh, I *should* so like it ! " sighed Angelena, clasping
her hands, and turning her bright eyes up to the ceiling.

" Well, then, say the word," replied his lordship hastily,
dreading an interruption to their *tête-a-tête*.

" I fear—I'm afraid—I——" faltered Angelena.

" Fear nothing ! " exclaimed the gallant old lord, drawing his chair close up to his fair friend's, and placing one
of her little hands between his, as if going to have a
game at hot hand with her—" fear nothing ! " repeated
he, pressing her hand most affectionately, adding, " I'll
take care of you, my little angel ! "

" Well," mused Angelena, without making any attempt
to withdraw her hand, " I should certainly like it uncommonly—the only difficulty would be about a horse,"

recollecting that Tom Hall would most likely be claiming
Lily of the Valley, which she now thought her papa had
made a mistake in selling him.

" Oh, a horse shall be no difficulty—none whatever,"
replied his lordship, throwing out his right hand; " our
people shall arrange all that—only say the word, and it
shall be managed as nice as can be."

" You're very kind, my lord—very."

" Not at all—not at all," repudiated the now impetuous
old peer.

" Indeed, but you are," replied Angelena, looking most
lovingly at him.

" The compliment's the other way, my darling—the
compliment's the other way," rejoined the old man, rising,
and giving her such a smack of a kiss as sent Mrs Blunt
spinning round on the other side of the partition, singing
to herself—

> " It's a very fine thing to be mother-in-law
> To a very magnificent four-balled bashaw."

" Oh, my lord !—oh, you naughty man !—fie for shame !
fie ! " ejaculated Angelena. " I must really have my
maid in to protect me," added she, pretending great alarm
as she adjusted her pink gauze ribbons.

" It's given you quite a colour," observed his lordship,
eyeing her now blood-mantling complexion.

" Well it might, I think," snapped Angelena, with a
toss of her head, as she stroked down her bright hair.

" You should thank me instead of being angry, my pretty
dear," replied he, not at all deceived by her pretended tiff.

" Thank you for nothing," retorted Angelena, re-
arranging her manacles, and looking down on her chemisette studs, one of which was hanging out.

" Let me put it right for you, my love ! " exclaimed
the lord, passing his hand inside the chemisette as adroitly
as a lady's-maid. Having adjusted the stud, he resumed
his seat by her side.

" Well, now, about the hunt," continued he, anxious
to get matters finally settled. " When shall it be ? "

" Hunt, indeed ! I'm not sure that I'll go, after such
rudeness," replied Angelena pettishly.

"Pooh! pooh! it'll do you a deal of good. Just look in the glass, and see what a fine complexion it's made you," retorted the peer.

"*Nonsense*," pouted Angelena. "I don't want complexions made that way. What would my ma say, do you think?"

"That her daughter is a very prudish young lady," replied the peer, again taking her unreluctant hand.

"But what would my *pa* say, do you think?" continued she archly.

"Oh, pooh! pas have no business with these matters —only for the ladies," answered he.

"But they make business sometimes," replied the young lady.

"Not yours, I should hope," rejoined the gay old Lothario.

"Don't know that," whispered the young lady, with a sly twinkle of her bright eye.

"Let us hope the best," exclaimed the old peer cheerily, who had every confidence in woman's wit.

"Well," sighed Angelena, with downcast eyes, "I suppose we must."

"Say the word, then; when shall it be?" resumed his lordship, again returning to the charge, for he was all for taking them when they were in the humour.

"Be!" said Angelena—"be!" repeated she, still dwelling on the sweet word.

"Yes, *be*," repeated his lordship boldly.

"Whenever your lordship likes," whispered the lady resignedly.

"That's right!—that's a darling!—that's a love of a girl!" exclaimed he, now encircling her slim waist with his arm. "Well, now," continued he, looking up at the ceiling, though he still kept squeezing and drawing her towards him; "let me see—Monday, Honeyball Hill— Tuesday, Rakelaw Gate—Thursday, Summerhail Tower —Saturday, Blunderfield—four good places—good as any we have. Rakelaw Gate's p'r'aps the best for a lady; but then it's a long way from here. Honeyball Hill there's always such a crowd at—nasty Beale and Brassey, and head-and-shoulders Brown, and all that set. I'll tell you

what," continued he, as if the idea had suddenly struck
him, though in reality he had been pondering upon it all
the way as he came—" I'll tell you what—how would it
do to have a quiet 'bye' to ourselves ?—meet, say, at
home—there's a litter of foxes that have scarce been
disturbed in Roughley Brake, just at the back of the
castle ; we could then throw off and finish as we liked,
without the bother and *surveillance* of a field."

" Well," mused Angelena, considering whether the
opportunities of privacy would compensate for the loss
of the distinction of having his gay lordship for a *cavalier
servante* before the country.

" I really think that would be the best way," resumed
his energetic lordship—" I really think that would be the
best way. You come quietly over, you know, with
Mr Horn."

" Mr Hall, you mean," observed Angelena.

" Ah, Hall, that's the name. I was thinking of Horns.
Not an unlikely man to wear them, I should say—he, he,
he ! " giggled his lordship, shrugging his old shoulders, as
if half shocked at what he had said.

" Mr Hall's not at home," observed Angelena, with a
prudish toss of her head.

" Not at home, isn't he," repeated his lordship briskly.
" Well, never mind ; get somebody else. I'll tell you
who," added he, " in a minute. There's my young friend
Jug—Jonathan Jug—you know him, I dare say ; of course
you do—he's in your pa's regiment, in fact. Well, Jonathan's the very man for us—nice, prudent, sensible, good-
natured little fellow. I promised his pa to call upon
him. 'Gad ! I'll go and do it directly ; and then you
and he can arrange to ride over together, and I'll have
horses and luncheon and everything ready, and we'll
have a nice quiet hunt to ourselves, undisturbed by
Brown or any of those horrors."

So saying, his lordship, raising the fair lady up from
her seat with himself, gave her a series of most impres-
sive salutes, and, laying down a couple of cards for papa
and mamma, backed, courtier-like, out of the little room,
and tripping gaily downstairs, mounted his hack, to canter
across the barrack-yard to card the proposed cat's-paw.

CHAPTER XXXIX.

ANGELENA ASTONISHES HER MOTHER.

SCARCE had Angelena finished waving her adieux through the window to the cantering-away old lord, ere mamma stood behind her in the room.

"And what d'ye think!" exclaimed the quick artful girl, turning short round on her inquisitive parent.

"Nay, I don't know!" replied Mrs Blunt, reddening up.

"*Guess,*" said Angelena in a significant tone.

"Nay," replied mamma, not venturing on the speculation women usually indulge in.

"*That I'm to be a lady,* then," said Angelena, spreading out her arms and hands on either side and dropping a very low curtsey.

"What! has he offered?" exclaimed Mrs Blunt, now in full flutter.

"*Offered!*" replied Angelena with another curtsey.

"Oh, my dear child! oh, my duck! oh, my angel! my beloved!" ejaculated mamma, hugging her daughter to her bosom, and then giving her a volley of kisses.

"*But don't tell pa,*" said Miss, with an ominous shake of her head.

"Why not, my beloved?" asked mamma, feeling it would be the death of her to keep it to herself.

"Oh, because, you see, my lord—that's to say, Lord Heartycheer—and I—I mean, Lord Heartycheer, I think, would like—indeed, I know he would prefer to—to come over to talk to papa about it himself, as soon as he and I have got matters a little further arranged, and he's——"

"Well, but you're *sure* he offered," interrupted Mrs Blunt, who well knew her daughter's imaginative powers.

" *Sure !* " retorted Angelena with a sneer—" sure," repeated she, " as if there could be any mistake about it."

" Why, you should know as well as any one," replied mamma, thinking of the number of offers she had had.

" I think I should, indeed," simpered Angelena, adding, " It's only for girls who've never had beaux to make mistakes about it."

" Well, you do 'stonish me," continued mamma, now regaining her breath with her confidence, as she thought of what she saw and heard through the crevice. " You do 'stonish me," repeated she.

" I saw it was coming," observed Angelena. " I believe he'd have offered out hunting if it hadn't been for the servants."

" What, he was very sweet, was he ? " asked mamma.

" Oh, very," replied Angelena ; " quite rapturous, in fact."

" You didn't tell me," observed mamma.

" No," mused Angelena, adding, " You see—you see, I thought it mightn't come to anything, and then you would only laugh at me, and p'r'aps feel disappointed, so I thought the best thing was just to wait and see if he took any steps."

" It was love at first sight, then," observed mamma.

" I should say it was," replied Angelena—" I should say it was. He was remarkably courteous and respectful as soon as I came up, and stuck to me the whole day, showing me the country, and getting me over the hedges and ditches and awkward places."

" He's a fine handsome man," said Mrs Blunt, thinking what a triumph it was for her daughter.

" Oh, he's a *charming* man," rejoined Angelena, thinking how severely he had kissed her.

" People talk of his age ; I don't believe he's half as old as they say," observed Mrs Blunt.

" They wouldn't think him old if they could get him," replied Angelena.

" No more they would, my darling," asserted Mrs Blunt, who was an ardent advocate of the doctrine that men are never too old to marry. " I always say," continued she, " that a man of fifty is infinitely preferable

30 3030302

30

302302302 302

to a boy of twenty, or five-and-twenty, who falls in love with every pretty face he meets, and whom no woman can be certain of till she's got him through the church. Then they get tired of their wives, and their sons come treading on their heels before they know where they are. It's an awkward thing when father and son want top-boots at the same time. That'll not be your case—and you'll be a countess, whatever happens. A countess! my w-o-r-r-d, but it will make some people stare," Mrs Blunt thinking over a select list of friends whom she would astonish with the great intelligence.

"And what will you do with Tom Hall?" she asked after a meditative pause.

"Oh, Tom may offer his fat hand to some one else. Jug says he's gone after Laura Giddyfowle, or whatever they call that great staring-eyed girl the men are all raving about."

"Ah, and Jug too," suggested Mrs Blunt.

"Oh, Jug and I will go on as before ; my lord'll arrange that—boys of his age are never jealous of those they consider their seniors. Jug's to be cat's-paw for the present—my lord's gone to see him about it, and Jug's to chaperone me over to the castle on Wednesday, after which, I make no doubt, his lordship will see pa, and arrange matters. See, his lordship has left his cards upon you," continued she, taking them up ; "so now," added Angelena, as she heard the well-known cough outside the back door, admonitory of her father's approach, "*whatever you do*, don't tell pa, if you please, for the present." So saying, she whisked out of the room, just clearing the landing with her smart dress as the colonel's great stomach pioneered the way for his body.

CHAPTER XL.

PARENTS IN COUNCIL.

" DON'T believe it—don't believe a word of it, hang me if I do ! " exclaimed the colonel, who came in in a very bad humour, having lost three-and-sixpence at skittles, when Mrs Blunt whispered him in the strictest confidence the great event of the day. " Not likely that hoary old rascal's goin' to be caught at his time o' life," continued he.

" Well, but I assure you it's the fact," replied Mrs Blunt, now speaking rather above her breath.

" Hoot, the divil ! you women are always fancyin' these things," growled he, stamping heavily with his plated high-low.

" Hush, my dear, hush ! don't make such a noise," rejoined Mrs Blunt soothingly, little doubting that her daughter, as was the fact, was now occupying her recent post of honour, listening.

" Well, well," growled the colonel, shaking his great cannon-ball-shaped head, " it makes no odds who hears what I say—I tell you, woman, it's not credible—it's not credible—wouldn't believe it if you were to swear to it."

" Well," mused Mrs Blunt, " it'll be difficult to persuade you—it'll be difficult to persuade you, I dare say."

" I know it will," growled the man of war, sousing himself on the old, hired, horse-hair sofa in a way that made it creak again ; " d—d difficult," added he, hoisting his legs up.

" Don't 'xactly see why it should, though," rejoined Mrs Blunt meekly.

" Don't ye," growled the colonel—" don't ye ; devilish

difficult to make me believe that a disreputable old dotard like that, who ought to be 'shamed to be seen out of his grave, is a-goin' to commit matrimony."

" Well, but Angelena assures me he does," asserted Mrs Blunt.

" She's mistaken, I tell ye," snarled the colonel ; " she's mistaken—doesn't know her man."

" He's offered to her certainly," replied Mrs Blunt boldly.

" Offered to her ! " exclaimed the colonel, startled at the information ; " offered to her ! " repeated he—" how, when, where ? "

" Well, he's just been here," observed Mrs Blunt, handing the colonel a card.

" Humph ! " grunted the monster, taking and eyeing it. " Humph ! what did he say ? "

" Oh, why (hem)—I wasn't (hem) present to (cough) hear 'xactly, that's to say—but (cough, hem, cough)—I know he's offered."

" Don't believe it," fumed the colonel again—" don't believe a word of it, curse me if I do."

" Well, you *may*," replied Mrs Blunt significantly.

" May believe a vast of things, if I'm fool enough," retorted the gallant officer ; " believe black's white, if I like, but I won't. I'll tell ye how it'll be," continued he— " I'll tell ye how it'll be," repeated he, raising his stentorian voice ; " you'll make a mess of it atween ye as sure as you're born—it'll be a reg'lar case of two stools—she'll never get him, and she'll lose Tom Hall to a certainty, and then I shall have to hand over the cheque for the mare, and there'll be no end of bother with the Christmas bills, and I don't know what," continued he, throwing out his right fin in a fury at the thought.

" Well, but you surely wouldn't have her throw away the chance ? " observed Mrs Blunt.

" Don't believe she has a chance. Don't believe the man has the slightest intention of anything of the sort," replied the colonel. " He's a reg'lar bad old goat— always has been—always will be. He's as wicked an old man as ever walked—don't know a worse."

" Well, but he may mend," replied Mrs Blunt, who

never despaired of the men, provided they had plenty of money.

"Mend! Damn him; he's too bad to mend—too bad for anything, 'cept a halter. Pretty thing it would be to lose Hall, with all his nice comfortable independence —'specially after the old usurer and I have talked matters over—for the chance of gettin' such an arrant old deceiver as that—a man whose very name is a by-word in society."

"Well, but Hall could be easily manished," replied Mrs Blunt; "there's nothin' bindin' there, you know."

"Nothin' bindin'!" ejaculated the colonel, flaring up —"nothin' bindin'! Is the honour of an English officer's daughter nothin'?"

"Well, but Tom may change his mind, you know," observed Mrs Blunt; "indeed, they do say he's gone to Carol Hill Green, and you may rely upon it he's not asked there for nothin'."

"Carol Hill Green, is he?" replied the colonel, staring, and dry-shaving his great chin—"Carol Hill Green, is he?" repeated he, considering how that would cut with regard to the cheque. Laura was the toast of the mess, and Tom Hall was under age, and altogether the colonel began to be uneasy, and to see things differently. If the Guineafowles caught Hall, Angelena was regularly thrown over; for Jug would never be worth looking after for any one—at least, not unless a whole row of other Jugs were disposed of. The colonel was inclined to pause. Perhaps the Heartycheer spec might be worth consideration after all.

"Well, but what makes you think he's offered?" asked the colonel in a more pacific tone.

"Think!" replied Mrs Blunt—"think!" repeated she. "Why, because, in the first place, Angelena says he did; and in the second place (cough, hem, cough), I overheard as much as makes me think so too."

"You did, did you?" replied the colonel, his blood-shot eyes staring wide—"you did, did you?" repeated he, adding, "That alters the case."

"Yes," said Mrs Blunt, "I was in our room, you see, lookin' over the washin', and I heard kissin' goin' on, so I stopped and listen'd, and distinctly heard the words,

U

'When shall it be, then?—when shall it be?' repeated several times, and then there was kissin' again; indeed, I saw it through the crack in the wainscot."

"Humph!" mused the colonel, pondering. The man was old—old certainly; but then there is no fool like an old fool, and more improbable things had happened. Might mean to reform—fresh man, though he was old, and age, after all, went more by constitution than by years; just as a horse, after a certain time of life, was to be judged more by his legs than his teeth. Fine thing it would be if Angelena did get him. What a dashing countess she would make! And he himself would have a room at the castle, and luxuriate on fat slices of venison, peaches, and wall-fruit without end. He wasn't sure that he wouldn't leave the army, and go and live there altogether.

And Mrs Blunt, having sworn the colonel to secrecy—at all events, sworn him not to mention the subject to Angelena until she gave him leave,—chimed in with him in discussing all the pros and cons, and expatiating on the magnificence of the prospect, with occasional speculations as to what Mrs Vainfield, Mrs Mouser, and Miss Quiz would think; and wished that she could see the Empress of Morocco's face when she heard it. Mrs Blunt was dying to be at her cream-laid note-paper, announcing the fact to all old friends and acquaintances.

So things gradually got into a more encouraging match-making mood, though when the colonel heard of the projected excursion to the castle with Jug, he put his foot upon it at once, unless Mrs Blunt accompanied them; and, after various ingenious efforts to shake off the old lady, Angelena was at length obliged to submit to be driven over, habited and garibaldied, in the old jingling mail-phaeton with posters, instead of cantering joyfully there with the cornet, who occupied a place in the rumble. And now, having got them so far advanced on their interesting excursion, we will take a peep at Lord Heartycheer's preparations for their reception.

CHAPTER XLI.

ARRANGING A QUIET BYE-DAY.

" WELL, Dicky," said Lord Heartycheer, in high glee, to his peculiar-dutied huntsman as they jogged homewards together after a capital run with a kill from Honeyball Hill, in which his well-mounted lordship had distinguished himself as usual—" well, Dicky, d'ye think you can manage us a quiet bye on Wednesday ? "

" Rayther quick, I fear, my lord—rayther quick," replied Dicky, with a half-supplicatory look. " These hounds'll go into a very small compass to-night," added he, looking down on the somewhat lagging pack as he spoke.

" Well, but you could manage us something that would pass muster with a lady, at all events," observed his lordship with a smile.

" Oh, certainly, by all means," rejoined Dicky, brightening up—" certainly—might take out a mixed pack for that matter, with a few of those we don't care much about : Lazarus here, for instance, and Lapwig, and Flasher. Benedict, too, might go, and Dangerous, also Royalty and Ferryman, and Baronet and Harbinger ; oh yes," added he, " we'll soon make up a lady's pack."

" I'll tell you what I want, then," said his lordship, thinking it better to make a confidant of Dicky at once— " I'll tell you what I want," said he, sidling his horse alongside of Dicky's. " You see, Miss Blunt, the colonel's daughter, is coming over to have a quiet hunt on the sly, and I want to arrange matters so as to have as much of her society as possible—you understand, eh ? "

" Jest so," replied Dicky, who was an adept at amatory

matters—" jest so," repeated he. " Well, then, I was
thinking," said he, after a pause, " the best plan will be
to have it near home—say, at Lovejoy Grove, or Kiss-me-
quick Hill—and then she could come in when she tired,
you know, poor thing—she could come in, you know,
when she's tired, you know."

" That's just my idea," exclaimed his lordship—" that's
just my idea. Have a little luncheon, show them the
pictures and things, and then have things ready to turn
out just when we like."

" By all means," assented Dicky, with a touch of his
cap.

" Keep it snug, you know," observed his lordship.

" By all means, my lord," assented Dicky. " Shall we
go in mufti or hunting things ? " asked he, looking at
his own smartly fitting scarlet.

" Oh—why—ha—hem—haw—let me see," mused his
lordship, thinking how it would act. " Perhaps," said
he after a pause—" perhaps the best plan will be to give
exercising orders, and then change all of a sudden, so
that it mayn't ooze out that we are going to hunt."

" By all means," assented Dicky, with another touch
of his cap, adding, " There are people who come out on
bye-days who don't come out on no other, jest, I believe,
for the sake of appearin' knowin'."

" There are," replied his lordship—" there are," adding,
" Monstrous bores they are, too. However, we'll trick
them this time. Have all things ready, you know, to
suit either order."

" By all means," assented Dicky.

" And tell Spurrier to exercise Lady Jane in a side-
saddle, with a rug, you know, like a habit—Miss Blunt
will ride her ; and tell him to have a steady horse for
Captain Jug, say old Solomon, or Brick's brown——"

" By all means, my lord," again assented Dicky ; and
the Cherryfield and Nutworth Chase cross-roads here
intervening, his lordship availed himself of the open for
mounting his hack and cantering off homewards, leaving
the complaisant Dicky to follow with the hounds.

CHAPTER XLII.

ONE TOO MANY.

" CON—FOUND it ! I *do* believe there's that nasty old woman coming," exclaimed his lordship, as, having got himself up in his most killing attire, he raked the distant sweeps of the long-winding approach with a telescope from his sumptuously furnished dressing-room in the western tower. " Coming, by Jove ! " repeated he in an agony of despair, after taking a second look, and seeing the now grinning Mrs Blunt, decked out like a cockatoo in all the colours of the rainbow. " Well, *con*—found it," continued he, swinging himself furiously into the room, and upsetting a chair as he caught it with his spur—" *con*—found it, but that's the stoopidest most asinine thing I ever knew done in the whole course of my life," and thereupon he slapped his forehead and white cords in an agony of despair.

He knew what it was to have an old woman coupled with a young one. While yet he meditated irresolutely what to do, the deep-sounding notes of the door-bell announced the arrival, and he hurried off almost mechanically to meet them.

" My dear Mrs Blunt ! my dear Mrs Blunt ! I'm *charmed*—I'm *overjoyed* to see you ! " he exclaimed, meeting her in the middle of the spacious entrance-hall, which the old lady was surveying in a very ownership sort of way. " This is, indeed, an unexpected, a most gratifying pleasure," continued he, seizing both her sky-blue, red-back-stitched gloved hands, and shaking them cordially. Then, glancing onwards, he exclaimed, " And the lovely Lady Angelena ! " to our fair, sprucely

habited, garibaldied friend, who contrived to show his
diamond pin in her delicate pink-and-white neckerchief
—" and the lovely Lady Angelena," repeated he, to the
delight of both mother and daughter, as he now seized
the ungloved hand of the latter. " And Jug, my dear
Jug ! " continued he, addressing him, too, with the utmost
glee, as the queerly put-on cornet stood a little behind
the mass of ermine, pea-green hat, and pink-tipped white
feathers that enveloped the now joint-stock mother-in-
law. Then, turning to Mrs Blunt again, his lordship
offered her his red-coated arm, and, preceded by a highly
scented, luxuriantly whiskered groom of the chamber
and two gigantic, quivering-calved footmen, they entered
a sumptuous sky-blue satined drawing-room, radiant with
mirrors, gilding, and ornaments from all parts of the
globe. " Come to the fire, my dear Mrs Blunt," continued
his lordship, leading her towards the first one, for the
room was large enough to require two—" come to the fire,
my dear Mrs Blunt, for there's a coolness in the air, and
you must have felt it in your phaeton, though," glancing
ardently at Angelena, " it seems to have agreed with
mademoiselle, who really looks quite bewitching," his
lordship wishing he could put the old curiosity up the
chimney, or anywhere else, to get rid of her.

" You've a beautiful—a splendid place here, certainly,
my lord," simpered Mrs Blunt, staring about her in
bewilderment, and thinking what a set-down it was for
her daughter.

" Glad you like it, ma'am—glad you like it," bowed
the gallant old cock ; " hope you'll come and stay here
very often."

" I'm sure I shall be most happy," replied the matter-
of-fact mamma-in-law.

" And the colonel, my old friend the colonel," continued his lordship, getting desperate, thinking as it
was over shoes, it might as well be over boots too.

" Oh, the colonel ! I'm sure the colonel 'll be happy,
too—nothin' he likes so much as a quiet billet i' the
country."

His lordship bowed again, thinking he would be very
sly if he got one there.

" Never thought to see the place under such (hem) circumstances," simpered Mrs Blunt, now unfolding one of her daughter's best kerchiefs.

Angelena, seeing her mamma was approaching tender ground, exclaimed, with a glance out of a deeply mullioned window in an apparently impregnable wall, " What a lovely dye it is ! "

" Charming ! " exclaimed the old peer—" charming," adding, " Shall we have a saunter round the terrace— into the garden—or would you prefer seeing the pictures first," continued he, adding, as he spoke, " I'll ring for Mrs Mansell—I'll ring for Mrs Mansell."

The lady so designated was the housekeeper, now somewhat advanced in life, but still retaining symptoms of the beauty that recommended her to his lordship, and raised her from the dairy to the head of the establishment.

Considering the questionable nature of her services, and the sort of people with whom she had to deal, Mrs Mansell was a very respectable-looking person ; and it was only under the scrutinising search of male eyes that the wince of deviation was apparent.

But though she was most decorous and respectful to all the guests before his lordship's face, treating them as if she thought they were what the servants call " quite quality," she took her change out of them behind his back, and let them see what she really thought of them.

" Well, I s'pose you'll be wantin' to see all the ins and outs of our place ? " observed she, as, having received mamma and miss from his lordship, she led the way across the spacious entrance-hall—" I s'pose you'll be wantin' to see all the ins and outs of our place ? " adding, " Women generally like to poke their noses into all the holes and corners they can."

" We want to see the castle, certainly," replied Mrs Blunt, bridling up, thinking the lady had better mind her p's and q's if she meant to stay there.

" Ah, well," rejoined Mrs Mansell, now ringing a con- cealed bell in the wall, which immediately produced an amazingly smart, handsomely dressed housemaid—for the old lord would have none but handsome women about him—of whom she said, addressing Mrs Blunt, " this

young 'oman will show you through the state apartments,
and by the time you've done with them, you'll find me
in the picter gallery."

So saying, Mrs Mansell made a sort of half-mock, half-
respectful curtsey to the " no-better-than-they-should-
be's," as she thought them, and looking at the maid as
much as to say " you'll not get much out of them," withdrew the way she came.

The housemaid, taking her cue from her predecessor,
just as the old post-boys used to take their threepenny
hints from those who brought up the chaise, proceeded to
open first one bedroom door and then another, announcing,
as she flourished her hand at the beds, this as the room
that Queen Caroline slept in, that as the one the Duke
of Somebody died in, another the room Lord Heartycheer
was born in—information which was a good deal lost
upon Mrs Blunt, busy thinking what room she would
choose for her daughter. Beautiful as they all were,
each succeeding one eclipsed its predecessor in splendour ;
so the more Mrs Blunt saw, the more she was bewildered.
And now, while the ladies are thus genially employed,
let us take a glance at the gentlemen below.

CHAPTER XLIII.

USEFUL JUG.

"WHAT the *deuce* did you bring that nasty old baggage
here for ? " asked his lordship, *sotto voce*, of Jug, as soon
as the folding-doors shut out the back views of the retreating ladies—" what the deuce did you bring that
nasty old baggage here for ? " repeated he, quite beside
himself with vexation.

"Why, she would come ! she would come ! " exclaimed
the half-frightened Jug. "I did all I could to prevent
her."

"Ord rot her ! " continued his lordship, stamping
furiously ; " she'll spoil all our sport—she'll spoil all our
sport. I didn't want *her*—I didn't want *her*. I thought
you and the girl would ride over together, and we'd
have a nice quiet day to ourselves. I made it expressly
for you, my dear fellow—I made it expressly for you.
Old Pitcher said to me the last time I saw him in Brooks's,
' Heartycheer, my boy, I wish you'd notice my grandson,
who's quartered beside you ' ; and I said to him, ' My
dear Pitcher, you're the oldest friend I have in the world,
the very oldest, and there's *nothing* I wouldn't do to
serve you. I'll not only call on your grandson, but I'll
call on the colonel, and so interest him in his behalf ' ;
and seeing the young lady, I thought it would be the
very thing to get you over together, for they all like a
sprig of nobility ; but I never wanted that old woman
for a moment—never wanted that old woman for a
moment."

"Well, I told her that ! I told her that ! " vociferated
little pig-eyes, "but she said the colonel insisted on her

coming—wouldn't hear of his daughter going without her—*indeed* she did," asserted Jug, now spluttering with vehemence.

"Well," mused his lordship, biting his lips and button-holing little Jug, "it's a bad job, a deuced bad job; but I'll tell you what you must do—you must ease me of the old body as much as you can, you know—ease me of the old body as much as you can, you know—you understand, eh?"

"Oh yes," replied Jug. "I'll do anything in that way; only tell me what to do."

"Why," said his lordship, "I can manage her here, you know; the difficulty will be about hunting, you know; and I shouldn't like to disappoint Miss Angelena, who's come in her habit, and all so smart."

"Just so," assented Jug, who had natural horror of hunting, though, like many jolly subs., he occasionally punished himself by partaking of the chase. "Well," continued he, "as far as hunting's concerned, I'm really quite indifferent about it to-day. Any other day would suit me quite as well—better, indeed, for I've got a pair of boots on that are anything but comfortable; and if one's boots don't fit, one's breeches seldom do either; and when one's garments arn't right," continued Jug, hitching and pulling away at a pair of his father's old leathers, that didn't seem to have the slightest idea of doing what they ought, "there's very little pleasure or enjoyment."

"Quite true," assented his lordship—"quite true. I know nothing so nasty as ill-fitting clothes, unless, indeed, it is a nasty old bundle of dirty finery such as that you've brought here. However," continued he, calming down, "we'll say no more about that—we'll say no more about that; you'll manage the old jade—you'll manage the old jade. And now, if you'll excuse me for half a minute," added his lordship, drawing the ivory-knobbed bell-handle, "I'll send for Dicky Thorndyke, and give him his cue."

CHAPTER XLIV.

SOOTHING SYRUP.

" OH, Dicky ! " said his lordship in an undertone, as that
hunting-equipped worthy emerged from the steward's
room, where he was having a little refreshment, and
approached his lordship respectfully in the grand entrance
hall—" oh, Dicky," repeated he in a tone of despair,
" here's a pretty kettle of fish ; Mrs Blunt's come with
her daughter, and whatever I'm to do I don't know."

" S-o-o-o," mouthed Dicky, drawing a long face.

" It's the most unfortunate thing that ever occurred,"
continued his lordship.

" It is so," said Dicky, conning the matter over.

" Mr Jug says he'll be good enough to keep her engaged
while we slip off with the daughter, so you must have all
things quick and ready for a start."

" By all means, my lord," assented Dicky, with a touch
of his forelock.

" The difficulty will be keeping her quiet after we've
gone," observed his lordship.

" Oh, I think that might be manished," replied Dicky
—" I think that might be manished. Lock up their
post-boy, and don't let him have any 'orses."

" Well," considered his lordship, " that might do."

" Or," continued Dicky briskly, " give her a little
somethin' soothin'."

" That was what I was thinking," whispered his lordship—" that was what I was thinking. If you could see
Doiley and tell him to mix her some—not over-strong,
you know, but just a moderate dose—we might reckon
upon having her quiet for a few hours at least."

" And Mr Jug ? " asked Dicky.

" Oh—why—ha—hem—Mr Jug must just take his chance, you know. It won't do for Doiley to tell him ; and if he has a mind to drink it, why—ha—hem—he'll just go to sleep too, that'll be all."

" Just so, my lord," assented Dicky—" just so," adding, " Then what would your lordship think of drawing first ? "

" First," mused his lordship—" first," repeated he, adding, " Don't know, I'm sure—this confounded interruption's put me so out—what would you think ? "

" There's the Grove, and Kiss-me-quick Hill, both sure finds," observed Dicky ; " but we might rouse young Mr Kyleycalfe, and if he was once to come to us we should never get rid on him, for he's no more sense nor delicacy nor a pig."

" No more he has," assented his lordship, who recollected how Kyleycalfe persecuted him one day when he had the beautiful Empress of Morocco out on the sly. " Dash it all ! what shall we do ? " continued his lordship, stamping furiously on the soft rug.

Dicky for once was mute.

" Couldn't you send to Kyleycalfe's, think you," asked his lordship, " with your compliments, and say you're going to draw Roughshaw Brake ; that would draw him off the other way ? "

" Well," said Dicky, " only it might stir up Harry Shoveller, or Mr Whickenrake, or some of the Fatacres people, for they're all of a litter like."

" They are so," assented his lordship, now more bothered than ever.

" How would it do," asked Dicky after a pause, " to run a drag, say, from Choplaw Wood over Broomfield Common, through Steventon Chase and Lingfield down to Mrs Easylove's ? "

" That would do ! " ejaculated his lordship—" that would do," repeated he, delighted at his huntsman's sagacity—" the very thing, I should say. Only it would be well to let Mrs 'Love know we're coming."

" By all means," assented Dicky—" by all means ; send little Charley Bates off with a note at once."

"Or stay," continued his lordship, thinking it over; "how would it do," asked he, "to send Mrs Mansell, think you, in the *incog.* chaise with dry things for us both in case we got wet?"

"A very good idea," replied Dicky—"a very good idea," repeated he; "then she'll be on the spot, and have everything ready against you arrive, for these old postin'-houses are not to be depended upon for comfort since railways were interduced."

"They're not," replied his lordship—"far from it. Mrs 'Love's was very cold the last time I was there; so now," continued he, button-holing his huntsman, "I'll send Mrs Mansell to you, and you'll see and start her at once with dry things of all sorts, you know, ladies' as well as gentlemen's, and then you be ready to turn out the instant you are wanted—the *instant* you are wanted," repeated his lordship energetically.

"By all means," assented Dicky.

"You must have the drag run in time, mind, and arrange to lift it occasionally, so that we may check and look about us a little, you know."

"By all means," assented Dicky.

"And don't forget the soothing syrup," enjoined the lord.

"Certainly not," replied the huntsman.

"Tell Doiley mulled claret's the best thing to give it in," added his lordship.

"By all means," assented the huntsman.

CHAPTER XLV.

BY BACK WAYS.

Just as his lordship got back to Jug, the faintest possible tinkle of a little bell in the cornice at the far end of the room announced that the ladies had entered the picture gallery, his lordship having had the bell placed in communication with the door, in order that he might know when visitors entered, and go and enjoy their admiration of the voluptuous paintings and statues with which it abounded from private peep-holes he had established in various parts of the wall.

"Now," said he to our pliant little friend Jug as he heard the significant bell, "we will join the ladies, if you please, and remember—I'll take care of the old lady now, if you'll have the kindness to relieve guard, as it were, when we go to hunt—that is to say, after luncheon, you know—I'll slip away, and you must ply her with wine, liqueurs, or whatever you think will do her good."

"I will," replied the dragoon, with great heartiness.

They then left the room arm-in-arm together, and found things just as his lordship anticipated, the housemaid having returned her charge to Mrs Mansell. With a sneer and a chuck of her chin, as much as to say, "there's fine copper company for you," that estimable lady had ushered them into the splendid picture-gallery ranging along the whole west side of the castle, and was commencing her horse-in-the-mill descriptions in a tone of hard-strained civility, when his lordship and Jug entered from the other end, and found our fair friends ranged before a voluptuous Etty that generally brought spectators up short.

"This," said Mrs Mansell, pointing to the picture, "is the great Mr Apollo, a gent much given to the ladies. He co'abited with Wenus in the Island of Rhodes, where it rained gold, and the earth was clothed, as you see, with lilies and roses. Among other young ladies he made love to was Miss Daphne, who, 'owever, liked a youngerer gent better nor him. Mr Apollo, therefore, who was an artful man, persuaded the youth to dress up as a gal, and keep company with the nymphs. They, you see, want him to bathe with them in the river near London, which the youth refusing to do, his sex was discovered, and he was stabbed to the 'eart with many daggers."

"Poor young man," sighed Mrs Blunt.

"Ah, that's a fine thing—a very fine thing, Mrs—Mrs —Mrs—Blunt," hemmed his lordship, coming too quickly upon them to allow of a retreat—"that's a very fine thing," repeated he; "the figures of the ladies, I take it to be quite perfection—you almost fancy you can feel them in the water, it's so lambent and clear." Then, turning to Mrs Mansell, he said, "Thank'ee, thank'ee—we needn't detain you, though," adding in a whisper, "Mr Thorndyke wants to see you."

Whereupon Mrs Mansell made a most respectful curtsey, leaving the further lionisation of the ladies to his lordship, whom she couldn't help thinking a good deal resembled Mr Apollo.

His lordship then took Mrs Blunt on his arm, and proceeded to explain and expatiate to a very uncultivated mind. Still she was all in the assenting enthusiastic mood, though her encomiums were sometimes misplaced. So they strolled down the fine gallery, followed by Angelena and Jug, the latter making faces at his lordship, and grimacing as he went.

"That," said his lordship, nodding at the back of a full-length statue occupying a newly erected pedestal on the floor of the gallery, "of course, you know: it's Power's Greek Slave, that was so much run after by all the young gentlemen at the Great Exhibition. That's an exact copy of it," continued he; "just got it home— gave a thousand—no, I'm wrong, fifteen hundred pounds for it. The figure's beautiful—very beautiful, certainly—

full and voluptuous, without any Hottentot Venusish exaggeration about it ; but there's a something about the face," continued he, turning the figure round on the pivot—" there's a something about the face that I don't like—an air of pensive melancholy, if you observe."

" Well, but she's a slave, you know," observed Angelena smartly, now falling into line with Jug before the statue.

" True, my dear—true," assented the owner. " It isn't the propriety of the expression that I question ; on the contrary, it's quite correct—quite correct—only the face reminds me of one of the most consummate hypocrites I ever met in my life—a girl with just the same mild subdued expression of countenance, but who was as heartless a hypocrite as ever breathed—a girl so full of artful purity that you would have thought she hadn't a worldly mercenary idea in her head, and yet whose soul ran upon money, and nothing but money. I really believe she'd have jilted a D'Orsay for any rich Bullock and Hulker out of the City."

" Horrid wretch ! " exclaimed Mrs Blunt, who, like many mammas, professed a thorough contempt for wealth.

Just as his lordship got to this virtuous period of his indignation, a softly stepping servant, in a gorgeous white tie and plain clothes that shone resplendently new, minced up, and announced in a half whisper that luncheon was on the table ; whereupon the peer vented the balance of his wrath upon the lady by declaring that he could " whip the figure " ; and then again getting Mrs Blunt on his arm, he led the way to the splendid banqueting-room that we had the pleasure of introducing to our readers on the Heartycheer Castle day, where, in newspaper phraseology, there was again a sumptuous display of every delicacy of the season. Our friends, after their long drive in the bracing wintry air, wanted little persuasion on the part of their noble host to induce them to fall to with hearty goodwill, while his lordship, who was not a luncheon eater, sat eyeing the party, and planning how to get the lively young lady away.

" Well," at length said he, looking at his diminutive watch as he rose from his chair on seeing Angelena was done, though mamma still plodded steadily on over a

third plateful of Perigord pie—" well, don't hurry yourself, my dear Mrs—Mrs—Mrs Blunt, whatever you do,"
laying his hand on her shoulder—" don't hurry yourself,
pray—make yourself quite at home, do ; and while you
are eating, if your lovely daughter will allow me, I'll
just take and show her the horse I propose putting her
upon, so that if there is any change or alteration to make
it may be done at once."

So saying, with a sly beckon to Angelena and a knowing
wink at Jug, he got the fair lady away, and in an instant
was squeezing her arm as lovingly within his on the far
side of the door as Jug had squeezed it on entering.
Away they hurried, by back passages and covered ways,
to the spacious courtyard of the castle stables behind.

Jug, who felt excessively relieved, as well by his lordship's departure as by his own escape from hunting, now
made an arm at all the bottles within reach, and began
helping himself and his mamma-in-law most plenteously
to their contents. Indeed, so far as Jug was concerned,
his lordship's order to drug them both was unnecessary,
for Jug very soon put himself *hors de combat;* but as the
beverage was mixed, the butler didn't care to waste it,
and very soon after it was placed upon the table, Jug
and Mrs Blunt were, as Mr Doiley said, " in the arms of
Murphy."

x

CHAPTER XLVI.

DAMPED HOPES.

ALTHOUGH the coast seemed clear as Lord Heartycheer
hurried our fair lady along, yet was every nook and
point of observation occupied by curious eyes, all bent
on seeing what the new favourite was like.

" 'Deed ! " sneered pretty Mary Smith, the stillroom-
maid, with a haughty toss of her neatly braided head,
" I'm sure she's nothin' to make a song about."

" Fine feathers make fine birds," remarked Jane
Softley, the third housemaid, to Roger Plush, the second
footman.

" Well, she's a contrast to the empress, anyhow ! "
exclaimed fat Bridget Brown, the head laundry-maid, to
Mr Smoothstep, the groom of the chamber.

" The tanner's wife's worth ten of her," rejoined the
polite Smoothstep, thereby conveying an indirect compliment to Bridget, who was as plump, if not as pretty, as
the empress.

When, however, his lordship, with the fair object of
these remarks, appeared on the top of the massive flight
of stone steps leading down into the spacious heavily
battlemented courtyard, symptoms of animation were
apparent, and Mr Spurrier, the bareheaded stud-groom,
instantly emerged from a stable leading the beautiful
Lady Jane, and had her sideways at the botton of the
steps as Angelena reached them.

" Stand by her head," said his lordship—" stand by
her head," repeated he, adding, " I'll put the lady on,"
stooping to take her foot as he spoke.

Angelena lifted her habit becomingly, and raising her

taper foot, his lordship vaulted her into the saddle as
light as a cork.

"That's capital!" exclaimed he, now standing erect,
and looking her over as she flounced about adjusting her
habit comfortably in the soft saddle—"that's capital!"
repeated he, now helping her to smooth it. "She'll carry
you like a bird ; and now, if you'll come this way, I'll
get my horse, and we'll be off."

So saying, his lordship led the way through the coach-
house courtyard into the one beyond, where there was an
instantaneous burst of red coats—Dicky Dyke emerging
from one stable, Billy Brick from another, Sam from a
third, and Mr Paxton, the scarlet-coated but now gaitered
second horseman, from a fourth. Quick as thought they
were in their saddles, and, at a nod from his lordship,
were trotting under the massive archway into the open
of the country beyond. The purple-coated feeder stood
with the kennel-door in his hand, and, at a signal from
Dicky, the glad pack came chiding and gambolling over
the green.

"Gently!" exclaimed Dicky—"gently!" repeated he,
shaking his head at the mirthful ones, as much as to say,
"Don't make a noise ; we're out on the sly to-day."

Billy then reined in his horse, and, preceded by Brick,
trotted gaily along at that pleasant post-boy pace so
familiar to fox-hunters. His lordship and Angelena
followed at a convenient distance, his lordship riding a
splendid three-hundred-guinea grey that had not been
out for a week. As soon as he got him settled on his bit,
he sidled up to the lady, and opened a profuse battery of
compliments upon her—

"Well, now, she did look lovely !—never saw her look
so well. Her brown Garibaldi was *so* becoming—the
colour matched her beautiful hair so nicely. The new
feather, too, was charming—the very poetry of a feather !
Never saw a habit fit so nicely—set off her bust and figure
to such advantage. Liked to see a lady got up with
taste—neatly fitting gloves, nice chemisettes, and tasty
kerchiefs," his lordship eyeing Angelena's delicate pink-
and-white one secured with the well-known diamond pin.

So they proceeded through the park, pleased with

themselves and each other. The day was still gloriously
fine, though the dancing sunbeams and water-marked
sun occasionally gave the old lord pause, and made him wish
he had brought out Paxton with his macintosh or greatcoat. However, one always hopes the best ; always
trusts that this day will be the exception to the rule ;
nor, so long as the bright sunshine lasts, will we believe
that so much splendour can be suddenly changed into
murky melancholiness.

So thought his lordship as he now proceeded silently
along, varying his inward admiration of Angelena with
congratulations at his sagacity in sending the dry things
to Mrs Easylove's, and speculations on the probable
result of the adventure. Angelena, who was equal to
any quantity of compliments, and not knowing how long
the opportunity might last, aroused his lordship from his
reverie by exclaiming—

" What a lovely tile ! What a lovely tile ! " repeated
she, his lordship evidently not catching the first shot.

" Ah ! ah, yes—a Lincoln and Bennett," replied his
lordship, uncovering his old frosty prow—" a Lincoln and
Bennett—capital tile-makers they are—have dealt with
them for many years," added he, putting it on again.

" No, it was the horse's tile I was admiring," laughed
Angelena.

" Oh ! ah, yes—the horse's *tail*," rejoined his lordship,
now better comprehending her dialect—" oh ! ah, yes,
he has a very beautiful tail—a very beautiful tail ; so
has yours—so has yours—carries it well, too—carries it
well, too—carry you well, I hope—carry you well, I
hope."

His lordship then again got up the steam of his compliments, all of which Angelena received with the utmost
composure and delight. She would have backed herself
at ten to one to be a countess. What a dasher she would
be, she thought !

It was not until his lordship heard the key again turn
in the lock of the private door in the park wall that he
was quite at his ease with regard to the start. He feared
the pursuit of Mrs Blunt, and doubted whether Jug was
enough of a diplomatist to keep her quiet. Now, how-

ever, that he was clear of the premises, and about to
dive into the bush of the country, he commenced banter-
ing Angelena on her boldness, wondering what mamma
would think, and hoping she wouldn't whip her when she
got back. Angelena, on her part, was all giggle and eyes,
anxious to fascinate—hardly knowing what to be doing.
So they chatted and chirped along the bridle-road through
Mr Dockenhead's fields, turning short to the left at the
village of Barnton to avoid passing Mr Cloverfog's farm at
Fodderington.

The hounds having now arrived on the long strip of
grass below the banks of Choplaw Wood, Billy Brick
looking inquiringly round on Dicky Dyke, who in turn
looked round at his lordship, when a nod from the peer
sent Billy scuttling one way, Sam another, while the
hounds made the old rotten fence crash with their weight
as they dashed into cover at the wave of Dicky's hand.

" Y-o-o-i over, good dogs ! Y-o-o-i yo-ver, and wind
him ! " cheered he, with a slight crack of his whip, when,
getting his horse by the head, he put him at the well-
accustomed gap in the fence, and presently commenced
his exhortations in cover.

My lord and my lady kept on the grassy strip outside,
my lord thinking about timing it cleverly for Mrs Easylove's, and the lady thinking of his lordship instead of
the hounds.

As the latter spread the cover, each following his own
line, it suddenly occurred to Dicky that he had forgotten
to tell the lad where to begin the drag ; and again, that
if they should chance to put up a fox, neither of the whips
had orders to stop the hounds. As he was riding, " yoicks-
ing," and meditating what he should do in such an emer-
gency, the whole pack suddenly burst forth in full cry ;
and while Dicky sat listening with his hand in the air,
hoping the best, fearing the worst, their short running,
quick turning, and increased music left no doubt on his
mind that they were on a fox, and that, too, with a burning
scent. Whipping out his horn, he got his horse by the
head, and shot up a ride, in hopes of heading and stopping
them in cover.

" Hark ! " exclaimed his lordship, breaking off in the

middle of an eulogium on Angelena's figure ; "that sounds very like a fox. Hark!" again exclaimed he, holding up his hand. "A fox for a hundred!" added he.

"No doubt," replied Angelena, reining in her horse, and depositing her kerchief in the saddle-pocket.

"A fox for a thousand! a fox for five-and-twenty hundred!" continued his lordship, listening. "Follow me!" added he, now clapping spurs to the grey, and hustling him up the ride as hard as ever he could lay legs to the ground.

When his lordship got to the top of the wood he heard Billy's cheery "Holloa, away," followed by a shrill "tweet, tweet, tweet" of a horn, that he knew proceeded from Billy's.

"Hang it, there must be some mistake," muttered his lordship, opening the bridle-gate out of cover—"there must be some mistake," repeated he, settling in his saddle for action, and looking about for Dicky.

Meanwhile, the hounds were racing away some three fields ahead, with none but Brick near hand.

"Well," said his lordship, dropping his elbows and settling for action, "needs must when a certain old gentleman drives, but I'm hanged if I know what he means."

"We are in for another Silverspring Firs day, I think!" exclaimed Angelena, now touching her mare gently with the whip to make her keep pace with his lordship.

"I'll bet you a kiss old Dick's made a mess of it," replied his lordship, smiling.

"How so?" asked Angelena, feeling if her habit was all right behind.

"*You'll see*," replied his lordship knowingly, as he gathered his horse to ride at a fence.

Over he went, with Angelena close upon him.

"A little more room, or I'll have to whip you myself!" exclaimed his lordship, who thought Angelena was atop of him.

"Beg pardon!" replied the lady, who felt she couldn't afford to kill the old gentleman who was to make her a countess.

Billy Brick.

His lordship then rose in his stirrups, and shot up a long strip of sound turf as if on a race-course. Still he gained nothing on the hounds.

" They're racing for Dusterton Woods—racing for Dusterton Woods ! " exclaimed his lordship, divided between joy at the prospect of a spinner and vexation at the apparent miscarriage of his project. " Hang it, never mind," thought he, " I have her with me at all events." So saying, he reined in his horse and made him break a high wattled fence on a bank, in order that Angelena might get over without difficulty.

" Oh, don't do that ! " exclaimed she, adding, " I like leaping ! "

" Do you, my darling," replied his lordship, adding, " You're the girl for my money."

They then went spluttering across a field of swede turnips together.

" Yonder he goes ! " now cried his eagle-eyed lordship, taking off his hat ; and some two fields ahead Billy Brick was sailing away, cheering and capping on the hounds, perfectly regardless of the great bullfinches that came in his way. Over he went, as if they were nothing. " I'll bet you a kiss he kills him," said his lordship, looking significantly at Angelena. " I'll bet you two kisses he kills him," continued he, increasing in energy.

" I'll bet you a pair of gloves," simpered Angelena prettily.

" Hang gloves ! " exclaimed his lordship ; " let's have something more substantial."

" I'm sure gloves are more substantial than kisses," rejoined the now laughing lady.

" Ah, but gloves are to be got anywhere ; kisses are not so common."

" You're a naughty man, and I must leave you," replied Angelena, pretending to turn her horse away from his lordship.

" Nonsense ! " exclaimed the old peer. " See how they're running," added he, pointing with his whip to the pack, now straining up the rising ground of Furrowflat Hill. " And yonder goes the fox ! " continued he, now taking off his hat as he again viewed the varmint rounding

the top of the rising ground. "*Forrard!—forrard!*"
screamed he, hustling his horse, and riding like a boy.

They were soon on the spot where his lordship viewed
the fox, Angelena handling and riding her horse most
beautifully. But hold, a check! The Sheepcome and
Delemere cross-roads intervene, and the fox has been
chased by a cur. The eager hounds spread like a rocket
for the scent, and Billy Brick, with upraised hand and
anxious eye, sits transfixed on his now smoking chestnut.
Lord Heartycheer and our fair friend pass over a gap at
the corner of a clover ley, and pull up a little short of
Brick. His lordship looks anxiously forward, in hopes
of a hint or a halloa; and Angelena, not less anxious
about herself, feels her hair, and her face, and her habit,
and hopes she's looking well. And well she is looking—
uncommonly well—warmed without being heated, with
a bright sparkle of animation imparted to her radiant
eyes.

"Ah, you'll do very nicely," whispered the old peer
in her ear, as she now began fingering the pretty pink-and-
white kerchief. "You'll do very nicely," repeated he.
"Only don't lose the pin, you know," which was now
rather sticking up.

"Shouldn't like to do that," replied Angelena, adjusting
it, and looking most lovingly at her lord as she hoped he
was to be.

She would have backed herself at this moment at
twenty to one for a countess.

"I'm afraid we've lost the fox," whispered she, shaking
her habit under her as she saw Billy Brick (Dicky, who
was nothing across country without Billy to bore holes
in the fences for him, having been floored at the first leap)
advancing to the assistance of the pack. "I'm afraid
we've lost the fox," repeated she, as his lordship sat
looking distrustful at Billy.

"Let's have a bet about it—let's bet half a dozen
kisses," replied his lordship coaxingly, taking hold of her
arm.

"Hush!" frowned Angelena, "the servants will hear,"
looking significantly at Sam, who now bustled past with
some tail hounds.

" Oh, never mind him," said his lordship, who was quite regardless of servants.

" Well, now, what do you say ? " resumed his lordship, *sotto voce.*

" Say about what ? " asked Angelena, pretending ignorance.

" About the kisses," replied his lordship ; " will you bet me half a dozen kisses we don't kill the fox ? "

" You must ask mamma," replied Angelena, with a stately bow.

" Oh, fiddle mammas," laughed his lordship ; " we young chaps like dealing with the daughters."

" Dare say you do, you naughty man," replied she, touching him lightly with her whip. Just then an envious drop of rain beat heavily on her fair forehead, causing her to shudder at the prospect of a storm. Who knew but a coronet depended on the weather ?

" I wish it mayn't be going to rine," observed she, looking anxiously up at the now cloud-cast sky.

" Hope not," muttered his lordship, who was watching Billy's cast, thinking he would make a huntsman. Another great drop confirmed Angelena's suspicions—it was indeed going to rain.

" Hark to Forester ! " cries Billy, as that fine black-and-white hound, after a preliminary feather up the inside of the high hedge between the turnip and pasture fields, at length gives one of his invaluable Bank of England notes, and the spreading pack rush to the summons. " Hark to Forester ! " again cries Billy, sticking spurs to his steed, and capping the rest on to their comrade.

" To him !—to him ! " cries Sam, riding and cracking his whip at the unbelieving ones.

They cluster and settle to the scent with undiminished perseverance.

" I shall want my kisses," observed his lordship knowingly, as he eyes their energy.

Another slight falter, and away they shot as before.

" He's away for the main earths at Tibberley Chase," observed his lordship to Angelena, considering how that would act for Mrs Easylove's.

" Indeed," smiled the fair coquette, not much wiser for the information.

" Tell me if you're tired, you know," said his lordship, squeezing her arm a little above the elbow as they again rode away together.

" Oh, I shan't tire," smiled the fair equestrian.

" You're a *darling!*" exclaimed his lordship, eyeing her intently, and thinking he would salute her rosy lips at the next check, whether the whips were there or not. " You're a *darling!*" repeated he, looking most lovingly at her.

" A countess for a hundred," thought Angelena, setting herself well in her saddle, sticking in her back, and holding up her head as if she was going to court all blazing in diamonds.

A smart blash of rain rather checked her aspirations. In truth, she was not got up for resisting the elements. Besides an abundant crinoline petticoat, she had on her best white silk eiderdown bustle, a thing not at all adapted for weather. Altogether she began to be nervous. Rain never improved any woman's looks.

" If the fox would only go to Scarrington Crags instead of the Chase," thought his lordship, " the rain would be all in our favour." Then he looked back for Dicky Dyke, wondering where that worthy had got, and how it was they had such a mistake about the drag. Then he wondered if Mrs Mansell would have got to Mrs Easylove's with the clothes, or if there was any mistake about them ; next, whether he should be able to dress himself without the aid of his valet ; and anon, he was imagining Jug and Mrs Blunt asleep together. Then he looked at Angelena, and wondered if she'd ever be as fat as her father ; next, he saw she would be more like her mother.

*Sweep !—blash !—howl !—*now came the rain in heavy driving showers, slackening the pace of the hounds, and causing the horses to duck and shake their heads.

" I wish it mayn't be going to rain," observed his lordship, pulling his coat collar up about his old ears.

" Going !" exclaimed Angelena ; " I should say it *was* rining."

" Won't be much," replied his lordship soothingly

—"won't be much ; besides," added he, " I know a
nice house where we can get shelter if it does—know a
nice house where we can get shelter if it does," repeated
he, his hazel eyes flashing as the hounds seemed rather
inclined to bend away to the south.

Vain hope ! Two fields more and they turned short to
the north.

" Hang them," muttered his lordship, vexed at the
change ; " we shall never get to Easylove's."

The storm now spoiled the scent, which the plodding
pack carried forward very languidly, falling into line,
with only a hound here and there throwing his tongue.
Billy cheered and telegraphed them on ; but do what
he would, he couldn't brew up a cry. Plough now intervened, and altogether things wore an unpromising aspect.
His lordship, recollecting it was only a " bye," and the
hunt altogether a sham, bethought him of leaving the
further enjoyment of it to Billy, retreating by the nearest
road he could find to Mrs Easylove's. Accordingly, he
began paving the way for a stop, observing to Angelena,
as he reined up the grey on a piece of rising ground, that
he feared it was all over for the day.

" Indeed ! " sighed the lady, flourishing her handkerchief, as the drifting rain took her sideways, to the
further discomfiture of her back and eiderdown bustle.

" Forrard on ! forrard on ! " still cheered Billy, holding
his hounds on to a meuse in a very tumble-down hedge,
when Forester again struck the scent most vehemently,
and they all scored to cry as before.

His lordship, mistaking Angelena's sigh for her bustle
into regret at the abrupt termination of the chase, resolved
to go on, and again getting his horse by the head was
presently sailing away with the pack, who now went
bustling and bristling over Benteygrass Moor in a way
that looked very like killing.

" Plenty of time both for the fox and the fair," thought
his lordship, eyeing the now streaming-away pack, and
the again elegantly sitting lady—" plenty of time both
for the fox and the fair," repeated he, eyeing Angelena's
masterly style of handling her horse to ride at a stiff
undisturbed fence. " Well done you ! " shouted his

lordship, as she cleared it in stride without touching a twig.

The hounds again slackened their pace. Dark lowering clouds obscured the late sun-bright sky, and the summit of the Hartsbourne Hills was shrouded in the distance.

" Bad sign that," thought his observing lordship, eyeing them—" bad sign that ; never knew them covered but it rained." And he again congratulated himself upon having sent the dry things to Mrs Easylove's. "Wish we were there," thought he, eyeing Botcherby steeple, and then the dark mass of Chillfield plantations ; wishing also that Angelena was not quite so game.

The poor girl's sigh had much to answer for ; but for it his lordship might have run his fair charge into the desired haven, if not dry, at all events without the disheartening consequences that ensued. The sigh, like many a sigh, upset his arrangements. He felt it would never do for him to give in while his inamorata wished to go on ; and so long as he had her with him he didn't so much mind the consequences. He therefore stuck to the hounds, notwithstanding they were now running in quite a contrary direction to that in which Mrs Easylove lived.

Angelena, now distressed and dispirited, cantered mechanically on, most anxiously wishing that his lordship was not so keen. The rain now became less capricious, but colder, more continuous and searching in its downpour. Angelena would have given anything to stop or get away from his lordship before she was quite spoiled. The lustre of the feathers was quite destroyed, and the dye of the Garibaldi began trickling down her face. Her hair, too, became loose, and fell wildly about her ears ; her pink and white kerchief was soaked, while her late looming-out habit stuck to her figure like a wet bathing-dress. Altogether she was regularly drenched.

His lordship marked the sad change, and his ardour began to cool. He was wet too, and blamed Angelena for the calamity. If he got the rheumatism, he might be laid up for the rest of the winter.

" Confound it, women never know when they have

enough of anything," thought he peevishly, as he felt the insidious rain penetrating the salient parts of his garments—a tinge of purple, too, began to descend upon his white cords.

The hounds, meanwhile, kept towling on with a very catchy scent, Billy still using his utmost efforts to accomplish that most desirable object in the eyes of a whip— the killing of a fox in the absence of the huntsman.

His lordship would gladly have seen them run out of scent.

They now got upon the wide expanse of Hatherton Moor, and looking at the dreary space before, the spongy clouds aloft—above all, at the red nose, pinched face, and crestfallen figure of the drenched girl, his lordship came to the determination that it was no use persevering to please her, so he just pulled up short, saying—

" Well, *I* go no farther."

" Nor *I*," faltered Angelena, who would have given anything to be anywhere else. Oh, that night would throw its sheltering shades over her forlorn, draggle-tailed figure ! She felt that her coronet chance was descending.

They then turned their backs upon the hounds, each thinking what a drowned rat the other looked.

The cold had struck into his lordship's old frame, and his teeth chattered and shook in his head. The wet had now even penetrated his pockets, and the water began to churn in his boots.

" If I don't catch my death of cold it'll be an odd thing to me," thought he, gathering up the grey and sticking spurs into his sides to make him quit the pack. He then went sailing away, straight across country, over hedges, ditches, and brooks, altogether regardless of the lady on whom so much care had been recently bestowed. Indeed, he seemed anxious to get away from her, and forget that he had been taken in by such a " shrimp of a thing," as he now called her. He felt that he had only taken up with her for the sake of contrast to the Empress of Morocco.

So he went splashing and crashing through the country, now wondering how he should get rid of Angelena when he got home, now anathematising Dicky Thorndyke for letting him in for such a chance.

" Could make as good a woman out of my whip," observed he to himself, gathering it together to ride full tilt at Foamington Brook, leaving the little lady to get over as she could.

The romance of the thing was fairly destroyed. The poetry of the feather, the sentiment of the hat, the taste of the tie were utterly ruined ; and in place of a bright-eyed, sunny-looking, well-set-up girl, the old peer saw nothing but a very downcast, draggle-tailed-looking Miss, who ere long would be very like her mother.

And he was almost glad that it was too dark for the grooms and people to see the figure she was when she got back to the castle.

The end of the Bye-day.

CHAPTER XLVII.

MYSTERY AND SOLUTION.

ALTHOUGH Jug took the most of the drugged drink, he was the first to awaken from his trance, when, seeing glasses and decanters scattered around on the table, he concluded he had been left drunk at the mess, and as there was still wine in the bottles, he made a grab at the nearest one, upsetting a tumbler of water into the joint-stock mother-in-law's lap. She then awoke with a start and a bound, nearly jumping on to Jug's knee; and then, after reseating herself and staring wildly around her, she burst into an incoherent fit of laughter.

" He, he, he ! he, he, he ! he, he, he ! " went she, as if she had been listening to the funniest story imaginable.

" He, he, he ! he, he ! " joined Jug, as if he participated in the fun.

" He, he, he ! he, he, he ! he, he, he ! " giggled the mother-in-law again, as if she couldn't help herself.

" Well," said Jug, now rubbing his eyes and staring intently at her through the misty confused gloom of the room.

" Well ! " responded Mrs Blunt, staring at him.

" Come, none of your nonsense. I know you," said Jug nervously.

" Know me ! " exclaimed Mrs Blunt. " Why, who d'ye think I am ? "

" Jaycock, to be sure," replied the cornet.

" Jaycock, to be sure," repeated Mrs Blunt ironically.

" Downeylipe, then," said Jug, thinking it wasn't Jaycock's voice.

"Where are we?" exclaimed Mrs Blunt, now looking wildly around her.

"Ay, where are we, indeed?" rejoined Jug, seeing by the size and fittings of the apartment that they were not in the messroom at the barracks.

"It's very dark," observed Mrs Blunt, straining her eyes into the misty confusion.

"It is," said Jug, half shutting his little pig ones to see better.

"Angelena!" exclaimed Mrs Blunt, looking wildly about her—"Angelena!" repeated she in a louder tone. "Well, now; where *can* we be?" added she.

"I know!" exclaimed Jug, brightening up.

"Well, where?" asked Mrs Blunt eagerly.

"Heartycheer Castle, to be sure," replied Jug.

"So we are!" assented Mrs Blunt, adding, "But what can have happened?"

"Happened—how d'ye mean happened?" asked Jug.

"Why, where's Angelena?" replied mamma, throwing out her arms.

"Angelena—Angelena—oh, Angelena went out with my lord; don't you remember?" asked Jug.

"I think I do," replied Mrs Blunt thoughtfully—"I think I do," adding, "But she ought to have been back before this. Naughty girl! what can she be doing?"

"Oh, she'll cast up presently," said Jug, who, like all young men, was never jealous of old ones. Jug, never thinking of marrying an old woman, never supposed that any young woman would think of marrying an old man.

"Well, but," said Mrs Blunt after a long pause, during which she endeavoured to recall and connect the events of the morning—"well, but we should be goin' home. The colonel 'll be expectin' us back."

"Can't go without Angelena," replied Jug, taking another venture at the bottles, and, getting hold of claret instead of sherry, he rose, and proceeded on a cruise round the room in search of the bell to ring for candles. Having at length hit it off in one of those out-of-the-way places that modern usage assigns to those articles, he gave it a pull that sounded very like taking his revenge for the trouble he had had.

Doiley was in the middle of a game at billiards with "my lord's gentleman," and Jug had to repeat the summons ere Doiley took any notice of it.

"That's that old divil in the dinin'-room," said he to his companion, putting on his coat ; "just leave the balls as they are till I come back." So saying he lit a candle by the billiard-table lamp, and proceeded leisurely to answer the summons. "Did you ring, mum ? " asked he in a sort of tone of astonishment, speaking at the heap of fur that alone was distinguishable in the gloom.

"Yes—no—yes, that's to say, Colonel Blunt—I mean Captain Jug did," replied she, not yet fairly recovered from her sleep.

"What might you please to want, sir ? " asked Doiley, addressing himself more respectfully to the cornet, who he knew was the grandson of a lord—though only a Baron one, as he told the earl's gentleman.

"W-a-a-nt," drawled Jug—" w—a—a—nt," repeated he, stretching himself out all fours. "Why, I should say, in the first place, we w—a—a—nt candles."

"Certainly, sir, certainly," replied Doiley, retiring to bring them.

When he returned, followed by a footman bearing the requisite illumination, he asked, in an offhand sort of way, as he began gathering up the napkins, if they would be dining there.

"Dinin'—why, haven't we dined ? " asked Mrs Blunt, staring wildly about, like an owl suddenly exposed to the sunshine.

"No, mum, no ; it was luncheon you took," replied Doiley contemptuously, thinking what a snob she must be to dine at two o'clock.

"Luncheon, was it ? " said she. "Well, I'm sure I thought it was dinner."

"Oh—yes—we'll dine, I s'pose," drawled Jug, who had been cogitating the matter over ; "may as well dine," added he.

"Then I'll tell monsieur you dine ? " observed Doiley interrogatively.

Y

" You may," responded Jug firmly.

" P'r'aps you'd like to go into the music-room or the drawing-room," suggested Doiley, thinking he might as well be getting the table laid.

" No, we'll do very well where we are," replied Mrs Blunt, yawning. " Is his lordship there ? " asked she.

" No, mum, no—his lordship's out, I think—not come in yet."

" Well, but where's my daughter—where's Angelena ? " demanded she, again returning to the charge.

" Oh, Angelena's safe enough," replied Jug.

" Not so sure of that," rejoined Mrs Blunt, who understood these gay old gentlemen better than the cornet. Then she began to think of all the colonel had said, and all she had heard about Lord Heartycheer's doings, which were not of a character to inspire much confidence in his discretion. However, she relied upon Angelena's prudence, and proceeded to recall all the conquests Angelena had made, and all the delicate positions she had been in.

Ere she had got half through the list, and just as Jug was dropping asleep again, Mr Doiley reappeared, and intimated, in the most respectful manner, that his lordship wished to speak to Captain Jug. Accordingly the sucking captain rose, and, shaking himself awake, proceeded to follow the servant along well-lighted corridors and passages, with scarlet cloth-covered outer doors, betokening the luxury within. Having reached one, at which another gentleman in full evening-dress stood sentry, Mr Doiley's jurisdiction ended, and with a respectful bow he transferred Jug to this second groom of the chamber, or whatever he was designated in the tax returns, who forthwith opened the doors, and ushered Jug into a sumptuously furnished room, where, amidst a splashing of water, a mournful voice was heard groaning—

" Come in, my dear Jug—come in."

It was his lordship getting parboiled after his soaking ; and in the midst of his turnings and splashings he proceeded to broach his misfortunes, talking as if he had been suffering martyrdom on account of the cornet.

" Oh, my dear fellow ! " bubbled he, with his mouth and nose only above water—" oh, my dear fellow ! you've let me in for such a mess !—you've let me in for such a mess !—bol-lol-lol-lol," as the water here came into his mouth. Having spluttered it out, he then proceeded with, " Never was so regularly taken in in my life— bol-lol-lol-lol," as he again got a mouthful of water. He then raised his old white head up a little, and proceeded to recount how that, to oblige the young lady, he had let Dicky draw for a fox ; and how that the unreasonable animal had led them such a dance as never was seen ; how wet he had got ; how he dreaded such an imperious domineering cold as he had the winter before last ; how he would have to go to bed as soon as he was enough boiled ; and how he should not get up till the next morning, if, indeed, he ever got up again ; and how he hoped Jug would make himself and the ladies quite at home, order whatever they liked, and stay all night if they liked—all of which Jug promised faithfully to do, and retired to carry out the intention.

Meanwhile, Mrs Blunt had been summoned to her dripping, draggle-tailed daughter ; and as she helped to take off each spoiled saturated garment, she felt an inward conviction that the sport of the day had not contributed at all to her " chance." Angelena was then boiled and put to bed ; and we are sure it will be satisfactory to our readers to learn that on the morrow this pattern old peer stole away by the back of the castle to hunt just as Mrs Blunt and her party drove away from the front.

CHAPTER XLVIII.

LORD LAVENDER'S BANK ACCOUNT.

CHRISTMAS ! Christmas ! that period to which some look
forward with such pleasure, others with such dread.
Christmas ! that period when our blunt, outspoken
country friends take the conceit out of one by exclamations at one's increasing age and altered looks, and our
once obsequious tradesmen no longer "any time that
suits you, sir," us, but, on the contrary, will trouble us
for that little account "on or before." Christmas, we
say again, drew on, bringing in its train the usual concomitants.

Among other parties interested in the period was our
old friend "sivin and four," whose peace of mind had
lately been greatly disturbed by the inundation of Lord
Lavender's cheques, who kept firing away on the strength
of having given Tom the Yeomanry commission, just as
if he had a balance to the good in Hall's hands. Day
after day old Trueboy came dribbling into the little pen
of a sweating-room, now bearing a cheque for a hundred
and fifty for a horse, now of ninety for a mare ; now for
a hundred and eight for a highly finished pony-chaise,
until the old banker began to dread the result. A cold
shiver came over him as the cautious cashier sidled from
his post at the counter for the sash-door, outside of which,
on a large board in white letters on a black ground, hung
the following pithy notice : " Call on a Business man in
Business hours, only on Business. Transact your Business,
and go about your Business, in order to give him time to
finish his Business."

" Sivin and four's elivin and twenty-nine is forty, and

thirty-three is sivinty-three, this'll niver do!" exclaimed
the old gentleman, as Trueboy, with his scratch-wig all
awry, and perturbation on his brow, now came in with one
for three hundred and eighty in favour of Sillery and
Fizzer, the accommodating wine merchants of ——.

"Sivin and four's elivin, and eighty is ninety-one, and
ninety's a 'under'd and eighty-one, the man'll break the
bank if we let him have his own way. Sivin and four's
elivin, and sixty is sivinty-one, I'll put a spoke in his
wheel."

So saying, Hall took a sheet of foolscap paper of the
dimensions that he wrote his London letters of advice
upon, and beginning at the very top of the page, as if he
thought he should have a difficulty in getting in all he
had to say, he wrote as follows :—

"Hall and Co. present their compliments to Lord
Lavender, and beg to call his lordship's attention to his
lordship's account, which is considerably out of cash.

> "The Bank, Fleecyborough,
> *Dec. . . .*"

And having given it to Trueboy to copy, who did it
with evident satisfaction, old Hall folded it with a very
diminutive double, and directing it to the Right Honourable Lord Lavender, sealed it with a large butter-pat
sort of seal, bearing the ominous, awe-striking words,
"Hall and Co.," in good, plain, bold, unmistakable letters
—letters that had struck terror into the mind of many a
recipient.

CHAPTER XLIX.

A CARD FROM HYACINTH HALL.

" ROT this old reprobate ! " exclaimed Lord Lavender, as the banker's missive reached him—" rot this old reprobate ! " repeated he, staring at the ill-written omened document ; " how can we give our Christmas festivities if this old usurer won't let us have money ? Oh dear ! oh dear ! " continued he, dashing his hand among his slightly silvery-streaked locks ; " what the deuce are these sort of people sent into the world for but to administer to the wants of the great. This, too, from an old snob, whose son I honoured with a commission in our regiment. Ingratitude's the worst of sins ! " exclaimed he, crumpling up the great letter, and making a mis-shot with it at the fire.

Lady Lavender, too, was shocked, for she had a neat little file of the expiring year's bills that she had been waiting for a favourable opportunity to present, to say nothing of several most "enchanting" shops that she wanted to do business with, by tantalising the keepers, in the first instance, with a little ready money.

In these emergencies the steward is generally the first person applied to, because on him devolves the onus of supplying the bank-hopper with coin, and so long as there are any arrears on the estate—no matter how small the amount—he is justly liable to censure for not getting them in, and so keeping the bank account square. How was his lordship to know that Jacob Browntops hadn't paid his rent, or that Mr Shuffler had decamped in the night carrying away all he had to Australia ?

Accordingly, Mr Gillyflower, his lordship's " commissioner," as they called him, was sent for, who, having made himself smart enough to wait upon her Majesty herself, was duly ushered into the presence, with a fine bunch of geraniums sticking in his button-hole.

Gillyflower was a great man of business—a great pen-and-ink man of business at least. Nothing was done on the estate without the most elaborate surveys, reports, plans, estimates, specifications, and detail. Not a barn was built, or hovel razed, without the minutest record of the whole transaction, and interminable negotiations relative to the purchase and disposal of the material. Everything was done through Mr Gillyflower, who issued instructions to poor Drearyman and his other sub-ordinates to inspect, and report, and suggest, and confer, and compare, and contract, so that in nine cases out of ten the season for doing the particular act was lost. Still, he had plenty of paper to vouch for his assiduity, and if pens and ink would have done as well as bricks and mortar, his lordship's would have been the best-managed estate in the county.

For all this unprofitable labour, and for smoothing over obdurate unreasonable creditors, Gillyflower had a thousand a year—a thousand made up in the following manner :—

A house and coals found, and bed .	.	£700
Keep of a cow	.	100
Cash	.	200
Total .	.	£1000

So that when anything went wrong his lordship blew up (behind Gillyflower's back, of course) at the rate of a thousand a year, expatiating on the absurdity of keeping such a highly salaried gentleman to " do nothing," verily believing he could get a man to do all he wanted for half the money.

The reader will now have the kindness to consider this elegant extract ushered into the library, in which were Lord and Lady Lavender, in the high state of indignation peculiar to great people when low-bred ones presume to ask for their money. His lordship briefly " opened the pleadings," as the lawyers say, by a mincing but vehement denunciation of that old humbug at Fleecyborough, a definition that Gillyflower's ready imagination immediately appropriated to old Hall, to whom he proposed Gillyflower's making a propitiatory visit and see if he couldn't get him to look benevolently on a few more cheques, which he had promised certain parties to draw in their favour.

Gillyflower had had so many conferences with old Hall, and knew his firm inflexible mode of doing business so well, that he felt it would be an absolute waste of time to go near him, unless he had money to pay in, so he at once recommended his lordship to give up all idea of anything of the sort, unless he could hit upon some expedient of mollifying the old cormorant apart from his beloved £ s. d.

" How would it do to send his son a ticket for our ball ? " asked Lady Lavender after a long pause, during which she recollected the favourable influence the Yeomanry commission had had on Madame Dentelle's bill.

His lordship shrugged his shoulders and raised his eyebrows, looking as if he thought it a desperate remedy —if not utterly impossible.

" Do no harm," rejoined her ladyship soothingly— " do no harm ; may make some fun for the Thistlewaite, the Ventnor, and Runnymede girls."

His lordship stood thinking the thing over, considering how it would do to have our Tom as a butt for his Christmas party.

" What sort of a cub is he ? " at length asked he of Gillyflower.

" Oh, the young man's very well—really very well," replied the commissioner, attitudinising ; " a great improvement on the old one, who hasn't an idea in his head but that of making money. The young one seems to have a turn for sporting—hunts with Lord Heartycheer— dines at the barracks—buys horses—does everything that a young man ought to do."

" Does he shoot ? " asked his lordship, who was all for
the trigger in opposition to the chase.

" Shoot," replied Gillyflower—" shoot," repeated he
thoughtfully—" well, I don't know whether he shoots or
not. I should think he did, though—most men do."

" Ah, but if there's any doubt about it, it wouldn't
do to have him at a *battue*," observed Lord Lavender,
recollecting the peppering he got in the legs from young
Mr Swellington, who thought he could shoot.

" But there'd be no occasion to take him out shooting,
my dear," observed Lady Lavender, who, the more she
thought of it, the more she was inclined to have our
Tom, if it was only to make fun for the girls, young
men being very scarce, as, indeed, they are in most
countries.

" There wouldn't," replied his lordship, thinking he
might couple him up with old Mr Barleymeale, and send
him on an agricultural excursion.

And so, after a little more doubt and hesitation and
ineffectual sounding of Gillyflower, whether he couldn't
first try his hand on the obdurate old banker, it was
arranged that a card should be enclosed for the ball in a
note of invitation from Lord Lavender to our Tom to
come and spend a few days at his lordship's seat, Hyacinth
Hall. And accordingly an enormous piece of pasteboard,
second only in size to those of a lord chamberlain's bearing
her Majesty's commands, surrounded with coronets and
heraldic devices, accompanied by a most diminutive
note, was put into a splendid, highly scented envelope,
sealed with the great family seal of state, and sent per
post to astonish the letter-carrier and the natives of
Fleecyborough generally.

The portentous document found our slippered, dressing-
gowned Tom ensconced in a luxuriously cushioned easy-
chair in the drawing-room, brooding over the beauties
and attractions of Laura Guineafowle, lamenting his ill-
luck in not having seen her beautiful blue eyes before
Angelena's sea-green ones, and wondering whether it was
possible to get off his engagement with the latter, so as
to enable him to offer his plump self to the former. Angelena, he thought, had stolen a march upon him—kid-

napped him, as it were—and he wouldn't have hesitated
about throwing her over if it wasn't for his fear of her
father, who, Major Fibs frequently assured him, was
one of the best pistol-shots in the kingdom. Indeed,
Tom's dreams of the lovely Laura were constantly interrupted by visions of the bulky colonel taking his stand
with the trifling distance of twelve paces measured out
between them. Had Tom but known of the hunt and
Heartycheer Castle expedition, he would have had no
difficulty in " crying off " with Angelena ; but, as usual,
everybody knew but the party most interested. And so
Tom grieved and fretted, wishing to be off with the old
love before he was on with the new. Worst of all, he had
no one in whom to confide—Mrs Hall, in her heart, not
favouring Laura a bit more than Angelena. She only
looked upon Laura as useful in diverting Tom's thoughts
from Angelena ; and in this state of the Cupid mart the
Lavender missive arrived. Mrs Hall, who knew of the
banker's letter, and suspected what it was, took it up to
her son herself, and shared in the exultation the invitation
produced.

" Well, now, that was nice ! that was delightful ! that
was a high compliment ! such a one as had never been
paid to any Fleecyborough gent before," and in her
prophetic mind she heard the marriage-bells ringing merrily
as our Tom handed the Honourable Mrs Hall into their
travelling carriage-and-four. And having exhausted
every species of panegyric, she restored the card and note
to the cover, and passed through the side door into old
Hall's den in the bank, who received the document with
a " Sivin and four's elivin, and twenty's thirty-one, I'd
rayther he'd paid some money to account," a wish that
Mrs Hall proceeded to combat with all the energy of an
ambitious woman.

And now, leaving the old people to discuss and settle
the point, we will again follow our Tom to the hunting-
field.

CHAPTER L.

LORD HEARTYCHEER, who had a large property in Glen-
fordshire, generally availed himself of the period of the
Christmas festivities to go and have a little shooting
there, a sport that he pursued in the most refined slaughter-
ing manner, leaving Dicky Dyke to amuse himself and
the country by rattling the large covers of Spygrove
Heath, Fullerby Woods, and Oakhampton Chase, which
Dicky did in the usual leisurely way of slack huntsmen
when "master's away." Nevertheless, it was rather a
favourite time with the country, as well on account of
the haughty earl's absence as because Billy Brick always
gave them a run, if by any chance he could manage it,
Billy, somehow or other, never being able to stop hounds,
let him be ever so well mounted, so long as they looked
like running. Many and curious were the excuses he
framed for Dicky—impossible bottoms, impenetrable
bullfinches, impervious raspers, that somehow or other
never intervened, or at least never stopped Billy when
Dicky was there ; but, as Dicky could claim the credit
of the feats to his lordship, and, moreover, didn't find it
convenient to quarrel with Billy, he did not inquire too
minutely into the facts. So Dicky, and Billy, and Sam
careered and capered through the country all very great
men in their way.

Shortly after his lordship's departure the plot thickened
considerably. Among other indications of winter, besides
oleaginous holly-stuck beef, seed-cake, citron, plums, and
mince-pies in profusion, was the sudden irruption of
no end of rough ponies, and little folks to ride them.

All the roads and lanes became alive with little scuttling scrambling things, worked by energetic, terrier-coated, worsted-comforted boys, exciting the terror of their mammas and the laughter of their papas. Oh, Charles! oh, James! oh, Thomas! Do, John (to the footman), for heaven's sake, run and stop them! I'm *sure* there'll be mischief! I'm *sure* they'll be killed!

And the cry was still " They come, they come," until every hall, every house, every place in the country seemed to have its complement of " Master Troublesomes " home for the holidays. And the work of the ponies increased : morning, noon, and night they were at work, their powers of endurance seeming to increase with each fresh demand, until they put the performance of the pampered hunter quite in the background. No sooner was one set of youngsters done than another set were ready to start, and races of every length and course were run at all hours of the day, with every species of start in order to bring them to an equality. A sudden change presently took place for hunting. The *Fleecyborough Independent and True Blue Champion* appeared with what in reality were four very so-so meets, but which caused great commotion among the holiday world, and great borrowing of saddles, bridles, and girths. Screws of all sorts rose in price, and plausible stablemen spoke in the handsomest terms of animals that had no more taste for hunting than the flys that were generally tackled to their tails. The little ponies were bottled up, and wondered what had happened to procure them so much care and corn. Great was the bragging and boasting among the youngsters how they would take the shine out of each other, and how five-barred gates and brooks—nay, rivers—should be nothing in their way.

Our friends at the barracks partook of the prevailing epidemic, and long and serious were the discussions as to the relative merits of Pippin's brown horse Blazer, Mattyfat's Hero, and Captain Spill's Harkaway, which it was thought his lordship's absence would favour the opportunity of testing.

In these discussions Jug, who always became an ardent sportsman after dinner, bore a conspicuous part, his known

intimacy with Lord Heartycheer and recent visit to the
Castle giving weight to what he said. Moreover, Jug had
heretofore managed to evade the exposure of his incompetence across country, having stoutly maintained throughout the summer that he was a regular " cut-'em-down
and hang-'em-up-to-dry man," only wanting opportunity
to exhibit his prowess. He got over his Heartycheer-
Castle day by saying that they had had a capital run, but
as he didn't know the country he couldn't give any account
of it. Lies, however, require a good deal of management,
and Angelena, we are sorry to say, did not assist her
quondam suitor in his endeavours. Indeed, she rather
went the other way, and hinted that Tom Hall and Jug
would make a very good match of it. The thing soon
came to the ears of the respective heroes, Downeylipe,
her new suitor, enlightening Jug, and Major Fibs taking
up the cudgels on behalf of Tom Hall. Of course, they
both went a good deal further than the exact truth,
adding expressions of defiance and contempt, and intimating that each only wanted opportunity to show the other
the way. The consequence was that a very deadly feud
was engendered between gentlemen who as yet had
scarcely had any communication with each other. Major
Fibs was quite sure that Mr Hall was a very respectable
performer, while the Heavysteeders generally patronised
Jug, and urged him, whatever he did, to take plenty of
jumping powder, and *sarve* Tom out handsomely. This
Jug, in his cups, promised faithfully to do, though the
morning's reflections sometimes didn't make the thing
look quite so easy. Indeed, the more they patted him
on the back, the greater man he thought Hall, until he
became quite afraid of him, and he wouldn't have been
at all sorry if the colonel had forbid his going out hunting
altogether ; in fact, he would have been very grateful.

There was no such luck, however, and on a very dark
December morning our shivering cornet was shaking
himself into his misfitting hunting clothes by the light
of a very meagre mould candle. They were all hereditary
garments, and had as much pretension to fitting as such
apologies ever have. The leather breeches were the
greatest failure, as, indeed, second-hand ones generally

are, having been made for a leg half as big again as the
cornet's, consequently there was a considerable fold at
the knee, which our friend flattered himself would never
be seen when he had his boots on. Indeed, he much
questioned that any one ever looked at the knees—just
as thick-legged ladies always flatter themselves that no
one looks at their feet. The boots were loose, white-
topped ones, with a sad propensity to turning round,
which they did in a most independent careless manner,
quite regardless of each other, so that the back seam of
one would be in front, while the other stood as it ought
to do. The coat, as coats go—when every man seems to
exert his skill in producing something uglier and more
outré than his neighbour—was not so far amiss, being a
roomy, dressing-gowney, old frock of the last century,
cut down into one of the queer half-coats, half-jackets,
many-pocketed, few-buttoned things of the present.

We question if there ever was a time when so many
hideous incongruous habiliments were to be seen in the
hunting field as there are now. Nay, we may go further,
and say that perhaps there never was a time when so little
care or taste was exhibited in dress generally, or when
such ugly misfitting garments were allowed to pass as
coats. What would have been thought in the dandy,
swallow-tailed days of George IV.—when coats were made
to fit like wax, and the slightest wrinkle was cut out and
fine drawn—of the baggy, sack-like things of the present
day, with sleeves that look like trousers put in by mistake ?
How pleasant it must be to ride or drive in the face of a
sleeting rain, with the wet drifting up to one's elbows,
without having the power of preventing it by buttoning
the wrists. But there is no absurdity that fashion will
not compass and even reconcile some people to.

Our Tom was better got up than Jug, his clothes having
been made for him, but Tights, having given Captain
Dazzler's groom a guinea (of Tom's money, of course) for
a most invaluable recipe for brown tops (another of the
hideous inventions or revivals of the day), had experienced
a " failyar," the tops having come out a bright red instead
of the nut-brown colour Tights expected. Being, however, a man of resources, Tights persuaded Tom they

would " come all right " as he proceeded to cover, and, trusting to Tights' word, Tom put on his grey terrier coat, and installed himself in the vacant seat of Major Fibs's jingling old dog-cart, as soon as that worthy drew up at the door to receive him. The major thought Tom looked rather warm about the legs, but not being much of a man for the chase, as his old white hat and mother-of-pearl buttoned, short-waisted, scarlet—or, rather, purple—coat testified, he kept his opinion to himself, and proceeded to expatiate on the ease of the vehicle and the merits of the steed as they drove out of town. When they got clear of the stones, the major began to divulge the real object of his mission, which was to try and smooth matters over between Tom and Angelena, so that the fair lady might not lose the second string to her bow.

Though Angelena still insisted on the unabated ardour of Lord Heartycheer, and maintained that he had over and over again promised to marry her, both the colonel and Mrs Blunt felt there were inconsistencies in the way, and that his lordship was not to be depended upon. Moreover, the colonel wanted to cash the Lily of the Valley cheque, Christmas operating upon his pocket much as it does upon the pockets of other people. So the major had plenty of scope for his diplomacy, a quality that he had no little difficulty in exercising, as well from the peculiar state of Tom's mind with regard to Laura as from the interruptions caused by passing sportsmen on their way to the meet. Whenever the major thought he was drawing nicely on to his point, and would compass his object, up cantered some one with an original observation about the weather, or inquiring if they weren't early or weren't late ? or if they'd breakfasted ? or if they had their horses on ? just as if anybody ever saw two men hunting one horse, and that, too, taken out of a gig ! The farther our gigmen went, however, the more impossible steady, business - like conversation became, for each by-road and green lane contributed its quota to the swelling throng, while the open space before Weary-field Wood was dotted with dark-clad horsemen, slightly sprinkled with pink. It was as yet but an early hour, and many of these sombre habiliments would be changed into livelier colours when the sporting masters cantered becomingly up.

The pinks that were there were most likely of the second and third-class order ; men who perhaps had been base enough to ride their own horses on, or who wanted to have a look at the hounds before they went into cover, proceedings to be utterly deprecated by all stylish sportsmen. However, there was a goodly throng of one sort and another, including a glorious muster of restless ponies, whose owners kept startling the high-bred hunters by rushing in among them, as the dismounted grooms fistled at the girths, the stirrups, or the mud sparks. Then the clamour and clatter on the road drew all eyes that way, and a charge of cantering swells might be seen, leaving a clear streak of smoke behind them like the vapour of an engine, and again behind them a second detachment hove in sight, to be in turn succeeded by another.

Wearyfield Wood was a fine central situation, approached by good roads, as well from Fleecyborough and Rattlinghope as from the smaller towns of Torrington and Moffat.

Dicky Dyke, of course, was late with the hounds, and at length came up pursing his mouth and simpering in the usual great-man style. Looking over the heterogeneous, blue-nosed, mud-stuck field, he only deigned to notice those whom his lordship would have recognised, or who toadied Dicky on his private account : Johnny Piper, who had lately sent him a basket of Kent filberts ; Tommy Kingsmill, who had marked the season with a turkey ; Andrew Dawson, whose apples were unexceptionable ; and Arthur Flintoff, who had promised him a sucking pig. He capped Jug, an example that was followed by the whips, greatly to Jug's enhancement. He looked at Hall, Head-and-shoulders Brown, Beale, Brassey, Kyleycalfe, and a whole host of others as if he had seen them before ; while he glanced at the variously grown, variously mounted, short-necked young Browns with a shudder, as he thought what a string of persecution there was coming on for some unfortunate master of hounds.

Having looked the people saucily over, and given him-

self as many airs as he could, Dicky looked at his gold
watch, and, seeing it only wanted five-and-twenty minutes
to twelve, he shut it against his cheek, and, drawing
on his red-lined dogskin gloves, took his grey horse short
by the head, and, rising in his stirrups, proceeded to
address the throng, for field we can hardly call it.

" Now, gen'l'men," said he, looking around him, " as
my lord's away, the conduct of affairs nattarally devolves
upon me, and I'll take it as a 'tickler favour if you'll all
come into cover, and keep there, and refrain from halloaing.
It's been well observed," continued he, " that every man
sees the hunted fox ; but as we only undertake to pursue
one at a time with our hounds—which I may observe
are bred with the greatest care and attention, containing
strains of almost every fashionable blood—the Belvoir,
the Burton, the Beaufort, the Quorn, to say nothin' of
a dash of the old Pytchley Furrier—I say, as we only
undertake to pursue one fox at a time, you'll p'r'aps have
the goodness to let the hounds select their own ! Stick
to him, and if they divide, my men here," looking at Billy
Brick (who now had his tongue in his cheek) and Sam,
" will stop 'em, and maintain to my halloa."

So saying, Dick sunk in his saddle, and turning his
horse the other way, at a slight cheer and wave of his
hand the glad pack dashed into the thick, moss-grown,
briary underwood, and the field proceeded to make their
first series of impressions up the clay of the deep-holding
ride.   Blob, blob, blob, squirt, squirt, squirt, flounder,
flounder, flounder, flounder, went the weary horses, while
the minor cavalry scuttled and scrambled over the surface
and through the boggy places in a way that must have
excited their bigger brothers' envy.   Dicky, of course,
was a little in advance, with Sam in the rear of the ill-
assorted field, while wide of Dicky, outside the cover on
the right, Billy's cheerful halloa was heard, accompanied
by an occasional crack of his whip.   Billy had strict orders
to head back the foxes, or at all events to stop the hounds
the instant they appeared outside.

The cover was some three hundred acres in extent—
perhaps more, for it was of that unprofitable nature that
no one we should think would be at the trouble of measur-

ing it. It was a wretched water-logged place, the trees
not having grown an inch in the memory of the " oldest
inhabitant." Trees, indeed, they could hardly be called,
being little better than poles ; while the brushwood had
ceased to be profitable since the introduction of coal
into the country by the Gobblegold Railway. The wood
was therefore left to itself a good deal, save where a
silvery birch or clean-grown hazel tempted a passing tramp
to add it to the miscellaneous contents of his cart.

The rough and tangled nature of the brake, coupled
with the intention of making a day of it in cover, induced
Dicky to draw very carefully, and any one unacquainted
with him would have said what a nice, patient, painstaking,
old huntsman this is ! how anxious he is not to miss a
chance ! while Head-and-shoulders Brown, Strutt, Beal,
Black, Brassey, and others indulged in coarse invectives
at his slow pottering dawdlings, wondering at his not
pushing on briskly for the dry thick lying at the top,
and talking as if they would dismiss Dicky, and take the
country away from his lordship.

Dicky, who sat with a quick ear cocked back to hear
their remarks and treasure them up for his lordship,
with such additions and variations as circumstances might
require, did not suffer himself to be at all put out of his
way, but went blobbing, and hold-up-ing, and gentle-ing,
and yoicking, and cheering, and cracking his whip in a
sort of way that as good as said, I don't care twopence
whether I find a fox or not.

Meanwhile Tom Hall and Jug were taking a mental
measure of each other, conjuring up a good deal more
equestrian prowess than either had ever invested the other
with before. Tom thought if he was on Jug's horse he
would cut Jug down ; and Jug thought if he was on
Tom's horse he would cut Tom down. So it is that we
generally fancy our neighbour's horse in preference to
our own, just as we often fancy our neighbour's wine-glass
is larger than our own.

Major Fibs, who was only backing Tom for an ulterior
object, not caring how soon he drew him off and resumed
the conversation he had made so little progress with in
coming, now advised Tom, seeing how he went floundering

and blundering about, to "get his orth a little tighter by the 'ead," observing that he would be having an "over-reach" if he didn't take care ; besides which, he would want all the steam he could raise against he got out of cover.

Jug's backers—Pippin, Spill, Dazzler, Mattyfat, and others of the Heavysteeds, stuck to our now half-drunken Jug, laughing at Hall's lumbering unsportsmanlike figure, and wishing that his still bright red boots mightn't take fire. Sundry disparaging observations they said Hall had made on the cornet and his horsemanship were reported, the speakers declaring they "wouldn't put up with it if they were him." And little pig-eyes waxed indignant at Tom, wishing that his horse might fall so that he might ride over him at once.

Long-continued yoickings, and crackings, and stir-him-up-ings, and rout-him-out-ings, will tire even the slackest funkster, and both Tom Hall and Jug had begun to wish for something more enlivening than Dicky's repeated exhortations, and the blobbing and floundering of their respective steeds, when a sudden Jullien-concert-like outburst of melody from the whole pack proclaimed that the varmint had started in view with every hound at his brush.

"Hoop—hoop—hoop! Talli-ho! talli-ho! talli-ho!" screeched Dicky, getting his horse by the head, and rising in his stirrups as though he were going to ride for the Derby. He then went hustling and bustling up the deep-holding ride, an object of unbounded admiration to the variously aged, variously clad, variously mounted youngsters behind. What a scrimmage ensued! How the mud flew, and how the half-blinded urchins wiped their faces with their jacket sleeves—up went a fresh volley on the instant. On they hurried, to the irresistible impetus of the hounds, Hall and Jug elbowing and racing with the best of them, each looking as though he would eat the other.

"Hold hard!" now cried Dicky, pulling up short across the ride—"hold hard!" repeated he, holding up his hand. "Don't you hear they're comin'?" asked he, casting an angry glance at the gallopers, muttering, "Wonder what half you fellers come out hunting for?"

"Talli-ho! Talli-ho! Talli-ho!" shrieked and screeched
a multitude of voices in every variety of intonation, as a
fine grey-backed old fellow, with his neat ears well laid
back and a well-tagged brush, crossed the ride about fifty
yards higher up at an easy listening pace, as if calculating
the amount of scent he was leaving behind, and whether
it was expedient to continue in cover or try his luck in
the open, either for Witherley Forest or the main earths
at Clumbercliffe Rocks. The concert behind was great,
but the ground was yet unfoiled, and while he had no
difficulty in meusing through the tangled thorns and
copsewood of the cover, he knew they would present
severe obstacles to his obstreperous pursuers, whose size
and capabilities he had had peculiar opportunities of
estimating; so he determined to make a wide swing of
the cover, and consider matters further after he had done
that. The sight of the glorious varmint infused fresh joy
into the field, and even Dicky, though every hound was
throwing his tongue on the line, couldn't resist the temptation of a "blow," so he out with his horn and joined its
shrill melody to the sweet music of the hounds. All
hands now grasped convulsively at the bridles, hats were
stuck firmer on the head, caps readjusted, and each
rider screwed himself up to the sticking point, as though
the success of the day depended on his individual exertions.

Having seen the hounds fairly across, Dicky reopened
the ball by catching his horse short round by the head,
and sticking spurs into his sides, bustling up the clayey,
water-logged ride as hard as ever he could lay legs to the
ground, thinking what an object of admiration he must
be to the rising generation behind.

Scuttle, scuttle, splash, splash, splash, blob, blob, blob,
blob, the field went as before, varied by the occasional
click, click, click of some little "stuck mud." Hall and
Jug spurred, and grinned, and rode like fools, each determined to be first, so long as there was nothing but galloping.

Up the long quagmire of a ride they all tore to within
sight of the crazy old gate that had been left sticking
half open in the mud ever since the hounds were there
cub-hunting; then, as they neared it, and the forward
funksters were preparing to fall back ere they came to

the dread chances of the stiff vale beyond, a short turn
to the left, followed by a slight diminution of melody,
relieved their anxieties, and proclaimed that the fox still
hugged the cover, and was bearing away to the left, giving
our friends a further chance of riding their horses' tails
off. Then the recent funkers came to the front again,
hustling and bustling away, as though they were quite
unacquainted with fear.

Round the wood the joyous pack raced, now showing
their stern-lashed speckled sides as they crossed some
recently cleared ground, now racing up a grassy avenue
between lines of feathering spruce, and anon diving into
the impenetrable thickets of the wilderness.

The longer they went the calmer the field became,
until, at each junction of the rides or cross-roads, knowing
sportsmen began pulling up, mopping their brows, and
speculating on the fox's future course, each having some
excellent reason to give why he *must* come back ; why
he couldn't go this way, or wouldn't go that ; though, if
the reasons had been sifted, they would have been found
to originate in the prophet's convenience. Strutt would
stay at the big oak at the cross-rides, at the high end,
feeling confident, with the " wind in that airt," the fox
would make for the rocks, while Brassey, who rode a
terrible roarer, planted himself beside a clump of hollies
that commanded a straight road to the forest.

On, on, however, Hall and Jug went, each slackening
of the one only seeming to increase the energy of the
other, though their horses by no means corresponded in
their exertions. Tom's horse, at all times a soft one,
began to heave and labour in his going ; but Tom, having
no more feeling or sympathy for a horse than he had for
a steam-engine, only spurred him the more, thinking to
pay him off for his misconduct on the Silverspring Firs
day. Jug, too, who was of the same order, spurred and
tugged his second charger, as if he thought his mouth
was made of india-rubber. The perspiration began to
pour down their legs and over their hoofs. The hounds
still careered on, round and round, back, and across—
here, there, and everywhere, now joined by this lagging
group, now deserted by that, now cheered by Dicky

Dyke, now halloaed on by Billy Brick. The ground was all foiled, and the rides dotted with hoof marks, like an over-pricked water-biscuit. Neither Hall or Jug, however, ever looked at that, nor do we believe they knew they were not going straight. Whenever the lulling music of the hounds seemed to prelude a stop, a view of the varmint set all ecstatic again. Many who had looked at their watches, with a keen eye to " pudding time," were thus inveigled again and again. Even " Head-and-shoulders," and the jumpers who despised all hunting that didn't involve good leaping, stayed for the chance of a spin at the end. Dicky, too, had looked at his ticker, thinking he had done enough, and more than enough for any humbugging holiday field, and seeing by the failing scent and diminishing pace of the pack that they had no chance either of catching the fox or making him flag, so wonderfully endowed is the varmint, was determining to pave the way for a stop, by halloaing " Fresh fox ! " at the next view, when a death of another sort ensued. Our Tom's horse, who had given him as many hints as would have served anything short of a wooden man, at length gave a series of convulsive staggering flounders, and fell, bearing Tom standing like a second Colossus of Rhodes astride him.

" Get clear of him ! " cried a dozen voices, thinking he might roll and damage our fat friend, but the warning was vain—a horse will never hurt a man if he can help it, —and the poor glassy-eyed brute stretched out its lifeless neck on the spot where he fell, a cutting reproof to his mutton-fisted master.

The end of the Hall *versus* Jug Hunt.

LIST OF SUBSCRIBERS
(as at 31st December 1986)

Michael J. Abberton
J. S. Abbott
Mrs. T. S. Acton
Mrs. A. R. Adamson
Robin Addison
H. W. Aidley, M. F. H.
R. N. Alington Maguire
J. A. Allen
J. H. Allen
James Allen
O. J. R. Allen
D. W. Allen
P. M. S. Allen
M. E. R. Allsopp
J. R. Allt
H. Ambrose
A. G. Amos
P. T. K. Anderson
Cecily Anderson
Graham P. Andrews
Miss Diane Andrews
G. A. N. Andrews
Dr. M. E. Anfilogoff
Mrs. H. E. Armitage
C. J. Armstrong
Frank Ash
P. Ashby
P. R. Ashley
R. A. C. Ashworth
J. P. Asquith
H. A. Atkinson

Douglas F. Bailey
Colonel G. O. Baker
W. J. Baker
H. A. S. Bancroft
D. W. Bardwell
John Barker

Robert D. Barnard
David J. Barnes
C. G. Barnett
H. L. Barrett
Mrs. P. M. Barton
D. S. Bass
Paul Bass
W. G. Bate
Peter Batty-Smith
Lt. Col. Sir John Baynes, Bt.
J. R. Beaumont, J. P., D. L.
Walter Bee
A. F. L. Beeston
Nicholas John Belcher
G. Bennett
Mrs. M. D. Berger
M. F. Berry
Peregrine Bertie
M. Ide Betts
Lt. Col. R. T. Betts
Major K. R. McK Biggs
D. Bilham
J. M. Binney
R. J. Bird
L. C. Blaaberg
The Rev. F. A. Black
His Honour Judge A. J. Blackett-Ord
Peter Blacklock
Mrs. Blair
E. C. Blake
M. D. Blake
The Rev. Michael Bland
A. H. Boddy
Sir Richard Body, M. P.
T. E. T. Bond
H. L. Boorer
C. V. C. Booth-Jones

L. A. F. Borrett
Stanley W. Botterill
Colonel M. C. Bowden
Miss Mary J. E. Bower
James T. Bowie
Mrs. John Bowlby
John G. Bowler
L. F. Bowyer
Jorgen Brandt
G. W. Brazendale, C. M. G.
Dr. O. B. Brears, O. B. E.
The Lord Bridges
A. F. B. Bridges
D. C. Bright
Frank Brightman
John E. Brindle
D. H. V. Brogan
K. C. Brookes
Col. J. M. Browell
W. A. Brown
M. G. Bruce-Squires
John Ross Buckley
Mrs. D. S. Bull
John S. Burgess
P. A. Burlton
Lieut. A. G. Burns, R. N.
John D. C. Burridge
D. V. S. Burroughs
A. M. Burton
E. J. Burton
Dr. J. D. K. Burton
Dr. J. W. Butler
Mrs. B. B. Buttenshaw
J. Byles

A. J. Cairns
G. A. Calver
Dr. J. A. Calvert

E. G. Cameron
A. J. C. Campbell
W. H. D. Campbell
L. R. Campfield
R. J. Canning
The Rev. W. R. D. Capstick
A. R. P. Carden
Robert Carew
Brigadier Caruthers
Paul Carver
A. G. Casewell
P. A. Cattermole
J. Cavey
Mrs. Eileen Cawkwell
Lord Charles Cecil
Major J. P. Chadwick
Philip Chadwick
Robert Chadwick
C. L. Chafer
W. T. Chaffer
Frank Chamberlain
Trevor J. Chapman
Captain L. W. L. Chelton,
R. N.
D. M. Child
E. F. Choppen, C. B. E.
Niall Christie
J. R. Clack
K. M. Clarke, B. Sc.
A. M. Clarkson
R. P. Clinton
W. Clunies-Ross
A. C. T. Cochrane
A. W. Cockerill
Robert Coggins
Christopher Newbury Coles
R. H. Collard
Miss A. Colliass
Edwin Collins
F. L. Collins
Ken Collins
M. L. Congdon
Major A. C. J. Congreve
F. A. Connelly
J. C. Conner
P. P. Cooke
E. J. Cooper
Mrs. E. Cooper
V. F. Cooper
W. H. Cooper

John Cope, M. P.
M. D. Corke
Lt. Col. J. N. Cormack
David Cormack
G. W. Cottrell
M. H. Couchman
Major W. D. Cox
S. R. Craddock
H. P. Craig
M. G. Cripps
Major J. S. Crisp
Major Sir John Croft, Bt.
Miss M. Crookes
Lt. Col. R. N. R. Cross
J. P. O. Crowe
John J. Crown
Lt. Col. F. M. Cunningham
John Curry
Geoffrey Cuttle

T. L. A. Daintith
Michael R. Dampier
M. R. M. Daniel
F. W. Daniel
J. P. S. Daniell
Clifford L. Daniels
Dr. M. L. R. Davies
J. E. Davies
R. W. Howard Davies
Mrs. J. A. Davis
Mrs. E. J. Dawkes
Mrs H. L. R. Day
Leut. Col. P. H. V. de
Clermont
The Rt. Hon. Lord de
Clifford
Robin de Wilde
Geoffrey J. Dear
Martyn J. Dearden
E. Dearing
Dennis Dee
Rowland P. Dell
Simon J. Dell
E. A. K. Denison
Anthony Dent
John Devaux
R. A. Dewhurst
Dr. A. M. Dixon
Mrs. Peter Dixon

Dr. William Dodd
P. J. Downs
Miss F. Duncombe
C. D. Dunstan
P. G. Durrans
M. H. Dyke

Col. D. F. Easten, M. C.,
M. H.
A. C. Eaton
Mr. & Mrs. J. R. Eccles
E. F. Edwards
John A. Edwards
P. S. A. Edwards
E. T. Eley
Mrs. B. Ellington
T. J. Ellis
M. G. Esther
Commander Raymond
Evans, R. N.
David A. H. Evans
L. J. C. Evans
J. M. Evans
Mrs. J. P. M. H. Evelyn

J. C. Fareham
T. C. Farmbrough
Major A. Farrant
W. R. Farrell
J. E. Farrer
T. M. Fawcett
The Rev. M. S. Feben,
S. T. L., P. H. L.
Mrs. M. R. Ferens
Dr. J. B. Ferguson
S. A. Ferris
Miss J. M. Field
D. H. Field
R. A. J. Finn
J. M. Fison
Mrs. Peter Fitzgerald
J. E. Fleeman
M. J. G. Fletcher
A. M. Florey
G. Ford
The Rev. Benjamin P. Ford
Mrs. B. J. Foster
Charles Fox

Major A. N. Fradgley
A. R. G. Frase
Dr. A. M. Freeman
Mrs. R. Fremantle
M. J. Frost
Dr. M. J. P. Furniss

Mrs. M. E. Gallop
Oliver Gardener
W. J. Garforth
Peter Gargett
A. F. Garnett
William J. Garnham
Professor J. C. A. Gaskin
Major R. H. C. Gates
Ivan Gault
Dr. Hugh Gibbs
T. M. & A. R. Gibson
Mrs. A. Gilchrist
His Hon. Judge S. S. Gill
Prof. R. W. Gilliatt
Richard Gilman, M. D.,
    F. A. C. S.
W. A. Gilmour
Anthony Goddard
John Godley
Captain W. E. B. Godsal,
    R. N.
C. A. Gold
Mrs. Bronwen Goldsmid
C. R. Goodall
Lt. Col. D. I. W. Goode
Paul Goodlet
M. P. Gordon-Jones
Capt. J. E. Gorst
Mrs. D. W. Gorton
Andrew H. Gould
Tony M. Gover
G. B. Graham
R. I. Graham
David Granger
Guy D. Grasby
J. Michael Green
Robin E. Greenwood
N. J. Grierson
Mrs. V. J. H. Grieve
Mrs. M. Griffin
His Hon. Judge B. Griffiths,
    Q.C.

Miss J. A. Groom
John D. Grossart
Simon Grove
A. D. Gunner
P. L. Guy, M. H.

Mrs. P. R. Hadfield
Gisbert Haefs
J. Hafok
J. A. Hall
Richard Hall
N. K. Halliday
J. A. L. Hamilton
R. M. Hannam
David T. Harcus
Frank Harding
J. I. Hardwick
Geoffrey N. H. Hardy
Mrs. M. Harris
Alan Harrison
Dr. Bernard James Harrison
Edwin Harrison
Lt. Col. J. A. Harrison
Dr. Nicholas Hart
Alan Hartnell
John H. Harvey
J. R. Havers-Strong
Joseph Hawes
Dr. P. W. Hawkes
A. W. Hawkins
Derek Hayes
I. S. Haynes, M. F. H.
John Heald
Wg. Cdr. N. V. O. P. Healey
John E. Heath
John Hefford
G. M. B. Helps
V. J. Helyar
Timothy Heneage
Robin Herdman
Mrs. A. M. Hesketh
Ms S. Heyworth
E. C. Hicks
Anthony Higgins
F. B. Hill
Miss Sophie Hill
Miss J. Hirschfeld
M. R. Hoare
James G. Hobden

J. A. Hock
Miss G. Hodges
P. Hodgkinson
Graham Holdsworth
Peter Hole, M. H.
W. Holt
Mr. & Mrs. R. W. J.
    Hopkins
H. L. Hoppe
M. Hord
J. M. Horsfall
Capt. M. A. Houghton
Mr. & Mrs. M. J. Howard
D. Howcroft
Mrs. D. C. Howe
Miss Wendy Howes
Lady Howick
Major C. J. C. Humfrey
Brigadier K. Hunt
J. C. V. Hunt
P. B. Hunter
James Hunter Blair
C. J. Hunter-Brown
I. W. M. Hurst, M. F. H.
T. F. Hutchinson

A. F. Iliffe
Nigel Ince
Col. F. J. Ingham
Intermotor Ltd.
G. W. Iredell

Mrs. J. M. Jachim
D. M. Jarvis
David Jeffcoat
V. R. M. Jeffery
C. P. Jenner, M. H.
J. M. Jerram
H. Thomson Jones
Terry Jones
Miss P. M. Jones
P. K. Jordan
Malcolm D. Joslyn
Frederick H. J. Jukes
H. L. Jukes

Michael Leo Keane
A. R. Keeping

Francis Kelly
J. E. Kelly
Dr. A. J. I. Kelynack
F. C. Kent
David Kenward
Dr. D. F. Kerr
W. H. Kibble
T. W. Killick
A. E. Kindred
Jonathan G. N. King
Lt. Col. R. D. Kinsella-
Bevan
Dr. Mary Ellen Kitler
David A. Knight
S. J. Knowles
Martin Kochanski

G. W. Laing
G. A. Lakin
Mrs. V. A. Langridge
Mrs. A. Langton
N. Lanham-Cook
M. A. Lavis
Richard Law
R. W. Lawrence, M. H.
The Hon. Hugh Lawson-
Johnston
Mrs. Mary G. Lawton
Owen Legg
G. C. M. Leggett
Frank Lehmann
L. Lelarge
L. P. F. L'Estrange, O. B. E.
J. W. P. Lewis
R. V. Lewis
Sir Anthony Lincoln,
K. C. M. G., C. V. O.
Dr. Charles Lipp
C. S. Lippell
Robin J. Lipscombe
William Lister
John Lockie
Anthony D. Loehnis
Mrs. B. Logan
G. A. Longbottom
Sir Gilbert Longden
T. R. W. Longmore
Miss S. Lonsdale
Edward Lord

A. D. Low
Dr. Nicholas J. Low
Dr. S. B. Lucas
Dr. Richard Luckett
H. C. R. Ludlow-Hewitt
Oliver Lynas
A. N. Lyndon-Skeggs

John MacFarlane
Lt. Col. C. H. T.
MacFetridge
Mrs. C. A. MacGregor
A. J. Mack
R. D. Mackay
The Revd. Hugh Mackay of
Talmine
Lt. Col. G. J. H. Mackie,
R. M.
Capt. M. J. MacKinlay
MacLeod
J. G. H. Mackrell
J. J. Macnamara
Miss Joan M. Mahony
Stephen Mahony
Capt. Dugald Malcolm
R. D. Mann
A. Marchant
Brian Margetts
R. D. Marshall
Mrs. B. M. Marshall
D. Marshall Evans
J. W. Martin
Major H. D. G. Martindale
Dr. D. Martyn-Johns
Peter I. Maslen
A. R. Mason
Philip Mason, C. I. E.,
O. B. E.
R. J. Mason, LL B., F. C. I.,
A. R. B.
S. C. W. Mason, B. A.
(Hons) & Mrs. P. J.
Mason, B. Ed. (Hons)
A. A. Mawby
R. T. Maylam
M. Maynard
The Hon. David M.
McAlpine
John McCaig

Denis J. McCarthy
Peter O. McDougall
P. McDougall
Dr. Ewen McEwen
D. J. McGlynn
Major C. McInnes
M. D. McMillan
M. A. Meacham
W. J. B. Meakin
C. J. Mears
David C. Mellors
Cdr. W. J. Melrose,
O. B. E., D. S. C.,
R. N. (Retd)
Keith Messenger
A. J. B. Mildmay-White
K. Miller
C. H. Millin
Peter Mimpriss
Dr. C. J. Mitchell
Mrs. G. M. Mitchell
A. G. Mitchell, C. B. E.,
D. F. M., M. A.
A. Moger
Mrs. Kathleen Moore
Kenneth A. Moore
David J. Morgan
G. E. Morris
P. A. Morton
Major A. R. C. Mott
E. D. Moylan
John Murray, Q. C.
John A. Mutimer

Mrs. S. J. Nash
John Wynne Naylor
P. E. Neal
Malcolm G. Neesam
David Negus, F. R. C. S.
Basil Newall
Mrs. John Newcomb
D. Newell
R. P. Newlands
M. W. Newton
C. D. Newton
M. J. Nicholas
Mark Nicholson
Mrs. D. Nicholson
Major George Nickerson

J. N. F. Norman
A. H. W. P. Norton

P. O'Neill
Miss M. R. O'Reilly
Major Gen. Odling
M. B. Ogle
D. A. Orton
C. D. Outred
R. Elwyn Owen

Henry Page
A. J. Palethorpe
D. J. Palmer
Anthony V. Parker
H. M. Parker
Dr. Miles Parkes, M. H.
Mrs. C. H. Parlby
Miss G. M. Partridge
K. G. Pates
C. T. Payne
C. Payne
Dennis Pearl
Mrs. N. F. K. Pearse
Johnathan R. H. Pearson
Dr. C. J. D. W. Peck
J. F. A. Peck
Mervyn R. C. Peckham
David Pennant
S. W. Percival
Robert Perfitt
D. J. Peters, J. P., M. A.
H. M. Peters
V. M. Pettifer
Mrs. V. M. Pettifer
Dr. A. J. B. Phillips, M. B.,
   B. S.
C. N. Phipps
Sir Charles Pickthorn, Bt.
Mrs. R. W. Pigott
B. W. Pitt
C. M. Plumbe
Michael J. Plummer
Robert H. Plumridge
George Pocklington
Henry Pomeroy
Richard Pomeroy
The Hon. R. W. Pomeroy

P. Potter
M. F. Powell
R. J. Pratt
Col. R. F. Preston
J. Maurice Price, Q. C.
A. T. Prince
Timothy Proctor
Miss S. Jasmine Profit
A. W. Pulley
Brion Purdey
Mrs. F. E. M. Puxon
Anthony Pye

M. Radakovic
Brig. E. Rait-Kerr
C. Ralton
G. H. Ramage
H. T. Randolph
A. E. Ranson
J. R. Stanley Raper
J. H. Ratcliff
Cyril Ray
Major David Rayner
Peter Read
Colonel A. H. N. Reade
P. F. Rednall
R. C. D. Rees
M. M. Reeve
Lt. Col. R. W. C. Reeves
Dr. R. W. Reid
Bruce Reid
W. F. Rendall
Dr. R. E. Rewell
David Reynolds
W. S. C. Richards
William Richardson,
   R. I. B. A.
C. W. Richmond-Watson
Andrew W. G. Rickett
H. W. Riddolls
Capt. N. J. Ridout
T. J. Riley
Mrs. Susan Roberts
R. F. Roberts
Brig. A. Robertson
Wg. Cdr. S. Robinson,
   R. A. F. (Rtd)
John Rolls
R. M. Romer

J. M. Rose
Joseph Rosenblum
C. M. Ross
Pamela Rowe
The Rev. A. G. B. Rowe
J. R. Russell Smith
J. F. Rutherford
Dr. Josephine Rutter
L. E. Rydings

D. W. Saint
C. G. C. Sayer
Rudy Schats
Philipp Schoeller
Richard Schutze
J. H. Scrutton
Gerald E. Seager
J. C. Sedgwick
M. Shannon
M. E. Sharp
G. D. C. Shaw
Frank Sheardown
Mark Sheardown
John Shearman
A. J. Shears
Clive Shenton
A. G. Sherratt
Mrs. W. E. Sherston
N. E. C. Sherwood
Mrs. G. M. Shipman
Mrs. F. R. Short
R. E. Silvey
R. E. Skelson
Mrs. J. Skinner
Mrs. J. Smallwood
N. L. H. Smith
J. C. S. F. Smithies
Timothy Smyth
Mrs. I. J. Barclay Sole
G. H. Southern
I. P. G. Southward
Sir John Sparrow
Major B. L. Speegle
Mrs. P. Spiller
S. A. Springate
Mrs. J. M. Stannah
Miss H. D. Stapleton
Miss Lesley Stark
Peter Starr

E. W. Stearn
David Steeds
F. F. Steele
B. G. Steff
R. P. Stevenson
A. W. Stewart
J. R. Stewart-Peter
J. S. R. Storer
Mrs. J. R. Strange
Mrs. R. W. Stratton
Dr F. S. Stych
D. Sullivan
C. W. Surtees
Dr. S. J. Surtees
Mrs. V. Surtees
Philip A. Surtees
R. V. N. Surtees
Colin Sutherland
Ian F. Swain
Sir Ronald Swayne
H. C. C. Swift
M. A. Syddall
Robert J. C. Symon
Lt. Col. G. Symonds
A. Symonds

Miss M. Tait
B. V. Talbott
C. E. Tatton-Brown
Alec I. Taylor
Maurice Taylor
Miss Anne Taylor
D. F. Taylor
Mrs M. E. Taylor
L. C. Thomas
P. C. F. Thomas
Major A. F. F. Thomson
R. M. Thorpe
Eric A. Tidy
M. J. Timms
Major J. V. Titley,
 R. A. M. C.
A. G. Todd
Bruce Todd
Maj. Gen. D. A. H. Toler
C. M. L. Toll
J. P. L. Tory
H. W. Townsend
Denis Tracey

L. E. Trafford
J. J. Trapp
A. F. Tremeer
Mrs. Jennifer M. Trippier
R. W. Trollope, M. F. H.
G. P. Tucker
Capt. A. C. Tupper, R. N.
I. M. Turner
A. A. Turner
Peter Thomspon-Tweddle
William J. Twibill

F. A. Underwood
T. G. S. Unite

D. B. Vale
George Vallance
S. van Praet D'Amerloo
D. J. Viveash
William von Raab

Michael Wace
T. Wainwright
Major M. P. Walker
Mrs. P. M. Walker
P. B. Walker
J. H. Walker
T. Walker
R. F. Walker
Major P. J. R. Waller,
 M. B. E., D. L.
J. E. Walsh
John H. Walton
Michael Ward-Thomas
A. T. Warwick C. Eng.,
 M. I. E. E.
H. A. Waterson
Ian R. Watson
E. D. B. Way
M. J. R. Wear
I. H. Wear
Mrs. A. J. Webb
The Rev. W. P. Webb
Mrs. H. D. Webb
W. R. B. Webb
Barbara Lilian Webster

Martin Webster
P. Webster
Dr. Paul Wellings
C. R. Wells
General Charles West
G. Westall
Terence Westgate
Mrs. Mary Davan Wetton
Royston Wheeler
B. C. Whitaker
Edmund H. White
Ralph White
A. P. Whitehead
D. Whiteley
The Revd. H. D. Wiard,
 M. A.
H. H. Wicks
J. L. R. Williams
J. P. Williams, M. Chir.
K. E. Williams
R. M. C. Williams
Major General E. A. W.
 Williams
Steven N. Wilshire
B. R. Wilson
Colonel E. B. Wilson
Edward Wilson
Herbert Wilson
Patrick Wilson
Major T. L. Wilson-Jerrim,
 M. C.
John Winch
K. R. Wing
John Winter
Harry Wolton, Q. C.
Douglas J. Wood
F. A. Woods
J. G. Wooldridge
Mrs David Wright
Patrick G. Wright
W. D. Wright
Dr. R. F. Wyatt
C. P. Wykeham-Martin

G. Yates
Ian Yeaman
N. W. S. Yonge
P. Youdale

PUBLICATIONS OF
THE R. S. SURTEES SOCIETY
R. S. SURTEES

Mr. Sponge's Sporting Tour. Facsimile of 1853 edition. 13 full-page coloured plates and 90 engravings by **John Leech.** Introduction by **Auberon Waugh.**

Mr. Facey Romford's Hounds. 24 coloured plates by **Leech** and **'Phiz'.** 50 engravings by **W. T. Maud.** Introduction by **Enoch Powell.**

"Ask Mamma". Facsimile of 1858 edition. 13 coloured plates and 70 engravings by **Leech.** Introduction by **Rebecca West.**

Handley Cross; or Mr. Jorrocks' Hunt. Facsimile of 1854 edition. 17 coloured plates and 100 engravings by **Leech.** Introduction by **Raymond Carr.**

Jorrocks' Jaunts and Jollities. Facsimile of 1874 edition. 31 coloured plates by **Henry Alken, 'Phiz'** and **W. Heath.** Introduction by **Michael Wharton** ('Peter Simple').

Hillingdon Hall or **The Cockney Squire** (Jorrocks). Facsimile of 1888 edition. 12 coloured plates by **Wildrake, W. Heath** and **Jellicoe.** Introduction by **Robert Blake.**

Plain or Ringlets? Facsimile of 1860 edition. 13 coloured plates and 45 engravings by **Leech.** Introduction by **Molly Keane.**

Young Tom Hall. 16 illustrations by **G. D. Armour.** Introduction by **Cyril Ray.**

Price **£16.95** in each case, packing and postage included.

SOMERVILLE AND ROSS

Some Experiences of an Irish R.M., Further Experiences of an Irish R.M., In Mr. Knox's Country. Facsimiles of the first editions of the Irish R.M. trilogy, which include the illustrations by **Miss Somerville.** Introduction by **Molly Keane.**

Prices (including p. & p.) **£8.70** each, **£24** for set of three.

CAPTAIN GRONOW

Reminiscences and Recollections. 17 coloured plates. **Last Recollections.** 12 coloured plates.

Price **£16.95** each or **£30** the pair (inc. p. & p).

W. W. JACOBS

Ship's Company. 12 short stories. Facsimile of first (1908) edition with 23 illustrations by **Will Owen.**

Price **£8.70** (including p. & p.).

RUDYARD KIPLING

Soldiers Three, The Story of the Gadsbys, In Black and White, Under the Deodars. Near-facsimiles of first editions in the Indian Railway Library series of 1888. Forewords by **Philip Mason, C.I.E.**

Prices (including p. & p.) **£2.95** for each of *Soldiers Three* and *The Story of the Gadsbys*, **£3.75** for each of *In Black and White* and *Under the Deodars.*

First published in this edition in 1987 by
The R. S. Surtees Society

Rockfield House
Nunney, Nr Frome
Somerset

© This Edition and Compilation The R. S. Surtees Society, 1987

ISBN 0 948560 05 3

Printed in Great Britain by Butler & Tanner Ltd,
Frome and London